"IT'S NO GAMBLE TO BET ON DICK FRANCIS,
and sure enough, he trots in with another
winner... In true Francis tradition, the villains
are mean and violent, and the
protagonists... are alive with human virtues and
failings... A galloping good book."
Publishers Weekly

TWICE SHY

"A DOWN-TO-THE-WIRE THRILLER ABOUT
THE EXOTIC WORLD OF HORSE RACING...
thoroughly frightening... vivid and diverse."
Houston Post

"SPLENDID... A FINELY CRAFTED CAPER...
The supergoon of the decade is a figure of such
sheer nightmare that you won't want to read
TWICE SHY when you're home alone."
Cosmopolitan

"THERE SEEMS TO BE NO END TO THE PLOT
VARIATIONS AND EXTRAORDINARY
SUSPENSE THAT FRANCIS CAN
GENERATE... HIS ABILITY TO TELL A STORY
AND ORCHESTRATE TENSION IS ALMOST
HYPNOTIC."
Philadelphia Inquirer

TWICE SHY

DICK FRANCIS

FAWCETT CREST • NEW YORK

A Fawcett Crest Book
Published by Ballantine Books

Library of Congress Catalog Card Number: 81-15814

ISBN 0-449-20756-0

This edition published by arrangement with G. P. Putnam's Sons

Manufactured in the United States of America

First International Edition: December 1982

First Ballantine Books Edition: March 1983
Fifth Printing: December 1984

With love and thanks
to my son
Felix
an excellent shot
who teaches physics

PART ONE

JONATHAN

ONE

I told the boys to stay quiet while I went to fetch my gun.

It usually worked. For the five minutes that it took me to get to the locker in the common room and to return to the classroom, thirty fourteen-year-old semi-repressed hooligans could be counted on to be held in a state of fragile good behavior, restrained only by the promise of a lesson they'd actually looked forward to. Physics in general they took to be unacceptably hard mental labor, but what happened when a gun spat out a bullet . . . that was *interesting*.

Jenkins delayed me for a moment in the common room: Jenkins with his sour expression and bad-tempered moustache, telling me I could teach momentum more clearly with chalk on a blackboard, and that an actual firearm was on my part simply self-indulgent dramatics.

"No doubt you're right," I said blandly, edging around him.

He gave me his usual look of frustrated spite. He hated my policy of always agreeing with him, which was, of course, why I did it.

"Excuse me," I said, retreating. "The boys are waiting."

The boys, however, weren't waiting in the hoped-for state of gently simmering excitement. They were, instead, in collective giggles fast approaching mild hysteria.

"Look," I said flatly, sensing the atmosphere with one foot through the door, "steady down, or you'll copy notes..."

This direst of threats had no result. The giggles couldn't be stifled. The eyes of the class darted between me and my gun and the blackboard, which was still out of my sight behind the open door, and upon every young face there was the most gleeful anticipation.

"OK," I said, closing the door, "So what have you writ—"

I stopped.

They hadn't written anything.

One of the boys stood there, in front of the blackboard, straight and still: Paul Arcady, the wit of the class. He stood straight and still because, balanced on his head, there was an apple.

The giggles all around me exploded into laughter, and I couldn't myself keep a straight face.

"Can you shoot it off, sir?"

The voices rose above a general hubbub.

"William Tell could, sir."

"Shall we call an ambulance, sir, just in case?"

"How long will it take a bullet to get through Paul's skull, sir?"

"Very funny," I said repressively, but indeed it *was* very funny, and they knew it. But if I laughed too much I'd lose control of them, and control of such a volatile mass was always precarious.

"Very clever, Paul," I said. "Go and sit down."

He was satisfied. He'd produced his effect perfectly. He took the apple off his head with a natural elegance and returned in good order to his place, accepting as his due the admiring jokes and the envious catcalls.

"Right then," I said, planting myself firmly where he had stood. "By the end of this lesson you'll all know how long it would take for a bullet traveling at a certain speed to cross a certain distance..."

The gun I had taken to the lesson had been a simple air gun, but I told them also how a rifle worked, and why in each case a bullet or a pellet came out fast. I let them handle the smooth metal: the first time many of them had seen an actual gun, even an air gun, at close quarters. I explained how bullets were made, and how they differed from the pellets I had with me. How loading mechanisms worked. How the grooves inside a rifle barrel rotated the bullet, to send it out spinning. I told them about air friction, and heat.

They listened with concentration and asked the questions they always did.

"Can you tell us how a bomb works, sir?"

"One day," I said.

"A nuclear bomb?"

"One day."

"A hydrogen...cobalt...neutron bomb?"

"One day."

They never asked how radio waves crossed the ether, which was to me a greater mystery. They asked about destruction, not creation; about power, not symmetry. The seed of violence born in every male child looked out of every face, and I knew how they were thinking, because I'd been there myself. Why else had I spent countless hours at their age practicing with a .22 cadet rifle on a range, improving my skill until I could hit a target the size of a thumbnail at fifty yards, nine times out of ten? A strange, pointless, sublimated skill, which I never intended to use on any living creature but had never since lost.

"Is it true, sir," one of them said, "that you won an Olympic medal for rifle shooting?"

"No, it isn't."

"What, then, sir?"

"I want you all to consider the speed of a bullet compared to the speed of other objects you are all familiar with. Now, do you think that you could be flying along in an airplane, and look out of the window, and see a bullet keeping pace with you, appearing to be standing still just outside the window?"

The lesson wound on. They would remember it all their lives, because of the gun. Without the gun, whatever Jenkins might think, it would have faded into the general dust they shook from their shoes every afternoon at four o'clock. Teaching, it often seemed to me, was as much a matter of imagery as of imparting actual information. The facts dressed up in jokes were the ones they got right in exams.

I liked teaching. Specifically I liked teaching physics, a subject I suppose I embraced with passion and joy, knowing full well that most people shied away in horror. Physics was only the science of the unseen world, as geography was of the seen. Physics was the science of all the tremendously powerful invisibilities—of magnetism, electricity, gravity, light, sound, cosmic rays... Physics was the science of the mysteries of the universe. How could *anyone* think it dull?

I had been for three years head of the physics department of the West Ealing School, with four masters and two technicians within my domain. My future, from my present age of thirty-three, looked like a possible deputy headmastership, most likely with a move involved, and even perhaps a headship, though if I hadn't achieved that by forty I could forget it. Headmasters got younger every year; mostly, cynics suggested, because the younger the man they appointed, the more the authorities could boss him about.

I was, all in all, contented with my job and hopeful of my prospects. It was only at home that things weren't so good.

The class learned about momentum and Arcady ate his apple when he thought I wasn't looking. My peripheral vision after ten years of teaching was, however, so acute that at times they thought I could literally see out of the back of my head. It did no harm: it made control easier.

"Don't drop the core on the floor, Paul," I said mildly. It was one thing to let him eat the apple—he'd deserved it—but quite another to let him think I hadn't seen. Keeping a grip on the monsters was a perpetual psychological game, but also priority number one. I'd seen stronger men than myself reduced to nervous breakdowns by the hunting-pack instincts of children.

When the end-of-lesson bell rang they did me the ultimate courtesy of letting me finish what I was saying before erupting into the going-home stampede. It was, after all, the last lesson on Friday...and God be thanked for weekends.

I made my way slowly around the four physics laboratories and the two equipment rooms, checking that everything was in order. The two technicians, Louisa and David, were dismantling and putting away all apparatus not needed on Monday, picking Five E's efforts at radio circuitry to pieces and returning the batteries, clips, bases and transistors to the countless racks and drawers in the equipment room.

"Shooting anyone special?" Louisa said, eyeing the gun which I was carrying with me.

"Didn't want to leave it unattended."

"Is it loaded?" Her voice sounded almost hopeful. By late Fridays one never asked her for an extra favor: not, that is, unless one was willing to endure a weepy ten minutes of "you don't realize how much this job entails," which, on most occasions, I wasn't. Louisa's tantrums, I reckoned, were based on her belief that life had cheated her, finding her at forty as a sort of storekeeper (efficient, meticulous and helpful) but not a Great Scientist. "If I'd gone to college..." she would say, leaving the strong impression that if she had, Einstein would have been relegated to second place. I dealt with Louisa by retreating at the warning signs of trouble, which was maybe weak, but I had to live with her professionally, and bouts of sullenness made her slow.

"My list for Monday," I said, handing it to her.

She glanced disparagingly down it. "Martin has ordered the oscilloscopes for third period."

The school's shortage of oscilloscopes was a constant source of friction.

"See what you can manage," I said.

"Can you make do with only two?"

I said I supposed so, smiled, hoped it would keep fine for her gardening, and left for home.

I drove slowly with the leaden feeling of resignation clamping down, as it always did on the return journey. Between Sarah and me there was no joy left, no springing love. Eight years of marriage, and nothing to feel but a growing boredom.

We had been unable to have children. Sarah had hoped for them, longed for them, pined for them. We'd been to every conceivable specialist and Sarah had had countless injections and pills and two operations. My own disappointment was bearable, though none the less deep. Hers had proved intractable and finally disabling, in that she had gone into a state of permanent depression from which it seemed nothing could rescue her.

We'd been told by encouraging therapists that many childless marriages were highly successful, husband and wife forging exceptionally strong bonds through their misfortune, but with us it had worked in reverse. Where once there had been passion there was now politeness; where plans and laughter, now a grinding hopelessness; where tears and heartbreak, silence.

I hadn't been enough for her, without babies. I'd been forced to face it that to her motherhood mattered most, that marriage had been but the pathway, that many a man would have done. I wondered unhappily from time to time how soon she would have divorced me had it been I who had proved infertile; and it was profitless also to guess that we would have been contented enough forever if she herself had been fulfilled.

I dare say it was a marriage like many another. We never quarreled. Seldom argued. Neither of us any longer cared enough for that; and as a total, prolonged way of life it was infinitely dispiriting.

It was a homecoming like thousands of others. I parked outside the closed garage doors and let myself into the house with arms full of air gun and exercise books. Sarah, home as usual from her part-time job as a dentist's receptionist, sat on the sofa in the sitting room reading a magazine.

"Hallo," I said.

"Hallo . . . good day?"

"Not bad."

She hadn't looked up from her pages. I hadn't kissed her. Perhaps for both of us it was better than total loneliness, but not much.

"There's ham for supper," she said. "And cole slaw. That all right?"

"Fine."

She went on reading; a slim fair-haired girl, still arrestingly pretty but now with a resentful expression. I was used to it, but in flashes suffered unbearable nostalgia for the laughing eagerness of the early days. I wondered sometimes if she noticed that the fun had gone out of me, too, although I could sometimes feel it still bubbling along inside, deeply buried.

On that particular evening I made an effort (as I did more and more rarely) to jog us out of our dimness.

"Look . . . let's just dump everything and go out to dinner. Maybe to Florestan's, where there's dancing."

She didn't look up. "Don't be silly."

"Let's just go."

"I don't want to." A pause. "I'd rather watch television." She turned a page, and added with indifference, "And we can't afford Florestan's prices."

"We could, if you'd enjoy it."

"No, I wouldn't."

"Well," I sighed. "I'll make a start on the books, then." She nodded faintly. "Supper at seven."

"All right."

I turned to go.

"There's a letter for you from William," she said with boredom in her voice. "I put it upstairs."

"Oh? Well, thanks."

She went on reading, and I took my stuff up to the third and smallest of our three bedrooms, which I used as a sort of study-cum-office. The real estate agent who had shown us the house had brightly described the room as "just right for the nursery," and had nearly lost himself the sale. I'd annexed the place for myself and made it as masculine as possible, but I was aware that for Sarah the spirit of unborn children still hovered there. She rarely went in. It was slightly unusual that she should have put the letter from my brother on my desk.

It said:

Dear Jonathan,

Please can I have thirty pounds? It's for going to the farm at half-term. I wrote to Mrs. Porter, and she'll have me. She says her rates have gone up because of inflation. It can't be for what I eat, as she mostly gives me bread and honey. (No complaints.) Also actually I need some money for riding, in case they won't let me earn any more rides at the stables by mucking out, they were a bit funny about it last time, something to do with the law and exploiting juveniles, I ask you. Can't wait to be sixteen and legally earn what I like. Anyway, if you could make it fifty quid it would be fine. If I can earn my riding, I'll send the extra twenty back, because if you don't want your heavy dough lifted at this high-class nick you have to have it embedded in concrete. Half-term is a week on Friday, early this year, so could you send it pronto?

Did you notice that Clinker did win the Wrap-Up 'chase at Stratford? If you don't want me to be a jockey, how about a tipster?

Hope you are well. And Sarah.

William

P.S. Can you come for Sports Day, or for Blah-Blah Day? I've got a prize for two plus two, you'll be astounded to hear.

Blah-Blah Day was Speech Day, at which the school prizes were handed out. I'd missed every one of William's, for one reason or another. I would go this time, I thought. Even William might sometimes feel lonely with no one close to him ever to see him collect his prizes, which he did with some monotony.

William went to private school thanks to a rich godfather who had left him a lot of money on trust "for his education and vocational training, and good luck to the little brat." William's trustees regularly paid his fees to the school and maintenance for clothes and etceteras to me, and I passed on cash to William as required. It was an arrangement which worked excellently on many counts, not least that it meant that William didn't have to live with Sarah and me. Her husband's noisy and independent-minded brother was not the child she wanted.

William spent his holidays on farms, and Sarah occasionally said that it was most unfair that William should have more money than I had and that William had been spoiled rotten from the day my mother had discovered she was pregnant again at the age of forty-six. Sarah and William, whenever they met, behaved mostly with wary restraint and only occasionally with direct truth. William had learned very quickly not to tease her, which was his natural inclination; and she had accepted that doling out sarcastic criticism invited a cutting response. They circled each other, in consequence, like exactly matched opponents unwilling to declare open war.

For as long as he could remember, William had been irresistibly attracted to horses and had long affirmed his intention to be a jockey, of which Sarah strongly and I mildly disapproved. Security, William said, was a dirty word. There were better things in life than a safe job. Sarah and I, I supposed, were happier with pattern and order and achievement. William increasingly as he grew through thirteen, fourteen, and now fifteen, seemed to hunger for air and speed and uncertainty. It was typical of him that he proposed to spend the week's midterm break in riding horses instead of working for the eight O level exams he was due to take immediately afterward.

I left his letter on my desk to remind myself to send him a check and unlocked the cabinet where I kept my guns.

The air gun that I'd taken to school was little more than a toy and needed no license or secure storage, but I also owned two Mauser 7.62's, an Enfield No. 4 7.62 and two Anschütz .22's, around which all sorts of regulations bristled, and also an old Lee Enfield .303, dating back from my early days and still as lethal as ever if one could raise the ammunition for it. The little I had, I hoarded, mostly out of nostalgia. There were no more .303 rounds being made, thanks to the army's switching to 7.62mm in the sixties.

I put the air gun back in its rack, checked that everything was as it should be, and locked the doors on the familiar smell of oil.

The telephone rang downstairs and Sarah answered it. I looked at the pile of exercise books, which would all have to be read and corrected and handed out to the boys again on Monday, and wondered why I didn't have a fixed-hours job that one didn't have to take home. It wasn't only for the pupils that homework was a drag.

I could hear Sarah's telephone-answering voice, loud and bright.

"Oh. Hallo, Peter. How nice . . ."

There was a long pause while Peter talked, and then from Sarah a rising wail.

"Oh, *no*. Oh, my *God*. Oh, no, Peter . . ." Horror, disbelief, great distress. A quality, anyway, which took me straight downstairs.

Sarah was sitting stiffly upright on the sofa, holding the telephone at the end of its long cord. "Oh, no," she was saying wildly. "It can't be true. It just *can't*."

She stared at me unseeingly, neck stretched upward, listening with even her eyes.

"Well, of course . . . of course, we will . . . Oh, Peter,

yes, of course . . . Yes, straight away. Yes . . . yes . . . we'll be there . . ." She glanced at her watch. "Nine o'clock. Perhaps a bit later. Will that do? All right then . . . and Peter, give her my love."

She clattered the receiver down with shaking hands.

"We'll have to go," she said. "Peter and Donna . . ."

"Not tonight," I protested. "Whatever it is, not tonight. I'm damn tired and I've got all those books . . ."

"Yes, at once, we must go at once."

"It's a hundred miles."

"I don't *care* how far it is. We must go *now. Now.*"

She stood up and practically ran toward the stairs.

"Pack a suitcase," she said. "Come on."

I followed her more slowly, half exasperated, half moved by her urgency. "Sarah, hold on a minute. What exactly has happened to Peter and Donna?"

She stopped four stairs up, and looked down at me over the bannister. She was already crying, her whole face screwed into agonized disorder.

"Donna." The words were indistinct. "Donna . . ."

"Has she had an accident?"

"No . . . not . . ."

"What, then?"

The question served only to increase the tears. "She . . . needs . . . me."

"You go, then," I said, feeling relieved at the solution. "I can manage without the car for a few days. Until Tuesday anyway. Monday I can get to school by bus."

"No . . . Peter wants you, too. He begged me . . . both of us."

"Why?" I said, but she was already running again up the stairs, and wouldn't answer.

I won't like it, I thought abruptly. Whatever had happened, she knew that I wouldn't like it and that my instincts would all be on the side of noninvolvement. I followed her upward with reluctance and found her already gathering clothes and toothpaste onto the bed.

"Donna has parents, hasn't she?" I said. "And Peter, too? So if something terrible's happened, why in God's name do they need *us?*"

"They're our friends." She was rushing about, crying and gulping and dropping things. It was much, much more than ordinary sympathy for any ill that might have befallen Donna: there was a quality of extravagance that both disturbed and antagonized.

"It's beyond the bounds of friendship," I said, "to go charging off to Norfolk hungry and tired and not knowing why. And I'm not going."

Sarah didn't seem to hear. The haphazard packing went ahead without pause and the tears developed into a low continuous grizzle.

Where once we had had many friends we now had just Donna and Peter, notwithstanding that they no longer lived five miles away and played squash on Tuesdays. All our other friends from before and after marriage had either dropped away or coupled and bred; and it was only Donna and Peter who like us had produced no children. Only Donna and Peter, who never talked nursery, whose company Sarah could bear.

She and Donna had once been long-time flat-mates. Peter and I, meeting for the first time as their subsequent husbands, had got on together amicably enough for the friendship to survive the Norfolk removal, though it was by now more a matter of birthday cards and telephone calls than of frequent house-to-house visits. We had spent a boating holiday together once on the canals. "We'll do it again next year," we'd all said, but we didn't.

"Is Donna ill?" I asked.

"No . . ."

"I'm not going," I said.

The keening grizzle stopped. Sarah looked a mess, standing there with vague reddened eyes and a clumsily folded nightdress. She stared down at the pale green froth that she wore against the chill of separate beds, and the disastrous news finally burst out of her.

"She was arrested," she said.

"Donna...arrested?" I was astounded. Donna was mouselike. Organized. Gentle. Apologetic. Anything but likely to be in trouble with the police.

"She's home now," Sarah said. "She's...Peter says she's ...well...*suicidal*. He says he can't cope with it." Her voice was rising. "He says he needs us *now*—this minute...He doesn't know what to do. He says we're the only people who can help."

She was crying again. Whatever it was, was too much.

"What," I said slowly, "has Donna done?"

"She went out shopping," Sarah said, trying at last to speak clearly. "And she stole...she stole..."

"Well, for heaven's sake," I said. "I know it's bloody for them, but thousands of people shoplift. So why all this excessive drama?"

"You don't listen," Sarah shouted. "Why don't you *listen?*"

"I—"

"She stole a *baby*."

TWO

We went to Norwich.

Sarah had been right. I didn't like the reason for our journey. I felt a severe aversion to being dragged into a highly charged emotional situation where nothing constructive could possibly be done. My feelings of friendship toward Peter and Donna were nowhere near strong enough. For Peter, perhaps. For Donna, definitely not.

All the same, when I thought of the tremendous forces working on that poor girl to impel her to such an action it occurred to me that perhaps the unseen universe didn't stop at the sort of electromagnetics that I taught. Every living cell, after all, generated electric charges: especially brain cells. If I put baby-snatching on a par with an electric storm, I could be happier with it.

Sarah sat silently beside me for most of the way, recovering, readjusting, preparing. She said only once what must have been in both of our minds.

"It could have been me."

"No," I said.

"You don't know . . . what it's like."

There was no answer. Short of having been born female and barren, there was no way of knowing. I had been told about five hundred times over the years in various tones from anguish to spite that I didn't know what it was like, and there was no more answer now than there had been the first time.

The long, lingering May evening made the driving easier than usual, although going northward out of London in the Friday night exodus was always a beast of a journey.

At the far, far end of it lay the neat new boxlike house with its big featureless net-curtained windows and its tidy oblongs of grass. One bright house in a street of others much the same. One proud statement that Peter had reached a certain salary level and still aspired to future improvement. A place and a way of life that I understood and saw no harm in: where William would suffocate.

The turmoil behind the uninformative net curtains was much as expected in some ways and much worse in others.

The usually meticulous tidy interior was in disarray, with unwashed cups and mugs making wet rings on every surface and clothes and papers scattered around. The trail, I came to realize, left by the in-and-out tramp of officialdom over the past two days.

Peter greeted us with gaunt eyes and the hushed voice of a death in the family; and probably for him and Donna what had happened was literally hurting them worse than a death. Donna herself sat in a silent huddle at one end of the big green sofa in their sitting room and made no attempt to respond to Sarah when she rushed to her side and put her arms around her in almost a frenzy of affection.

Peter said helplessly, "She won't talk . . . or eat . . ."

"Or go to the bathroom?"

"What?"

Sarah looked up at me with furious reproach, but I said mildly, "If she goes off to the bathroom when she feels the need, it's surely a good sign. It's such a *normal* act."

"Well, yes," Peter said limply. "She does."

"Good, then."

Sarah clearly thought that this was another prime example of what she called my general heartlessness, but I had meant only to reassure. I asked Peter what exactly had taken place, and as he wouldn't tell me in front of Donna herself, we removed to the kitchen.

In there, too, the police and medics and court officials and social workers had made the coffee and left the dishes. Peter seemed not to see the mess that in past times would have set both him and Donna busily wiping up. We sat at the table with the last remnants of daytime fading to dusk, and in that gentle light he slowly unlocked the horrors.

It was on the previous morning, he said, that Donna had taken the baby from its pram and driven off with it in her car. She had driven seventy-odd miles northeast to the coast, and had at some point abandoned the car with the baby inside it, and had walked off along the beach.

The car and the baby had been traced and found within hours, and Donna herself had been discovered sitting on the sand in pouring rain, speechless and stunned.

The police had arrested her, taken her to the station for a night in the cells, and paraded her before a magistrate in the morning. The bench had called for psychiatric reports, set a date for a hearing a week ahead and, despite protests from the baby's mother, set Donna free. Everyone had assured Peter she would only be put on probation, but he still shuddered from their appalling future of ignominy via the press and the neighborhood.

After a pause, and thinking of Donna's trancelike stare, I said, "You told Sarah she was suicidal."

He nodded miserably. "This afternoon I wanted to warm her. To put her to bed. I ran the bath for her." It was a while before he could go on. It seemed that the suicide attempt had been in deadly earnest: he had stopped her on the instant before she plunged herself and her switched-on hair-drier into the water. "And she still had all her clothes on," he said.

It seemed to me that what Donna urgently needed was

some expert and continuous psychiatric care in a comfortable private nursing home, all of which she was probably not going to get.

"Come on out for a drink," I said.

"But I *can't.*" He was slightly trembling all the time, as if his foundations were in an earthquake.

"Donna will be all right with Sarah."

"But she might try—"

"Sarah will look after her."

"But I can't face—"

"No," I said. "We'll buy a bottle."

I bought some Scotch and two glasses from a philosophical publican just before closing time, and we sat in my car to drink in a quiet tree-lined street three miles from Peter's home. Stars and streetlights between the shadowy leaves.

"What are we going to do?" he said despairingly.

"Time will pass."

"We'll never get over it. How can we? It's bloody... impossible." He choked on the last word and began to cry like a boy. An outrush of unbearable, pent-up, half-angry grief.

I took the wobbling glass out of his hand. Sat and waited and made vague sympathetic noises and wondered what to God I would have done if, as she said, it had been Sarah.

"And to happen now," he said at length, fishing for a handkerchief to blow his nose, "of all times."

"Er...oh?" I said.

He sniffed convulsively and wiped his cheeks. "Sorry about that."

"Don't be."

He sighed. "You're always so calm."

"Nothing like this has happened to me."

"I'm in a mess," he said.

"Well...it'll get better."

"No, I mean, besides Donna. I didn't know what to do...before...and now, after, I can't even *think.*"

"What sort of mess? Financial?"

"No. Well, not exactly." He paused uncertainly, needing a prompt.

"What then?"

I gave him his glass back. He looked at it vaguely, then drank most of the contents in one mouthful.

"You don't mind if I burden you?" he said.

"Of course not."

He was a couple of years younger than I, the same age as both Donna and Sarah; and all three of them, it had sometimes seemed to me, saw me not only as William's older brother but as their own. At any rate it was as natural to me as to him that he should tell me his troubles.

He was middling tall and thin and had recently grown a lengthy moustache which had not given him the overpoweringly macho appearance he might have been aiming for. He still looked an ordinary inoffensive competent guy who went around selling his computer know-how to small businesses on weekdays and tinkered with his boat on Sundays.

He dabbed his eyes again and for several minutes took slow, deep, calming breaths.

"I got into something which I wish I hadn't," he said.

"What sort of thing?"

"It started more or less as a joke." He finished the last inch of drink and I stretched across and poured him a refill. "There was this fellow. Our age, about. He'd come up from Newmarket, and we got talking in that pub you bought the whisky from. He said it would be great if you could get racing results from a computer. And we both laughed."

There was a silence.

"Did he know you worked with computers?" I said.

"I'd told him. You know how one does."

"So what happened next?"

"A week later I got a letter. From this fellow. Don't know how he got my address. From the pub, I suppose. The barman knows where I live." He took a gulp from his drink and was quiet for a while, and then went on, "The letter asked if I would like to help someone who was working out a computer program for handicapping horses. So I thought, why not? All handicaps for horse races are sorted out on computers, and the letter sounded quite official."

"But it wasn't?"

He shook his head. "A spot of private enterprise. But I still thought, why not? Anyone is entitled to work out his own program. There isn't such thing as *right* in handicapping unless the horses pass the post in the exact order that the computer weighted them, which they never do."

"You know a lot about it," I said.

"I've learned, these past few weeks." The thought brought no cheer. "I didn't even notice I was neglecting Donna, but she says I've hardly spoken to her for ages." His throat closed and he swallowed audibly. "Perhaps if I hadn't been so occupied . . ."

"Stop feeling guilty," I said. "Go on with the handicapping."

After a while he was able to.

"He gave me pages and pages of stuff. All handwritten in diabolical handwriting. He wanted it organized into programs that any fool could run on a computer." He paused. "You do know about computers."

"More about microchips than programming, which isn't saying much."

"The other way around from most people, though."

"I guess so," I said.

"Anyway, I did them. Quite a lot of them. It turned out they were all much the same sort of thing. They weren't really very difficult, once I'd got the hang of what the notes all meant. It was understanding those which was the worst. So anyway, I did the programs and got paid in cash." He stopped and moved restlessly in his seat, glum and frowning.

"So what is wrong?" I asked.

"Well . . . I said it would be best if I ran the programs a few times on the computer he was going to use, because so many computers are different from each other, and although he'd told me the make of the computer he'd be using and I'd made allowances, you never can really tell you've got no bugs until you actually try things out on the actual type of machine. But he wouldn't let me. I said he wasn't being reasonable and he told me to mind my own business. So I just shrugged him off and thought if he wanted to be so stupid it was his own affair. And then these other two men turned up."

"What other two men?"

"I don't know. They just sneered when I asked their names. They told me to hand over to them the programs I'd made on the horses. I said I already had. They said they were nothing to do with the person who'd paid for the job, but all the same I was to give them the programs."

"And did you?"

"Well, yes... in a way."

"But Peter—" I said.

He interrupted, "Yes, I know, but they were so bloody *frightening*. They came the day before yesterday—it seems years ago—in the evening. Donna had gone out for a walk. It was still light. About eight o'clock, I should think. She often goes for walks..." He trailed off again and I gave his glass a nudge with the bottle. "What?" he said. "Oh no, no more, thanks. Anyway, they came, and they were so *arrogant*, and they said I'd regret it if I didn't give them the programs. They said Donna was a pretty little missis, wasn't she, and they were sure I'd like her to stay that way." He swallowed. "I'd never have believed...I mean, that sort of thing doesn't *happen*."

It appeared, however, that it had.

"Well," he said, rallying. "What I gave them was all that I had in the house, but it was really only first drafts, so to speak. Pretty rough. I'd written three or four trial programs out in longhand, like I often do. I know a lot of people work on typewriters or even straight onto a computer, but I get on better with pencil and eraser, so what I gave them *looked* all right, especially if you didn't know the first thing about programming, which I should think they didn't, but not much of it would run as it stood. And I hadn't put the file names on anyway, or any REMs or anything, so even if they debugged the programs they wouldn't know what they referred to."

Disentangling the facts from the jargon; what he had done had been to deliver to possibly dangerous men a load of garbage, knowing full well what he was doing.

"I see," I said slowly, "what you meant by a mess."

"I'd decided to take Donna away for a few days, just to be safe. I was going to tell her as a nice surprise when I got home from work yesterday . . . and then the police turned up in my office, and said she'd taken . . . taken . . . oh Christ, how *could* she?"

I screwed the cap onto the bottle and I looked at my watch. "It's getting on for midnight," I said. "We'd better go back."

"I suppose so."

I paused with my hand on the ignition key. "Didn't you tell the police about your two unpleasant visitors?" I said.

"No, I didn't. I mean, how could I? They've been in and out of the house, and a policewoman too, but it was all about Donna. They wouldn't have listened . . . and anyway . . ."

"Anyway what?"

He shrugged uncomfortably. "I got paid in cash. Quite a lot. I'm not going to declare it for tax. If I told the police— well, I'd more or less have to."

"It might be better," I said.

He shook his head. "It would cost me a lot to tell the police, and what would I gain? They'd make a note of what I said and wait until Donna got bashed in the face before they did anything. I mean, they can't go around guarding everyone who's been vaguely threatened night and day, can they? And as for guarding *Donna* . . . well, they weren't very nice to her, you know. Really rotten, most of them were. They made cups of tea for each other and spoke over her head as if she was a lump of wood. You'd think she'd poked the baby's eyes out, the way they treated her."

It didn't seem unreasonable to me that official sympathy

had been mostly on the side of the baby's frantic mother, but I kept the thought to myself.

"Perhaps it would be best, then," I said, "if you did take Donna away for a bit, straight after the hearing. Can you get leave?"

He nodded.

"But what she really needs is proper psychiatric care. Even a spell in a mental hospital."

"No," he said.

"I'm not so sure you're right. They have a high success rate with mental illness nowadays. Modern drugs, and hormones, and all that."

"But she's not—" He stopped.

The old taboos died hard. "The brain is part of the body," I said. "It's not separate. And it goes wrong sometimes, just like anything else. Like the liver. Or the kidneys. You wouldn't hesitate if it was her kidneys."

He shook his head, though, and I didn't press it. Everyone had to decide things for themselves. I started the car and wheeled us back to the house, and Peter said as we turned into the short concrete driveway that Donna was usually happy on their boat, and he would take her away on that.

The weekend dragged on. I tried surreptitiously now and then to mark the inexorable exercise books, but the telephone rang more or less continuously, and as answering it seemed to be the domestic chore I was best fitted for, I slid into a routine of chat. Relatives, friends, press, officials, busybodies, cranks and stinkers, I talked with the lot.

Sarah cared for Donna with extreme tenderness and devotion and was rewarded with, at first, wan smiles and, gradually, low-toned speech. After that came hysterical tears, a brushing of hair, a tentative meal, a change of clothes, and a growth of invalid behavior.

When Peter talked to Donna it was in a miserable mixture of love, guilt and reproach, and he found many an opportunity of escaping into the garden. On Sunday morning he went off in his car at pub-opening time and returned late for lunch, and on Sunday afternoon I said with private relief that I would now have to go back home ready for school on Monday.

"I'm staying here," Sarah said. "Donna needs me. I'll ring my boss and explain. He owes me a week's leave anyway."

Donna gave her the by now ultra-dependent smile she had developed over the past two days, and Peter nodded with eager agreement.

"OK," I said slowly. "But take care."

"What of?" Sarah said.

I glanced at Peter, who was agitatedly shaking his head. All the same, it seemed sensible to take simple precautions.

"Don't let Donna go out alone," I said.

Donna blushed furiously, and Sarah was instantly angry, and I said helplessly, "I didn't mean—I meant keep her safe . . . from people who might want to be spiteful to her."

Sarah saw the sense in that and calmed down, and a short while later I was ready to leave.

I said goodbye to them in the house because there seemed to be always people in the street staring at the windows with avid eyes, and right at the last minute Peter thrust into my hand three cassettes for playing in the car if I should get bored on the way home. I glanced at them briefly: *The King and I, Oklahoma!,* and *West Side Story.* Hardly the latest hits, but I thanked him anyway, kissed Sarah for appearances, kissed Donna ditto, and with a regrettable lightening of spirits took myself off.

It was on the last third of the way home, when I tried *Oklahoma!* for company, that I found that what Peter had given me wasn't music at all, but quite something else.

Instead of "Oh, What a Beautiful Mornin'," I got a loud vibrating scratchy whine interspersed with brief bits of one-note plain whine. Shrugging, I wound the tape forward a bit, and tried again.

Same thing.

I ejected the tape, turned it over, and tried again. Same thing. Tried *The King and I* and *West Side Story*. All the same.

I knew that sort of noise from way back. One couldn't forget it, once one knew. The scratchy whine was made by two tones alternating very fast so that the ear could scarcely distinguish the upper from the lower. The plain whine indicated simply an interval with nothing happening. On *Oklahoma!*, fairly typical, the stretches of two-tone lasted anywhere from ten seconds to three minutes.

I was listening to the noise a computer produced when its programs were recorded onto ordinary cassette tape.

Cassettes were convenient and widely used, especially with smaller computers. One could store a whole host of different programs on cassette tapes, and simply pick out whichever was needed, and use it: but the cassettes were still just ordinary cassettes, and if one played the tape straightforwardly in the normal way on a cassette player, as I had done, one heard the vibrating whine.

Peter had given me three sixty-minute tapes of computer programs: and it wasn't so very difficult to guess what those programs would be about.

I wondered why he had given them to me in such an indirect way. I wondered, in fact, why he had given them to me at all. With a mental shrug I shoveled the tapes and their misleading boxes onto the dashboard and switched on the radio instead.

School on Monday was a holiday after the greenhouse emotions in Norfolk, and Louisa-the-technician's problems seemed moths' wings beside Donna's.

On Monday evening, while I was watching my own choice on the television with my feet on the coffee table, and eating cornflakes and cream, Peter telephoned.

"How's Donna?" I said.

"I don't know where she'd be without Sarah."

"And you?"

"Oh, pretty fair. Look, Jonathan, did you play any of those tapes?" His voice sounded tentative and half-apologetic.

"A bit of all of them," I said.

"Oh. Well, I expect you'll know what they are?"

"Your horse-handicapping programs?"

"Yes . . . er . . . will you keep them for me for now?" He gave me no chance to answer and rushed on. "You see, we're hoping to go off to the boat straight after the hearing on Friday. Well, we do have to believe Donna will get probation, even the nastiest of those officials said it would be so in such a case, but obviously she'll be terribly upset with having to go to court and everything and so we'll go away as soon as we can . . . and I didn't like the thought of leaving those cassettes lying around in the office, which they were, so I went over to fetch them yesterday morning, so I could give them to you. I mean, I didn't really think it out. I could have put them in the bank, or anywhere. I suppose what I really wanted was to get those tapes right out of my life so that if those two brutes came back asking for the programs I'd be able to say I hadn't got them and that they'd have to get them from the person I made them for."

It occurred to me not for the first time that for a computer programer Peter was no great shakes as a logical thinker, but maybe the circumstances were jamming the circuits.

"Have you heard from those men again?" I asked.

"No, thank God."

"They probably haven't found out yet . . ."

"Thanks very much," he said bitterly.

"I'll keep the tapes safe," I said. "As long as you like."

"Probably nothing else will happen. After all, I haven't done anything illegal. Or even faintly wrong."

It's the "if-we-don't-look-at-the-monster-he'll-go-away" syndrome, I thought. But maybe he was right.

"Why didn't you tell me what you were giving me?" I inquired. "Why *The King and I* dressing, and all that?"

"What?" His voice sounded almost puzzled, and then

cleared to understanding. "Oh, it was just that when I got home from the office you were all sitting down to lunch, and I didn't get a single chance to catch you away from the girls, and I didn't want to have to start explaining in front of them—so I just shoved them into those cases to give to you."

The faintest twitch of unease crossed my mind, but I smothered it. Peter's world since Donna took the baby had hardly been one of general common sense and normal behavior. He had acted pretty well, all in all, for someone hammered from all directions at once, and over the weekend I had felt an increase of respect for him, quite apart from liking.

"If you want to play those programs," he said, "you'll need a Grantley computer."

"I don't suppose—" I began.

"They might amuse William. He's mad on racing, isn't he?"

"Yes, he is."

"I spent so much time on them. I'd really like to know how they work out in practice. I mean, from someone who knows horses."

"All right," I said. But Grantley computers weren't scattered freely around the landscape, and William had his exams ahead, so the prospect of actually using the programs seemed a long way off.

"I wish you were still here," he said. "All the telephone calls, they're really getting me down. And did you have any of those poisonous abusive beastly voices spitting out hate against Donna, when you were answering?"

"Yes, several."

"But they've never even *met* her."

"They're unbalanced. Just don't listen."

"What did you say to them?"

"I told them to take their problems to a doctor."

There was a slightly uncomfortable pause, then he said explosively, "I wish to God Donna had gone to a doctor." A gulp. "I didn't even *know* . . . I mean, I knew she'd wanted children, but I thought, well, we couldn't have them, so that was that. I never *dreamed*... I mean, she's always so quiet and wouldn't hurt a fly. She never showed any signs... We're pretty fond of each other, you know. Or at least I thought—"

"Peter, stop it."

"Yes." A pause. "Of course, you're right. But it's difficult to think of anything else."

We talked a bit more, but only covering the same old ground, and we disconnected with me feeling that somehow I could have done more for him than I had.

Two evenings later he went down to the river to work on his two-berth cabin cruiser, filling its tanks with water and fuel, installing new cooking-gas cylinders and checking that everything was in working order for his trip with Donna.

He had been telling me earlier that he was afraid the ship's battery was wearing out and that if he didn't get a new one they would run it down flat with their lights at night and in the morning find themselves unable to start the engine. It had happened once before, he said.

He wanted to check that the battery still had enough life in it.

It had.

When he raised the first spark, the rear half of the boat exploded.

THREE

Sarah told me.

Sarah on the telephone with the stark over-controlled voice of exhaustion.

"They think it was gas, or petrol vapor. They don't know yet."

"Peter..."

"He's dead," she said. "There were people around. They saw him moving...with his clothes on fire. He went over the side into the water, but when they got him out—" A sudden silence, then, slowly, "We weren't there. Thank God Donna and I weren't there."

I felt shaky and slightly sick. "Do you want me to come?" I said.

"No. What time is it?"

"Eleven." I had undressed, in fact, to go to bed.

"Donna's asleep. Knockout drops."

"And how...is she?"

"Christ, how would you expect?" Sarah seldom spoke in that way: a true measure of the general awfulness. "And

Friday," she said. "The day after tomorrow. She's due in court."

"They'll be kind to her."

"There's already been one call, just now, with some beastly woman telling me it served her right."

"I'd better come," I said.

"You can't. There's school. No, don't worry. I can cope. The doctor at least said he'd keep Donna heavily sedated for several days."

"Let me know, then, if I can help."

"Yes," she said. "Good night, now. I'm going to bed. There's a lot to do tomorrow. Good night."

I lay long awake in bed and thought of Peter and the unfairness of death: and in the morning I went to school and found him flicking in and out of my mind all day.

Driving home I saw that his cassettes were still lying in a jumble on the dashboard. Once parked in the garage I put the tapes back into their boxes, slipped them in my jacket pocket, and carried my usual burden of books indoors.

The telephone rang almost at once, but it was not Sarah, which was my first thought, but William.

"Did you send my check?" he said.

"*Hell*, I forgot." I told him why, and he allowed that forgetting in such circs could be overlooked.

"I'll write it straight away, and send it direct to the farm."

"OK. Look, I'm sorry about Peter. He seemed a nice guy, that time we met."

"Yes." I told William about the computer tapes, and about Peter wanting his opinion on them.

"Bit late now."

"But you still might find them interesting."

"Yeah," he said without much enthusiasm. "Probably some nutty betting system. There's a computer here somewhere in the math department. I'll ask what sort it is. And look, how would it grab you if I didn't go to university?"

"Badly."

"Yeah. I was afraid so. Anyway, work on it, big brother. There's been a lot of guff going on this term about choosing a career, but I reckon it's the career that chooses *you*. I'm going to be a jockey. I can't help it."

We said goodbye and I put the receiver down thinking that it wasn't much good fighting to dissuade someone who at fifteen already felt that a vocation had him by the scruff of the neck.

He was slim and light: past puberty but still physically a boy, with the growth into man's stature just ahead. Perhaps nature, I thought hopefully, would take him to my height of six feet and break his heart.

Sarah rang almost immediately afterward, speaking crisply with her dentist's-assistant voice. The shock had gone, and the exhaustion. She spoke to me with edgy bossiness, a leftover, I guessed, from a very demanding day.

"It seems that Peter should have been more careful," she said. "Everyone who owns a boat with an inboard engine is repeatedly told not to start up until they are sure that no gas or petrol or petrol vapor has accumulated in the bilge. Boats blow up every year. He must have known. You wouldn't think he would be so stupid."

I said mildly, "He had a great deal else on his mind."

"I suppose he had, but all the same everyone says—"

If you could blame a man for his own death, I thought, it diminished the chore of sympathy. "It was his own fault . . ." I could hear the sharp voice of my aunt over the death of her neighbor. "He shouldn't have gone out with that cold."

"The insurance company," I said to Sarah, "may be trying to wriggle out of paying all they might."

"What?"

"Putting the blame onto the victim is a well-known ploy."

"But he should have been more careful."

"Oh, sure. But for Donna's sake, I wouldn't go around saying so."

There was a silence which came across as resentful. Then she said, "Donna wanted me to tell you . . . she'd rather you didn't come here this weekend. She says she could bear things better if she's alone with me."

"And you agree?"

"Well, yes, frankly, I do."

"OK, then."

"You don't mind?" She sounded surprised.

"No. I'm sure she's right. She relies on you." And too much, I thought. "Is she still drugged?"

"Sedated." The word was a reproof.

"Sedated, then?"

"Yes, of course."

"And for the court hearing tomorrow?" I asked.

"Tranquilizers," Sarah said decisively. "Sleeping pills after."

"Good luck with it."

"Yes," she said.

She disconnected almost brusquely, leaving me with the easement of having been let off an unpleasant task. Once upon a time, I supposed, we would have clung together to help Donna. At the beginning our reactions would have been truer, less complicated, less distorted by our own depressions. I mourned for the dead days, but undoubtedly I was pleased not to be spending the weekend with my wife.

On the Friday I went to school still with the computer tapes in my jacket pocket, and, feeling that I owed it to Peter at least to try to play them, sought out one of the math masters in the common room. Ted Pitts, short-sighted, clear-headed, bilingual in English and algebra.

"That computer you've got tucked away somewhere in a cubbyhole in the math department," I said. "It's your special baby, isn't it?"

"We all use it. We teach the kids."

"But it's you who plays it like Beethoven while the rest are still at chopsticks?"

He enjoyed the compliment in his quiet way. "Maybe," he said.

"Could you tell me what make it is?" I asked.

"Sure. It's a Harris."

"I suppose," I said unhopefully, "that you couldn't run a tape on it that was recorded on a Grantley?"

"It depends," he said Ie was earnest and thoughtful,

twenty-six, short on humor but full of good intentions and ideals of fair play. He suffered greatly under the sourly detestable Jenkins who was head of the math department and extracted from his assistants the reverential attitude he never got from me.

"The Harris had no language built into it," Ted said. "You can feed it any computer language, FORTRAN, COBOL, ALGOL, Z–80, BASIC, you name it, the Harris will take it. Then you can run any programs written in those languages. But the Grantley is a smaller affair which comes all ready preprogramed with its own form of BASIC. If you had a Grantley BASIC language tape, you could feed it into our Harris's memory, and then you could run Grantley BASIC programs." He paused. "Er . . . is that clear?"

"Sort of." I reflected. "How difficult would it be to get a Grantley BASIC language tape?"

"Don't know. Best to write to the firm direct. They might send you one. And they might not."

"Why might they not?"

He shrugged. "They might say you'd have to buy one of their computers."

"For heaven's sake," I said.

"Yeah. Well, see, these computer firms are very awkward. All the smaller personal computers use BASIC, because it's the easiest language and also one of the best. But the firms making them all build in their own variations, so that if you record your programs from their machines, you can't run them on anyone else's. That keeps you faithful to *them* in the future, because if you change to another make, all your tapes will be useless."

"What a bore," I said.

He nodded. "Profits getting the better of common sense."

"Like all those infuriating incompatible video recorders."

"Exactly. But you'd think the computer firms would have more sense. They may hang on to their own customers by force, but they're sure as Hades not going to persuade anyone else to switch."

"Thanks anyway," I said.

"You're welcome." He hesitated. "Do you actually have a tape that you want to use?"

"Yes." I fished in my pocket and produced *Oklahoma!* "This one and two others. Don't be misled by the packaging. It's got computer noise all right on the tape."

"Were they recorded by an expert or an amateur?"

"An expert. Does it make any difference?"

"Sometimes."

I explained about Peter's making the tapes for a client who had a Grantley, and I added that the customer wouldn't let Peter try out the programs on the machine they were designed to run on.

"Oh, really?" Ted Pitts seemed happy with the news. "In that case, if he was a conscientious and careful chap, it's just possible that he recorded the machine language itself on the first of the tapes. TOMs can be very touchy. He might have thought it would be safer."

"You've lost me," I said. "What are TOMs?"

"Computers." He grinned. "Stands for Totally Obedient Moron."

"You've made a joke," I said disbelievingly.

"Not mine, though."

"So why should it be safer?"

He looked at me reproachfully. "I thought you knew more about computers than you appear to."

"It's ten years at least since I knew more. I've forgotten and they've changed."

"It would be safer," he said patiently, "because if the client rang up and complained that the program wouldn't run, your friend could tell them how to stuff into their computer a brand-new version of its own language, and then your friend's programs *would* run from that. Mind you," he added judiciously, "you'd use up an awful lot of computer space putting the language in. You might not have much room for the actual programs."

He looked at my expression and sighed.

"OK," he said. "Suppose a Grantley has a 32K store, which is a pretty normal size. That means it has about forty-nine thousand store-slots, of which probably the first seventeen thousand are used in providing the right circuits to function as BASIC. That would leave you about thirty-two thousand store-slots for punching in your programs. Right?"

I nodded. "I'll take it on trust."

"But then if you feed in the language all over again it would take another seventeen thousand store-slots, which would leave you with under fifteen thousand store-slots to work with. And as you need one store-slot for every letter you type, and one for every number, and one for every space, and comma, and bracket, you wouldn't be able to do a great deal before all the store-slots were used and the whole thing was full up. And at that point the computer would stop working." He smiled. "So many people think computers are bottomless pits. They're more like bean bags. Once they're full you have to empty the beans out before you can start to fill them again."

"Is that what you teach the kids?"

He looked slightly confused. "Er... yes. Same words. One gets into a rut."

The bell rang for afternoon registration and he stretched out his hand for the tape. "I could try that," he said, "if you like."

"Yes. If it isn't an awful bother."

He shook his head encouragingly, and I gave him *The King and I* and *West Side Story* for good measure.

"Can't promise it will be today," he said. "I've got classes all afternoon and Jenkins wants to see me at four." He grimaced. "Jenkins. Why can't we call him Ralph and be done with it."

"There's no hurry," I said, "with the tapes."

Donna got her probation.

Sarah reported, again sounding tired, that even the baby's mother had quieted down because of Peter's being killed, and Donna had gently wept in court, and even some of the policemen had been fatherly.

"How is she?" I said.

"Miserable. It's just hitting her, I think, that Peter's really gone." Her voice sounded protective.

"No more suicide?" I asked.

"I don't think so, but the poor darling is so *vulnerable*. So easily hurt. She says it's like living without skin."

"Have you enough money?" I said.

"That's just like you!" she exclaimed. "Always so damned practical."

"But—"

"I've got my bank card."

I hadn't wanted to wallow too long in Donna's emotions and it had irritated her. We both knew it. We knew each other too well.

"Don't let her wear you out," I said.

Her voice came back still sharply, "I'm perfectly all right. There's no question of wearing me out. I'm staying here for a week or two longer at least. Until after the inquest and the funeral. And after that, if Donna needs me. I've told my boss, and he understands."

I wondered fleetingly whether I might not become too fond of living alone if she were away a whole month. I said, "I'd like to be there at the funeral."

"Yes. Well, I'll let you know."

I got a tart and untender goodnight: but then my own to her hadn't been loving. We wouldn't be able to go on, I thought, if ever the politeness crumbled.

The building had long been uninhabited, and we were only a short step from demolition.

On Saturday I put the Mausers and the Enfield No. 4 in the car and drove to Bisley and let off a lot of bullets over the Surrey ranges.

During the past few months my visits there had become less constant, partly, of course, because there was no delight in the winter in pressing one's stomach to the cold earth, but mostly because my intense love of the sport seemed to be waning.

I had been a member of the British rifle team for several

years but now never wore any of the badges to prove it. I kept quiet in the bar after shooting and listened to others analyze their performances and spill the excitement out of their systems. I didn't like talking of my own scores, present or past.

A few years back I had taken the sideways jump of entering for the Olympics, which was a competition for individuals and quite different from my normal pursuits. Even the guns were different (at that time all small bore) and all the distances the same (300 meters). It was a world dominated by the Swiss, but I had shot luckily and well in the event and had finished high for a Briton in the placings. It had been marvelous. The day of a lifetime; but it had faded into memory, grown fuzzy with time passing.

In the British team, which competed mostly against the old Commonwealth countries and often won, one shot 7.62mm guns at varying distances, 300, 500, 600, 900, and 1,000 yards. I had always taken immense delight in accuracy, in judging wind velocity and air temperature and getting the climatic variables exactly right. But now, both internally and externally, the point of such skill was fading.

The smooth elegant Mausers that I cherished were already within sight of being obsolete. Only long-distance assassins, these days, seemed to need totally accurate rifles, and *they* used telescopic sights, which were banned and anathema to target shooters. Modern armies tended to spray out bullets regardless. None of the army rifles shot absolutely straight, and in addition, every advance in effective killing-power was a loss to aesthetics. The marksman's special skill was drifting toward sport, as archery had, as swordplay had, as throwing the javelin and the hammer had; the commonplace weapon of one age becoming the Olympic medal of the next.

I didn't shoot very well on that particular afternoon and found little appetite afterward for the camaraderie in the clubhouse. The image of Peter stumbling over the side of his boat on fire and dying made too many things seem irrelevant.

I was pledged to shoot in the Queen's Prize in July and in a competition in Canada in August, and I reflected driving home that if I didn't put in a little more practice I would disgrace myself. The trips overseas came up at fairly regular intervals, and because of the difficulties involved in transporting guns from one country to another I had designed my own carrying case. About four feet long and externally looking like an ordinary extra-large suitcase, it was internally lined with aluminum and divided into padded shock-absorbing compartments. It held everything I needed for competitions, not only three rifles but all the other paraphernalia, such as scorebook, ear-defenders, telescope, cleaning things, ammunition, thick jersey for warmth, and a supporting canvas and leather jacket. Unlike many people I usually carried the guns fully assembled and ready to go, legacy of having missed my turn once because of traffic hold-ups, a firearm still in pieces and fingers trembling with haste. I was not actually supposed to leave them with the bolt in place, but I often did. Only when the special gun suitcase went onto airplanes did I strictly conform to regulations, and then it was bonded and sealed and hedged about with red tape galore; and also, perhaps because it didn't look like what it was, I'd never lost it.

Sarah, who had been enthusiastic at the beginning and had gone with me often to Bisley, had in time got tired of the bang bang bang, as most wives did. She had tired also of my spending so much time and money and had been only partly mollified by the Olympic Games. All the jobs I applied for, she had pointed out crossly, let us live south of London, convenient for the ranges. "But if I could ski," I said, "it would be silly to move to the tropics."

She had a point, though. Shooting wasn't cheap, and I wouldn't have been able to do as much as I did without support from indirect sponsors. The sponsors expected in return that I would not only go to the international competitions, but go to them practiced and fit: conditions that until very recently I'd been happy to fulfill. I was getting old, I thought. I would be thirty-four in three months.

TWICE SHY

I drove home without haste and let myself into the quiet house, which was no longer vibrant with silent tensions. Dumped my case on the coffee table in the sitting room with no one to suggest I take it straight upstairs. Unclipped the locks and thought of the pleasant change of being able to go through the cleaning and oiling routine in front of the television without tight-lipped disapproval. Decided to postpone the clean-up until I'd chosen what to have for supper and poured out a reviving Scotch.

Chose a frozen pizza. Poured the Scotch.

The front doorbell rang at that point and I went to answer it. Two men, olive-skinned, dark-haired, stood on the doorstep: and one of them held a pistol.

I looked at it with a sort of delayed reaction, not registering at once, because I'd been looking at peaceful firearms all day. It took me at least a whole second to realize that this one was pointing at my midriff in a thoroughly unfriendly fashion. A Walther .22, I thought: as if it mattered.

My mouth, I dare say, opened and shut. It wasn't what one expected in a moderately crime-free suburb.

"Back," he said.

"What do you want?"

"Get inside." He prodded toward me with the long silencer attached to the automatic and because I certainly respected the blowing-away power of hand guns I did as he said. He and his friend advanced through the front door and closed it behind them.

"Raise your hands," said the gunman.

I did so.

He glanced toward the open door of the sitting room and jerked his head toward it.

"Go in there."

I went slowly and stopped, and turned, and said again, "What do you want?"

"Wait," he said. He glanced at his companion and jerked his head again, this time at the windows. The companion switched on the lights and then went across and closed the curtains. It was not yet dark outside. A shaft of evening sunshine pierced through where the curtains met.

I thought: why aren't I desperately afraid. They looked so purposeful, so intent. Yet I still thought they had made some sort of weird mistake and might depart if nicely spoken to.

They seemed younger than myself, though it was difficult to be sure. Italian, perhaps; from the South. They had the long straight noses, the narrow jaws, the black-brown eyes. The sort of faces which went fat with age and grew moustaches and became godfathers.

That last thought shot through my brain from nowhere and seemed as nonsensical as the pistol.

"What do you want?" I said again.

"Three computer tapes."

My mouth no doubt went again through the fish routine. I listened to the utterly English sloppy accent and thought that it couldn't have less matched the body it came from.

"What . . . computer tapes?" I said, putting on bewilderment.

"Stop messing. We know you've got them. Your wife said so."

Jesus, I thought. The bewilderment this time needed no acting.

He jerked the gun a fraction. "Get them," he said. His eyes were cold. His manner showed he despised me.

I said with a suddenly dry mouth, "I can't think why my wife said . . . why she thought—"

"Stop wasting time," he said sharply.

"But—"

"The King and I, and *West Side Story,"* he said impatiently, "and *Okla-fucking-homa."*

"I haven't got them."

"Then that's too bad, buddy boy," he said; and there was in an instant in him an extra dimension of menace. Before, he had been fooling along in second gear, believing no doubt that a gun was enough. But now I uncomfortably perceived that I was not dealing with someone reasonable and safe. If these were the two who had visited Peter, I understood what he had meant by frightening. There was a volatile quality, an absence of normal inhibition, a powerful impression of recklessness. The brakes-off syndrome which no legal deterrents deterred. I'd sensed it occasionally in boys I'd taught, but never before at such magnitude.

"You've got something you've no right to," he said. "And you'll give it to us."

He moved the muzzle of the gun an inch or two sideways and squeezed the trigger. I heard the bullet zing past close to my ear. There was a crash of glass breaking behind me. One of Sarah's mementoes of Venice, much cherished.

"That was a vase," he said. "Your television's next. After that, you. Ankles and such. Give you a limp for life. Those tapes aren't worth it."

He was right. The trouble was that I doubted if he would believe that I really hadn't got them.

He began to swing the gun around to the television.

"OK," I said.

He sneered slightly. "Get them then."

With my capitulation he relaxed complacently, and so did his obedient and unspeaking assistant, who was standing a pace to his rear. I walked the few steps to the coffee table and lowered my hands from the raised position.

"They're in the suitcase," I said.

"Get them out."

I lifted the lid of the suitcase a little and pulled out the jersey, dropping it on the floor.

"Hurry up," he said.

He wasn't in the least prepared to be faced with a rifle; not in that room, in that neighborhood, in the hands of the man he took me for.

It was with total disbelief that he looked at the long deadly shape and heard the double click as I worked the bolt. There was a chance he would realize that I'd never transport such a weapon with a bullet up the spout, but then if he took his own shooter around loaded, perhaps he wouldn't.

"Drop the pistol," I said. "You shoot me, I'll shoot you both, and you'd better believe it. I'm a crack shot." There was a time for boasting, perhaps; and that was it.

He wavered. The assistant looked scared. The rifle was an ultra-scary weapon. The silencer slowly began to point downward, and the automatic thudded to the carpet. The anger could be felt.

"Kick it over here," I said. "And gently."

He gave the gun a furious shove with his foot. It wasn't near enough for me to pick up, but too far for him also.

"Right," I said. "Now you listen to me. I haven't got those tapes. I've lent them to someone else, because I thought they were music. How the hell should I know they were computer tapes? If you want them back you'll have to wait until I get them. The person I lent them to has gone away for the weekend and I've no way of finding out where. You can have them without all this melodrama, but you'll have to wait. Give me an address, and I'll send them to you. I frankly want to get shut of you. I don't give a damn about those tapes or what you want them for. I just don't want you bothering me . . . or my wife. Understood?"

"Yeah."

"Where do you want them sent?"

His eyes narrowed.

"And it will cost you two quid," I said. "For packing and postage."

The mundane detail seemed to convince him. With a disgruntled gesture he took two pounds from his pocket and dropped them at his feet.

"Cambridge main post office," he said. "To be collected."

"Under what name?"

After a pause he said, "Derry."

I nodded. "Right," I said. A pity, though, that he'd given my own name. Anything else might have been informative. "You can get out, now."

Both pairs of eyes looked down at the automatic now on the carpet.

"Wait in the road," I said. "I'll throw it to you through the window. And don't come back."

They edged to the door with an eye on the sleek steel barrel following them, and I went out after them into the hall. I got the benefit of two viciously frustrated expressions before they opened the front door and went out, closing it again behind them.

Back in the sitting room I put the rifle on the sofa and picked up the Walther to unclip it and empty its magazine into an ashtray. Then I unscrewed the silencer from the barrel, and opened the window.

The two men stood on the pavement, balefully staring across twenty feet of grass. I threw the pistol so that it landed in a rose bush not far from their feet. When the assistant had picked it out and scratched himself on the thorns I threw the silencer into the same place.

The gunman, finding he had no bullets, delivered a verbal parting shot.

"You send those tapes, or we'll be back."

"You'll get them next week. And stay out of my life."

I shut the window decisively and watched them walk away, every line of their bodies rigid with discomfiture.

What on *earth*, I wondered intensely, had Peter programed onto those cassettes?

FOUR

"Who," I said to Sarah, "asked you for computer tapes?"

"What?" She sounded vague; a hundred miles away, on this planet but in another world.

"Someone," I said patiently, "must have asked you for some tapes."

"Oh . . . you mean cassettes?"

"Yes, I do." I tried to keep any grimness out of my voice, to sound merely conversational.

"But you can't have got his letter already," she said, puzzled. "He only came this morning."

"Who was he?" I said.

"Oh!" she exclaimed. "I suppose he telephoned. He could have got our number from information."

"Sarah . . ."

"Who was he? I've no idea. Someone to do with Peter's work."

"What sort of man?" I asked.

"What do you mean? Just a man. Middle-aged, gray-haired, a bit plump." Sarah herself, like many naturally slim people, saw plumpness as a moral fault.

"Tell me what he said," I pressed.

"If you insist. He said he was so sorry about Peter. He said Peter had brought home a project he'd been working on for his firm, possibly in the form of handwritten notes, possibly in the form of cassettes. He said the firm would be grateful to have it all back, because they would have to reallocate the job to someone else."

It all sounded a great deal more civilized than frighteners with waving guns.

"And then?" I prompted.

"Well, Donna said she didn't know of anything Peter had in the house, though she did of course know he'd been working on *something*. Anyway, she looked in a lot of cupboards and drawers, and she found these three loose cassettes, out of their boxes, stacked between the gin and the Cinzano in the liquor cabinet. Am I boring you?"

She sounded overpolite and as if boring had been her intention, but I simply answered fervently, "No, you're not. Please do go on."

The shrug traveled almost visibly down the wire. "Donna gave them to the man. He was delighted until he looked at them closely. Then he said they were tapes of musicals and not what he wanted, and please would we look again."

"And then either you or Donna remembered—"

"I did," she affirmed. "We both saw Peter give them to you, but he must have got them mixed up. He gave you his firm's cassettes by mistake."

Peter's firm . . .

"Did the man give you his name?" I said.

"Yes," Sarah said. "He introduced himself when he arrived. But you know how it is. He mumbled it a bit and I've forgotten it. Why? Didn't he tell you when he rang up?"

"No visiting card?"

"Don't tell me," she said with exasperation, "that you didn't take his address. Wait a moment, I'll ask Donna."

She put the receiver down on the table and I could hear

her calling Donna. I wondered why I hadn't told her of the nature of my visitors and decided it was probably because she would try to argue me into going to the police. I certainly didn't want to do that, because they were likely to take unkindly to my waving a rifle about in such a place. I couldn't prove to them that it had been unloaded, and it did not come into the category of things a householder could reasonably use to defend his property. Bullets fired from a Mauser 7.62 didn't at ten paces smash vases and embed themselves in the plaster, they seared straight through the wall itself and killed people outside walking their dogs.

Firearms certificates could be taken away faster than given.

"Jonathan?" Sarah said, coming back.

"Yes..."

She read out the full address of Peter's firm in Norwich and added the telephone number.

"Is that all?" she said.

"Except... you're both still all right?"

"I am, thank you. Donna's very low. But I'm coping."

We said our usual goodbyes: almost formal, without warmth, deadly polite.

Duty took me back to Bisley the following day: duty and restlessness and dreadful prospects on the box. I shot better and thought less about Peter, and when the light began to fade I went home and corrected the ever-recurring exercise books: and on Monday Ted Pitts said he hadn't yet done anything about my computer tapes but that if I cared to stay on at four o'clock we could both go down to the computer room and see what there was to see.

When I joined him he was already busy in the small sideroom that with its dim cream walls and scratchily polished floor had an air of being everybody's poor relation. A single light hung without a shade from the ceiling, and the two wooden chairs were regulation battered school issue. Two nondescript tables occupied most of the floor space;

and upon them rested the uninspiring-looking machines which had cost a small fortune. I asked Ted mildly why he put up with such cramped, depressing quarters.

He looked at me vaguely, his mind on his task. "You know how it is. You have to teach boys individually on this baby to get good results. There aren't enough classrooms. This is all that's available. It's not too bad. And anyway, I never notice."

I could believe it. He was a hiker, an ex-youth-hosteler, and embracer of earnest discomforts. He perched on the edge of the hard wooden chair and applied his own computerlike brain to the one on the tables.

There were four separate pieces of equipment. A box like a small television set with a typewriter keyboard protruding forward from the lower edge of the screen. A cassette player. A large upright uninformative black box marked simply "Harris"; and something which looked at first sight like a typewriter, but which in fact had no keys. All four were linked together, and each to its own wall socket, by black electric cables.

Ted Pitts put *Oklahoma!* into the cassette player and typed CLOAD "BASIC" on the keyboard. CLOAD "BASIC" appeared in small white capital letters high up on the left of the television screen, and two asterisks appeared, one of them rapidly blinking on and off, up on the right. On the cassette player, the wheels of the tape reels quickly revolved.

"How much do you remember?" Ted said.

"About enough to know that you're searching the tape for the language, and that CLOAD means load from the cassette."

He nodded and pointed briefly to the large upright box. "The computer already has its own BASIC stored in there. I put it in at lunchtime. Now just let's see..." He hunched himself over the keyboard, pressing keys, stopping and starting the cassette player and punctuating his activity with grunts.

"Nothing useful," he muttered, turning the tapes over and repeating the process. "Let's try . . ." A fair time passed. He shook his head now and then, and said finally, "Give me those other two tapes. It must logically be at the *beginning* of one of the sides . . . unless of course he added it at the end simply because he had space left. Or perhaps he didn't do it at all."

"Won't the programs run on your own version of BASIC?"

He shook his head. "I tried before you came. The only response you get is ERROR IN LINE 10. Which means that the two versions aren't compatible." He grunted again and tried *West Side Story,* and toward the end of the first side he sat bolt upright and said, "Well, now."

"It's on there?"

"Can't tell yet. But there's something filed under 'Z.' Might just try that." He flicked a few more switches and sat back beaming. "Now all we do is wait a few minutes while that"—he pointed at the large upright box—"soaks up whatever it is on the tape under 'Z,' and if it should happen to be Grantley BASIC, we'll be in business."

"Why does 'Z' give you hope?"

"Instinct. Might be a hundred percent wrong. But it's a much longer recording than anything else I've found so far on the tapes, and it feels the right length. Four and a quarter minutes. I've fed BASIC into the Harris thousands of times."

His instinct proved reliable. The word READY suddenly appeared on the screen, white and bright and promising. Ted sighed heavily with satisfaction and nodded three times.

"Sensible fellow, your friend," he said. "So now we can see what you've got."

When he ran *Oklahoma!* again the file names came up clearly beside the flashing asterisk at top right of the screen, and although some of them were mysterious to me, some of them were definitely not.

DONCA EDINB EPSOM FOLKE FONTW GOODW HAMIL HAYDK HEREF HEXHM

"Names of towns," I said. "Towns with racecourses."

Ted nodded. "Which would you like to try?"

"Epsom."

"OK," he said. He rewound the tape with agile fingers and typed CLOAD "EPSOM" on the keyboard. "This puts the program filed under EPSOM into the computer, but you know that, of course. I keep forgetting."

The encouraging word READY appeared again, and Ted said, "Which do you want to do, list it or run it?"

"Run," I said.

He nodded and typed RUN on the keyboard, and in bright little letters the screen inquired:

WHICH RACE AT EPSOM? TYPE NAME OF RACE AND
PRESS 'ENTER'.

"My God," I said. "Let's try the Derby."

"Stands to reason," Ted said, and typed DERBY. The screen promptly responded with:

TYPE NAME OF HORSE AND PRESS 'ENTER'.

Ted typed JONATHAN DERRY and pressed the double-sized key on the keyboard marked ENTER; and the screen obliged with:

EPSOM: THE DERBY.
HORSE: JONATHAN DERRY.
TO ALL QUESTIONS ANSWER YES OR NO AND PRESS
'ENTER'.

A couple of inches lower down there was a question:

HAS HORSE WON A RACE?

Ted typed YES and pressed ENTER. The first three lines remained, but the question was replaced with another:

HAS HORSE WON THIS YEAR?

Ted typed NO. The screen responded:

HAS HORSE WON ON COURSE?

Ted typed NO. The screen responded:

HAS HORSE RUN ON COURSE?

Ted typed YES.

There were questions about the horse's sire, its dam, its jockey, its trainer, the number of days since its last run, and its earnings in prize money; and one final question:

IS HORSE QUOTED ANTE-POST AT 25—1 OR LESS?

Ted typed YES and the screen said merely

ANY MORE HORSES?

Ted typed YES again, and we found ourselves back at

TYPE NAME OF HORSE AND PRESS 'ENTER'.

"That's not handicapping," I said.
"Is that what it's supposed to be?" Ted shook his head. "More like statistical probabilities, I should have thought. Let's go through it again and answer NO to ANY MORE HORSES?"

He typed TED PITTS for the horse's name and varied the answers, and immediately after his final NO we were presented with a cleared screen and a new display.

HORSE'S NAME	WIN FACTOR
JONATHAN	
DERRY	27
TED PITTS	12

"You've *no* chance," I said. "You might as well stay in the stable."

He looked a bit startled, and then laughed. "Yes. That's what it is. A guide to gamblers."

He typed LIST instead of RUN, and immediately the bones of the program appeared, but scrolling upward too fast to read, like flight-information changes at airports. Ted merely hummed a little and typed LIST 10–140, and after some essential flickering the screen presented the goods:

```
LIST 10–140
10 PRINT "WHICH RACE AT EPSOM? TYPE NAME OF
RACE AND PRESS 'ENTER'"
20 INPUT A$
30 IF A$ = "DERBY" THEN 330
40 IF A$ = "OAKS" THEN 340
50 IF A$ = "CORONATION CUP" THEN 350
60 IF A$ = "BLUE RIBAND STAKES" THEN 360
```

The list went down to the bottom of the screen in this fashion, and Ted gave it one appraising look and said, "Dead simple."

The dollar sign, I seemed to remember, meant that the input had to be in the form of letters. Input A, without the dollar sign, would have asked for numbers.

Ted seemed perfectly happy. He typed LIST 300–380 and got another set of instructions.

At 330 the program read:

```
LET A = 10: B = 8: C = 6: D = 2: D1 = 2
```

Lines 332, 334 and 336 looked similar, with numbers being ascribed to letters.

"That's the weighting," Ted said. "The value given to each answer. Ten points for the first question, which was...um...has the horse won a race. And so on. I see that ten points are given also for the last question, which was about...er...ante-post odds, wasn't it?"

TWICE SHY

I nodded.

"There you are, then," he said. "I dare say there's a different weighting for every race. There might of course be different *questions* for every race. Ho hum. Want to see?"

"If you've the time," I said.

"Oh sure. I've always got time for TOMs. Love 'em, you know."

He went on typing LIST followed by various numbers and came up with such gems as:

```
520 IF N$ = "NO" THEN GOTO 560: X = X + B
530 INPUT N$ : AB = AB + 1
540 IF N$ = "NO" THEN GOTO 650: X = X + M
550 T = T + G2
560 GOSUB 4000
```

"What does all that mean?" I asked.

"Um...well...it's much easier to *write* a program than to read and understand someone else's. Programs are frantically individual. You can get the same results by all sorts of different routes. I mean, if you're going from London to Bristol you go down the M4 and it's called M4 all the way, but on a computer you can call the road anything you like, at any point on the journey, and *you* might know that at different moments L2, say, or RQ3 or B7(2) equaled M4, but no one else would."

"Is that also what you teach the kids?"

"Er, yes. Sorry, it's a habit." He glanced at the screen. "I'd guess that these top lines are to do with skipping some questions if previous answers make them unnecessary. Jumping to later bits of program. If I printed the whole thing out onto paper I could work out their exact meaning."

I shook my head. "Don't trouble. Let's try a different racecourse."

"Sure."

He rewound the tape to the beginning and typed CLOAD

"DONCA," and when the screen said READY, typed RUN.
Immediately we were asked:

WHICH RACE AT DONCASTER? TYPE NAME OF RACE
AND PRESS 'ENTER'.

"OK," Ted said, pressing switches. "What about further
down the tape? Say, GOODW?"
We got:

WHICH RACE AT GOODWOOD? TYPE NAME OF RACE
AND PRESS 'ENTER'.

"I don't know any races at Goodwood," I said.
Ted said, "That's easy," and typed LIST 10–140. When
the few seconds of flickering had stopped, we had:

```
LIST 10–140
10 PRINT "WHICH RACE AT GOODWOOD? TYPE
NAME OF RACE AND PRESS 'ENTER'"
20 INPUT A$
30 IF A$ = "GOODWOOD STAKES" THEN 330
40 IF A$ = "GOODWOOD CUP" THEN 340
```

There were fifteen races listed altogether.
"What happens if you type in the name of a race there's
no program for?" I asked.
"Let's see," he said. He typed RUN, and we were back
to:

WHICH RACE AT GOODWOOD?

He typed DERBY, and the screen informed us:

THERE IS NO INFORMATION FOR THIS RACE.

"Neat and simple," Ted said.

TWICE SHY

We sampled all the sides of the three tapes, but the programs were all similar.

WHICH RACE AT REDCAR? WHICH RACE AT ASCOT? WHICH RACE AT NEWMARKET?

There were programs for about fifty racecourses, with varying numbers of races listed at each. Several lists contained not actual titles of races but general categories like STRAIGHT 7 FURLONGS FOR 3 YR OLDS AND UPWARDS, or THREE MILE WEIGHT-FOR-AGE STEEPLECHASE: and it was not until quite late that I realized with amusement that *none* of the races were handicaps. There were no questions at all about how many lengths a horse had won by, while carrying such and such a weight.

All in all, there was provision for scoring for any number of horses in each of more than eight hundred named races, and in an unknown quantity of *un*named races. Each race had its own set of weightings and very often its own set of questions. It had been a quite monumental task.

"It must have taken him days," Ted said.

"Weeks, I think. He had to do it in his spare time."

"They're not complicated programs, of course," Ted said. "Nothing really needing an expert. It's more organization than anything else. Still, he hasn't wasted much space. Amateurs write very long programs. Experts get to the same nitty-gritty in a third of the time. It's just practice."

"We'd better make a note of which side of which tape contains the Grantley BASIC," I said.

Ted nodded. "It's at the end. After York. Filed under 'Z.'" He checked that he had the right tape, and wrote on its label in pencil.

For no particular reason I picked up the other two tapes and briefly looked at the words I had half-noticed before: the few words Peter had penciled onto one of the labels: "Programs compiled for C. Norwood."

Ted, glancing over, said, "That's the first side you're

looking at. Ascot and so on." He paused. "We might just as well number the sides properly, one to six. Get them in order."

Order, to him as to me, was a habit. When he'd finished the numbering he put the cassettes back in their gaudy boxes and handed them over. I thanked him most profoundly for his patience and took him out for a couple of beers: and over his pint he said, "Will you be trying them out?"

"Trying what out?"

"Those races, of course. It's the Derby next month some time. If you like we could work out the scores for all the Derby horses, and see if the program comes up with the winner. I'd actually quite *like* to do it. Wouldn't you?"

"I wouldn't begin to know the answers to all those questions."

"No." He sighed. "Pity. The info must be *somewhere*, but unearthing it might be a bore."

"I'll ask my brother," I said, explaining about William. "He sometimes mentions form books. I'd guess the answers would be in those."

Ted seemed pleased with the idea, and I didn't immediately ask him which he was keener to do, to test the accuracy of the programs or to make a profit. He told me, however.

He said tentatively, "Would you mind very much...I mean...would you mind if I took a *copy* of those tapes?"

I looked at him in faint surprise and he smiled awkwardly.

"The fact is, Jonathan, I could do with a boost to the economy. I mean...if these tapes actually come up with the goods, why not use them?" He squirmed a little on his seat, and when I didn't rush to answer, he went on, "You know how bloody small our salaries are. It's no fun with three kids to feed. And their clothes, their shoes cost a bomb, and the little devils grow out of them before you've paid for them, practically. I'm never under my limit on my credit cards. Never."

"Have another beer," I said.

"It's better for you," he said gloomily, accepting the

offer. "You've no children. It isn't so hard for you to manage on a pittance. And you earn more anyway, with being a head of department."

I said thoughtfully, "I don't see why you shouldn't make copies, if you want to."

"Jonathan!" He was clearly delighted.

"But I wouldn't use them," I said, "without finding out if they're any good. You might lose a packet."

"I'll be careful," he said, but his eyes gleamed behind his black-rimmed spectacles, and I wondered uneasily if I were seeing the birth of a compulsion. There was always a slight touch of the fanatic about Ted. "Can you ask your brother where I can get a form book?" he said.

"Well . . ."

He scanned my face. "You're regretting saying I could copy them. Do you want them for yourself, now, is that it?"

"No. I just thought . . . gambling's like drugs. You can get addicted and go down the drain."

"But all I want—" He stopped and shrugged. He looked disappointed but nothing more; and I sighed and said, "OK. But for God's sake be sensible."

"I will," he said fervently. He looked at me expectantly and I took the tapes out of my pocket and gave them back to him.

"Take good care of them," I said.

"With my life."

"Not that far." I thought briefly of gun-toting visitors and of much I didn't understand, and I added slowly, "While you're about it, make copies for me, too."

He was puzzled. "But you'll have the originals."

I shook my head. "They belong to someone else. I'll have to give them back. But I don't see why, if copies are possible, that I shouldn't also keep what I return."

"Copies are dead easy," he said. "Also they're prudent. All you do is load the program into the computer, from the cassette, like we did, then change to a fresh cassette and load the program back from the computer onto the new tape.

You can make dozens of copies, if you like. Any time I've written a program I especially don't want to lose I record it onto several different tapes. That way, if one tape gets lost or some idiot rerecords on top of what you've done, you've always got a back-up."

"I'll buy some tapes, then," I said.

He shook his head. "You give me the money, and I'll get them. Ordinary tapes are OK if you're pushed, but special digital cassettes made for computer work are better."

I gave him some money, and he said he would make the copies the following day, either at lunch time or after school. "And get the form book," he reminded me, "won't you?"

"Yes," I said. And later, from home, I telephoned the farm and spoke to William.

"How's it going?"

"What would you say if I tried for a racing stable in the summer?"

"I'd say stick to farms," I said.

"Yeah. But the hunters are all out at grass in July and August, and this riding school here's cracking up; they've sold off the best horses, there's nothing much to ride, and there's weeds and muck everywhere. Mr. Askwith's taken to drink. He comes roaring out in the mornings clutching the hard stuff and swearing at the girls. There are only two of them left now, trying to look after fourteen ponies. It's a mess."

"It sounds it."

"I've been reduced to doing some revision for those grotty exams."

"Things must be bad," I said.

"Thanks for the check."

"Sorry it was late. Listen, I've a friend who wants a racing form book. How would he get one?"

William, it transpired, knew of about six different types of form book. Which did my friend want?

One which told him a horse's past history, how long since it had last raced and whether its ante-post odds were less than 25 to 1. Also its sire's and dam's and jockey's and trainer's history, and how much it had won in prize money. For starters.

"Good grief," said my brother. "You want a combination of the form book and the *Sporting Life.*"

"Yes, but *which* form book?"

"*The* form book," he said. "*Raceform and Chaseform.* Chaseform's the jumpers. Does he want jumpers as well?"

"I think so."

"Tell him to write to Turf Newspapers, then. The form book comes in sections; a new updated section every week. Best on earth. I covet it increasingly, but it costs a bomb. Do you think the trustees would consider it vocational training?" He spoke, however, without much hope.

I thought of Ted Pitts's financial state and inquired for something cheaper.

"Hum," William said judiciously. "He could try the weekly *Sporting Record,* I suppose." A thought struck him. "This wouldn't be anything to do with your friend Peter and his betting system, would it? You said he was dead."

"Same system, different friend."

"There isn't a system born," William said, "that really works."

"You'd know, of course," I said dryly.

"I do read."

We talked a little more and said goodbye in good humor, and I found myself regretting, after I'd put down the receiver, that I hadn't asked him if he'd like to spend the week with me rather than on the farm. But I didn't suppose he would have done. He'd have found even the drunken Mr. Askwith more congenial than the decorum of Twickenham.

Sarah telephoned an hour later, sounding strained and abrupt.

"Do you know anyone called Chris Norwood?" she asked.

"No, I don't think so." The instant I'd said it I remembered Peter's handwriting on the cassette. "Program compiled for C. Norwood." I opened my mouth to tell her, but she forestalled me.

"Peter knew him. The police have been here again, asking questions."

"But what—" I began in puzzlement.

"I don't *know* what it's all about, if that's what you're going to ask. But someone called Chris Norwood has been shot."

FIVE

Ignorance seemed to surround me like a fog.

"I thought Peter might have mentioned him to you," Sarah said. "You always talked with him more than to Donna and me."

"Doesn't Donna know this Norwood?" I asked, ignoring the bitter little thrust.

"No, she doesn't. She's still in shock. It's all too much."

Fogs could be dangerous, I thought. There might be all manner of traps waiting, unseen.

"What did the police actually say?" I said.

"Nothing much. Only that they were inquiring into a death, and wanted any help Peter could give."

"Peter!"

"Yes, Peter. They didn't know he was dead. They weren't the same as the ones who came before. I think they said they were from Suffolk. What does it matter?" She sounded impatient. "They'd found Peter's name and address on a pad beside a telephone. This Norwood's telephone. They said that in a murder investigation they had to follow even the smallest lead."

"Murder!"

"That's what they said."

I frowned and asked, "When was he killed?"

"How do I know? Sometime last week. Thursday. Friday. I can't remember. They were talking to Donna, really, not to me. I kept telling them she wasn't fit, but they wouldn't listen. They wouldn't see for ages that the poor darling is too dazed to care about a total stranger, however he died. And to crown it all, when they did finally realize, they said they might come back when she was better."

After a pause I said, "When's the inquest?"

"How on earth should I know?"

"I mean . . . on Peter."

"Oh." She sounded disconcerted. "On Friday. We don't have to go. Peter's father is giving evidence of identity. He won't speak to Donna. He somehow thinks it was her fault that Peter was careless with the boat. He's been perfectly beastly."

"Mm," I said noncommittally.

"A man from the insurance company came here, asking if Peter had ever had problems with leaking gas lines and wanting to know if he always started the engine without checking for petrol vapor."

Peter hadn't been careless, I thought. I remembered that he'd been pretty careful on the canals, opening up the engine compartment every morning to let any trapped vapor escape. And that had been diesel, not petrol: less inflammable altogether.

"Donna said she didn't know. The engine was Peter's affair. She was always in the cabin unpacking food and so on while he was getting ready to start up. And anyway," Sarah said, "why all this fuss about vapor? It isn't as if there was any actual *petrol* sloshing about. They say there wasn't."

"It's the vapor that explodes," I said. "Liquid petrol won't ignite unless it's mixed with air."

"Are you serious?"

"Absolutely."

"Oh."

There was a pause, a silence, some dying-fall goodbyes. Not with a bang, I thought, but with a yawn.

On Tuesday Ted Pitts said he hadn't yet had a chance to buy the tapes for the copies and on Wednesday I sweet-talked a colleague into taking my games duty for the afternoon and straight after my last class set off to Norwich. Not to see my wife, but to visit the firm where Peter had worked.

It turned out to be a three-room, two-men-and-a-girl affair tucked away in a suite of offices in a building on an industrial estate: one modest component among about twenty others listed on the directory-board in the lobby, *Mason Miles Associates, Computer Consultants* rubbing elbows with *Direct Access Distribution Services* and *Sea Magic, Decorative Shell Importers.*

Mason Miles and his Associates showed no signs of overwork, but neither was there any of the gloom which hangs about a business on the brink. The inactivity, one felt, was normal.

The girl sat at a desk reading a magazine. The younger man fiddled with a small computer's innards and hummed in the manner of Ted Pitts. The older man, beyond a wide-open door labeled "Mason Miles," lolled in a comfortable chair with an arm-stretching expanse of newspaper. All three looked up without speed about five seconds after I'd walked through their outer, unguarded defenses.

"Hallo," the girl said. "Are you for the job?"

"Which job?"

"You're not, then. Not Robinson, D. F.?"

"Afraid not."

"He's late. Dare say he's not coming." She shrugged. "Happens all the time."

"Would that be Peter Keithly's job?" I asked.

The young man's attention went back to his eviscerated machine.

"Sure is," said the girl. "If you're not for his job, er . . . how can we help you?"

I explained that my wife, who was staying in Peter's house, was under the impression that someone from the firm had visited Peter's widow, asking for some tapes he had been working on.

The girl looked blank. Mason Miles gave me a lengthy frown from a distance. The young man dropped a screwdriver and muttered under his breath.

The girl said, "None of us has been to Peter's house. Not even before the troubles."

Mason Miles cleared his throat and raised his voice. "What tapes are you talking about? You'd better come in here."

He put down the newspaper and stood up reluctantly, as if the effort was too much for a weekday afternoon. He was not in the least like Sarah's description of a plump, gray-haired, ordinary middle-aged man. There was a crinkly red thatch over a long white face, a lengthy stubborn-looking upper lip and cheekbones of Scandinavian intensity; the whole extra-tall body being, as far as I could judge, still under forty.

"Don't let me disturb you," I said without irony.

"You are not."

"Would anyone else from your firm," I asked, "have gone to Peter's house, asking on your behalf for the tapes he was working on?"

"What tapes were those?"

"Cassettes with programs for evaluating racehorses."

"He was working on no such project."

"But in his spare time?" I suggested.

Mason Miles shrugged and sat down again with the relief of a traveler after a wearisome journey. "Perhaps. What he did in his spare time was his own affair."

"And do you have a gray-haired, middle-aged man on your staff?"

He gave me a considering stare and then said merely, "We employ no such a person. If such a person has visited Mrs. Keithly purporting to come from here, it is disturbing."

I looked at his totally undisturbed demeanor and agreed.

"Peter was writing the programs for someone called Chris Norwood," I said. "I don't suppose you've ever heard of him?" I made it a question but without much hope, and he shook his head and suggested I ask his Associates in the outer office. The Associates also showed nil reactions to the name of Chris Norwood, but the young man paused from his juggling of microchips long enough to say that he had put everything Peter had left concerning his work in a shoebox in a cupboard, and he supposed it would do no harm if I wanted to look.

I found the box, took it out, and began to sift through the handwritten scraps of notes which it contained. Nearly all of them concerned his work and took the form of mysterious memos to himself. "Remember to tell R. T. of modification to PET." "Pick up floppy discs for L.M.P." "Tell ISCO about L's software package." "The bug in R's program must be a syntax error in the subroutine." Much more of the same, and none of it of any use.

There was a sudden noise and flurry at the outer door, and a wild-eyed, breathless, heavily flushed youth appeared, along with a suitcase, a hold-all, an overcoat and a tennis racket.

"Sorry," he panted. "The train was late."

"Robinson?" the girl said calmly. "D. F.?"

"What? Oh. Yes. Is the job still open?"

I looked down at another note, the writing as neat as all the others: "Borrow Grantley BASIC tape from G. F." Turned the piece of paper over. On the back he'd written "C. Norwood, Angel Kitchens, Newmarket."

I persevered to the bottom of the box, but there was nothing else that I understood. I put all the scrappy notes back again and thanked the Associates for their trouble. They hardly listened. The attention of the whole firm was intently fixed on D. F. Robinson, who was wilting under their probing questions. Miles, who had beckoned them all into the inner office, was saying, "How would you handle a client who made persistently stupid mistakes but blamed *you* for not explaining his system thoroughly?"

I sketched a farewell which nobody noticed, and left.

Newmarket lay fifty miles to the southwest of Norwich, and I drove there through the sunny afternoon thinking that the fog lay about me as thick as ever. Radar, perhaps, would be useful. Or a gale. Or some good clarifying information. Press on, I thought: press on.

Angel Kitchens, as listed in the telephone directory in the post office, were to be found in Angel Lane, to which various natives directed me with accuracy varying from vague to absent, and which proved to be a dead-end pavement tributary to the east of the town, far from the mainstream of High Street.

The Kitchens were just what they said: the kitchens of a mass food-production business, making frozen gourmet dinners in single-portion foil pans for the upper end of the market. "Posh nosh," one of my route directors had said; "fancy muck," said another. "You can buy that stuff in the town, but give me a hamburger any day" from another, and "real tasty" from the last. They'd all known the product, if not the location.

At a guess the Kitchens had been developed from the back half and outbuildings of a defunct country mansion; they had that slightly haphazard air and were surrounded by mature trees and the remnants of a landscaped garden. I parked in the large but well-occupied expanse of concrete outside a new-looking white single-story construction marked "Office," and pushed my way through its plate-glass double-door entrance.

Inside, in the open-plan expanse, the contrast to Mason Miles Associates was complete. Life was taken at a run, if not a stampede. The work in hand, it seemed, would overwhelm the inmates if they relaxed for a second.

My tentative inquiry for someone who had been a friend of Chris Norwood reaped me a violently unexpected reply.

"That *creep?* If he had any friends they'd be down in Veg Preparation, where he worked."

"Er . . . Veg Preparation?"

"Two-story gray stone building past the freezer sheds."

I went out to the parking lot, wandered around and asked again.

"Where them carrots is being unloaded."

Them carrots were entering a two-story stone building by the sackload on a fork-lift truck, the driver of which mutely pointed me to a less cavernous entrance around a corner.

Through there one passed through a small lobby beside a large changing-room where rows of outdoor clothing hung on pegs. Next came a white-tiled scrub-up room smelling like a hospital, followed by a swinging door into a long narrow room lit blindingly by electricity and filled with gleaming stainless steel, noisily whirring machines and people dressed in white.

At the sight of me standing there in street clothes a large man wearing what looked like a cotton undervest over a swelling paunch advanced with waving arms and shooed me out.

"Cripes, mate, you'll get me sacked," he said, as the swinging door swung behind us.

"I was directed here," I said mildly.

"What do you want?"

With less confidence than before, I inquired for any friend of Chris Norwood.

The shrewd eyes above the beer-stomach appraised me. The mouth pursed. The chef's hat sat comfortably over strong dark eyebrows.

"He's been murdered," he said. "You from the press?"

I shook my head. "He knew a friend of mine, and he got both of us into a bit of trouble."

"Sounds just like him." He pulled a large white handkerchief out of his white trousers and wiped his nose. "What exactly do you want?"

"I think just to talk to someone who knew him. I want to know what he was like. Who he knew. Anything. I want to know why and how he got us into trouble."

"I knew him," he said. He paused, considering. "What's it worth?"

I sighed. "I'm a schoolmaster. It's worth what I can afford. And it depends *what* you know."

"All right then," he said judiciously. "I finish here at six. I'll meet you in the Purple Dragon, right? Up the lane, turn left, quarter of a mile. You buy me a couple of pints and we'll take it from there. OK?"

"Yes," I said. "My name is Jonathan Derry."

"Akkerton." He gave a short nod, as if sealing a bargain. "Vince," he added as an afterthought. He gave me a last unpromising inspection and barged back through the swinging doors. I heard the first of the words he sprayed into the long busy room: "You, Reg, you get back to work. I've only to take my eyes off you . . ."

The door closed discreetly behind him.

I waited for him at a table in the Purple Dragon, a pub a good deal less colorful than its name, and at six-fifteen he appeared, dressed now in gray trousers and a blue-and-white shirt straining at its buttons. Elliptical views of hairy chest appeared when he sat down, which he did with a wheeze and a licking of lips. The first pint I bought him disappeared at a single draught, closely followed by half of the second.

"Thirsty work, chopping up veg," he said.

"Do you do it by hand?" I was surprised and sounded it.

"Course not. Washed, peeled, chopped, all done by machines. But nothing hops into a machine by itself. Or out, come to that."

"What . . . er . . . veg?" I said.

"Depends what they want. Today, mostly carrots, celery, onions, mushrooms. Regular every day, that lot. Needed for Burgundy Beef. Our best seller, Burgundy Beef. Chablis Chicken, Pork and Port, next best. You ever had any?"

"I don't honestly know."

He drank deeply with satisfaction. "It's good food," he said seriously, wiping his mouth. "All fresh ingredients. No mucking about. Pricey, mind you, but worth it."

"You enjoy the job?" I asked.

He nodded. "Sure. Worked in kitchens all my life. Some of them, you could shake hands with the cockroaches. Big as rats. Here, so clean you'd see a fruit fly a mile off. I've been in Veg three months now. Did a year in Fish, but the smell hangs in your nostrils after a while."

"Did Chris Norwood," I said, "chop up veg?"

"When we were pushed. Otherwise he cleaned up, checked the input, and ran errands." His voice was assured and positive: a man who had no need to guard his tongue.

"Er . . . checked the input?" I said.

"Counted the sacks of veg as they were delivered. If there were twenty sacks of onions on the day's delivery note, his job to see twenty sacks arrived." He inspected the contents of the pint glass. "Reckon it was madness giving him that job. Mind you, it's not millionaire class, knocking off sacks of carrots and onions, but it seems he was supplying a whole string of bleeding village shops with the help of the truck drivers. The driver would let the sacks fall off the truck on the way here, see, and Chris Norwood would count twenty where there was only sixteen. They split the profits. It goes on everywhere, that sort of thing, in every kitchen I've ever worked in. Meat too. Sides of ruddy beef. Caviar. You name it, it's been nicked. But Chris wasn't just your usual opportunist. He didn't know what to keep his hands off."

"What didn't he keep his hands off?" I asked.

Vince Akkerton polished off the liquid remains and put down his glass with suggestive loudness. Obediently I crossed to the bar for a refill, and once there had been a proper inspection of the new froth and a sampling of the first two inches, I heard what Chris Norwood had stolen.

"The girls in the office said he pinched their cash. They didn't cotton on for ages. They thought it was one of the women there that they didn't like. Chris was in and out all the time, taking in the day-sheets and chatting them up. He thought a lot of himself. Cocky bastard."

I looked at the well-fleshed worldly-wise face and thought of chief petty officers and ship's engineers. The same easy assumption of command: the ability to size men up and put them to work. People like Vince Akkerton were the indispensable getters of things done.

"How old," I said, "was Chris Norwood?"

"Thirtyish. Same as you. Difficult to say, exactly." He drank. "What sort of trouble did he get you in?"

"A couple of bullies came to my house looking for something of his."

Fog, I thought.

"What sort of thing?" said Akkerton.

"Computer tapes."

If I'd spoken in Outer Mongolian it couldn't have meant less to him. He covered his bewilderment with beer and in disappointment I drank some of my own.

"Course," said Akkerton, rallying, "there's a computer or some such over in the office. They use it for keeping track of how many tons of Burgundy Beef and so on they've got on order and in the freezers, stuff like that. Working out how many thousands of ducks they need. Lobsters. Even coriander seeds." He paused and with the first glint of humor said, "Mind you, the results are always wrong, on account of activities on the side. There was a whole shipment of turkeys missing once. Computer error they said." He grunted. "Chris Norwood with his carrots and onions, he was peanuts."

"These were computer tapes to do with horseracing," I said.

The dark eyebrows rose. "Now that makes more sense. Every bleeding thing in this town practically is to do with horseracing. I've heard they think the knacker's yard has a direct line to our Burgundy Beef. It's a libel."

"Did Chris Norwood bet?"

"Everyone in the firm bets. Cripes, you couldn't live in this town and not bet. It's in the air. Catching, like the pox."

I seemed to be getting nowhere at all and I didn't know what else to ask. I cast around and came up with, "Where was Chris Norwood killed?"

"Where? In his room. He rented a room in a council house from a retired old widow who goes out cleaning in the mornings. See, she wasn't supposed to take in lodgers, the council don't allow it, and she never told the welfare, who'd been doling out free meals, that she was earning, so the fuss going on now is making her crazy." He shook his head. "Next street to me, all this happened."

"What *did* exactly happen?"

He showed no reluctance to tell. More like relish.

"She found Chris dead in his room when she went in to clean it. See, she thought he'd have gone to work; she always went out before him in the mornings. Anyway, there he was. Lot of blood, so I've heard. You don't know what's true and what isn't, but they say he had bullets in his *feet*. Bled to death."

Christ Almighty . . .

"Couldn't walk, you see," Akkerton said. "No telephone. Back bedroom. No one saw him."

With a dry mouth I asked, "What about . . . his belongings?"

"Dunno, really. Nothing stolen, that I've heard of. Seems there were just a few things broken. And his stereo was shot up proper, same as him."

What do I do, I thought. Do I go to the police investigating Chris Norwood and tell them I was visited by two men who threatened to shoot my television and my ankles? Yes, I thought, this time I probably do.

"When . . ." My voice sounded hoarse. I cleared my throat

and tried again. "Which day did it happen?"

"Last week. He didn't show up Friday morning, and it was bloody inconvenient as we were handling turnips that day and it was his job to chop the tops and roots off and feed them into the washer."

I felt dazed. Chris Norwood had been dead by Friday morning. It had been *Saturday afternoon* when I'd flung my visitors' Walther out into the rose bush. On Saturday they had still been looking for the tapes, which meant ... dear God ... that they hadn't got them from Chris Norwood. They'd shot him, and left him, and they still hadn't got the tapes. He would have given them to them if he'd had them: to stop them shooting him; to save his life. The tapes weren't worth one's life: they truly weren't. I remembered the insouciance with which I faced that pistol and was, in retrospect, terrified.

Vince Akkerton showed signs of feeling it was time he was paid for his labors. I mentally tossed between what I could afford and what he might expect and decided to try him with the least possible. Before I could offer it, however, two girls came into the bar and prepared to sit at the next table. One of them, seeing Akkerton, changed course abruptly and fetched up at his side.

"Hullo, Vince," she said. "Do us a favor. Stand us a rum and Coke and I'll pay you tomorrow."

"I've heard that before," he said indulgently. "But this friend of mine's buying."

Poorer by two rum and Cokes, another full pint and a further half (for me), I sat and listened to Akkerton explaining that the girls worked in the Angel Kitchens office.

Carol and Janet. Young, medium bright, full of chatter and chirpiness, expecting from minute to minute the arrival of their boyfriends.

Carol's opinion of Chris Norwood was straightforwardly indignant. "We all worked out it had to be him dipping into our handbags, but we couldn't *prove* it, see? We were just going to set a trap for him when he got killed, and I suppose

I should feel sorry for him, but I don't. He couldn't keep his hands off anything. I mean, not anything. He'd take your last sandwich when you weren't looking and laugh at you while he ate it."

"He didn't see anything wrong in pinching things," Janet said.

"Here," Akkerton said, leaning forward for emphasis, "young Janet here, she works the computer. You ask her about those tapes."

Janet's response was a raised-eyebrow thoughtfulness.

"I didn't know he had any actual tapes," she said. "But of course he was always *around*. It was his job, you know, collecting the day-sheets from all the departments and bringing them to me. He'd always hang around a bit, especially the last few weeks, asking how the computer worked, you know? I showed him how it came up with all the quantities, how much salt, you know, and things like that, had to be shifted to each department, and how all the others went through, mixed container loads to Bournemouth or Birmingham, you know. The whole firm would collapse, you know, without the computer."

"What make is it?" I said.

"What *make?*" They all thought it an odd question, but I'd have gambled on the answer.

"A Grantley," Janet said.

I smiled at her as inoffensively as I knew how and asked her if she would have let Chris Norwood run his tapes through her Grantley if he'd asked her nicely, and after some guilty hesitation and a couple of downward blushes into her rum and Coke, said she might have done, you know, at one time, before they discovered, you know, that it was Chris who was stealing their cash.

"We should have guessed it ages ago," Carol said, "but then the things he took, like our sandwiches and such, and things out of the office, staples, envelopes, rolls of tape, well we *saw* him take those, we were used to it."

"Didn't anyone ever complain?" I said.

Not officially, the girls said. What was the use? The firm never sacked people for nicking things; if they did, there would be a strike.

"Except that time, do you remember, Janet?" Carol said. "When the poor old lady turned up, wittering on about Chris stealing things from her house. *She* complained, all right. She came back three times, making a fuss."

"Oh, sure," Janet nodded. "But it turned out it was only some old bits of paper she was on about, you know, nothing like money or valuables, and anyway Chris said she was losing her marbles, and had thrown them away, most like, and it all blew over, you know."

I said, "What was the old lady's name?"

The girls looked at each other and shook their heads. It was weeks ago, they said.

Akkerton said he hadn't known of that, he'd never heard about the old lady, not down with his Veg.

The girls' boyfriends arrived at that moment and there was a general reshuffle around the tables. I said I would have to be going, and by one of those unspoken messages Akkerton indicated that I should see him outside.

"O'Rorke," said Carol suddenly.

"What?"

"The old lady's name," she said. "I've remembered. It was Mrs. O'Rorke. She was Irish. Her husband had just died, and she'd been paying Chris to carry logs in for her fire, and things like that she couldn't manage."

"I don't suppose you remember where she lived?"

"Does it matter? It was only a great fuss over nothing."

"Still..."

She frowned slightly with obliging concentration, though most of her attention was on her boyfriend, who was tending to flirt with Janet.

"Stetchworth," she exclaimed. "She complained about the taxi fare." She gave me a quick glance. "To be honest, we were glad to be rid of her in the end. She was an awful old nuisance, but we couldn't be too unkind because of her old man dying, and that."

"Thanks very much," I said.

"You're welcome." She moved away from me and sat herself decisively between her boyfriend and Janet, and Akkerton and I went outside to settle our business.

He looked philosophically at what I gave him, nodded and asked me to write my name and address on a piece of paper in case he thought of anything else to tell me. I tore a page out of my diary, wrote, and gave it to him thinking that our transaction was over, but when I'd shaken his hand, said goodbye and walked away from him, he called after me.

"Wait, lad."

I turned back.

"Did you get your money's worth?" he said.

More than I'd bargained for, I thought. I said, "Yes, I think so. Can't really tell yet."

He nodded, pursing his lips. Then with an uncharacteristically awkward gesture he held out half of the cash. "Here," he said. "You take it. I saw into your wallet in the pub. You're nearly cleaned out.. Enough's enough." He thrust his gift toward my hand, and I took it back with gratitude. "Teachers," he said, pushing open the pub door. "Downtrodden underpaid lot of bastards. Never reckoned to school myself." He brushed away my attempt at thanks and headed back to the beer.

SIX

By map and in spite of misdirections, I eventually found the O'Rorke house in Stetchworth. Turned into the driveway. Stopped the engine. Climbed out of the car, looking at what lay ahead.

A large, rambling, untidy structure; much wood, many gables, untrained creeper pushing tendrils onto the slated roof, and sash windowframes long ago painted white. The garden in the soft evening light seemed a matter of grasses and shrubs growing wherever they liked; and a large bush of lilac, white and sweet-scented, almost obliterated the front door.

The bell may have rung somewhere deep inside in response to my finger on the button, but I couldn't hear it. I rang again and tried a few taps on the inadequate knocker, and when the blank seconds mounted to minutes stepped back a few paces, looking up at the windows for signs of life.

I didn't actually see the door open behind the lilac bush, but a sharp voice spoke to me from among the flowers.

"Are you Saint Anthony?" it said.

"Er, no." I stepped back into the line of sight and found standing in the shadowy half-open doorway a short, white-haired old woman with yellowish skin and wild-looking eyes.

"About the fate?" she said.

"Whose fate?" I asked, bewildered.

"The church's, of course."

"Oh," I said. "The *fête*."

She looked at me as if I were totally stupid, which from her point of view, I no doubt was.

"If you cut the peonies tonight," she said, "they'll be dead by Saturday."

Her voice was distinguishably Irish, but with the pure vowels of education, and her words were already a dismissal. She was holding onto the door with one hand and its frame with the other, and was on the point of irrevocably rejoining them.

"Please," I said hastily, "show me the peonies . . . so that I'll know which to pick . . . on Saturday."

The half-begun movement was arrested. The old woman considered for a moment and then stepped out past the lilac into full view, revealing a waif-thin frame dressed in a rust-colored jersey, narrow navy-blue trousers, and pink-and-green-checked bedroom slippers.

"'Round the back," she said. She looked me up and down, but saw nothing apparently to doubt. "This way."

She led me around the house along a path whose flat sunken paving stones merged at the edges with the weedy overgrowth of what might have been flowerbeds. Past a shoulder-high stack of sawn logs, contrastingly neat. Past a closed side door. Past a greenhouse filled with the straggly stalks of many dead geraniums. Past a wheelbarrow full of cinders, about whose purpose one could barely guess. Around an unexpected corner, through a too-small gap in a vigorously growing hedge, and finally into the riotous mess of the back garden.

"Peonies," she said, pointing, though indeed there was

no need. Around the ruin of a lawn huge swaths of the fat luxurious blowsy heads, pink, crimson, frilly white, raised themselves in every direction from a veritable ocean of glossy dark leaves, the sinking sun touching all with gold. Decay might lie in the future but the present was a triumphant shout in the face of death.

"They're magnificent," I said, slightly awed. "There must be thousands of them."

The old woman looked around without interest. "They grow every year. Liam couldn't have enough. You can take what you like."

"Um." I cleared my throat. "I'd better tell you I'm not from the church."

She looked at me with the same sort of bewilderment as I'd recently bent on her. "What did you want to see the peonies for, then?"

"I wanted to talk to you. For you not to go inside and shut your door when you learned what I want to talk about."

"Young man," she said severely, "I'm not buying anything. I don't give to charities. I don't like politicians. What do you want?"

"I want to know," I said slowly, "about the papers that Chris Norwood stole from you."

Her mouth opened. The wild eyes raked my face like great watery searchlights. The thin body shook with powerful but unspecified emotion.

"Please don't worry," I said hastily. "I mean you no harm. There's nothing at all to be afraid of."

"I'm not afraid. I'm angry."

"You did have some papers, didn't you, that Chris Norwood took?"

"Liam's papers. Yes."

"And you went to Angel Kitchens to complain?"

"The police did nothing. Absolutely nothing. I went to Angel Kitchens to make that beastly man give them back. They said he wasn't there. They were lying. I know they were."

Her agitation was more than I was ready to feel guilty

for. I said calmingly. "Please . . . could we just sit down?" I looked around for a garden bench but saw nothing suitable. "I don't want to upset you. I might even help."

"I don't know you. It's not safe." She looked at me for a few more unnerving seconds with full beam and then turned and began to go back the way we had come. I followed reluctantly, aware that I'd been clumsy but still not knowing what else to have done. I had lost her, I thought. She would go in behind the lilac and shut me out.

Back through the hedge, past the cinders, past the cemetery in the greenhouse: but not past the closed side door. To my slightly surprised relief she stopped there and twisted the knob.

"This way," she said, going in. "Come along. I think I'll trust you. You look all right. I'll take the risk."

The house was dark inside and smelled of disuse. We seemed to be in a narrow passage, along which she drifted ahead of me, silent in her slippers, light as a sparrow.

"Old women living alone," she said, "should never take men they don't know into their houses." As she was addressing the air in front of her, the admonishment seemed to be to herself. We continued along past various dark-painted closed doors, until the passage opened out into a central hall where such light as there was filtered through high-up windows of patterned stained glass.

"Edwardian," she said, following my upward gaze. "This way."

I followed her into a spacious room whose elaborate bay window looked out onto the glory in the garden. Indoors, more mutedly, there were deep-blue velvet curtains, good-looking large rugs over the silver-gray carpet, blue velvet sofas and armchairs . . . and dozens and dozens of seascapes crowding the walls. Floor to ceiling. Billowing sails. Four-masters. Storms and seagulls and salt spray.

"Liam's," she said briefly, seeing my head turn around them.

When Liam O'Rorke liked something, I thought fleetingly, he liked a lot of it.

"Sit down," she said, pointing to an armchair. "Tell me who you are and why you've come here." She moved to a sofa where, to judge from the book and glass on the small table adjacent, she had been sitting before I arrived, and perched her small weight on the edge as if ready for flight.

I explained about Peter's link with Chris Norwood, saying that Chris Norwood had given what I thought might be her husband's papers to Peter for him to organize into computer programs. I said that Peter had done the job and had recorded the programs on tape.

She brushed aside the difficult technicalities and came straight to the simple point. "Do you mean," she demanded, "that your friend Peter has my papers?" The hope in her face was like a light.

"I'm afraid not. I don't know where the papers are."

"Ask your friend."

"He's been killed in an accident."

"Oh." She stared at me, intensely disappointed.

"But the tapes," I said. "I do know where those are— or at least I know where copies of them are. If the knowledge that's on them is yours, I could get them for you."

She was a jumble of renewed hope and puzzlement. "It would be wonderful. But these tapes...wherever they are...didn't you bring them with you?"

I shook my head. "I didn't know you existed until an hour ago. It was a girl called Carol who told me about you. She works in the office of Angel Kitchens."

"Oh, yes." Mrs. O'Rorke made a small movement of embarrassment. "I screeched at her. I was so *angry*. They wouldn't tell me where to find Chris Norwood in all those buildings and sheds. I'd said I'd scratch his eyes out. I've an Irish temper, you know. I can't always control it."

I thought of the picture she must have presented to those girls and reckoned their description of her "making a fuss" had been charitable.

"The trouble is," I said slowly, "that someone else is looking for those tapes." I told her a watered-down version of the visit to my house of the gunmen, to which she listened with open-mouthed attention. "I don't know who they are," I said, "or where they come from. I began to think that so much ignorance might be dangerous. So I've been trying to find out what's going on."

"And if you know?"

"Then I'll know what *not* to do. I mean, one can do such stupid things, with perhaps appalling consequences, just through not knowing some simple fact."

She regarded me steadily with the first glimmer of a smile. "All you're asking for, young man, is the secret that has eluded *Homo sapiens* from day one."

I was startled not so much by the thought as by the words she phrased it in, and as if sensing my surprise she said with dryness, "One does not grow silly with age. If one was silly when young, one may be silly when old. If one was acute when young, why should acuteness wane?"

"I have done you," I said slowly, "an injustice."

"Everyone does," she said indifferently. "I look in my mirror. I see an old face. Wrinkles. Yellow skin. As society is now constituted, to present this appearance is to be thrust into a category. Old woman, therefore silly, troublesome, can be pushed around."

"No," I said. "It's not true."

"Unless of course," she added as if I hadn't spoken, "one is an *achiever*. Achievement is the savior of the very old."

"And are you not... an achiever?"

She made a small regretful movement with hands and head. "I wish I were. I am averagely intelligent, but that's all. It gets you nowhere. It doesn't save you from rage. I apologize for my reaction in the garden."

"But don't," I said. "Theft's an assault. Of course you'd be angry."

She relaxed to the extent of sitting back into the sofa, where the cushions barely deflated under her weight.

"I will tell you as much as I can of what has happened. If it saves you from chasing Moses across the Red Sea, so much the better."

To know what *not* to do...

I grinned at her.

She twitched her lips and said, "What do you know about racing?"

"Not a great deal."

"Liam did. My husband. Liam lived for the horses all his life. In Ireland, of course, when we were children. Then here. Newmarket, Epsom, Cheltenham, that's where we've lived. Then back here to Newmarket. Always the horses."

"Were they his job?" I asked.

"In a way. He was a gambler." She looked at me calmly. "I mean a professional gambler. He lived on his winnings. I still live on what's left."

"I thought it wasn't possible," I said.

."To beat the odds?" The words sounded wrong for her appearance. It was true, I thought, what she'd said about categories. Old women weren't expected to talk gambling; but this one did. "In the old days it was perfectly possible to make a good living. Dozens did it. You worked on a profit expectation of ten percent on turnover, and if you had any judgment at all, you achieved it. Then they introduced the Betting Tax. It took a slice off all the winnings, reduced the profit margin to almost nil, killed off all the old pros in no time. Your ten percent was all going into the Revenue, do you see?"

"Yes," I said.

"Liam had always made more than ten percent. He took a pride in it. He reckoned he could win one race out of three. That means that every third bet, on average, would win. That's a very high percentage, day after day, year after year. And he *did* beat the tax. He tried new ways, added new factors. With his statistics, he said you could always win in the long run. None of the bookies would take his bets."

"Er . . . what?" I said.

"Didn't you know?" She sounded surprised. "Bookmakers won't take bets from people who repeatedly win."

"But I thought that's what they were in business for. I mean, to take people's bets."

"To take bets from ordinary mug punters, yes," she said. "The sort who may win occasionally but never do in the end. But if you have an account with almost any bookie and you keep winning, he'll close your account."

"Good grief," I said weakly.

"At the races," she said, "all the bookies knew Liam. If they didn't know him to talk to, they knew him by sight. They'd only let him bet in cash at starting price, and then as soon as he'd got his money on they'd tic-tac it around the ring and they'd all reduce the price of that horse to ridiculously small odds, making the starting price very low, so that he wouldn't win much himself, and so that the other racegoers would be put off backing that horse, and stake their money on something else."

There was a longish pause while I sorted out and digested what she'd said.

"And what," I said, "about the pari-mutuel?"

"The pari-mutuel is unpredictable. Liam didn't like that. Also the pari-mutuel in general pays worse odds than the bookies. No, Liam liked betting with the bookies. It was a sort of war. Liam always won, though most times the bookies didn't know it."

"Er," I said, "how do you mean?"

She sighed. "It was a lot of work. We had a gardener. A friend, really. He lived here in the house. Down that passage where we came in just now, those were his rooms. He used to like driving around the country, so he'd take Liam's cash and drive off to some town or other and put it all on in the local betting shops, bit by bit, and if the horse won, which it usually did, he'd go around and collect, and come home. He and Liam would count it all out. So much for Dan—that was our friend—and so much for the working funds, and the rest for us. No more tax to pay, of course. No income tax. We went on for years like that. Years. We all got on so well together, you see."

She fell silent, looking into the gentle past with the incongruously wild eyes.

"And Liam died?" I said.

"Dan died. Eighteen months ago, just before Christmas. He was ill for only a month. It was so quick." A pause. "And Liam and I, we didn't realize until after . . . we didn't know how much we depended on Dan, until he wasn't there. He was so strong. He could lift things . . . and the garden . . . Liam was eighty-six, you see, and I'm eighty-eight, but Dan was younger, not over seventy. He was a blacksmith from Wexford, way back. Full of jokes, too. We missed him so much."

The golden glow of sunlight outside had faded from the peonies, the great vibrant colors fading to grays in the approaching dusk. I listened to the young voice of the old woman telling the darker parts of her life, clearing the fog from my own.

"We thought we'd have to find someone else to put the bets on," she said. "But who could we trust? Some of the time last year Liam tried to do it himself, going around betting shops in places like Ipswich and Colchester, places where they wouldn't know him, but he was too old, he got dreadfully exhausted. He had to stop it, it was too much. We had quite a bit saved, you see, and we decided we'd have to live on that. And then this year a man we'd heard of, but never met, came to see us, and he offered to *buy* Liam's methods. He said to Liam to write down how he won so consistently, and he would buy what he'd written."

"And those notes," I said, enlightened, "were what Chris Norwood stole?"

"Not exactly," she said, sighing. "You see there was no need for Liam to write down his method. He'd written it down years ago. All based on statistics. Quite complicated. He used to update it when necessary. And of course, add new races. After so many years, he could bet with a thirty-three-percent chance of success in nearly a thousand particular races every year."

She coughed suddenly, her white thin face vibrating with the muscular spasm. A fragile hand stretched out to the glass on the table, and she took a few tiny sips of yellowish liquid.

"I'm so sorry," I said contritely. "Making you talk."

She shook her head mutely, taking more sips, then put down the glass carefully and said, "It's great to talk. I'm glad you're here, to give me the opportunity. I have so few people to talk to. Some days I don't talk at all. I do miss Liam, you know. We chattered all the time. He was a terrible man to live with. Obsessive, do you see? When he had something in his mind he'd go on and on and on with it. All these sea pictures, it drove me mad when he kept buying them, but now he's gone, well, they seem to bring him close again, and I won't move them, not now."

"It wasn't so very long ago, was it, that he died?" I said.

"On March first," she said. She paused, but there were no tears, no welling distress. "Only a few days after Mr. Gilbert came. Liam was sitting there"—she pointed to one of the blue armchairs, the only one that showed rubbed dark patches on the arms and a shadow on its high back—"and I went to make us some tea. Just a cup. We were thirsty. And when I came back he was asleep." She paused again. "I thought he was asleep."

"I'm sorry," I said.

She shook her head. "It was the best way to go. I'm glad for him. We'd both loathed the thought of dying in a hospital stuck full of tubes. If I'm lucky and if I can manage it, I'll die here too, like that, one of these days. I'll be glad to. It is comforting, do you see?"

I did see, in a way, though I had never before thought of death as a welcome guest to be patiently awaited, hoping that he would come quietly when one was asleep.

"If you'd like a drink," she said in exactly the same matter-of-fact tone, "there's a bottle and some glasses in the cupboard."

"I have to drive home..."

She didn't press it. She said, "Do you want to hear about Mr. Gilbert? Mr. Harry Gilbert?"

"Yes, please. If I'm not tiring you."

"I told you. Talking's a *pleasure*." She considered, her head to one side, the white hair standing like a fluffy halo around the small wrinkled face. "He owns bingo halls," she said; and there was for the first time in her voice the faintest hint of contempt.

"You don't approve of bingo?"

"It's a mug's game." She shrugged. "No skill in it."

"But a lot of people enjoy it."

"And pay for it. Like mug punters. The wins keep them hooked but they lose in the end."

The same the world over, I thought with amusement: the professional's dim view of the amateur. There was nothing amateur, however, about Mr. Gilbert.

"Bingo made him rich," the old woman said. "He came here one day to see Liam, just drove up one day in a Rolls and said he was buying a chain of betting shops. He wanted to buy Liam's system so he'd always be six jumps ahead of the mugs."

I said curiously, "Do you always think of a gambler as a mug?"

"Mr. Gilbert does. He's a cold man. Liam said it depends on what they want. If they wanted excitement, OK. They're mugs but they're getting their money's worth. If they want profit and they still bet on instinct, they're just mugs."

She coughed again, and sipped again, and after a while gave me the faint smile, and continued.

"Mr. Gilbert offered Liam a lot of money. Enough for us to invest and live on comfortably for the rest of our days. So Liam agreed. It was wisest. They argued a bit about the price, of course. They spent almost a week ringing each other up with offers. But in the end it was settled." She paused. "Then before Mr. Gilbert paid the money, and before Liam gave him all the papers, Liam died. Mr. Gilbert telephoned me to say he was sorry, but did the bargain still stand, and I said yes it did. It certainly did. I was very pleased to be going to be without money anxieties, do you see?"

I nodded.

"And then," she said, and this time with anger, "that *hateful* Chris Norwood stole the papers out of Liam's office—stole all his life's work." Her body shook. It was the fact of *what* had been stolen which infuriated her, I perceived, more than the fortune lost. "We'd both been glad to have him come here, to carry coal and logs and clean the windows, and then I'd begun to wonder if he'd been in my handbag, but I'm always pretty vague about how much I have there . . . and then Liam died." She stopped, fighting against agitation, pressing a thin hand to her narrow chest, squeezing shut those wide-staring eyes.

"Don't go on," I said, wanting her to desperately.

"Yes, yes," she said, opening her eyes again. "Mr. Gilbert came to collect the papers. He brought the money all in cash. He showed it to me, in a briefcase. Packets of notes. He said to spend it, not invest it. That way there would be no fuss with tax. He said he would give me more if I ever needed it . . . but there was enough, you know, for years and years, living as I do. And then we went along to Liam's office, and the papers weren't there. Nowhere. Vanished. I'd put them all ready, you see, the day before, in a big folder. There were so many of them. Sheets and sheets, all in Liam's spikey writing. He never learned to type. Always wrote by hand. And the only person who'd been in there besides Mrs. Urquart was Chris Norwood. The only person."

"Who," I said, "is Mrs. Urquart?"

"What? Oh, Mrs. Urquart comes to clean for me. Or she did. Three days a week. She can't come now, she says. She's in trouble with the welfare people, poor thing."

Akkerton's voice in the pub floated back: ". . . she never told the welfare she was earning . . ."

I said, "Was it in Mrs. Urquart's house that Chris Norwood lodged?"

"Yes, that's right." She frowned. "How did you know?"

"Something someone said." I sorted through what I had first said to her to explain my visit and belatedly realized that I'd taken for granted she'd known something which I now saw that perhaps she didn't.

"Chris Norwood . . ." I said slowly.

"I'd like to strangle him."

"Didn't your Mrs. Urquart tell you...what had happened?"

"She rang in a great fuss. Said she wasn't coming anymore. She sounded very upset. Saturday morning, last week."

"And that was all she said, that she wasn't coming anymore?"

"We hadn't been very good friends lately, not with Chris Norwood stealing Liam's papers. I didn't want to quarrel with her. I needed her, for the cleaning. But since that hateful man stole from us, she was very defensive, almost rude. But she needed the money, just like I needed her, and she knew I'd never give her away."

I looked out toward the peonies, where the grays were darkening to night, and debated whether or not to tell her what had befallen Chris Norwood. Decided against, because hearing of the murder of someone one knew, even someone one disliked, could be incalculably shattering. To thrust an old lady living alone in a big house into a state of shock and fear couldn't do any possible good.

"Do you read newspapers?" I said.

She raised her eyebrows over the oddness of the question but answered simply enough. "Not often. The print's too small. I've good eyes, but I like big-print books." She indicated the fat red-and-white volume on her table. "I read nothing else, now." She looked vaguely around the dusk-filled room. "Even the racing pages. I've stopped reading those. I just watch the results on television."

"Just the results? Not the races?"

"Liam said watching the races was the mugs' way of betting. Watch the results, he said, and add them to statistical probabilities. I do watch the races, but the results are more of a habit."

She stretched out a stick-thin arm and switched on the table-light beside her, shutting the peonies instantly into blackness and banishing the far corners of the room into deep shadows. On herself the instant effect was to enhance her physical degeneration, putting skin-folds cruelly back where the dusk had softened them, anchoring the ageless mind into the old, old body.

I looked at the thin, wizened yellow face, at the huge eyes that might once have been beautiful, at the white unstyled hair of Liam O'Rorke's widow, and I suggested that maybe, if I gave her the computer tapes, she could still sell the knowledge that was on them to her friend Mr. Gilbert.

"It did cross my mind," she said, nodding, "when you said you had them. I don't really understand what they are, though. I don't know anything about computers."

She'd been married to one, in a way. I said, "They are just cassettes—like for a cassette player."

She thought for a while, looking down at her hands. Then she said, "If I pay you a commission, will you do the deal for me? I'm not so good at dealing as Liam, do you see? And I don't think I have the strength to haggle."

"But wouldn't Mr. Gilbert pay the agreed price?"

She shook her head doubtfully. "I don't know. That deal was struck three months ago, and now it isn't the papers themselves I'm selling, but something else. I don't know. I think he might twist me into corners. But you *know* about these tapes, or whatever they are. You could talk to him better than me." She smiled faintly. "A proper commission, young man. Ten percent."

It took me about five seconds to agree. She gave me Mr. Harry Gilbert's address and telephone number and said she would leave it all to me. I could come back and tell her when it was done. I could bring her all the money, she said, and she would pay me my share, and everything would be fine.

"You trust me?" I said.

"If you steal from me, I'll be no worse off than I am at present."

She came with me to the lilac-shrouded front door to let me out, and I shook her thistledown hand, and drove away.

The Red Sea parted for Moses, and he walked across.

SEVEN

On Thursday I trundled blearily around school, ineffective from lack of the sleep I'd forfeited in favor of correcting the elder boys' exercise books. They too, like William, had decisive exams ahead. One of the most boring things about myself, I'd discovered, was this sense of commitment to the kids.

Ted Pitts didn't turn up. Jenkins, when directly asked, said scratchily that Pitts had laryngitis, which was disgraceful as it put the whole math department's timetable out of order.

"When will he be back?"

Jenkins gave me a sour sneer, not for any particular reason but because it was an ingrained mannerism.

"His wife telephoned," he said. "Pitts has lost his voice. When he regains it, doubtless he will return."

"Could you give me his number?"

"He isn't on the telephone," Jenkins said repressively. "He says he can't afford it."

"His address, then?"

"You should ask in the office," Jenkins said. "I can't be

expected to remember where my assistant masters live."

The school secretary was not in his office when I went to look for him during morning break, and I spent the last two periods before lunch (Five C, magnetism; Four D, electrical power) fully realizing that if I didn't send computer tapes to Cambridge on that very day they would not arrive by Saturday: and if no computer tapes arrived at Cambridge main post office by Saturday I could expect another and much nastier visit from the man behind the Walther.

At lunchtime food came low on the priorities. Instead I first went out of school along to the nearest row of shops and bought three blank sixty-minute cassettes. They weren't of the quality beloved by Ted Pitts, but for my purpose they were fine. Then I sought out one of Ted Pitts's colleagues and begged a little help with the computer.

"Well," he said hesitantly. "OK, if it's only for ten minutes. Straight after school. And don't tell Jenkins, will you?"

"Never."

His laugh floated after me as I hurried down the passage toward the coin-box telephone in the main entrance hall. I rang up Newmarket police station (via information) and asked for whoever was in charge of the investigation into the murder of Chris Norwood.

That would be Detective Chief Superintendent Irestone, I was told. He wasn't in. Would I care to talk to Detective Sergeant Smith? I said I supposed so, and after a few clicks and silences a comfortable Suffolk voice asked me what he could do for me.

I had mentally rehearsed what to say, but it was still difficult to begin. I said tentatively, "I might know a bit about why Chris Norwood was murdered and I might know perhaps roughly who did it, but I also might easily be wrong, it's just that—"

"Name, sir?" he said, interrupting. "Address? Can you be reached there, sir? At what time can you be reached there, sir? Detective Chief Superintendent Irestone will get in touch with you, sir. Thank you for calling."

I put the receiver down not knowing whether he had paid

extra-fast attention to what I'd said, or whether he had merely given the stock reply handed out to every crackpot who rang up with his or her pet theory. In either case it left me with just enough time to catch the last of the hamburgers in the school canteen and to get back to class on the dot.

At four I was held up by Louise's latest grudge (apparatus left out all over the benches—Martin would never do that) and I was fearful as I raced along the corridors the boys were not allowed to run in, and slid down the stairs with both hands on the bannisters and my feet touching only about every sixth tread, a trick I had learned in my far-back youth, that Ted Pitts's colleague would have tired of waiting, and gone home.

To my relief, he hadn't. He was sitting in front of the familiar screen shooting down little random targets with the zest of a seven-year-old.

"What's that?" I said, pointing at the game.

"Starstrike. Want a go?"

"Is it yours?"

"Something Ted made up to amuse and teach the kids."

"Is it in BASIC?" I asked.

"Sure. BASIC, graphics and special characters."

"Can you list it?"

"Bound to be able to. He'd never stuff it into ROM if he wanted to teach from it."

"What exactly," I said frustratedly, "is ROM?"

"Read only memory. If a program is in ROM you can only run it, you can't list it."

He typed LIST, and Ted's game scrolled up the screen to seemingly endless flickering rows.

"There you are," Ted's colleague said.

I looked at part of the last section of the program, which was now at rest on the screen:

```
410 RESET (RX, RY): RX = RX − RA : RY : RY − 8
420 IF RY > 2 SET (RX, RY): GOTO 200
430 IF ABS (1 * 8 − RX) > 4 THEN 150
460 FOR Q = 1 TO 6: PRINT 64 + 4 * v, "****";
```

A right load of gibberish to me, though poetry to Ted Pitts.

To his colleague I said, "I came down here to ask you to record something—anything—on these cassettes." I produced them. "Just so they have computer noise on them, and a readable program. They're for, er, demonstration."

He didn't query it.

I said, "Do you think Ted would mind me using his game?"

He shrugged. "I shouldn't think so. Two or three of the boys have got tapes of it. It's not secret."

He took the cassettes out of my hands and said, "Once on each tape?"

"Er, no. Several times on each side."

His eyes widened. "What on earth for?"

"Um." I thought in circles. "To demonstrate searching through file names."

"Oh. All right." He looked at his watch. "I'd leave you to do it, but Jenkins goes mad if one of the department doesn't check the computer's switched off and put the door key in the common room. I can't stay long anyway, you know."

He put the first of the tapes obligingly into the recorder, however, typed CSAVE "A", and pressed 'ENTER.' When the screen announced READY, he typed CSAVE "B", and after that CSAVE "C", and so on until the first side of the tape was full of repeats of Starstrike.

"This is taking ages," he muttered.

"Could you do one side of each tape, then?" I asked.

"OK."

He filled one side of the second tape and approximately half of a side on the third before his growing restiveness overcame him.

"Look, Jonathan, that's enough. It's taken nearer an hour than ten minutes."

"You're a pal."

"Don't you worry, I'll hit you one of these days for my games duty."

I picked up the cassettes and nodded agreement. Getting someone else to do games duty wasn't only the accepted way of wangling Wednesday afternoons off, it was also the coin in which favors were paid for.

"Thanks a lot," I said.

"Any time."

He began putting the computer to bed and I took the cassettes out to my car to pack them in a padded envelope and send them to Cambridge, with each filled side marked "Play this side first."

Since there was a Parents' Evening that day, I went for a pork pie with some beer in a pub, corrected books in the common room, and from eight to ten, along with nearly the whole complement of staff (as these occasions involved a three-line whip) reassured the parents of all the fourteen-year-olds that their little horrors were doing splendidly. The parents of Paul apple-on-the-head Arcady asked if he would make a research scientist. "His wit and style will take him far," I said noncommittally, and they said "He enjoys your lessons," which was a nice change from the next parent I talked to, who announced belligerently, "My lad's wasting his time in your class."

Placate, agree, suggest, smile: above all, show concern. I supposed those evenings were a Good Thing, but after a long day's teaching they were exhausting. I drove home intending to flop straight into bed, but when I opened the front door I found the telephone on the boil.

"Where have you been?" Sarah said, sounding cross.

"Parents' meeting."

"I've been ringing and ringing. Yesterday too."

"Sorry."

With annoyance unmollified she said, "Did you remember to water my house plants?"

Hell, I thought. "No, I didn't."

"It's so *careless*."

"Yes. Well, I'm sorry."

"Do them now. Don't leave it."

I said dutifully, "How's Donna?"

"Depressed." The single word was curt and dismissive. "Try not to forget," she said acidly, "the croton in the spare bedroom."

I put the receiver down, thinking that I positively didn't want her back. It was an uncomfortable, miserable thought. I'd loved her once so much. I'd have died for her, literally. I thought purposefully for the first time about divorce and in the thinking found neither regret nor guilt, but relief.

At eight in the morning when I was juggling coffee and toast the telephone rang again, and this time it was the police. A London accent, very polite.

"You rang with a theory, sir, about Christopher Norwood."

"It's not exactly a theory. It's...at the least...a coincidence." I had had time to cut my words down to essentials. I said, "Christopher Norwood commissioned a friend of mine, Peter Keithly, to write some computer programs. Peter Keithly did them and recorded them on cassette tapes, which he gave to me. Last Saturday two men came to my house, pointed a gun at me, and demanded the tapes. They threatened to shoot my television set and my ankles if I didn't hand them over. Are you, er, interested?"

There was a silence, then the same voice said, "Wait a moment, sir."

I drank some coffee and waited, and finally a different voice spoke in my ear, a bass voice, slower, less stilted, asking me to repeat what I'd said to the inspector.

"Mm," he said, when I'd finished. "I think I'd better see you. How are you placed?"

School, he agreed, was unavoidable. He would come to my house in Twickenham at four-thirty.

He was there before me, sitting not in a labeled and light-flashing police car, but in a fast four-door sedan. When I'd braked outside the garage he was already on his feet, and I found myself appraising a stocky man with a craggy young-old face, black hair dusting gray, unwavering light brown eyes and a skeptical mouth. Not a man, I thought, to save his time for fools.

"Mr. Derry?"

"Yes."

"Detective Chief Superintendent Irestone." He briefly produced a flip-over wallet and showed me his certification. "And Detective Inspector Robson." He indicated a second man emerging from the car, dressed casually like himself in gray trousers and sports jacket. "Can we go inside, sir?"

"Of course." I led the way in. "Would you like coffee, or tea?"

They shook their heads and Irestone plunged straight into the matter in hand. It appeared that what I'd told them so far did indeed interest them intensely. They welcomed, it seemed, my account of what I'd learned on my trek via Angel Kitchens to Mrs. O'Rorke. Irestone asked many questions, including how I persuaded the gunmen to go away empty-handed.

I said easily, "I didn't have the tapes here, because I'd lent them to a friend. I said I'd get them back and post them to them and luckily they agreed to that."

His eyebrows rose, but he made no comment. It must have seemed to him merely that I'd been fortunate.

"And you'd no idea who they were?" he said.

"None at all."

"I don't suppose you know what sort of pistol it was?"

He spoke without expectation, and it was an instant before I answered: but I said, "I think, a Walther .22. I've seen one before."

He said intently, "How certain are you?"

"Pretty certain."

He reflected. "We'd like you to go to your local station to see if you can put together Identi-kit pictures."

"Of course I will," I said, "but you might be able to see these men themselves, if you're lucky."

"How do you mean?"

"I did send them some tapes, but not until yesterday. They were going to pick them up from Cambridge main post office, and I should think there's a chance they'll be there tomorrow."

"That's helpful." He sounded unexcited, but wrote it all down. "Anything else?"

"They aren't the tapes they wanted. I still haven't got those back. I sent them back some other tapes with a computer game on."

He pursed his lips. "That wasn't very wise."

"But the real ones morally belong to Mrs. O'Rorke. And those gunmen won't come stampeding back here while they think they've got the goods."

"And how long before they find out?"

"I don't know. But if they're the same two people who threatened Peter, it might be a while. He said they didn't seem to know much about computers."

Irestone thought aloud. "Peter Keithly told you that two men visited him on the Wednesday evening, is that right?" I nodded. "Christopher Norwood was killed last Friday morning. Eight and a half days later." He rubbed his chin. "It might be unwise to suppose it will take them another eight and a half days to discover what you've done."

"I could always swear those *were* the tapes Peter Keithly gave me."

"And I don't think," he said flatly, "that this time they'd believe you." He paused. "The inquest on Peter Keithly was being held today, wasn't it?"

I nodded.

"We consulted with the Norwich police. There's no room to doubt your friend's death was an accident. I dare say you've wondered?"

"Yes, I have."

"You don't need to. The insurance inspector's report says the explosion was typical. There were no arson devices. No dynamite or plastics. Just absence of mind and rotten bad luck."

I looked at the floor.

"Your gunmen didn't do it," he said.

I thought that maybe he was trying to defuse any hatred I might be brewing, so that my testimony might be more impartial, but in fact what he was giving me was a kind of comfort, and I was grateful.

"If Peter hadn't died," I said, looking up, "they might have gone back to him when they found what they'd got from him was useless."

"Exactly," Irestone said dryly. "Do you have friends you could stay with for a while?"

On Saturday morning, impelled, I fear, by Mrs. O'Rorke's ten-percent promise, I drove to Welwyn Garden City to offer her tapes to Mr. Harry Gilbert.

Not that I exactly had the tapes with me, as they were still locked up with Ted Pitts's laryngitis, but at least I had the knowledge of their existence and contents, and that should be enough, I hoped, for openers.

From Twickenham to Welwyn was twenty miles in a direct line but far more in practice and tedious besides around the North Circular Road and narrow shopping streets. In contrast, the architects' dream city, when I got there, was green and orderly, and I found the Gilbert residence in an opulent cul-de-sac. Bingo, it seemed, had kept poverty a long, long way from his doorstep, which was reproduction Georgian, flanked with two pillars and surrounded by a regular regiment of windows. A house of red, white and sparkle on a carpet of green. I pressed the shiny brass doorbell, thinking it would be a bore if the inhabitants of this bijou mansion were out.

Mr. Gilbert, however, was in.

Just.

Mr. Gilbert opened his front door to my ring and said whatever I wanted I would have to come back later, as he was just off to play golf. Clubs and a cart for transporting them stood just inside the door, and Mr. Gilbert's heavy frame was clad appropriately in check trousers, open-necked shirt and blazer.

"It's about Liam O'Rorke's betting system," I said.

"What?" he said sharply.

"Mrs. O'Rorke asked me to come. She says she might be able to sell it to you after all."

He looked at his watch; a man of about fifty, in appearance unimpressive, more like a minor official than a peddler of pinchbeck dreams.

"Come in," he said. "This way."

His voice was no-nonsense middle-of-the-road, nearer the bingo hall than Eton. He led me into an unexpectedly functional room furnished with a desk, typewriter, wall maps with colored drawing pins dotted over them, two swivel chairs, one tray of drinks and five telephones.

"Fifteen minutes," he said. "So come to the point." He made no move to sit down or offer me a seat, but he was not so much rude as indifferent. I saw what Mrs. O'Rorke had meant about his being a cold man. He didn't try to clothe the bones of his thoughts with social top-dressing. He'd have made a lousy schoolmaster, I thought.

"Liam O'Rorke's notes were stolen," I began.

"I know that," he said impatiently. "Have they turned up?"

"Not his notes, no. But computer programs made from them, yes."

He frowned. "Mrs. O'Rorke has these programs?"

"No. I have. On her behalf. To offer to you."

"And your name?"

I shrugged. "Jonathan Derry. You can check with her, if you like." I gestured to the rank of telephones. "She'll vouch for me."

"Did you bring these . . . programs with you?"

"No," I said. "I thought we should make a deal first."

"Humph."

Behind his impassive face a fierce amount of consideration seemed to be taking place, and at length I had a powerful feeling that he couldn't make up his mind.

I said, "I wouldn't expect you to buy them without a demonstration. But I assure you they're the real thing."

It produced no discernible effect. The interior debate

continued: and it was resolved not by Gilbert or myself but by the arrival of someone else.

A car door slammed outside and there were footsteps on the polished parquet in the hall. Gilbert's head lifted to listen, and a voice outside the open door called, "Dad?"

"In here," Gilbert said.

Gilbert's son came in. Gilbert's son, who had come to my house with a pistol.

I must have looked as frozen with shock as I felt: but then so did he. I glanced at his father, and it came to me too late that this was the man Sarah had described—middle-aged, ordinary, plump—who had gone to Peter's house asking for the tapes. The one to whom she had said, "My husband's got them."

I seemed to have stopped breathing. It was as if life itself had been punched out of me. To know what *not* to do . . .

For all my instinct that ignorance was dangerous I had not learned enough. I hadn't learned the simple fact that would have stopped me from walking into that house: that Mr. Bingo Gilbert had a marauding Italian-looking son.

It was never a good idea to pursue Moses across the Red Sea . . .

"My son Angelo," Gilbert said.

Angelo made an instinctive movement with his right hand toward his left armpit as if reaching for his gun, but he wore a bloused suede jerkin over his jeans, and was unarmed. Thank the Lord, I thought, for small mercies.

In his left hand he carried the package I had sent to Cambridge. It had been opened, and he was holding it carefully upright to save the cassettes from falling out.

He recovered his voice faster than I did. His voice and his arrogance and his sneer.

"What's this mug doing here?" he said.

"He came to sell me the computer tapes."

Angelo laughed derisively. "I told you we'd get them for nothing. This mug sent them. I told you he would." He lifted the package jeeringly. "I told you you were an old fool to offer that Irish witch any cash. You'd've done better to let me shake the goods out of her the minute her old man died. You've no clues, Dad. You should have cut me in months ago, not tell me when it's already a mess."

His manner, I thought, was advanced son-parent rebellion: the young bull attacking the old. And part of it, I suspected, was for my benefit. He was showing off. Proving that even if I'd got the better of him the last time we'd met, it was he, Angelo, who was the superior being.

"How did this creep get here?"

Gilbert either ignored the peacockery or indulged it. "Mrs. O'Rorke sent him," he said.

Neither of them thought to ask the very awkward question of how I knew Mrs. O'Rorke. I'd have given few chances for my health if they'd worked it through. I reckoned that this was one exceptional occasion when ignorance was emphatically the safest path, and that in prudence I should be wholly ignorant of the life and death of Chris Norwood.

"How come he still has the tapes to sell," Angelo said cunningly, "if he's already sent them to me?"

Gilbert's eyes narrowed and his neck stiffened, and I saw that his unprepossessing exterior was misleading: that it was indeed a tough bull Angelo was challenging, one who still ruled his territory.

"Well?" he said to me.

Angelo waited with calculation and triumph growing in his eyes and throughout his face like an intoxication, the scarifying lack of inhibition ballooning as fast as before. It was his utter recklessness, I thought, which was to be feared above all.

"I sent a copy," I said. I pointed to the package in his hand. "Those are copies."

"Copies?" It stopped Angelo for a moment. Then he said suspiciously, "Why did you send copies?"

"The originals belonged to Mrs. O'Rorke. They weren't mine to give you. But I certainly didn't want you and your friend coming back again waving your gun all over the place, so I did send some tapes. I had no idea I would ever see you again. I just wanted to be rid of you. I had no idea you were Mr. Gilbert's son."

"Gun?" Gilbert said sharply. *"Gun?"*

"His pistol."

"Angelo!" There was no mistaking the anger in the father's voice. "I've forbidden you—*forbidden* you, do you hear—to carry that gun. I sent you to *ask* for those tapes. To ask. To buy."

"Threats are cheaper," Angelo said. "And I'm not a child. The days when I took your orders are over."

They faced each other in unleashed antagonism.

"That pistol is for protection," Gilbert said intensely. "And it is mine. You are not to threaten people with it. You are not to take it out of this house. You still depend on me for a living, and while you work for me and live in this house you'll do what I say. You'll leave that gun strictly alone."

God in Heaven, I thought: *he doesn't know about Chris Norwood*.

"You taught me to shoot," Angelo said defiantly.

"But as a sport," Gilbert said, and didn't understand that sport for his son was a living target.

I interrupted the filial battle and said to Gilbert, "You've got the tapes. Will you pay Mrs. O'Rorke?"

"Don't be bloody stupid," Angelo said.

I ignored him. To his father I said, "You were generous before. Be generous now."

I didn't expect him to be. I wanted only to distract him, to keep his mind on something trivial, not to let him *think*.

"Don't listen to him," Angelo said. "He's only a mug."

Gilbert's face mirrored his son's words. He looked me up and down with the same inner conviction of superiority, the belief that everyone was a mug except himself.

If Gilbert felt like that, I thought, it was easy to see why Angelo did. Parental example. I would often at school know the father by the behavior of the son.

I shrugged. I looked defeated. I let them get on with their ill will. I wanted above all to get out of that house before they started to put bits of knowledge together and came up with a picture of me as a real towering threat to Angelo's liberty. I didn't know if Gilbert would stop his son—or *could* stop him—if Angelo wanted me dead: and there was a lot of leafy Welwyn Garden City lying quietly in the back garden.

"Mrs. O'Rorke's expecting me," I said. "To know how I got on."

"Tell her nothing doing," Angelo said.

Gilbert nodded.

I edged past Angelo to the door, looking suitably meek under his scathing sneer.

"Well," I said weakly, "I'll be going."

I walked jerkily through the hall, past the attendant golf clubs and out of the open front door, taking with me a last view of Gilbert locking psychological horns with the menace that would one day overthrow him.

I was sweating. I wiped the palms of my hands on my trousers, fumbled open the car door, put a faintly trembling hand on the ignition key and started the engine.

If they hadn't been so busy fighting each other...

As I turned out of the drive into the cul-de-sac itself I had a glimpse of the two of them coming out onto the step to stare after me: and my mouth was uncomfortably dry until I was sure Angelo hadn't leaped into his car to give chase.

I had never felt my heart flutter that way before. I had never, I supposed, felt real fear. I couldn't get it to subside. I felt shaky, restless, short of breath, slightly sick.

Reaction, no doubt.

EIGHT

Somewhere between Welwyn and Twickenham I pulled into a parking space to work out where to go.

I could go home, collect my guns, and drive to Bisley. I looked down at my hands. On present form, I'd miss the target by a yard. No point in wasting money on the ammunition.

It should take a fair while for the Gilberts to discover that they had "Starstrike" instead of racing programs, but not as long as that to work out that while I had the original tapes, they had no exclusive control of Liam's system. I needed somewhere they wouldn't find me when they came looking. Pity, I thought, that Sarah and I had so few friends.

I walked across the road to a public telephone booth and telephoned to William's farm.

"Well of course, Jonathan," Mrs. Porter said. "Of course I'd have you. But William's gone. He got fed up with no horses to ride here and he packed up and went off to Lambourn this morning. He'd a friend there, he said, and he's going straight back to school from there tomorrow evening."

"Was he all right?"

"So much *energy*!" she said. "But he won't eat a thing. Says he wants to keep his weight down, to be a jockey."

I sighed. "Thanks anyway."

"It's a pleasure to have him," she said. "He makes me laugh."

I rang off, counted the small stack of coins I had left, and public spiritedly spent them on the Newmarket police.

"Chief Superintendent Irestone isn't here, sir," they said. "Do you want to leave a message?"

I hesitated, but in the end all I said was, "Tell him Jonathan Derry called. I have a name for him. I'll get in touch with him later."

"Very good, sir."

I got back into the car, consulted a slip of paper in my wallet and drove to Northolt to visit Ted Pitts, knowing that quite likely he wouldn't be pleased to see me. When I had finally tracked down the school secretary he had parted with the requested information reluctantly, saying that the masters' addresses were sacrosanct to save them from over-zealous parents. Ted Pitts, he said, had particularly made him promise not to divulge.

"But I'm not a parent."

"Well, no."

I'd had to persuade, but I got it. And one could see, I thought, why Ted wanted to guard his privacy, because where he lived, I found, was in a mobile home on a caravan site. Neat enough, but not calculated to impress some of the social climbers in the PTA.

Ted's wife, who opened the door to my knock, looked surprised but not unwelcoming. She was as earnest as Ted, small, bright-eyed, an occasional visitor to school football matches, where Ted tore up and down the side lines refereeing. I sought for a name and thought "Jane," but wasn't sure. I smiled hopefully instead.

"How's Ted?" I said.

"Much better. His voice is coming back." She opened

the door wider. "He'd like to see you, I'm sure, so do come in." She gestured to the inside of the caravan, where I couldn't yet see, and said, "It's a bit of a mess. We didn't expect visitors."

"If you'd rather I didn't—"

"No. Ted will want you."

I stepped up into the van and saw what she meant. In every direction spread an untidy jumble of books and newspapers and clothes and toys, all the normal clutter of a large family but condensed into a very small space.

Ted was in the minuscule sitting room with his three little girls, sitting on a sofa and watching while they played on the floor. When he saw me he jumped to his feet in astonishment and opened his mouth, but all that came out was a squeaky croak.

"Don't talk," I said. "I just came to see how you are." Any thoughts I had about cadging a bed from him had vanished. It seemed silly, indeed, to mention it.

"I'm better." The words were recognizable, but half a whisper, and he gestured for me to sit down. His wife ordered coffee and I accepted. The children squabbled and he kicked them gently with his toe.

"Jane will take them out soon," he said huskily.

"I'm being a nuisance."

He shook his head vigorously. "Glad you came." He pointed to a ledge running high along one wall and said, "I bought your new tapes. They're up there, with your cassettes, out of reach. The children climb so. Haven't done the copying yet, though. Sorry." He rubbed his throat as if massage would help, and made a face of frustration.

"Don't talk," I said again, and passed on William's information about form books. He seemed pleased enough but also subdued, as if the knowledge no longer interested him.

Jane returned with one mug of coffee and offered sugar. I shook my head and took a sip of the liquid, which looked dark brown but tasted weak.

I said, more to make conversation than anything else, "I don't suppose either of you know where I could put up for a night or two? Somewhere not too expensive. I mean, not a hotel." I smiled lopsidedly. "I've spent so much on petrol and other things this week that I'm a bit short."

"End of the month," Ted said, nodding. "Always the same."

"But your house!" Jane said. "Ted says you've got a house."

"Er, um, er, I haven't been getting on too well with Sarah." The convenient half-truth arrived just in time and they made small sad noises in sympathetic comprehension. Ted, all the same, shook his head, sorry not to be able to help.

"Don't know of anywhere," he said.

Jane, standing straight, tucking her elbows into her sides and clasping her hands tightly together, said, "You could stay here. On the sofa."

Ted looked extremely surprised but his wife very tensely said, "Would you pay us?"

"Jane!" Ted said despairingly, but I nodded.

"In advance?" she said rigidly, and I agreed again. I gave her two of the notes I'd got from the bank a day earlier and asked if it was enough. She said yes looking flushed and bundled the three children out of the room, out of the caravan, and down toward the road. Ted, hopelessly awkward and embarrassed, stuttered a wheezy apology.

"We've had a bad month...they've put the land rent up here...and I had to pay for new tires, and for the car license. I must have the car and it's falling to bits...and I'm overdrawn..."

"Do stop, Ted," I said. "I know all about being broke. Not starving broke. Just penniless."

He smiled weakly. "I suppose we've never had the bailiffs...but this week we've been living on bread mostly. Are you sure you don't mind?"

"Positive."

So I stayed with the Pitts. Watched television, built bright brick towers for the children, ate the egg supper my money had bought, took Ted for a pint.

The talking couldn't have done his throat much good, but between the froth and the dregs I learned a good deal about the Pitts. He'd met Jane one summer in a youth hostel in the Lake District, and they'd married while he was still at college because the oldest of the little girls was imminent. They were happy, he said, but they'd never been able to save a deposit for a house. Lucky to have the mobile home. Mortgaged, of course. During the holidays he looked after the children while Jane took temporary secretarial jobs. Better for the family income. Better for Jane. He still went hiking on his own, though, one week every year. Backpacking. Sleeping in a tent, in hilly country: Scotland or Wales. He gave me a shy look through the black-framed glasses. "It sorts me out. Keeps me sane." It wasn't everyone, I thought, who was his own psychotherapist.

When we got back the caravan was tidy and the children asleep. One had to be quiet, Ted said, going in: they woke easily. The girls all slept, it appeared, in the larger of the two bedrooms, with their parents in the smaller. There were a pillow, a car traveling blanket and a clean sheet awaiting me, and although the sofa was a bit short for comfort it was envelopingly soft.

It was only on the point of sleep, far too late to bother, that I remembered that I hadn't called back to talk to Irestone. Oh well, I thought, yawning, tomorrow would do.

In the morning I did call from a telephone booth near the public park where Ted and I took the children to play on the swings and seesaw.

Irestone, as usual, wasn't in. Wasn't he *ever* in? I asked. A repressive voice told me the chief superintendent was off duty at present, and would I please leave a message. I perversely said that no, I wouldn't, I wanted to speak to the chief superintendent personally. If I would leave a number, they said, he would in due course call me. Impasse, I thought: Ted Pitts had no telephone.

"If I call you at nine tomorrow morning," I said, "will Chief Superintendent Irestone be there? If I call at ten? At eleven? At midday?"

I was told to wait and could hear vague conversations going on in the background, and going on for so long that I had to feed more coins into the box, which scarcely improved my impatience. Finally, however, the stolid voice returned. "Detective Chief Superintendent Irestone will be in the Incident Room tomorrow morning from ten o'clock onward. You may call him at the following number."

"Wait a minute." I unclipped my pen and dug out the scrap of paper which held Ted's address. "OK."

He gave me the number, and I thanked him fairly coolly, and that was that.

Ted was pushing his tiniest girl carefully around on a sort of turntable, holding her close to him and laughing with her. I wished quite surprisingly fiercely that I could have had a child like that, that I could have taken her to a sunny park on Sunday mornings, and hugged her little body and watched her grow. Sarah, I thought. Sarah... this is the way you've ached, perhaps; and for the baby to cuddle, and the young woman to see married. This is the loss. This, that Ted Pitts has. I watched his delight in the child and I envied him with all my heart.

We sat on a bench a bit later while the girls played in a sandbox, and for something to say I asked him why he'd lost his first intense interest in the racing form books.

He shrugged, looked at his children, and said in the husky voice which was slowly returning to normal, "You can see how it is. I can't risk the money. I can't afford to buy the form books. I couldn't even afford to buy a set of tapes for myself this week, to copy the programs onto. I bought some for you with the money you gave me, but I just didn't have enough. I told you, we've been down to counting pennies for food, and, although next month's pay will be in the bank tomorrow, I still haven't paid the electricity..."

"It's the Derby soon," I said.

He nodded morosely. "Don't think I haven't thought of

it. I look at those tapes sitting up on that shelf, and I think, shall I or shan't I? But I've had to decide not to. I can't risk it. How could I possibly explain to Jane if I lost? We need every pound, you know. You can see we do."

It was ironic, I thought. On the one hand, there was Angelo Gilbert, who was prepared to kill to get those tapes, and on the other, Ted Pitts, who had them and set them lower than a dustup with his wife.

"The programs belong to an old woman named O'Rorke," I said. "Mrs. Maureen O'Rorke. I went to see her this week."

Ted showed only minor signs of interest.

"She said a few things I thought you'd find amusing."

"What things?" Ted said.

I told him about the bookmakers' closing the accounts of regular winners, and about the system the O'Rorkes had used with their gardener, Dan, going around betting shops to put their money on anonymously.

"Great heavens," Ted said. "What a palaver." He shook his head. "No, Jonathan, it's best to forget it."

"Mrs. O'Rorke said her husband could bet with an overall certainty of winning once every three times. How does that strike you statistically?"

He smiled. "I'd need a hundred percent certainty to bet on the Derby."

One of the children threw sand in the eyes of another and he got up in a hurry to scold, to comfort, to dig around earnestly with the corner of his handkerchief.

"By the way," I said, when order was restored. "I took some copies of your game 'Starstrike.' I hope you don't mind."

"You're welcome," he said. "Did you play it? You have to type in F or S at the first question mark. I haven't written the instructions out yet, but I'll let you have them when I do. The kids"—he looked pleased and a touch smug—"say it's neat."

"Is it your best?"

"My best?" He smiled a fraction and shrugged, and said,

"I teach from it. I had to write it so that the kids could understand the program and how it worked. Sure, I could write a far more sophisticated one, but what would be the point?"

A pragmatist, Ted Pitts, not a dreamer. We collected the children together, with Ted brushing them down and emptying sand from their shoes, and drove back to the caravan to homemade hamburgers for lunch.

In the afternoon under Ted's commiserating eyes I corrected the load of exercise books which I happened not to have carried into my house on Friday night. The boys had Irestone to thank for that. And on Monday morning, with Ted's voice in good enough shape, he thought, to quell the monsters in the classroom, we both went back to school.

We each drove our own cars. I felt I'd used up my welcome in the caravan and although Jane said I could stay if I liked I could see I was no longer a blessing from heaven. The new paycheck would be in the bank. There would be more than bread this week, and I would have to think of somewhere else.

Ted stretched up in the last minutes before we left and plucked the six cassettes from the high shelf. "I could do these at lunchtime today," he said. "If you like."

"That would be great," I said. "Then you can keep one set and the others will be Mrs. O'Rorke's."

"But don't you want some yourself?"

"Maybe later I could get copies of yours . . . but I can't see me chasing around betting shops for the rest of my life."

He laughed. "Nor me. Though I wouldn't have minded a flutter . . ." A sort of longing gleamed in his eyes again and was quickly extinguished. "Ah, well," he said, "forward to the fray." He kissed Jane and the little girls, and off we went.

During the midmorning break I yet again tried to reach Chief Superintendent Irestone, this time from the pay telephone in the common room. Even with the new number I got no joy. Chief Superintendent Irestone wasn't available at that time.

"This is boring," I said. "I was told he would be."

"He was called away, sir. Will you leave a message?"

I felt like leaving a couple of round oaths. I said, "Tell him Jonathan Derry called."

"Very good, sir. Your message timed at ten thirty-three."

To hell with it, I thought.

I had taken about five paces down the room in the direction of the coffee machine when the telephone rang behind me. It was the time of day when masters' wives tended to ring up to get their dear ones to run errands on their way home, and the nearest to the bell answered its summons as a matter of course. My wife, at least, I thought, wouldn't be calling, but someone shouted, "Jonathan, it's for you."

Surprised, I retraced my steps and picked up the receiver.

"Hello," I said.

"*Jonathan,*" Sarah said. "Where have you been? Where in God's name have you *been*?"

She sounded hysterical. Her voice was high, vibrating with tension, strung tighter than I'd ever heard before. Near snapping point. Frightening.

"What's happened?" I asked. I was aware that my voice sounded too calm, but I couldn't help it. It always seemed to come out that way when there was a jumbled turmoil going on inside.

"Oh, my *Christ!*" She still had time to be exasperated with me: but no time to say more.

After the shortest of pauses another voice spoke, and this time every hair of my body rose in protest.

"Now you listen to me, creep."

Angelo Gilbert.

"You listen to me," he said. "Your little lady wifey's sitting here snug as you like. We tied her to a chair so's not to hurt her." He sniggered. "Her friend, too, the wet little bird. Now you listen, mug, because you're going to do just what I tell you. Are you you listening?"

"Yes," I said. I was in fact listening with all my might and with one hand clamped over my other ear because of the chatter and coffee cups all around me. It was macabre.

It also seemed to have divorced me from any feeling in my feet.

"That was your last runaround, that was," Angelo said, "sending us those fake tapes. This time you'll give us the real ones, get it?"

"Yes," I said mildly.

"You wouldn't like to get your little wifey back with her face all smashed up, would you?"

"No."

"All you got to do is give us the tapes."

"All right," I said.

"And no bloody runaround." He seemed disappointed that I'd shown so little reaction to his dramatics but even in that dire moment it seemed second nature to use on him the techniques I'd unconsciously developed in the years of teaching: to deflate the defiance, to be bored by the super-ego, to kill off the triumphant cruelty by an appearance of indifference.

It worked on the kids, it worked a treat on Jenkins, and it had already worked twice on Angelo. He should have learned by now, I thought, that I didn't rise to sneers or arrogance: not visibly anyway. He was too full of himself to believe that someone might not show the fear he felt the urge to induce. He might not be ultra-bright, but he was incalculably dangerous.

He held the receiver to Sarah's mouth, and against her I had fewer defenses.

"Jonathan . . ." It was half anger, half fright: high and vehement. "They came yesterday. *Yesterday.* Donna and I have been tied up here all *night.* Where have you damned well *been?*"

"Are you in Donna's house?" I said anxiously.

"*What?* Yes, of *course.* Of *course* we are. Don't ask such damn silly questions."

Angelo took the phone back again. "Now you listen, mug. Listen good. This time there's to be no messing. This time we want the real McCoy, and I'm telling you, it's your last chance."

I didn't answer.

"Are you there?" he said sharply.

"Sure," I said.

"Take the tapes to my father's house in Welwyn. Have you got that?"

"Yes. But I haven't got the tapes."

"Then *get* them." His voice was nearly a screech. "Do you hear?" he demanded. "Get them."

"It'll take some time," I said.

"You haven't got time, creep."

I took a deep breath. He wasn't safe. He wasn't reasonable. He wasn't a schoolchild. I simply couldn't play him too far.

"I can get the tapes today," I said. "I'll take them to your father when I get them. It might be late."

"Sooner," he said.

"I can't. It's impossible."

I didn't know exactly why I wanted to delay. It was an instinct. To work things out; not to rush in. This time the Egyptians would have more sense.

"When you get there," he said, seeming to accept it, "my father will test the tapes. On a computer. A Grantley computer. Get it, mug? My father bought a Grantley computer, because that's the sort of computer those tapes were written for. So no funny tricks like last time. He'll try the tapes, see? And they'd better be good."

"All right," I said again.

"When my father is satisfied," he said, "he'll ring me here. Then I'll leave your little wifey and the wet chick tied up here, and you can come and rescue them like a right little Galahad. Got it?"

"Yes," I said.

"Don't you forget, creep, any funny stuff and your little wifey will keep the plastic surgery business in work for years. Starting with her nice white teeth, creep."

He apparently again held the receiver for Sarah because it was her voice which came next. Still angry, still frightened, still high.

"For God's sake, get those tapes."

"Yes, I will," I said. "Has Angelo got his pistol?"

"Yes. Jonathan, do as he says. *Please* do as he says. Don't fool about." It was an order just as much as a prayer.

"The tapes," I said with an attempt at reassurance, "are not worth a tooth. Keep him calm if you can. Tell him I'll do what he says. Tell him I've promised you."

She didn't answer. It was Angelo who said, "That's all, creep. That's enough. You get those tapes. Right?"

"All right," I said. And the line abruptly went dead.

I felt pretty dead myself.

The common room had emptied and I was already going to be late for class. I picked up the necessary books mechanically and propelled myself on unfelt feet along the passages to the laboratories.

Get the tapes...

I couldn't get them until I could find Ted Pitts, which would probably not be until lunchtime at twelve-fifteen. I had an hour and a half until then in which to decide what to do.

The senior boys were studying radioactivity. I told them to continue the set of experiments with alpha particles that they had started last week and I sat on my high stool by the blackboard from where I often taught, and watched the Geiger counters, with my mind on Angelo Gilbert.

Options, I thought.

I could yet once again ring the police. I could say an unstable man is holding my wife hostage at gunpoint. I could say I thought it was he who had killed Christopher Norwood. If I did, they might go chasing out to the Keithly house and try to make Angelo surrender. And then Sarah could be a hostage not for three little cassettes, but for Angelo's personal liberty. An escalation not to be thought of.

No police.

What, then?

Give Harry Gilbert the tapes. Trust that Angelo would leave Sarah and Donna undamaged. Do, in fact, precisely what I'd been told: and believe that Angelo wouldn't wait for me to walk into Donna's house and then leave three dead bodies behind when he walked out of it.

It wasn't logically likely, but it was possible.

It would have been better if I could have thought of a good valid reason for the murder of Chris Norwood. He hadn't given Angelo the finished computer programs because if he had there would have been no need for Angelo to come to *me*. I speculated, not for the first time, on exactly what had happened to the tapes Peter told me he had sent to the person who had commissioned them. To C. Norwood, Angel Kitchens, Newmarket.

To Chris Norwood, comprehensive thief. Cocky little bastard, Akkerton had said. Vegetable chef Akkerton, feeding his paunch in the pub.

I had supposed that Chris Norwood, when first faced with Angelo, had simply said that Peter Keithly was writing the programs and had all the notes, and that Angelo should get them from *him*. Angelo had then gone threateningly to Peter, who had been frightened into giving him programs which he knew were incomplete. By the time the Gilberts discovered they were useless, Peter was dead. Back must have gone Angelo to Chris Norwood, this time waving a gun. And again Chris Norwood must have said Peter Keithly had the programs on tapes. That if he was dead, they were in his house. He would have told him that, I thought, *after* Angelo had shot up the stereo. He would have begun to be really frightened: but he would still have wanted to keep the programs if he could, because he knew they were a meal ticket for life.

Chris Norwood, I guessed, had twice not given Angelo what he wanted; and Chris Norwood was dead.

I also had fooled and obstructed Angelo twice; and I couldn't be sure that I wasn't alive because I'd had a handy rifle. Without his father there to restrain him, Angelo could still be as volatile as the petrol vapor that had killed Peter, even if he thought he finally had his hands on the treasure he'd been chasing for so long.

Some of the boys were getting their nuclei into knots. Automatically I descended from the heights of the stool and reminded them that cloud chambers didn't cloud if one neglected to add dry ice.

No more runarounds, Angelo had said.

Well . . .

What tools did I have, I thought. What skills that I could use?

I could shoot.

I couldn't, on the other hand, shoot Angelo. Not while he had a Walther to Sarah's head. Not without landing myself in jail for manslaughter at the least.

Shooting Angelo was out.

I had the knowledge that physics had given me. I could construct a radio, a television, a thermostat, a digital clock, a satellite tracker and, given the proper components, a laser beam, a linear accelerator and an atomic bomb. I couldn't exactly make an atomic bomb before lunch.

The two boys who were using the alpha particle scattering analogue were arguing over the apparatus, which consisted of one large magnet bombarded by a host of small ones. One boy insisted that the power of permanent magnets decayed with time, and the other said that was rubbish; permanent meant permanent.

"Who's right, sir?" they asked.

"Permanence is relative," I said. "Not absolute."

There was a flash of impermanent electrical activity at that moment in my brain. The useful knowledge was at hand.

God bless all boys, I thought.

NINE

Ted Pitts hunched over the Harris all through lunchtime, making and testing the copies on the new tapes.

"There you are," he said finally, rubbing his neck. "As far as I can see, they're perfect."

"Which set do you want?"

He peered at me earnestly through the black frames. "Don't you mind?"

"Choose which you like," I said. "I'll take the others."

He hesitated, but decided on the originals. "If you're sure?"

"Certain," I said. "But give me the original boxes— *Oklahoma* and so on. It might be better if I hand them over in the right wrappings."

I slid the copies into the gaudy boxes, thanked Ted, returned to the common room, and told my four long-suffering lieutenants that I had developed a stupefying sick shivery headache and would they please take my afternoon classes between them. There were groans, but it was a service we regularly did for each other when it was unavoidable. I was going home, I said. With luck, I would be back in the morning.

Before I left I made a detour to the prep room where Louisa was counting out springs and weights for the juniors' class that afternoon. I told her about the headache and got scant sympathy, which was fair. While she took the load of batteries through into one of the laboratories to distribute them along the benches, I opened one of her tidy cupboards and helped myself to three small objects, hiding them smartly in my pocket.

"What are you looking for?" Louisa asked, coming back and seeing me in front of the still-open doors.

"Nothing particular," I said vaguely. "I don't really know."

"Get home to bed," she said, sighing, casting herself for martyrdom. "I'll cope with the extra work."

My absence meant in reality less work for her, not more, but there was nothing to be gained by pointing it out. I thanked her profusely to keep her in a good mood for the others, and went out to the car to drive home.

No need to worry about Angelo's being there: he was in the Keithlys' house a hundred miles away in Norfolk.

Everything felt unreal. I thought of the two girls, tied to the chairs, uncomfortable, scared, exhausted. Don't fool about, Sarah had said. Do what Angelo says.

Somewhere in one of the sideboard drawers we had a photograph album, thrust out of sight since we had lost the desire to record our joyless life. I dug it out and turned the pages, looking for the picture I had taken once of Peter, Donna and Sarah standing out on the pavement in front of Peter's house. The sun had been shining, I found. All three were smiling, looking happy. A pang to see Peter's face, no moustache, looking so pleased with himself and young. Nothing special about that photograph: just people, a house, a street. Reassuring to me, however, at that moment.

I went upstairs to my own small room, unlocked the gun cabinet and took out one of the Mauser 7.62's and also one of the Olympic-type rifles, the Anschütz .22. Packed them both into the special suitcase along with some ammunition of both sizes. Carried the case down to the car and locked it into the trunk.

Reflected and went upstairs to fetch a large brown bath towel from the linen cupboard. Locked that also into the trunk.

Locked the house.

After that, I sat in the car for three or four minutes thinking things out, with the result that I went back into the house yet again, this time for a tube of extra-strength glue.

All I didn't have enough of, I thought, was time.

I started the engine and set off, not to Welwyn, but to Norwich.

Propelled by demons I did the trip in shorter time than usual, but it was still four-thirty when I reached the city outskirts. Six hours since Angelo had telephoned. Six long hours for his hostages.

I drew up beside a telephone booth in a shopping mall not far from Donna's house and dialed her number. Praying, I think, that Angelo would answer, that all would be at least no worse than it had been in the morning.

"Hello," he said. Eagerly, I thought. Expecting his father.

"It's Jonathan Derry," I said. "I've got the tapes."

"Let me talk to my father."

"I'm not at your father's house. I haven't gone there yet. It's taken me all day to get the tapes."

"Now you listen, creep." He was roughly, nastily angry. "I warned you."

"It's taken me all day, but I've got them," I interrupted insistently. "I've got the tapes. I've got the tapes."

"All *right*," he said tautly. "Now take them to my father. Take them there, do you hear?"

"Yes," I said. "I'll go there straight away, but it'll take me some time. It's a long way."

Angelo muttered under his breath and then said, "How long? Where are you? We've been waiting all fucking night and all fucking day."

"I'm near Bristol."

"Where?" It was a yell of fury.

"It'll take me four hours," I said, "to reach your father."

There was a brief silence. Then Sarah's voice, tired beyond tears, numb with too much fright.

"Where are you?" she said.

"Near Bristol."

"Oh, my God." She sounded no longer angry, but hopeless. "We can't stand much more of this—"

The receiver was taken away from her in midsentence, and Angelo came back on the line.

"Get going, creep," he said, and hung up.

Breathing space, I thought. Four hours before Angelo expected the message from his father. Instead of pressure mounting inexorably, dangerously, in that house, there would at worst, I hoped, be a bearable irritation, and at best a sort of defusing of suspense. They wouldn't for another four hours be strung up with a minute-to-minute expectation.

Before getting back into the car I opened the trunk, took the telescope and the two rifles out of their nonjolt beds in the suitcase and wrapped them more vulnerably in the brown towel. Put them into the car on the brown upholstery of the back seat. Put the boxes of bullets beside them, also hidden by the towel. Looked then at my fingers. No tremors. Not like in my heart.

I drove around into the road where the Keithly house stood and stopped at the curb just out of sight of the net-curtained window. I could see the roof, part of a wall, most of the front garden . . . and Angelo's car in the driveway.

There weren't many people in the street. The children would be home from school, indoors having tea. The husbands wouldn't be back yet from work: there was more space than cars outside the houses. A peaceful suburban scene. Residential street, middle-income prosperous, not long built. An uncluttered street with no big trees and no forests of electricity and telegraph poles: new-laid cables tended to run underground for most of their journey, emerging only occasionally into the daylight. In the photograph of Peter's house there had been one telegraph pole nearby with wires distributing from it to the individual houses all around, but not much else. No obstructions. Neat flat asphalt pavements, white curbstones, blacktop roadway. A few neat little hedges bordering some of the gardens. A lot of neat green rectangular patches of repressed grass. Acres of net curtains ready to twitch. I-can-see-out-but-you-can't-see-in.

The first essential for pinpoint rifle shooting was to know how far one was from the target. On ranges the distances were fixed, and always the same. I was accustomed to precisely three, four, and five hundred yards. To nine hundred and a thousand yards, both of them further than half a mile. The distance affected one's angle of aim: the longer the distance, the further above the target one had to aim in order to hit it.

Olympic shooting was all done at three hundred meters, but from different body positions: standing, kneeling and lying prone. In Olympic shooting also one was allowed ten sighters in each position—ten chances of adjusting one's sights before one came to the forty rounds which counted for scoring.

In that street in Norwich I was not going to get ten sighters. I could afford barely one.

No regular lines of telegraph poles meant no convenient help with measuring the distance. The front gardens though, I reckoned, should all be of more or less the same width because all the houses were identical, so as inconspicuously and casually as possible I slipped out of the car and paced slowly along the street, going away from Peter's house.

Fourteen paces per garden. I did some mental arithmetic and came up with three hundred yards meaning twenty-two houses.

I counted carefully. There were only twelve houses between me and my target: say one hundred and seventy yards. The shorter distance would be to my advantage. I could reckon in general to hit a target within one minute of a degree of arc: or in other words to hit a circular target of about one inch wide at a hundred yards, two inches wide at two hundred, three inches wide at three hundred, and so on to a ten-inch dinner plate at a thousand.

My target on that evening was roughly rectangular and about four inches by six, which meant that I mustn't be further away from it than four hundred yards. The main problem was that from where I stood, even if I used the telescope, I couldn't see it.

An old man came out of the house against whose curb I was parked and asked if I wanted anything.

"Er, no," I said. "Waiting for someone. Stretching my legs."

"My son wants to park there," he said, pointing to where my car was. "He'll be home soon."

I looked at the stubborn old face and knew that if I didn't move he would be staring at me through the curtains, watching whatever I did. I nodded and smiled, got into the car, backed up into his next-door driveway, and left the street by the way I'd come.

All right, I thought, driving around. I have to come into the street from the opposite end. I have to park where I can see the target. I do not, if possible, park outside anyone's house fully exposed to one of those blank-looking one-way viewing screens. I do not park where Angelo can see me. I count the houses carefully to get the distance right; and above all I don't take much time.

It's a cliché in movies that when an assassin looks through the telescopic sight, steadies the crossed lines on the target and squeezes the trigger, the victim drops dead. Quite often the assassin will perform this feat while standing up, and nearly always it will be with his first shot: all of which makes serious marksmen laugh, or wince, or both. The only film I ever saw that got it right was *The Day of the Jackal*, where the gunman went into a forest to pace out his distance, to strap his rifle to a tree for steadiness, to adjust his sights and take two or three trial shots at a head-sized melon before transferring it all to the place of execution. Even then there was no allowance for wind—but one can't have everything.

TWICE SHY

I drove into the top end of Peter's road, with which I was less familiar, and between two of the houses came across the wide entrance gates to the old estate upon which the new houses had been built. The double gates themselves, wrought iron, ajar, led to a narrow road that disappeared into parkland, and they were set not flush with the roadway or even with the fronts of the houses, but slightly farther back. Between the gates and the road there was an area of moderately well-kept gravel and a badly weathered notice board announcing that all callers to the Paranormal Research Institute should drive in and follow the arrows to Reception.

I turned without hesitation onto the gravel area and stopped the car. It was ideal. From there, even with the naked eye, I had a clear view of the target. A slightly sideways view certainly, but good enough.

I got out of the car and counted the houses which stretched uniformly along the street: the Keithlys' was the fourteenth on the opposite side of the road and my target was one house nearer.

The road curved slightly to my right. There was a slight breeze from the left. I made the assessments almost automatically and eased myself into the back of the car.

I had gone through long patches of indecision over which rifle to use. The 7.62 bullets were far more destructive, but if I missed the target altogether with the first shot, I could do terrible damage to things or people I couldn't see. People half a mile away, or more. The .22 was much lighter: still potentially deadly if I missed the target, but not for such a long distance.

In a car I obviously couldn't lie flat on my stomach, the way I normally fired the Mauser. I could kneel, and I was more used to kneeling with the .22. But when I knelt in the car I wouldn't have to support the rifle's weight; I could rest it on the door and shoot through the open window.

For better or worse I chose the Mauser. The stopping power was so much greater, and if I was going to do the job it was best done properly. Also I could see the target clearly and it was near enough to make hitting it with the second shot a certainty. It was the *first* shot that worried.

A picture of Paul Arcady rose in my mind. "Could you shoot the apple off his head, sir?" What I was doing was much the same. One slight mistake could have unthinkable results.

Committed, I wound down the rear window and then fitted the sleek three-inch round of ammunition into the Mauser's breech. I took a look at the target through the telescope, steadying that too on the window ledge, and what leaped to my eye was a bright, clear, slightly oblique close-up of a flat shallow box, fixed high up and to one side on the telegraph pole: gray, basically rectangular, fringed with wires leading off to all the nearby houses.

The junction box.

I was sorry for all the people who were going to be without telephones for the rest of the day, but not too sorry to put them out of order.

I lowered the telescope, folded the brown towel, and laid it over the doorframe to make a nonslip surface. Wedged myself between the front and rear seats as firmly as possible, and rested the barrel of the Mauser on the towel.

I thought I would probably have to hit the junction box two or three times to be sure. The 7.62mm bullets tended to go straight through things, doing most of the damage on the way out. If I'd cared to risk shooting the junction box *through the pole* one accurate bullet would have blown it apart, but I would have to have been directly behind it, and I couldn't get there unobserved.

I set the sights to what I thought I would need for that distance, lowered my body into an angle that felt right, corrected a fraction for the breeze, and squeezed the trigger. Hit the pole, I prayed. High or low, hit the pole. The bullet might indeed go through it, but with the worst of its impetus spent.

7.62-caliber rifles make a terrific noise. Out in the street it must have cracked like a bullwhip. In the car it deafened me like in the old days before ear-defenders.

I reloaded. Looked through the telescope. Saw the bullet hole, round and neat, right at the top of the gray junction box casing.

Allelujah, I thought gratefully, and breathed deeply from relief.

Lowered the sight a fraction, keeping my body position unchanged. Shot again. Reloaded. Shot again. Looked through the telescope.

The second and third holes overlapped, lower down than the first, and maybe because I wasn't shooting at it directly face on, but from a little to one side, the whole casing seemed to have split.

It would have to do. It was all too noisy.

I put the guns and telescope on the floor with the towel over them and scrambled through onto the front seat.

Started the engine, reversed slowly onto the road and drove away at a normal pace, seeing in the rear-view mirror a couple of inhabitants come out inquiringly into the street. The net curtains must all have been twitching, but no one shouted after me, no one pointed and said, "That's the man."

And Angelo . . . what would he think? And Sarah . . . who knew the sound of a rifle better than church bells? I hoped to God she'd keep quiet.

Going out of Norwich I stopped for gas and used the telephone there to ring Donna's number.

Nothing.

A faint humming noise, like wind in the wires.

I blew out a lungful of air and wondered with a smile what the repair men would say when they climbed the pole on the morrow. Unprintable, most like.

There were perhaps ways of interfering with incoming calls by technical juggling, by ringing a number, waiting for it to be answered, saying nothing, waiting for the receiver to be put down, and then not replacing one's own receiver, leaving the line open and making it impossible for the number to ring again. I might have trusted that method for a short while, but not for hours: and with some exchanges it didn't work.

Farther along the road I stopped again, this time to tidy and reorganize the car. I returned the Mauser and the telescope to their beds in the suitcase in the trunk, along with the 7.62mm ammunition; then I broke all my own and everyone else's rules and loaded a live .22 round into the breech of the Anschütz.

I laid the towel on the back seat and rolled the Olympic rifle in it lengthways, and then stowed it flat on the floor behind the front seats. The towel blended well enough with the brown carpet, and I reckoned that if I didn't accelerate or brake or corner too fast, the gun should travel without moving.

Next I put four extra bullets into my righthand pocket, because the Anchütz had no magazine and each round had to be loaded separately. After so many years of practice I could discharge the spent casing and load a new bullet within the space of two seconds, and even faster if I held the fresh bullet in my right palm. The two rifles were physically the same size, and I'd have taken the Mauser with its available magazine if it hadn't been for its horrific power in a domestic setting. The .22 would kill, but not the people in the next house.

After that I juggled around a bit with the cassettes and their boxes and the glue and the bits I'd pinched from school, and finally drove on again, this time to Welwyn.

Harry Gilbert was expecting me. From the way he came bustling out of his house the moment I turned into his driveway he had been expecting me for a long time and had grown thoroughly tired of it.

"Where have you *been?*" he said. "Did you bring the tapes?"

He had come close to me as I emerged from the car, thrusting his chin forward belligerently, sure of his power over a man at a disadvantage.

"I thought you didn't approve of Angelo threatening people with your pistol," I said.

Something flickered in a muscle in his face.

"There are times when only threats will do," he said. "Give me the tapes."

I took the three tapes out of my pocket and showed them to him; the three tapes themselves, out of their boxes.

I said, "Now ring Angelo and tell him to untie my wife."

Gilbert shook his head. "I try the tapes first. Then I ring Angelo. And Angelo leaves your wife tied up until you yourself go to release her. That is the arrangement. It's simple. Come into the house."

We went again into his functional office, which this time had an addition in the shape of a Grantley computer sitting on his desk.

"The tapes." He held his hand out for them, and I gave them to him. He slotted the first one into the recorder which stood beside the computer and began to fumble around with the computer's typewriterlike keys in a most disorganized fashion.

"How long have you had that computer?" I said.

"Shut up."

He typed RUN, and not surprisingly nothing happened, as he hadn't fed the program in from the cassette. I watched him pick up the instruction book and begin leafing through it, and if there had been all the time in the world I would have let him stew in it longer. But every minute I wasted meant one more dragging minute for Donna and Sarah, so I said, "You'd better take lessons."

"Shut *up*." He gave me a distinctly bull-like glare and typed RUN again.

"I want Angelo out of that house," I said, "so I'll show you how to run the tapes. Otherwise we'll be here all night."

He would have given much not to allow me the advantage, but he should have done his homework first.

I ejected the tape to see which side we'd got, then reinserted it and typed CLOAD "EPSOM". The asterisks began to blink at the top righthand corner as the computer searched the tape, but at length it found "EPSOM", loaded the Epsom program, and announced READY.

"Now type RUN and press 'ENTER'," I said.

Gilbert did so, and immediately the screen said:

WHICH RACE AT EPSOM?
TYPE NAME OF RACE AND PRESS 'ENTER'.

Gilbert typed DERBY, and the screen told him to type the name of the horse. He typed in 'ANGELO', and made the same sort of fictional replies Ted Pitts and I had done. Angelo's win factor was 46, which must have been the maximum. It also said quite a lot about Gilbert's estimate of his son.

"How do you get Ascot?" he said.

I ejected the tape and inserted the first side of all. Typed CLOAD "ASCOT", pressed "ENTER", and waited for READY.

"Type RUN, press 'ENTER'," I said.

He did so, and at once got

WHICH RACE AT ASCOT?
TYPE NAME OF RACE AND PRESS 'ENTER'.

He typed GOLD CUP and looked enthralled by the ensuing questions, and I thought that he'd played with it long enough.

"Telephone Angelo," I said. "You must surely be satisfied that this time you've got the real thing."

"Wait," he said heavily. "I'll try all the tapes. I don't trust you. Angelo was insistent that I shouldn't trust you."

I shrugged. "Test what you like."

He tried one or two programs on each of the sides, finally realizing that CLOAD plus the first five letters of the racecourse required, inserted between quotation marks, would unlock the goodies.

"All right," I said at length. "Now call Angelo. You can run the programs all you like when I've gone."

He could find no further reason for putting it off. With a stare to which his own natural arrogance was fast returning he picked up one of the telephones, consulted a note pad beside it, and dialed the number.

Not surprisingly he didn't get through. He dialed again. Then, impatiently, again. Then, muttering under his breath, he tried one of the other telephones with ditto nil results.

"What is it?" I said.

"The number doesn't ring."

"You must be dialing it wrong," I said. "I've got it here."

I fished into my jacket pocket for my diary and made a show of fluttering through the leaves. Came to the number. Read it out.

"That's what I dialed," Gilbert said.

"It can't be. Try again." I'd never thought of myself as an actor but I found it quite easy to pretend.

Gilbert dialed again, frowning, and I thought it time to be agitated and anxious.

"You *must* get through," I said. "I've worried and rushed all day to get those tapes here, and now you *must* call Angelo, he *must* leave my wife."

In experience of command he had tough years of advantage, but then I was too accustomed to having to control wily opponents, and when I took a step toward him it was clear to both of us that physically I was taller and fitter and quite decisively stronger.

He said hastily, "I'll try the operator," and I fidgeted and fumed around him in simulated anxiety while the operator tried without success and reported the number out of order.

"But it can't be," I yelled. *"You've got to call Angelo."*

Harry Gilbert simply stared at me, knowing that it was impossible.

I cut the decibels a shade but looked as furious as I could and said, "We'll have to go there."

"But Angelo said—"

"I don't give a damn what Angelo said," I said forcefully. "He won't leave the house until he knows you've got the tapes, and now it seems you can't tell him you have. So we'll bloody well have to go there and tell him. And I'm absolutely fed up with all this buggering about."

"You can go," Gilbert said. "I'm not coming."

"Yes you are. I'm not walking up to that house alone with Angelo inside it with that pistol. He said I was to give the tapes to *you*, and that's what I've done, and you've got to come with me to tell him so. And I promise you," I said threateningly, warming to the part, "that I'll take you with me one way or another. Knocked out or tied up or just sitting quietly in the front seat beside me. Because you're the only one Angelo will listen to." I snatched up the cassettes lying beside the computer. "If you want these tapes back you'll come with me."

He agreed to come. He hadn't much choice. I pulled the cases for the tapes out of my pocket and showed him the labels, *Oklahoma!*, *The King and I*, *West Side Story*. Then I ejected the cassette which was still in the recorder and put all three of the tapes into their cases. "And we'll take these," I said, "to prove to Angelo that you have them."

He agreed to that also. He came out with me to my car, slamming his own front door behind him, and sat in the front passenger seat.

"I'll hold the tapes," he said.

I put them however on the dashboard out of his immediate reach and told him he could have them once we got to Norwich.

It was a strange journey.

He was a far more powerful man than I would normally have thought of opposing, yet I was discovering that I had probably always thought of myself as being weaker than I was. For the whole of my life I had gone in awe of headmasters; as a pupil, as a student, as a teacher. Even when I'd disagreed or despised or rebelled, I'd never tried actively to defeat. One could easily be chucked out of school and out of college and out of the better jobs in physics.

Harry Gilbert couldn't chuck me out of anything, and perhaps that was the difference. I could face his belief in his own superiority and not be intimidated by it. I could use my wits and my muscles to get him to do what I wanted.

It was heady stuff. Have to be careful, I reflected, not to develop delusions of grandeur of my own.

Angelo, I thought suddenly, feels just as I do. Feels the spreading of the wings of internal power. Feels he can do more than he realized. Sees his world isn't as constricting as he thought. Angelo too was emerging into a new conception of ability—but in him there were no brakes.

"There is someone there with Angelo," I said. "My wife said 'they.'" I spoke neutrally, without aggression.

Gilbert sat heavily silent.

"When Angelo came to my house," I said, "there was another man with him. Very like Angelo in looks. Did what Angelo told him."

After a pause Gilbert shrugged and said, "Eddy. Angelo's cousin. Their mothers were twins."

"Italian?" I said.

Another pause. Then, "We are all Italian by descent."

"But born in England?"

"Yes. Why do you ask?"

I sighed. "Just to pass the journey."

He grunted but gradually a good deal of his resentment of my behavior subsided. I had no idea whether or not he considered it justified.

Anxiety on my part didn't need to be acted. I found myself drumming my fingers on the steering wheel when stopped by red lights and cursing long trucks which delayed my passing. By the time we got to Norwich it would be over the four hours I'd warned Angelo to expect, and of all things that I didn't want, it was Angelo ballooning into premature rage.

"Will you pay Mrs. O'Rorke anything for these tapes?" I said.

A pause. "No."

"Not even without Angelo knowing?"

He gave me a fierce sideways glare. "Angelo does what I tell him. Whether I pay or don't pay Mrs. O'Rorke is nothing to do with him."

If he believed all that, I thought, he was deluding himself. Or perhaps he still wanted to believe what had so far been true. Perhaps he truly didn't see that his days of domination over Angelo were ticking away fast.

Just let them last, I thought, for another two hours.

TEN

The long lingering evening was slowly dying by the time we reached Norwich, though it wouldn't be totally dark for another hour. I drove into the Keithlys' road from the direction that would place Gilbert nearest to the house when I pulled up at the curb: Angelo had seen my car at his father's house as I had seen his, and the sight of it would alarm him.

"Please get out of the car as soon as I stop," I said to Gilbert. "So that Angelo can see you."

He grunted, but when I pulled up he opened the door as I'd suggested and gave any watchers from behind the curtains a full view of his lumbering exit from the front seat.

"Wait," I said, standing up on my own side and talking to him across the top of the car. "Take the tapes." I reached across the top of the car and gave them to him. "Hold them up," I said, "so that Angelo can see them."

"You give too many orders."

"I don't trust your son any more than he trusts me."

He gave me a bullish stare of fully revived confidence,

but he did in fact turn and lift the tapes, showing them to the house.

Behind his back I leaned down and picked up the towel-wrapped rifle, holding it longways with the stock to my chest and the flap of my jacket falling over it.

Angelo opened the front door, shielding himself half behind it.

"Go in," I said to Gilbert. "This street is full of people watching through the curtains."

He gave an automatically alarmed look at being spied on and began to walk toward his son. I slid around the car fast and walked close behind him, almost stepping on his heels.

"Explain," I said urgently.

His head lifted ominously, but he said loudly to Angelo, "Your telephone's out of order."

"What?" Angelo exclaimed, opening the door a fraction wider. "It can't be."

Gilbert said impatiently, "It is. Don't be a fool. Why else would I come all this way?"

Angelo turned away from the door and strode into the sitting room, which was where the telephone was located. I heard him pick up the receiver and rattle the cradle, and slam the instrument down again.

"But he brought the tapes," Gilbert said, walking to the sitting room door and showing the bright cases. "I tried them. All of them. This time they're the real thing."

"Come in here, you creep," Angelo called.

I propped the wrapped rifle, barrel downward to the carpet, against the small chest of drawers which stood within arm's reach of the sitting room door and showed myself in the doorway.

The sitting room furniture was all pushed awry. Sarah and Donna sat back-to-back in the center of the room, with their wrists and ankles strapped to the arms and legs of two of the chairs from the dining room. To one side stood Angelo, holding the Walther, with, beyond the two girls, his look-alike, Eddy. There were glasses and plates sprinkled about, and the smell of long hours of cigarette smoke.

Sarah was facing me.

We looked at each other with a curious lack of emotion, I noticing almost distantly the dark smudges under her eyes, the exhausted sag of her body, the strain and pain round her mouth.

She said nothing. No doubt she considered I was showing too little concern and was too calm as usual: the message on her face wasn't love and relief but relief and disgust.

"Go home," I said wearily to Angelo. "You've got what you wanted."

I prayed for him to go. To be satisfied, to be sensible, to be ruled by his father, to be approximately normal.

Harry Gilbert began to turn from his son back toward me, saying, "That's it, then, Angelo. We'd best be off."

"No," Angelo said.

Gilbert stopped. "What did you say?" he said.

"I said no," Angelo said. "This creep's going to pay for all the trouble he's put me to. You come here, creep."

Gilbert said, "No, Angelo." He gestured to the girls. "This is enough."

Angelo pointed his pistol with its bulbous silencer straight at Donna's head. "This one," he said viciously, "has been screaming at me for hours that they'll report me to the police, the stupid little bitch."

"They won't," I said quickly.

"Dead right they won't."

Even to Gilbert his meaning was clear. Gilbert made movements of extreme disapproval and active fear and said, "Put down the gun. Angelo, put it down." His voice thundered with parental command and from long long habit Angelo began to obey. Even in the same second he visibly reversed his instinct; and I knew that for me it was then or never.

I stretched out my right arm, thrust my hand down into the towel and grasped the stock of the rifle. Swung the towel off the barrel and in the same fluid movement stood in the doorway with the barrel pointing straight at Angelo and the safety catch unlocking with a click.

"Drop it," I said.

They were all utterly astounded, but perhaps Angelo most of all because I'd twice played on him the same trick. The three men stood there as if frozen, and I didn't look at Sarah, not directly.

"Drop the pistol," I said. He was still pointing it toward Donna.

He couldn't bear to drop it. Not to lose that much face.

"I'll shoot you," I said.

Even then he hesitated. I swung the barrel to the ceiling and squeezed the trigger. The noise crashed in the small room. Pieces of plaster fell from the ceiling. The sharp smell of cordite prevailed over stale cigarette, and all the mouths were open, like fish. The rifle was pointing back at his heart with the next round in the breech almost before he'd moved an inch, and he looked at it with dazed disbelief.

"Drop the pistol," I said. "Drop it."

He was still undecided. I'll have to hit him, I thought despairingly. I don't want to. Why won't he drop the bloody thing? There's nothing he can gain.

The air seemed to be still ringing with the aftermath of explosion, but it was into silence that Sarah spoke.

With a sort of sullen ferocity, which seemed as much directed at me as at Angelo, she said loudly, "He shot in the Olympic Games."

Angelo's eyes developed doubt.

"Drop the pistol," I said quietly, "or I'll shoot your hand."

Angelo dropped it.

His face was full of fury and hate, and I thought him capable of flinging himself upon me regardless of consequences. I looked at him stolidly, showing no triumph, showing nothing to inflame.

"You've got the tapes," I said. "Get in the car, all three of you, and get out of my life. I'm sick of your faces." I stepped back a pace into the hall and nodded with my head toward the front door.

"Just get out," I said. "One at a time. Angelo first."

He came toward me with his dark eyes like pits in the olive face, the light too dim now to give them wicked life. I stood back a few steps further and followed his progress to the front door, as in my own house, with the black barrel.

"I'll get you," he said.

I didn't answer.

He pulled open the door with the force of rage and stepped outside.

"Now you," I said to Harry Gilbert.

He was almost as angry as his son, but perhaps it was fanciful of me to guess that there was also some recognition that I'd been able to stop Angelo where he couldn't, and that that had been a good thing.

He followed Angelo out onto the driveway and I saw them both opening the doors of Angelo's car.

"Now you," I said to Eddy. "You pick up Angelo's gun. Pick it up by the silencer. Do you know how to unload it?"

Eddy, the carbon copy, nodded miserably.

"Do it, then," I said. "Very, very carefully."

He looked at the rifle and at Angelo getting into the car, and shook the bullets out of the clip, letting them drop on the carpet.

"Right," I said. "Take the pistol with you." I gestured with the rifle barrel and jerked my head toward the open front door, and of the three of them it was Eddy who left with the least reluctance and the most speed.

From inside the hall I watched Angelo start the engine, slam the gears into reverse and make a rough exit into the road. Once there he deliberately sideswiped my car, damaging his own rear fender in the process, and accelerated down the street as if to prove his superior manhood.

With a feeling of terrible tension I closed the front door and went into the sitting room. Crossed to Sarah; looked at the rubber straps which fastened her wrists and unbuckled them. Unbuckled those around her ankles. Then those around Donna.

Donna started crying. Sarah shoved herself stiffly off the chair and collapsed onto the softer contours of the sofa.

"Do you realize how long we've been sitting there?" she demanded bitterly. "And before you damned well ask, yes they did untie us now and then for us to go to the bathroom."

"And to eat?"

"I hate you," she said.

"I really wanted to know."

"Yes, to eat. Twice. He made me cook."

Donna said between sobs, "It's been awful. *Awful.* You've no idea."

"They didn't...?" I began anxiously.

"No they didn't," Sarah said flatly. "They just sneered."

"Hateful," Donna said. "Called us mugs." She hobbled across the carpet and lowered herself gingerly into an armchair. "I hurt all over." Tears trickled down her cheeks. I thought of Angelo's description of "wet chick" and stifled it quickly.

"Look," I said, "I know you don't feel like it, but I'd be much happier if you'd stuff a few things into a suitcase and we all left this house."

Donna helplessly shook her head, and Sarah said "Why?" with mutiny.

"Angelo hated having to go. You saw him. Suppose he comes back? When he thinks we're off guard...he might."

The idea alarmed them as much as me and also angered Sarah. "Why did you give them the pistol?" she demanded. "That was *stupid*. You're such a *fool*."

"Are you coming?"

"You can't expect us..." Donna wailed.

I said to Sarah, "I have to make a phone call. I can't do it from here." I indicated the dead telephone. "I'm going away in the car to do it. Do you want to come or not?"

Sarah took stock of that rapidly and said that yes, they were coming, and despite Donna's protests she drove her stiffly upstairs. They came down a few minutes later carrying a hold-all each, and I noticed that Sarah had put on some lipstick. I smiled at her with some of the old pleasure in seeing her resurfacing briefly, and she looked both surprised and confused.

"Come on, then," I said, and took the hold-alls from them to put in the trunk. "Best be off." I fetched the rifle, once again wrapped loosely in the towel to confuse the neighbors, and stowed it in the suitcase. Checked that Donna had brought the door keys; shut the front door; drove away.

"Where are we going?" Sarah said.

"Where would you like?"

"What about *money?*"

"Credit cards," I said.

We drove a short way in a silence broken only by Donna's occasional sniffs and sobs, going along now with lights on everywhere and the long soft evening turning to full dark.

I pulled up beside a telephone booth and put through a collect call to the Suffolk police.

"Is Detective Chief Superintendent Irestone there?" I said. Hopeless question but had to be asked.

"Your name, sir?"

"Jonathan Derry."

"One moment."

I waited through the usual mutterings and clicks, and then a voice that was still not Irestone's said, "Mr. Derry, Chief Superintendent Irestone left instructions that if you telephoned again, your message was to be taken down in full and passed on to him directly. Chief Superintendent Irestone asked me to say that owing to, er, a hitch in communications he was not aware that you had tried to reach him so often, not until this afternoon. I am Detective Inspector Robson. I came to your house with the chief superintendent, if you remember."

"Yes," I said. A man nearing forty, fair-headed, reddish skin.

"If you tell me why you rang, sir?"

"You'll take notes?"

"Yes, sir. And a recording."

"Right. Well . . . the man who came to my house with a pistol is called Angelo Gilbert. His father is Harry Gilbert, who runs bingo halls all over Essex and northeast London. The man who came with Angelo is his cousin Eddy—don't know his last name. He does what Angelo tells him."

I paused and Inspector Robson said, "Is that the lot, sir?"

"No, it isn't. At this moment all three of them are traveling from Norwich in Angelo's car." I told him the make, the color, the number, and that it had a bashed-in rear fender. "They are probably going to Harry Gilbert's house in Welwyn Garden City. I think Angelo also lives there, but perhaps not Eddy." I gave him the address. "They should arrive there in about an hour and a quarter to an hour and a half. In the car there is a Walther .22 pistol with a silencer. There may or may not be bullets in it. It may or may not be the pistol which Angelo waved at me, but it looks identical. It might be the pistol which killed Christopher Norwood."

"That's very useful, sir," Robson said.

"There's one more thing . . ."

"Yes?"

"I don't think Harry Gilbert knows anything at all about Chris Norwood's death. I mean, I don't think he even knows he's dead. If you go to arrest Angelo, Harry Gilbert won't know why."

"Thank you, sir."

"That's all," I said.

"Er," he said. "The chief superintendent will be in touch with you."

"All right, but—" I hesitated.

"Yes, sir?"

"I'd be glad to know—"

"Just a minute, sir," he interrupted, and kept me hanging on through some lengthy unintelligible background talk. "Sorry, sir, you were saying?"

"You remember I sent Angelo some computer tapes with games on them?"

"Yes, I do. We went to Cambridge main post office and alerted the man whose job it was to hand out letters-to-be-called-for, but unfortunately he went for his tea break without mentioning it to anyone, and during that short period your package was collected. A girl clerk handed it over. We didn't find out until it was too late. It was . . . infuriating."

"Mm," I said. "Well, Angelo came back with more threats, demanding the real tapes, and I've just given them to him. Only . . ."

"Only what, sir?"

"Only they won't be able to run them on their computer. I think when they get home they might try those tapes straight away, and when they find they don't work they might . . . well they *might* set out to look for me. I mean . . ."

"I know *exactly* what you mean," he said dryly.

"So, er, I'd be glad to know if you plan to do anything about Angelo this evening. And if you think there's enough to hold him on."

"Instructions have already gone off," he said. "He'll be picked up tonight as soon as he reaches the house in Welwyn. We have some fingerprints to match . . . and some girls who saw two men arrive at Norwood's. So don't worry, once we've got him, we won't let him go."

"Could I ring up to find out?"

"Yes." He gave me a new number. "Call there. I'll leave a message. You'll get it straight away."

"Thank you," I said gratefully, "very much."

"Mr. Derry?"

"Yes?"

"What's wrong with the tapes this time?"

"Oh . . . I stuck magnets into the cases."

He laughed. "I'll see you later, perhaps," he said. "And thanks. Thanks a lot."

I put the receiver down smiling, thinking of the three powerful Magnadur magnets distorting the programs on the tapes. The permanent magnets which were black and flat; two inches long, three quarters of an inch wide, three sixteenths of an inch thick. I'd stuck one into the inside of each case, flat on the bottom, black as the plastic, looking like part of the case itself. I'd taken the tapes and the cases separately to Harry Gilbert's—the tapes in one pocket, the cases in another—and only after he'd played them had I married them all together. Sandwiching electromagnetic recording tapes between such magnets was like wiping a blackboard roughly with a wet sponge: there would be traces of what had been recorded there, but not enough to make sense.

It might take Angelo all the way home to see what I'd done, because the magnets did look as if they belonged there.

Or it might not.

I drove wearily in the direction of home. I seemed to have been driving forever. It had been a very long day. Extraordinary to think it was only that morning that I'd set out from Ted Pitt's.

Both of the girls went to sleep as the miles unrolled, the deep sleep of release and exhaustion. I wondered briefly what would become of us in the future, but mostly I just thought about driving and keeping my own eyelids apart.

We stayed in a motel on the outskirts of London and slept as if dead. The alarm call I'd asked for dragged me from this limbo at seven in the morning, and yawning like a great white shark I got through to the number Inspector Robson had given me.

"Jonathan Derry," I said. "Am I too early?"

It was a girl's voice that answered, fresh and unofficial. "No, it's not too early," she said. "John Robson asked me to tell you that Angelo Gilbert and his cousin Eddy are in custody."

"Thank you very much."

"Any time."

I put the receiver down with a steadily lightening heart and shook Sarah awake in the next bed.

"Sorry," I said. "But I've got to be in school by nine o'clock."

ELEVEN

There was a period when Sarah went back to work and Donna drooped around our house trying to come to terms with the devastation of her life. Sarah's manner to her grew gradually less overprotective and more normal, and when Donna found she was no longer indulged and pampered every waking moment, she developed a pout in place of the invalid smile and went home. Home to sell her house, to collect Peter's insurance money, and to persuade her probation officer to take Sarah's psychological place.

On the surface things between myself and Sarah continued much as before: the politeness, the lack of emotional contact, the daily meetings of strangers. She seldom met my eyes and seemed to speak only when it was essential, but I slowly realized that the deeply embittered set of her mouth, which had been so noticeable before the day we set off to Norwich, had more or less gone. She looked softer and more as she had once been and, although it didn't seem to have altered her manner toward me, it was less depressing to look at.

In my inner self a lot had changed. I seemed to have stepped out of a cage. I did everything with more confidence and more satisfaction. I shot better. I taught with zest. I even found the wretched exercise books less of a drag. I felt that one day soon I would stretch the spreading wings, and fly.

One night as we lay in the dark, each in our frostily separate cocoon, I said to Sarah, "Are you awake?"

"Yes."

"You know that at the end of the term I'm going to Canada with the rifle team?"

"Yes."

"I'm not coming back with them."

"Why not?"

"I'm going to the United States. Probably for the rest of the school holidays."

"Whatever for?"

"To see it. Perhaps to live there, eventually."

She was silent for a while; and what she said in the end seemed only obliquely to have anything to do with my plans.

"Donna talked to me a lot, you know. She told me all about the day she stole that baby."

"Did she?" I said noncommittally.

"Yes. She said that when she saw it lying there in its pram she had an overpowering urge to pick it up and cuddle it. So she did. She just did. Then when she had it in her arms she felt as if it belonged to her, as if it was hers. So she carried it to her car, which was just there, a few steps away. She put the baby on the front seat beside her and drove off. She didn't know where she was going. She said it was a sort of dream, in which she had at last had the baby she'd pined for for so long."

She stopped. I thought of Ted Pitts's little girls and the protective curve of his body as he held his smallest one close. I could have wept for Sarah, for Donna, for every unwillingly barren parent.

"She drove for a long way," Sarah said. "She got to the sea and stopped there. She took the baby into the back of the car and it was perfect. She was in utter bliss. It was still like a dream. And then the baby woke up." She paused. "I suppose it was hungry. Time for its next feeding. Anyway it began to cry, and it wouldn't stop. It cried and cried and cried. She said that it cried for an hour. The noise started driving her mad. She put her hand over its mouth, and it cried harder. She tried to hug its face into her shoulder so that it would stop, but it didn't. And then she found that its diaper was dirty, and the brown stuff had oozed down the baby's leg and was on her dress."

Another long pause, then Sarah's voice: "She said she didn't know babies were like that. Screaming and smelly. She'd thought of them as sweet and smiling at her all the time. She began to hate that baby, not love it. She said she sort of threw it down onto the back seat in a rage, and then she got out of the car and just left it. Walked away. She said she could hear the baby crying all the way down the beach."

This time the silence was much longer.

"Are you still awake?" Sarah said.

"Yes."

"I'm reconciled now to not having a child. I grieve . . . but it can't be helped." She paused and then said, "I've learned a lot about myself these past weeks, because of Donna."

And I, I thought, because of Angelo.

After another long while she said, "Are you still awake?"

"Yes."

"I don't really understand, you know, all that happened. I mean, I know that that hateful Angelo has been arrested for murder, of course I do, and that you have been seeing the police . . . but you've never told me exactly what it was all about."

"You seriously want to know?"

"Of course I do, otherwise, I wouldn't ask." The familiar note of impatience rang out clearly. She must have heard it herself, because she immediately said more moderately, "I'd like you to tell me. I really would."

"All right," I said; and I told her pretty well everything,

starting from the day that Chris Norwood set it all going by stealing Liam O'Rorke's notes. I told her events in their chronological order, not in the jumbled way I learned of them, so that a clear pattern emerged of Angelo's journeyings in search of the tapes.

When I'd finished she said slowly, "You knew all through that day when he had us tied up that he was a murderer."

"Mm."

"My God." She paused. "Didn't you think he might kill us? Donna and me?"

"I thought he *might*. I thought he might do it anytime after he knew his father had the tapes. I thought he might kill all three of us, if he felt like it. I couldn't tell, but couldn't risk it."

A long silence. Then she said, "I think, looking back, that he did mean to. Things he said . . ." She paused. "I was glad to see you."

"And angry."

"Yes, angry. You'd been so *long*. And Angelo was so bloody *frightening*."

"I know."

"I heard the rifle shots. I was in the kitchen cooking."

"I was afraid you might tell Angelo you heard them."

"I only spoke to him when I absolutely had to. I loathed him. He was so *arrogant*."

"You shook him," I said, "telling him I'd shot in the Games. It was the clincher."

"I just wanted to—to kick him in the ego."

I smiled in the darkness. Angelo's ego had taken quite a pummeling at the hands of the Derrys.

"Do you realize," I said, "that we haven't talked like this for months?"

"Such a lot has happened. And I feel . . . different."

Nothing like a murderer, I thought, for changing one's view of the world. He'd done a good job for both of us.

"Do you want to come, then?" I said. "To America?"

To America. To go on together, to try a bit longer. I didn't really know which I wanted: to clear out, cut loose, divorce, start again, remarry, have children . . . or to make what one might of the old dead love, to pour commitment into the shaky foundations, to rebuild them solid.

It was Sarah, I thought, who would have to decide.

"Do you want us to stay together?" I asked.

"You've thought of divorce?"

"Haven't you?"

"Yes." I heard her sigh. "Often, lately."

"It's pretty final, being divorced," I said.

"What then?"

"Wait a bit," I said slowly. "See how we go. See what we both really want. Keep on talking."

"All right," she said. "That'll do."

INTERVAL

TWICE SHY

Letter from Vince Akkerton to Johnathan Derry:

Angel Kitchens
Newmarket
July 12th

Dear Mr. Derry:

You remember you were asking about Chris Norwood, that day back in May? I don't know if you're still interested in those computer tapes you were talking about, but they've turned up here at the Kitchens. We were clearing out the room we change from outdoor clothes in, prior to its being repainted, you see, and there was this bag there that everyone said didn't belong to them. So I looked in it, and there were a lot of old papers of writing and three cassettes. I thought I'd give them a run on my cassette player, because they didn't have any labels on saying what was on them, but all that came out was a screeching noise. Well, a mate of mine who heard it said don't throw them away, because I was going to, that's computer noise, he said. So I took the tapes in to Janet to see what she could make of them, but she said the firm has got rid of their old computer, it wasn't big enough for all it was having to do, and they've now got a company computer or something with disc drives, she says, and it doesn't use cassettes.

So, anyway, I remembered about you all of a sudden, and I found I'd still got your address, so I thought I'd ask you if you thought this was what you were talking about. I threw the pages of writing into the rubbish, and that's that, they're gone, but if you want these tapes, you send me a tenner for my trouble and you can have them.

Yours truly,
Vince Akkerton

Letter from the executors of Mrs. Maureen O'Rorke to Jonathan Derry:

September 1st

Dear Sir:

We are returning the note you wrote to Mrs. O'Rorke, together with your enclosure of three cassettes.

Unfortunately Mrs. O'Rorke had died peacefully in her sleep at home three days before your gift was posted. In our opinion, therefore, the contents of the package should be regarded as belonging to yourself, and we herewith return them.

We are,
Yours faithfully,
Jones, Pearce and Block,
Solicitors

TWICE SHY

Letter from Harry Gilbert to Marty Goldman, Ltd., Turf Accountants:

October 15th

Dear Marty,

In view of what has happened, I'm asking you to release me from the transfer that we had agreed. I haven't the heart, old friend, to build any more king-doms. With Angelo jailed for life there's no point in me buying all your betting shops. You knew, of course, that they were for him—for him to manage, anyway.

I know you had some other offers, so I hope you won't be coming after me for compensation.

Your old friend,
Harry

Letter from the University of Eastern California selection board to Jonathan Derry:

London
October 20th

Dear Mr. Derry:

Subsequent to your interview in London last week, we have pleasure in offering you a three-year teaching post in the Department of Physics. Your salary for the first year will be Scale B (attached) to be reviewed thereafter. One full semester's notice to be given in writing on either side.

We understand that you will be free to take up the post on January 1st next, and we await your confirmation that you accept this offer.

Further details and instructions will be sent to you upon receipt of your acceptance.

Welcome to the university!

Lance K. Barowska, D.Sc.
Director of Selections,
  Science Faculty
University of Eastern California

TWICE SHY

Excerpt from a private letter from the Governor of Albany Prison, Parkhurst, Isle of Wight, to his friend the Governor of Wakefield Prison, Yorkshire.

. . . .

Well, Frank, we're letting Angelo Gilbert out on parole this week, and I wish between you and me that I felt better about it. I'd like to have advised against it, but he's served fourteen years and there's been a lot of pressure from the Reformers group on the Home Sec to release him. It's not that Gilbert's actively violent or even hostile, but he's been trying hard to get this parole so for the last two years there's been no breath of trouble.

But as you know with some of them they're never stable, however meek they look, and I've a feeling Gilbert's like that. You remember, when you had him about five years ago, you felt just the same. It isn't in the cards, I suppose, to keep him locked up for life, but I just hope to God he doesn't go straight out and shoot the first person who crosses him.

See you soon, Frank.

Donald

PART TWO

WILLIAM

TWELVE

I put my hand on Cassie's breast, and she said, "No, William. No."

"Why not?" I said.

"Because it's never good for me, twice, so soon. You know that."

"Come on," I said.

"No."

"You're lazy," I said.

"And you're greedy." She picked my hand off and gave it back to me.

I replaced it. "At least let me hold you," I said.

"No." She threw my hand off again. "With you, one thing leads to another. I'm going to get some orange juice and run the bath, and if you're not careful you'll be late."

I rolled onto my back and watched her walk about the bedroom, a tall thin girl with too few curves and very long feet. Seen like that in all her angular nakedness she still had the self-possessed quality which had first attracted me: a natural apartness, a lack of cling. Her self-doubts, if any, were well hidden, even from me. She went downstairs and came back carrying two glasses of juice.

"William," she said. "Stop staring."

"I like to."

She walked to the bathroom to turn on the taps and came back brushing her teeth.

"It's seven o'clock," she said.

"So I've noticed."

"You'll lose that cushy job of yours if you're not out on the gallops in ten minutes."

"Twenty will do."

I rose up, however, and pinched the bath first, drinking the orange juice as I went. Count your blessings, I said to myself, soaping. Count Cassandra Morris, a better girl than I'd ever had before; seven months bedded, growing more essential every day. Count the sort of job that no one could expect to be given at twenty-nine. Count enough money, for once, to buy a car that wasn't everyone's cast-off held together by rust and luck.

The old ache to be a jockey was pretty well dead, but I supposed there would always be regret. It wasn't as if I'd never ridden in races; I had, from sixteen to twenty, first as an amateur, then a professional, during which time I'd won eighty-four steeplechases, twenty-three hurdle races, and wretchedly cursed my unstoppably lengthening body. At six foot one I'd broken my leg in a racing fall, been imprisoned in traction for three months, and grown two more inches in bed.

It had been practically the end. There *had* been very tall jump jockeys in the past, but I'd progressively found that even if I starved to the point of weakness I couldn't keep my weight reliably below eleven stone. Trainers began saying I was too tall, too heavy, sorry, lad, and employing someone else. So at twenty I'd got myself a job as an assistant trainer, and at twenty-three I'd worked for a bloodstock agent, and at twenty-six on a stud farm, which kept me off the racecourse too much. At twenty-seven I'd been employed in a sort of hospital for sick racehorses which went out of business because too many owners preferred to shoot their liabilities, and after that there had been a spell of selling horse feed, and then a few months in the office of a bloodstock auctioneer, which had paid well but bored me to death; and each time between jobs I'd spent the proceeds of the last one in wandering around the world, drifting homeward when the cash ran out and casting around for a new berth.

It had been at one of the points of no prospects that Jonathan had sent the cable.

CATCH THE NEXT FLIGHT. GOOD JOB IN ENGLISH RACING POSSIBLE IF YOU INTERVIEW HERE IMMEDIATELY. JONATHAN

I'd turned up that night on his Californian doorstep sixteen hours later, and early the next morning he had sent me off to see "a man I met at a party." A man, it transpired, of middle height, middle years and middling gray hair: a man I knew instantly by sight. Everyone in racing, world-wide, knew him by sight. He ran his racing as a big business, taking his profits in the shape of bloodstock, selling his stallions for up to a hundred times more than they'd earned on the track.

"Luke Houston," he said neutrally, extending his hand.

"Yes, sir," I said, retrieving some breath. "Er, William Derry."

He offered me breakfast on a balcony overlooking the Pacific, eating grapefruit and boiled eggs and giving me smiling genial glances which were basically as casual as X-rays.

"Warrington Marsh, my racing manager in England, had a stroke four days ago," he said. "Poor guy, he's doing well—I have bulletins every A.M.—but it is going to be some time, a long time, I'm afraid, before he'll be active again." He gestured to my untouched breakfast. "Eat your toast."

"Yes, sir."

"Tell me why I should give you his job. Temporarily, of course."

Good grief, I thought. I hadn't the experience or the connections of the stricken revered maestro. "I'd work hard," I said.

"You know what it entails?"

"I've seen Warrington Marsh everywhere, on the racecourse, at the sales. I know what he does . . . but not the extent of his authority."

He cracked his second egg. "Your brother says you've gotten a lot of general know-how. Tell me about it."

I listed the jobs, none of which sounded any more impressive than they had in fact been.

He said, "College degrees?" pleasantly.

"No. I left school at seventeen and didn't go to university."

"Private income?" he said. "Any?"

"My godfather left some money for my schooling. There's still enough for food and clothes. Not enough to live on."

He drank some coffee and hospitably poured me a second cup.

"Do you know which trainers I have horses with in the British Isles?"

"Yes, sir. Shell, Thompson, Miller, and Sandlache in England and Donavan in Ireland."

"Call me Luke," he said. "I prefer it."

"Luke," I said.

He stirred sweetener into his coffee.

"Could you handle the finance?" he said. "Warrington always has full responsibility. Do millions frighten you?"

I looked out at the vast blue ocean and told the truth. "I think they do in a way, yes. It's too easy in the upper reaches to think of a zero or two as not mattering one way or another."

"You need to spend to buy good horses," he said. "Could you do it?"

"Yes."

"Go on," he said mildly.

"Buying potentially good horses isn't the problem. Looking at a great yearling, seeing it move, knowing its breeding is as near perfect as you can predict, and being able to afford it, that's almost easy. It's picking the excellent from among the second rank and the unknowns, that's where the judgment comes in."

"Could you guarantee that every horse you bought for me, or advised my trainers to buy, would win?"

"No, I couldn't," I said. "They wouldn't."

"What percentage would you expect to win?"

"About fifty percent. Some would never race, others would disappoint."

He unaggressively, quietly, slowly and without pressure asked me questions for almost an hour, sorting out what I'd done, what I knew, how I felt about taking ultimate powers of decision over trainers who were older than myself, how I felt about dealing with the racing authorities, what I'd learned about bookkeeping, banking and money markets, whether I could evaluate veterinarian and nutritive advice. By the end I felt inside out, as if no cranny of my mind stayed gently unprobed. He would choose someone older, I thought.

"How do you feel," he said finally, "about a steady job, nine to five, weekends off, pension at the end of it?"

I shook my head from deep instinct, without thinking it out. "No," I said.

"That came from the heart, fella," he observed.

"Well . . ."

"I'll give you a year and a ceiling beyond which you're not to spend. I'll be looking over your shoulder, but I won't interfere unless you get in a fix. Want to take it?"

I drew a deep breath and said, "Yes."

He leaned smilingly forward to shake my hand. "I'll send you a contract," he said. "But go right on home now and take over at once. Things can fall apart too fast with no one in charge. So you go straight to Warrington's house, see his wife, Nonie—I'll call her you're coming—and you operate from his office there until you find a place of your own. Your brother told me you're a wanderer, but I don't mind that." He smiled again. "Never did like tame cats."

Like so much else in American life the contract, when it swiftly followed me over the Pond, was in complete contrast to the relaxed approach of the man who'd offered it. It set out in precise terms what I must do, what I had discretion to do, what I must not do. It stated terms of reference I'd never thought of. He had given me a great deal of freedom in some ways and none at all in others; but that, I supposed, was fair enough. He wouldn't want to stake his whole British operation on an unknown without enforceable safeguards. I took it to a solicitor, who read it and whistled and said it had been drawn up by corporation lawyers who were used to munching managers as snacks.

"But do I sign it?" I said.

"If you want the job, yes. It's tough, but as far as I can see, fair."

That had been eight months ago. I had come home to widespread and understandable disbelief that such a plum should have fallen my way. I had survived Nonie Marsh's resentment and Warrington's incoherent unhelpfulness; had sold several of Luke's unpromising two-year-olds without great loss, had cajoled the trainers into provisionally accepting me and done nothing sweat-makingly disastrous. Despite all the decisions and responsibility, I'd enjoyed every minute.

Cassie appeared in the doorway.

"Aren't you going to get out of that bath?" she demanded. "Just sitting there smiling."

"Life's good."

"And you'll be late."

I stood up in the water and as she watched me straighten she said automatically, "Mind your head." I stepped out onto the floor, and kissed her, dripping down her neck.

"For God's sake get dressed," she said. "And you need a shave." She gave me a towel. "The coffee's hot, and we're out of milk."

I flung a few clothes on and went downstairs, dodging

beams and low doorways on the way. The cottage we'd rented in the village of Six Mile Bottom (roughly six miles south of Newmarket) had been designed for seventeenth-century man, who hadn't suffered the dietetic know-how of the twentieth. And would seven feet, I wondered, ducking into the kitchen, be considered normal in the twenty-fifth?

We had lived in the cottage all summer and in spite of its low ceilings it suited us fine. There were apples now in the garden, and mists in the mornings, and sleepy wasps trying to find warm cracks in the eaves. Red tiled floors and rugs downstairs, dining room surrendered to office, sitting room cozy around an as-yet-untried hearth; red-checked curtains, rocking chairs, corn dollies and soft lights. A townspeople's country toy, but enough, I sometimes thought, to make one want to put down roots.

Bananas Frisby had found it for us. Bananas, long-time friend, who kept a pub in the village. I'd called in there one day on my way to Newmarket and told him I was stuck for somewhere to live.

"What's wrong with your old boat?"

"I've grown out of it."

He gave me a slow glance. "Mentally?"

"Yeah. I've sold it. And I've met a girl."

"And this one," he suggested, "isn't ecstatic about rubbing down dead varnish?"

"Far from."

"I'll keep it in mind," he said, and indeed he called me a week later at Warrington's house and said there was a tarted-up cottage down the road from him that I could go and look at: the London-based owners didn't want to sell but could do with some cash, and they'd be willing to let it to someone who wouldn't stay forever.

"I told them you'd the wanderlust of an albatross," he said. "I know them, they're nice people, don't let me down."

Bananas personally owned his almost equally old pub, which was very slowly crumbling under his policy of neglect. Bananas had no family, no heirs, no incentive to preserve his worldly goods; so when each new patch of damp appeared inside his walls he bought a luxurious green potted plant to hide it. Since I'd known him the shiny-leafed camouflage had multiplied from three to eight: and there was a vine climbing now through the windows. If anyone ever remarked about the dark patches on the walls, Bananas said the plants had caused them, and strangers never realized it was the other way around.

Bananas' main pride and joy was the small restaurant, next door to the bar, in which he served *cuisine minceur* of such perfection that half the passing jockeys of England ate there religiously. It had been over his dried, crisp, indescribable roast duck that I'd first met him, and like a mark well hooked had become an addict. Couldn't count the *délices* I'd paid for since.

He was already up as usual when I waved to him on my way to the gallops; sweeping out, cleaning up, opening his windows wide to get rid of the overnight fug. A fat man himself he nonetheless had infinite energy and ran the whole place with the help of two women, one in the bar and one in the kitchen, both of whom he bossed around like a feudal lord. Betty in the kitchen cooked stolidly under his eagle eye and Bessie in the bar served drinks with speed bordering on sleight-of-hand; Bananas was head waiter and every other sort of waiter, collecting orders, delivering food, presenting bills, cleaning and relaying tables, all with a deceptive show of having all day to chat. I'd watched him at it so often that I knew his system; he practically never wasted time by going into the kitchen. Food appeared from Betty through a vast serving hatch shielded from the public view, and dirty dishes disappeared down a gentle slide.

"Who washes up?" I'd said once in puzzlement.

"I do," Bananas said. "After closing time I feed it all through the washer."

"Don't you ever sleep?"

"Sleep's boring."

He needed, it seemed, only four hours a night.

"And why work so hard? Why not have more help?"

He looked at me pityingly. "Staff cause as much work

as they do," he said. And I'd found out later that he closed the restaurant every year toward the end of November and took off to the West Indies, returning in late March when the flat racing stirred back to life. He hated the cold, he said; he worked at a gallop for eight months for four months' palm trees and sun.

That morning on the Limekilns, Simpson Shell was working his best young prospect and looking smug. The eldest of Luke Houston's five trainers, he had been least resigned to me and he still had hang-ups which showed on his face every day.

"Morning, William," he said, frowning.

"Morning, Sim." I watched with him the rangy colt upon whom the Houston hope of a Classic next season was faintly pinned. "He's moving well," I said.

"He always does." The voice was slighting and impatient. I smiled to myself. Neither compliments nor soft soap, he was saying, were going to change his opinion of the upstart who had overruled him in the matter of selling two two-year-olds. He had told me he disagreed strongly with my weeding-out policy, even though I'd put it to him beforehand and discussed every dud to be discarded. "Warrington never did that," he'd thundered, and he'd warned me he was writing to Luke to complain. I never heard the result. Either he'd never written or Luke had backed me up; but it had consolidated his Derry-wards hostility, not least because, although I had saved Luke Houston a stack of pointless training fees, I had at the same time deprived Simpson Shell. He was waiting, I knew, for the duds to win for their new owners so that he could crow, and it was my good luck that so far they hadn't.

Like all Luke's trainers he trained for many other owners besides. Luke's horses at present constituted about a sixth of his string, which was too high a percentage for him to risk losing them altogether: so he was civil to me, but only just.

I asked him about a filly who had had some heat in her leg the previous evening, and he grumpily said it was better.

He hated me to take a close interest in his eight Houston horses, yet I guessed that if I didn't another letter would be winging to California complaining that I was neglecting my duties. Sim Shell, I thought ruefully, couldn't be pleased.

Over in the Bury Road, Mort Miller, younger, neurotic, fingers snapping like firecrackers, told me that Luke's ten darlings were eating well and climbing the walls with eagerness to slaughter the opposition. Mort had considered the sale of three no-gooders a relief, saying he hated the lazy so-and-sos and grudged them their oats. Mort's horses were always as strung up as he was, but they certainly won when it mattered.

I dropped in on Mort most days because it was he, for all his positive statements, who in fact asked my opinion most.

Once a week, usually fitting in with race meetings, I visited the other two trainers, Thompson and Sandlache, who lived thirty miles from each other on the Berkshire Downs, and about once a month I spent a couple of days with Donavan in Ireland. With them all I had satisfactory working arrangements, they on their part admitting that the two-year-olds I'd got rid of were of no benefit to themselves, and I promising that I would spend the money I'd saved on the training fees to buy extra yearlings in October.

I would be sorry, I thought, when my year was over.

Driving home from Mort's I stopped in town to collect a radio I'd been having repaired, and again to fill up with petrol, and again at Bananas' pub to pick up some beer.

Bananas was in the kitchen prodding some marinating veal. Opening time still lay an hour ahead. Everything in the place was gleaming and fresh and the plants grew damply in their pots.

"There was a fellow looking for you," Bananas said.

"What sort of fellow?"

"Big man. Didn't know him. I told him where your cottage was." He scowled at Betty, who was obviously peeling grapes. "I told him you were out."

"Did he say what he wanted?"

"Nope."

He shed an apron and took his bulk into the bar. "Too early for you?" he said, easing behind the counter.

"Sort of."

He nodded and methodically assembled his usual breakfast: a third of a tumbler of brandy topped up with two scoops of vanilla-walnut ice cream.

"Cassie went off to work," he said, reaching for a spoon.

"You don't miss much."

He shrugged. "You can see that yellow car a mile off, and I was out front cleaning the windows." He stirred the ice cream into the brandy and with gourmand enjoyment shoveled the first installment into his mouth. "That's better," he said.

"It's no wonder you're fat."

He merely nodded. He didn't care. He'd told me once that his size made his fat customers feel better and spend more, and that his fat customers in search of a miracle outnumbered the thin.

He was a natural eccentric, himself seeing nothing unusual in anything he did. In various late-night sessions he'd unbuttoned a little of his inner self, and under the surface geniality I'd had glimpses of a deep pessimism, a moroseness which looked with despair at the inability of the human race to live harmoniously on the beautiful earth. He had no politics, no god, no urge to agitate. Peoples, he said, were known to starve on rich fertile tropical earth; peoples stole their neighbors' lands; peoples murdered peoples from racial hate; peoples tortured and killed in the name of freedom. It sickened him, he said. It had been going on from prehistory, and it would go on until the vindictive ape was wiped out.

"But you yourself seem happy enough," I'd once said.

He'd looked at me darkly. "You're a bird. Always on the wing. You'd be a sparrowhawk if you hadn't such long legs."

"And you?"

"The only option is suicide," he said. "But right now it's

not necessary." He'd deftly poured himself another brandy, and lifted the glass in a sort of salute. "Here's to civilization, damn it."

His real forenames, written over the pub doorway, were John James, but his nickname was a pudding. "Bananas Frisby," a hot fluffy confection of eggs, rum, bananas and orange, was an item nearly always on his menu, and "Bananas" he himself had become. It suited his outer persona well, but his inner not at all.

"You know what?" he said.

"What?"

"I'm growing a beard."

I looked at the faint shadow on the dark jaw. "It needs compost," I said.

"Very funny. The days of the big fat slob are over. What you see is the start of the big fat distinguished innkeeper." He took a large spoonful of ice cream and drank some of the liquid as a chaser, wiping the resulting white moustache off on the back of his hand.

He wore his usual working clothes: open-necked shirt, creaseless gray flannels, old tennis shoes. Thinning dark hair scattered his scalp haphazardly, with one straight lock falling over an ear; and as Frisby in the evenings wasn't all that different from Frisby in the mornings I couldn't see a beard transforming the image. Particularly not, I thought interestedly, while it grew.

"Can you spare a tomato or two?" I said. "Those Italian ones?"

"For your lunch?"

"Yeah."

"Cassie doesn't feed you."

"It's not her job."

He shook his head over the waywardness of our domestic arrangements, but if he had had a wife I wondered which one of them would have cooked. I paid for the beer and the tomatoes, promised to bring Cassie to admire the whiskers, and drove home.

Life for me was good, as I'd told Cassie. Life at that

moment was a long way from Bananas' world of horrors.

I parked in front of the cottage and walked up the path juggling radio, beer and tomatoes in one hand and fishing for keys with the other.

One doesn't expect people to leap out of nowhere waving baseball bats. I had merely a swift glimpse of him, turning my head toward the noise of his approach, seeing the solid figure, the savagery, the raised arm. I hadn't even the time to think incredulously that he was going to hit me before he did it.

The crashing blow on my moving head sent me dazed and headlong, shedding radio, beer cans, tomatoes on the way. I fell half on the path and half on a bed of pansies and lay in a pulsating semi-consciousness in which I could smell the earth but couldn't think.

Rough fingers twined themselves into my hair and pulled my head up from its face-down position, As if from a great distance away from my closed eyes a harsh deep voice spoke nonsensical words.

"You're not..." he said. "*Fuck* it."

He dropped my head suddenly and the small second knock finished the job. I wasn't aware of it. In my conscious mind things simply stopped happening.

The next thing that impinged was that someone was trying to lift me up, and that I was trying to stop him.

"All right, lie there," said a voice. "If that's how you feel."

How I felt was like a shapeless form spinning in a lot of outer space. He tried again to pick me up and things inside the skull suddenly shook back into order.

"Bananas," I said weakly, recognizing him.

"Who else? What happened?"

I tried to stand up and staggered a bit, trampling a few more long-suffering pansies.

"Here," Bananas said, catching me by the arm. "Come into the house." He semisupported me and found the door was locked.

"Keys," I mumbled.

"Where are they?"

I waved a vague arm, and he let go of me to look for them. I leaned against the doorpost and throbbed. Bananas found the keys and came toward me and said in anxiety. "You're covered in blood."

I looked down at my red-stained shirt. Fingered the cloth. "That blood's got seeds in," I said.

Bananas peered at my chest. "Your lunch." He sounded relieved. "Come on."

We went into the cottage where I collapsed into a chair and began to sympathize with migraine sufferers. Bananas searched in random cupboards and asked plaintively for the brandy.

"Can't you wait until you get home?" I said without criticism.

"It's for you."

"None left."

He didn't press it. He may have remembered that it had been he, a week ago, who'd emptied the bottle.

"Can you make tea?" I said.

He said resignedly, "I suppose so," and did.

While I drank the resulting ambrosia he told me that he'd seen a car driving away from the direction of the cottage at about eighty miles an hour down the country road. It was the car, he said, of the man who'd asked for me earlier. He had been at first puzzled and then disquieted, and had finally decided to amble down to see if everything was all right.

"And there you were," he said, "looking like a poleaxed giraffe."

"He hit me," I said.

"You don't say."

"With a baseball bat."

"So you saw him."

"Yeah. Just for a second."

"Who was he?"

"No idea." I drank some tea. "Mugger."

"How much did he take?"

I put down the tea and patted the hip pocket in which I

carried a small notecase. The wallet was still there. I pulled it out and looked inside. Nothing much in there, but also nothing missing.

"Pointless," I said. "What did he want?"

"He asked for you," Bananas said.

"So he did." I shook my head, which wasn't a good idea as it sent little daggers in all cranial directions. "What exactly did he say?"

Bananas gave it some thought. "As far as I can remember," he said, "it was, 'Where does Derry live?'"

"Would you know him again?" I asked.

He pensively shook his head. "I shouldn't think so. I mean, I've a general impression—not young, not old, roughish accent—but I was busy, I didn't pay all that much attention."

Oddly enough, though I'd seen him for only a fraction of the time Bananas had, I had a much clearer recollection of my attacker. A freeze view, like a snapshot, standing framed in my mind. A thick-set man with yellowish skin, grayish about the head, intent eyes darkly shadowed. The blur on the edge of the snapshot was the downward slash of his arm. Whether the memory was reliable, or whether I'd know him again, I couldn't tell.

Bananas said, "Are you all right to leave?"

"Sure."

"Betty will finish those grapes and stare into space," he said. "The old cow's working to rule. That's what she says. Working to rule, I ask you. She doesn't belong to a union. She's invented her own bloody rules. At the moment rule number one is that she doesn't do anything I don't directly tell her to."

"Why not?"

"More pay. She wants to buy a pony to ride on the Heath. She can't ride, and she's damn near sixty."

"Go on back," I said smiling. "I'm OK."

He semi-apologetically made for the door. "There's always the doctor, if you're worse."

"I guess so."

He opened the door and peered out into the garden. "There are beer cans in your pansies."

He went out saying he would pick them up, and I shoved myself off the chair and followed him. When I got to the door he was standing on the path holding three beer cans and a tomato and staring intently at the purple-and-yellow flowers.

"What is it?" I said.

"Your radio."

"I've just had it fixed."

He looked up at me. "Too bad."

Something in his tone made me totter down the path for a look. Sure enough, my radio lay in the pansies: what was left of it. Casing, dials, circuits, speaker, all had been comprehensively smashed.

"That's nasty," Bananas said.

"Spite," I agreed. "And a baseball bat."

"But *why*?"

"I think," I said slowly, "that maybe he thought I was someone else. After he'd hit me, he seemed surprised. I remember him swearing."

"Violent temper," said Bananas, looking at the radio.

"Mm."

"Tell the police," he said.

"Yeah."

I took the beer from him and sketched a wave as he walked briskly up the road. Then I stared for a while at the shattered radio thinking slightly disturbing thoughts: like what would my head have looked like if he hadn't stopped after one swipe.

With a mental shiver I went back indoors and applied my concussion to writing up my weekly report sheet for Luke Houston.

THIRTEEN

I never did get around to consulting the doctor or calling the police. I couldn't see anything productive coming from spending the time.

Cassie took the whole affair philosophically but said that my skull must be cracked if I didn't want to make love.

"Double ration tomorrow," I said.

"You'll be lucky."

I functioned on two cylinders throughout the next day and in the evening Jonathan rang, as he sometimes did, keeping a long-distance finger on little brother's pulse. He had never grown out of the *in loco parentis* habit, nor, to be honest, did I want him to. Jonathan, six thousand miles away, was still my anchor, my most trusted friend.

A pity about Sarah, of course. I would have seen more of Jonathan all my life if I could have got on better with Sarah. She irritated me like an allergy rash with her bossiness and her sarcasm, and I'd never been able to please her. I'd thought at one time that their marriage was on the way to the cemetery and I hadn't grieved much, but somehow or other they'd retreated from the brink. She certainly seemed softer with Jonathan nowadays, but when I was around the old acid rose still in her voice, and I never stayed long in their house. Never staying long in one place was in fact, according to her, one of my least excusable faults. I ought to buckle down, she said, and get a proper job.

She was looking splendid these days, slender as a girl and tawny with the sun. Many, I supposed, seeing the fair hair, the good bones, the still-tight jawline, the grace of movement, would have envied Jonathan his young-at-forty-five wife. And all, as far as I knew, without the plastic surgeon's knife.

"How's Sarah?" I said automatically. I'd been asking after her religiously most of my life, and not caring a jot. The truce she and I maintained for Jonathan's sake was fragile; a matter of social form, of empty politeness, of unfelt smiles, of asking after health.

"She's fine," he said. "Just fine." His voice after all these years had taken on a faint inflection and many of the idioms of his adopted country. "She sends you her best."

"Thanks."

"And you?" he said.

"Well enough considering some nut hit me on the head."

"What nut?"

"Some guy who came here and lay in wait, and took a bash at me."

"Are you all right?"

"Yeah. No worse than a racing fall."

"Who was he?" he asked.

"No idea. He asked for directions from the pub, but he'd got the wrong man. Maybe he asked for Terry . . . it sounds much the same. Anyway, he blasted off when he found he'd made a slight error, so that's that."

"And no harm done?" he asked insistently.

"Not to me, but you should see my radio."

"What?"

"When he found I was the wrong guy, he took it out on my radio. I wasn't awake, mind you, at that point. But when I came around, there it was, mashed."

There was a silence on the other end, and I said, "Jonathan? Are you still there?"

"Yes," he said. "Did you see the man? What did he look like?"

I told him: fortyish, grayish, yellowish. "Like a bull," I said.

"Did he say anything?"

"Something about me not being who he expected, and fuck it."

"How did you hear him if you were knocked out?"

I explained. "But all that's left is a sore spot for the hairbrush," I said, "so don't give it another thought."

We talked about this and that for the rest of our customary six minutes, and at the end he said, "Will you be in tomorrow night?"

"Yes, I should think so."

"I might call you back," he said.

"OK." I didn't bother to ask him why. He had a habit of not answering straightforward questions with straightforward answers if it didn't suit him, and his noncommittal announcement told me that this was one of those times.

We said amicable goodbyes, and Cassie and I went to bed and renewed our normal occupation.

"Do you think we'll ever be tired of it?" she asked.

"Ask me when we're eighty."

"Eighty is impossible," she said, and indeed it seemed so to us both.

Cassie went to Cambridge every day in her little yellow car to spend eight hours behind a building society desk discussing mortgages. Cassie's mind was full of terms like "with-profits endowment" and "early redemption charges," and I thought it remarkable, sometimes, that she'd never suggested a twenty-five-year millstone around my own neck.

I'd once before tried living with someone—nearly a year with a cuddly blonde who wanted marriage and nestlings. I'd felt stifled and gone off to South America and behaved abominably, according to her parents. But Cassie wasn't like that: if she wanted the same things she didn't say so, and maybe she realized, as I did, that I always came back to England, that the homing instinct was fairly strong. One day, I thought, one *distant* day ... and maybe with Cassie ... I might, just perhaps, and with all options open, buy a house.

One could always sell it again, after all.

Jonathan did telephone again the following evening and came straight to the point.

"Do you," he said, "remember that summer when Peter Keithly got killed in his boat?"

"Of course I do. One doesn't actually forget one's own brother being tangled up in a murder."

"It's fourteen years ago," he said doubtfully.

"Things that happen when you're fifteen stay sharp in your mind forever."

"I guess you're right. Anyway ... you know who I mean by Angelo Gilbert."

"The bumper-off," I said.

"As you say. I think the man who hit you on the head may be Angelo Gilbert."

A great one, my brother, for punching the air out. On a distinctly short breath I said, "You sound very calm about it." But then of course he would. He was always calm. In the scariest crisis it would be Jonathan who spoke and acted as if nothing unusual was happening. He'd carried me out of a fire once as a small child and I'd thought that somehow nothing was the matter, nothing was really wrong with the flames and the roaring and crashing all around us, because he'd looked down at me and smiled.

"I checked up," he said. "Angelo Gilbert got out of prison seventeen days ago, on parole."

"Out—"

"It would take him a while to orientate himself and to find you. I mean ... if it was him, he would have thought you were me."

I sorted my way through that and said, "What makes you think it was him?"

"Your radio, really. He seemed to enjoy destroying things like that. Televisions. Stereos. And he'd be forty now . . . and his father reminded me of a bull. What you said took me right back."

"Good grief."

"Yes."

"You really think it was him?"

"I'm afraid it's possible."

"Well," I said, "now that he knows he got the wrong guy, maybe he won't bother me again."

"Monsters don't go away because you don't look at them."

"What?"

"He may come back."

"Thanks very much."

"William, take it seriously. Angelo was dangerous in his twenties and it sounds as if he still is. He never did get the computer programs he killed for, and he didn't get them because of me. So take care."

"It might not have been him."

"Act as if it was."

"Yeah," I said. "So long, Professor." The wryness in my voice must have been plain to him.

"Keep off horses," he said.

I put the receiver down ruefully. Horses, to him, meant extreme risk.

"What's the matter?" Cassie said. "What did he say?"

"It's all a very long story."

"Tell it."

I told it on and off over the next few hours, remembering things in pieces and not always in the order they'd happened, much as Jonathan had told it to me all those years ago. Before going off to Canada to shoot, he had collected me straight from school at the end of that summer term and we'd gone to Cornwall, just the two of us, for a few day's sailing. We'd had great holidays there two or three times before, but that year it blew a gale and poured with rain continuously, and to amuse me while we sat and stared through the dripping yacht club windows, waiting for the improvement which never came, he'd told me about Mrs. O'Rorke and Ted Pitts and the Gilberts, and how he'd stuck magnets in the cassettes. I'd been so fascinated that I hadn't minded missing the sailing.

I wasn't sure that I'd been shown every alley of the labyrinth; my quiet schoolmasterly brother had been reticent in patches, and I'd always guessed that it was because probably in some way he'd used his guns. He never would let me touch them, and the only thing I ever knew him to be scared of was having his precious firearms certificate taken away.

"So there you are," I said finally. "Jonathan got Angelo tossed into clink. And now he's out."

Cassie had listened with alternating alarm and amusement, but it was doubt that remained in the end.

"So what now?" she said.

"So now, if Angelo's on the rampage, hostilities may be resumed."

"Oh no."

"And there are certain disadvantages that Derry number two may have to contend with." I ticked them off on my fingers. "One, I can't shoot. Two, I know practically nothing about computers. And three, if Angelo's come charging out of jail intending to track down his lost crock of gold, I've no idea where it is or even if it still exists."

She frowned. "Do you think that's what he wants?"

"Wouldn't you?" I said gloomily. "You spend fourteen years in a cell brooding over what you lost and dreaming of vengeance and, yes, you're going to come out looking for both—and a small detail like having attacked the wrong man isn't going to put you off."

"Come to bed," Cassie said.

"I wonder if he thinks the way he used to." I looked at her increasingly loved face. "I don't want him busting in here to hold you hostage."

"With no Jonathan to cut the telephone wires and send for the posse? Come to bed."

"I wonder how he did it?"

"What?"

"Cut the wires. It isn't that easy."

"Climbed the pole with a pair of scissors," she said.

"You can't climb a pole. There aren't any footholds except at the top."

"Why are you wondering about it after all these years? Come to bed."

"Because of a bang on the head."

She said, "Are you really anxious?"

"Uneasy."

"You must be. I've mentioned bed three times and you're still sitting down."

I grinned at her and rose to my feet; and at that moment an almighty crash on the front door burst it open with splintering wood and a broken lock.

Angelo stood in the gap. Stood for less than a second regaining his balance from the kick which had brought him in, stood with the baseball bat swinging and his face rigid with ill intent.

Neither Cassie nor I had time to protest or yell. He waded straight in, laying about him, smashing anything near him, a lamp, some corn dollies, a vase, a picture . . . the television. Like a whirlwind demented he devastated the pretty interior, and when I leaped at him I met a fist in the face and a fast knee, which missed my groin, and I smelled his sweat and heard his breath rasp from exertion and took in what he was grittily saying: and it was just my name and Jonathan's, over and over.

"Derry . . . Derry . . . fucking *Derry*."

Cassie tried to help me, and he slashed at her with the heavy wooden bat and connected with her arm. I saw her stumble from the pain of it, and in a fury I put one of my own arms around his neck and tried to yank his head back, to hurt him enough to make him drop his weapon and probably if the truth were told to throttle him. But he knew more about dirty fighting than I'd ever learned and it took him about two elbow jabs and a scrunching backhand jerk of my fingers to pry me loose. He shook me off with such force that I half fell, but still clung to his clothes with octopus tentacles, not wanting to be thrown clear so that he could get another swing with that bat.

We crashed around the broken room with me sticking to him with ferocity at least equal to his and him struggling to get free; and it was Cassie, in the end, who finished it. Cassie who grabbed the brass coal scuttle from the hearth by its shining handle and swung it in an arc at arm's length, aiming at Angelo's head. I saw the flash of its gleaming surface and felt the jolt through Angelo's body: and I let go of him as he fell in a sprawl on the carpet.

"Oh, God," Cassie was saying. "Oh, God." There were tears on her face and she was holding her left arm away from her body in a way I knew all too well.

Angelo was visibly breathing. Stunned only. Soon to awake.

"Have to tie him," I said breathlessly. "What've we got?"

Cassie painfully said "Clothesline," and before I could stop her she'd vanished into the kitchen, returning almost at once with a new line still in its package. Wire wrapped in plastic, the bright label said. Strong enough, indeed, for a bull.

While I was still uncoiling it with unsteady fingers, there was the sound outside of someone thudding up the path; and I had time for a feeling of absolute despair before I saw who it was.

Bananas came to the dark doorway with a rush and stood there stock still taking in the ravaged scene.

"I saw his car come back. I was just closing up—"

"Help me tie him," I said, nodding at Angelo, who was stirring ominously. "He did all this. He's coming around."

Bananas turned Angelo onto his face and held his hands together behind his back while I built knots around the wrists, and then continued with the job himself, leading the line down from the wrists to join it to two more knots around the ankles.

"He's broken Cassie's arm," I said.

Bananas looked at her and at me and at Angelo, and

walked purposefully over to where the telephone stood miraculously undamaged on its little table.

"Wait," I said. "Wait."

"But Cassie needs a doctor. And I'll get the police."

"No," I said. "Not yet."

"But you must."

I wiped my nose on the back of my hand and looked remotely at the resulting smear of blood. "There's some pethidine and a syringe in the bathroom," I said. "It'll do a lot to stop Cassie hurting."

He nodded in understanding and said he would fetch it.

"Bring the box marked 'Emergency.' It's on the shelf over the bath taps."

While he went and came back with his surprising speed I helped Cassie to sit on a chair and to rest her left arm on a cushion, which I put on the telephone table. It was the forearm, I found, which was broken: both bones, probably, from the numb uselessness of her hand.

"William," she said whitely, "don't. It hurts. Don't."

"Darling...darling...it has to have support. Just let it lie there. Don't fight it."

She did mutely what I said and looked paler than ever.

"I didn't feel it," she said. "Not like this, not at first."

Bananas brought the emergency box and opened it. I tore the syringe out of its sterile package and filled it from the ampul of pethidine. Pulled Cassie's skirt up high over the sun-browned legs and fed the muscle-relaxing pain-killer into the long muscle of her thigh.

"Ten minutes," I said, pulling the needle out and rubbing the place with my knuckles. "A lot of the pain will go. Then we'll be able to take you to the casualty department of Cambridge hospital to get it set. Nowhere nearer will be open at this time of night."

She nodded slightly with the first twitch of a smile, and on the floor Angelo started trying to kick.

Bananas again walked toward the telephone, and again I stopped him.

"But, William—"

I looked around at the jagged evidence of a passionate need for revenge; the explosion of fourteen years of pent-up hate. I said, "He did this because my brother got him jailed for murder. He's out on parole. If we call the police he'll be back inside—"

"Then of *course*," Bananas said, picking up the receiver.

"No," I said. "Put it down."

He looked bewildered. Angelo on the floor began mumbling as if in delirium—a mixture of atrocious swearwords and loud incomprehensible unfinished sentences.

"That's stir talk," said Bananas, listening.

"You've heard it before?"

"You hear everything in the end in my trade."

"Look," I said. "I get him sent back to jail and then what happens? It wouldn't be so long before he was out . . . and he'd have a whole new furious grudge to avenge. And by that time he might have learned some sense and not come waving a piece of wood and going off half-cocked, but wait until he'd managed a pistol, and sneak up on me one day three, four years from now, and finish me off. This"—I waved a hand—"isn't an act of reason. I'm only Jonathan's brother. I myself did him no harm. This is anger against life. Blind, colossal, ungovernable rage. I can do without him focusing it all on me personally in the future." I paused. "I have to find a better—a final—solution. If I can."

"You can't mean—" Bananas said tentatively.

"What?"

"To . . . to . . . no, you couldn't."

"Not that final solution, no. Though it's quite a thought. Cement boots and a downward trip in the North Sea."

"Tankful of piranhas," Cassie said.

Bananas looked at her with relief and almost laughed, and finally put the telephone receiver back in its cradle.

Angelo stopped mumbling and came full awake. When he realized where he was and in what condition, the skin which had until then been pale became redly suffused: the face, the neck, even the hands. He rolled halfway over onto his back and filled the room with the intensity of his rage.

"If you start swearing," I said, "I'll gag you."

With an effort he said nothing, and I looked at his face squarely and fully for the first time. There wasn't a great deal left of the man whose picture I had once pored over in a newspaper—not youth, not black hair, not narrow jaw, not long thin nose. Age, heredity, prison food, all had given him fatty deposits to blur the outlines of the head and bulk the body.

Average brains, Jonathan had said. Not clever. Relies on his frightening-power and gets his results from that. Despises everyone. Calls them creeps and mugs.

"Angelo Gilbert," I said.

He jerked and looked surprised, as if he had thought I wouldn't know him: nor would I have, if Jonathan hadn't called.

"Let's get it straight," I said. "It was not my brother who sent you to prison. You did it to yourself."

Cassie murmured, "Criminals in jail are there voluntarily."

Bananas looked at her in surprise.

"My arm feels better," she said.

I stared down at Angelo. "You chose jail when you shot Chris Norwood. Those fourteen years were your own fault, so why take it out on *me?*"

It made no impression. I hadn't really thought it would. Blaming one's troubles on someone else was average human nature.

Angelo said, "Your fucking brother tricked me. He stole what was mine."

"He stole nothing of yours."

"He did." The words were bass-voiced, fierce and positive, a growl in the throat. Cassie shivered at the menace Angelo could generate even tied up in ignominy on a cottage floor.

The crock of gold, I thought suddenly, might have its uses.

Angelo seemed to be struggling with himself but in the end the words tore out of him, furious, frustrated, still bursting with an anger that had nowhere to go. *"Where is he?"* he said. "Where's your fucking brother? I can't find him."

Saints alive . . .

"He's dead," I said coldly.

Angelo didn't say whether or not he believed me, but the news did nothing for his general temper. Bananas and Cassie displayed a certain stillness but fortunately kept quiet.

I said to Bananas, "Could you watch him for a minute while I make a phone call?"

"Hours if you like."

"Are you all right?" I asked Cassie.

"That stuff's amazing."

"Won't be long." I picked the whole telephone off the table beside her and carried it into the office, closing the door as I went.

I called California, thinking that Jonathan would be anywhere but home, that I'd get Sarah, that it would be siesta time under the golden sun. But Jonathan was in, and he answered.

"I just had a thought," I said. "Those tapes that Angelo Gilbert wanted—have you still got them?"

"Good grief," he said. "I shouldn't think so." A pause while he reflected. "No, we cleared everything out when we left Twickenham. You remember, we sold the furniture and bought new out there. I got rid of pretty well everything. Except the guns, of course."

"Did you throw the tapes away?"

"Um," he said. "There was a set I sent to Mrs. O'Rorke and got back again . . . oh yes, I gave them to Ted Pitts. If anyone still has them, it would be Ted. But I shouldn't think they'd be much use after all these years."

"The tapes themselves, or the betting system?"

"The system. It must be long out of date."

It wouldn't matter too much, I thought.

"There are a lot of computer programs out here now for helping you win on horses," Jonathan said. "Some of them work, they say."

"You haven't tried them?"

"I'm not a gambler."

"Oh, yeah?"

"What do you want the tapes for?" he said.

"To tie Angelo up in knots again."

"Take care."

"Sure. Where would I find Ted Pitts?"

He told me doubtfully to try the West Ealing School, where they'd both been teaching, but said it was unlikely that he was still there. They hadn't been in touch with each other at all since he'd emigrated. Perhaps I could trace Ted through the Schoolmasters Union, who might have his address.

I thanked him and disconnected, and went back into the sitting room, where everyone looked much as I'd left them.

"I have a problem," I said to Bananas.

"Just one?"

"Time."

"Ah. The essence."

"Mm." I stared at Angelo. "There's a cellar under this cottage."

Angelo had no fear; one had to give him that. I could see quite clearly that he understood I meant not to let him go, yet his only reaction was aggressive and set him struggling violently against the clothesline.

"Watch him," I said to Bananas. "There's some stuff in the cellar. I'm going to clear it out. If he looks like getting free, give him another bash on the head."

Bananas looked at me as if he'd never seen me before; and perhaps he hadn't. I put a quick apologetic hand on Cassie's shoulder as I went, and in the kitchen I opened the latched wooden door which led to the cellar steps.

Down there it was cool and dry: a brick-lined room with a concrete floor and a single light bulb swinging from the ceiling. When we had come to the cottage we had found the garden chairs stacked in there, but they were now outside on the grass, leaving only oddments like a paraffin stove, some tins of paint, a stepladder and a stack of fishing gear. I carried everything in relays up the steps and dumped it all in the kitchen.

When I'd finished, there was nothing in the cellar to help a captive; yet I would still have to keep him tied because of the nature of the lockless door. It was made simply of upright planks screwed together with the screwheads fortunately on the kitchen side. Across near the top there were six thumb-sized holes, presumably for ventilation. A good enough barrier against most contingencies but not to be trusted to withstand the sort of kick with which the enemy had battered his initial way in.

"Right," I said, going back into the sitting room. "Now, you, Angelo, are going into the cellar. Your only alternative is an immediate return to jail, as all this"—I indicated the room—"and that"—Cassie's arm—"will cancel your parole and send you straight behind bars."

"You bloody can't," he said furiously.

"I bloody can. You started this. You damn well take the consequences."

"I'll get you *busted.*"

"Yeah. You try it. You got it wrong, Angelo. I'm not my brother. He was clever and wily and he tricked you silly, but he would never use physical force; and I will, you mug, I will."

Angelo used words that made Bananas wince and glance apprehensively at Cassie.

"I've heard them before," she said.

"You've a choice, Angelo," I said. "Either you let my friend and me carry you carefully down the steps without you struggling, or you struggle and I pull you down by the legs."

The loss of face in not struggling proved too much. He tried to bite me as I bent down to put my arms under his armpits, so I did what I'd said—grasped the line tying his ankles and dragged him feet foremost out of the sitting room, through the kitchen and down the cellar steps, with him yelling and swearing the whole way.

FOURTEEN

I tugged him well away from the stairs, let go of his legs and returned to the kitchen. He shouted after me blasphemously and I could still hear him when the door was shut. Let him get on with it, I thought callously; but I left on the single light, whose switch was outside on the kitchen wall.

I wedged the latch shut by sliding a knife handle through the slot, and for good measure stacked the stepladder, the table and a couple of chairs into a solid line between the refrigerator and the cellar door, making it impossible for it to open normally into the kitchen.

In the sitting room, and without hustling, I said, "OK. Decision time, mates." I looked at Bananas. "It's not your fight. If you'd rather, you can go back to your dishwashing and forget this ever happened."

He looked resignedly around the room. "I promised you'd leave this place as you found it. Practically pledged my soul."

"I'll replace what I can. Pay for the rest. And grovel. Will that do?"

"You can't manage that brute on your own." He shook

his head. "How long do you mean to keep him?"

"Until I find a man called Pitts." I explained to him and Cassie what I wanted to do and why, and Bananas sighed and said it seemed fairly sensible in the circs, and that he would help where he could.

We shoehorned Cassie gently into my car and I drove her to Cambridge while Bananas in his effective way set himself to tidy the sitting room. There wasn't a great deal one could do at that point about the splintered and uncloseable front door, and he promised to stay in the cottage until we got back.

In the event it was only I who returned. I sat with Cassie through the long wait in the silent hospital while they tried to find someone to X-ray her arm, but it seemed that after midnight the radiology department was firmly shut, with all the radiologists asleep in their own homes, and only the direst surgical emergency would recall them.

Cassie was given a careful splint from shoulder to fingernails and also another pain-killer and a bed; and when I kissed her and left she said, "Don't forget to feed the bull," which the nurses put down to drug-induced light-headedness.

Bananas was asleep when I got back, flat out on the sofa and dreaming I dare say of palm trees. The mess I'd left behind was miraculously cleared with every broken fragment out of sight. There were many things missing but overall it looked more like a room the owners would recognize. Gratefully I went quietly into the kitchen and found my barricade altered and strengthened with four planks which had been lying in the garage, the door now wedged shut from top to bottom.

The light switch was up. Except for whatever dim rays were crawling through the ventilation holes, Angelo was lying in the dark.

Although I'd been quiet, I'd woken Bananas, who was sitting up, pinching the bridge of his nose and blinking heavy eyelids open and shut.

"All the pieces are in the garage," he said. "Not in the

trash can. I reckoned you might need them, one way or another."

"You're great," I said. "Did Angelo try to get out?"

Bananas made a face. "He's a horrible man, that."

"You talked to him?"

"He was shouting through the door that you'd stopped his circulation by tying his wrists too tight. I went in to see, but you hadn't; his fingers were pink. He was halfway up the stairs and he tried to knock me over. Tried to sweep my legs from under me and make me fall. God knows what he thought it would achieve."

"Probably to scare me into letting him go."

Bananas scratched himself around the ribs. "I came up into the kitchen and shut the door on him, and switched his light off, and he went on howling for ages about what he'd do to you when he got out."

Keeping his courage up, I thought.

I looked at my watch. Five o'clock. Soon be light. Soon be Friday with all its problems. "I guess," I said yawning, "that a couple of hours shut-eye would do no harm."

"And that one?" He jerked his head toward the kitchen.

"He won't suffocate."

"You're a revelation to me," Bananas said.

I grinned at him and I think he thought me as ruthless as our visitor. But he was wrong. I was fairly sure that Angelo that night had come back to kill, to finish off what he had earlier started, knowing by then who I was and not expecting a Cassie. I was soft compared with him.

Bananas walked home to his dishwasher and I took his place on the sofa, feeling the bedroom too far away, out of touch. Despite the hectic night I went to sleep immediately and woke with mind-protesting reluctance to switch off the alarm clock at seven o'clock. The horses would be working on the Heath. Simpson Shell had set up a trial of two late-developing three-year-olds, and if I wasn't there to watch he'd be writing to Luke Houston to say I was a shirker. And I wanted anyway, Angelo or no Angelo, to see how those horses went.

I loved the Heath in the early mornings with the manes blowing under the wide skies. My affection for horses was so deep and went back so far that I couldn't imagine life without them. They were a friendly foreign nation living in our land, letting their human neighbors tend them and feed them, accepting them as servants as much as masters. Fast, fascinating, essentially untamed, they were my landscape, my old shoes, the place to where my heart returned, as necessary to me as the sea to sailors.

Even on that morning they lifted my spirits and I watched the trial with a concentration Angelo couldn't disrupt. One of the three-year-olds finished most decisively fast and Simpson said with careful civility that he hoped I would report to Luke how well the colt was looking.

"I'll tell Luke you've done wonders with him. Remember how unbalanced he looked in May? He'll win next week, don't you think?"

He gave me the usual ambivalent stare, needing my approbation but hating it. I smiled internally and left him to drive the short distance to where Mort was directing his string.

"All OK?" I asked.

"Well, yes," Mort said. "Genotti's still shaping up well for the Leger." He flicked his fingers six times rapidly. "Can you come back to the house for breakfast? The Bungay filly is still not eating well, and I thought we might discuss what we could do. You sometimes have ideas. And there's Luke's bill. I want to explain one or two items before you query them."

"Mort," I interrupted him regretfully, "could we postpone it for a day or two? Something's come up that I'll have to deal with first."

"Oh? Oh." He sounded put out, because I'd never refused him before. "Are you sure?"

"Really sorry," I said.

"I might see you this afternoon," he said, fidgeting badly.

"Um . . . yes. Of course."

He nodded with satisfaction and let me go with good grace, and I doubted whether I would in fact turn up on Newmarket racecourse for that day's program, even though three of Luke's horses were running.

On my way back through the town I stopped at a few shops which were open early and did some errands on my prisoner's account, buying food and one or two small comforts. Then I rocketed the six miles to the village and stopped first at the pub.

Bananas, looking entirely his usual self, had done his dishes, cleaned the bar, and put Betty's back up by saying she was too old to start learning to ride.

"The old cow's refusing to make the celery mousse for lunch. Working to her stupid rules." He disgustedly assembled his breakfast, adding chopped ginger as a topping to the ice cream and pouring brandy lavishly over the lot. "I went down to the cottage again. Not a peep from our friend." He stirred his mixture with anticipation. "You can't hear him from outside, however loud he yells. I found that out last night. You'll be all right if you keep any callers in the garden."

"Thanks."

"When I've finished this I'll come and help you."

"Great."

I hadn't wanted to ask him, but I was most thankful for his offer. I drove on down to the cottage and unloaded all the shopping into the kitchen, and Bananas appeared in his tennis shoes while I was packing food into a carrier. He looked at the small heap of things I'd put ready by the door.

"Let's get it over," he said. "I'll carry this lot."

I nodded. "He'll be blinded at first by the light, so even if he's got himself free we should have the advantage."

We began to remove the barricade from against the door, and when it would open satisfactorily I took the knife out of the latch, picked up the carrier, switched on the cellar light and went into the cage.

Angelo was lying face down in the middle of the floor,

still trussed the way we'd left him: arms behind his back, white clothesline leading slackly between tied wrists and tied ankles.

"It's morning," I said cheerfully.

Angelo barely moved. He said a few low words of which "turd" was the only one distinguishable.

"I've brought you some food." I dumped in one corner the carrier bag, which in fact contained two sliced loaves, several cartons of milk, some water in a plastic bottle, two large cooked chickens, some apples and a lot of various candy bars and chocolate. Bananas silently dumped his own load, which consisted of a blanket, a cheap cushion, some paperback books and two disposable polystyrene chamber pots with lids.

"I'm not letting you out," I said to Angelo. "But I'll untie you."

"Fuck you," he said.

"Here's your watch." I had slipped it off his wrist the evening before to make the tying easier. I took it out of my pocket and put it on the floor near his head. "Lights out tonight at eleven," I said.

It seemed prudent at that point to search Angelo's pockets, but all he was carrying was money. No knives, no matches, no keys: nothing to help him escape.

I nodded to Bananas and we both began to untie the knots, I the wrists, Bananas the ankles, but Angelo's struggles had so tightened our original work that it took time and effort to remove it. Once Angelo was free we coiled the line and retreated up the stairs, from where I watched him move stiffly into a kneeling position with his arms loose and not yet working properly.

The air in the cellar had seemed quite fresh. I closed the door and fixed the latch, and Bananas restacked the barricade with methodical thoroughness.

"How much food did you give him?" he asked.

"Enough for two to four days. Depends on how fast he eats it."

"He's used to being locked up, there's that about it."

Bananas, I thought, was busy stifling remaining doubts. He shoved the four planks into place between the cellar door and the refrigerator, casually remarking that during the night he'd sawn the wood to fit.

"More secure that way," he said. "He won't get out."

"Hope you're right."

Bananas stood back, hands on hips, to contemplate his handiwork, and indeed I was as sure as one could be that Angelo couldn't kick his way out, particularly as he would have to try it while standing on the stairs.

"His car must be somewhere," I said. "I'll look for it after I've phoned the hospital."

"You phone, I'll look," Bananas said, and he went on the errand.

Cassie, I was told, would be having her arm set under anesthetic during the morning. I could collect her at six that evening if all went well.

"May I speak to her?"

"One moment."

Her voice came slowly and sleepily onto the line. "I'm pie-eyed with pre-med," she said. "How's our guest?"

"Happy as a kangaroo with blisters."

"Hopping . . . mad?"

"That pre-med isn't working," I said.

"Sure is. My body's floating but my brain's fizzing along in zillions of sparks. It's weird."

"They say I can fetch you at six."

"Don't . . . be late."

"I might be," I said.

"You don't love me."

"Yeah."

"Sweet William," she said. "A pretty flower."

"Cassie, go to sleep."

"Mm."

She sounded infinitely drowsy. "Goodbye," I said, but I don't think she heard.

I telephoned next to her office and told her boss she'd fallen down the cellar steps and broken her arm, and that she'd probably be back at work sometime the next week.

"How irritating," he said. "Er, for her, of course."

"Of course."

Bananas came back as I was putting down the receiver and said that Angelo's car was parked harmlessly at the top of the lane where the hard surface petered out into muddy cart track. Angelo had left the keys in the ignition. Bananas dumped them on the table.

"Want anything, shout," he said. I nodded gratefully and he padded off, a powerhouse in a suit of blubber.

I set about the task of finding Ted Pitts, telephoning first to Jonathan's old school at West Ealing. A female voice there crisply told me that no one of that name was presently on the staff, and that none of the present staff could help me as they were not there: the new term would not start for another week. The only master who had been teaching in the school fourteen years ago would be, she imagined, Mr. Ralph Jenkins, assistant headmaster, but he had retired at the end of the summer term and in any case it would be unlikely that any of his past assistants would have kept in touch with him.

"Why not?" I asked curiously.

After the faintest of hesitations the voice said levelly, "Mr. Jenkins himself would have discouraged it."

Or in other words, I thought, Mr. Jenkins had been a cantankerous old bastard. I thanked her for as little as I had realistically expected and asked if she could tell me the address of the Schoolmasters Union.

"Do you want their number as well?"

"Yes, please."

She told me both, and I put through a call to their offices. Ted Pitts? Edward? I suppose so, I said. Could I wait? Yes, I could.

The answering voice, a man's this time, shortly told me that Edward Farley Pitts was no longer a member. He had resigned his membership five years previously. His last known address was in Middlesex. Did I want it? Yes, please, I said.

Again I was given a telephone number along with the address. Another female voice answered it, this time with music and children's voices loud in the background.

"What?" she said. "I can't hear you."

"Ted Pitts," I shouted. "Can you tell me where he lives?"

"You've got the wrong number."

"He used to live in your house."

"What? Wait a minute. Shut up, you lousy kids. What did you say?"

"Ted Pitts—"

"Terry, shut off that bleeding stereo. Can't hear myself think. Shut it off. Go on, shut if off."

The music suddenly stopped.

"What did you say?" she said again.

I explained that I wanted to find my lost friend, Ted Pitts.

"Guy with three daughters?"

"That's right."

"We bought this house off of him. Terry, you knock Michelle's head on that wall one more time and I'll rattle your teeth. Where was I? Oh, yes, Ted Pitts. He gave us an address to send things on to, but it's years ago and I don't know where my husband put it."

It was really important, I said.

"Well if you hold on I'll look. Terry... *Terry!*" There was the sound of a slap and a child's wail. The joys of motherhood, I thought.

I held on for an age listening to the scrambled noise of the squabbling siblings, held on so long that I thought she had forgotten all about me and simply left me off the hook, but in the end she did come back.

"Sorry I've been so long, but you can't put your hand on a thing in this house. Anyway, I've found where he moved to."

"You're a doll," I said, writing it down.

She laughed in a pleased fashion. "Want to call around? I'm fed to the teeth with these bloody kids."

"School starts next week."

"Thank the Lord."

I disconnected and tried the number she had given me, but to this one there was no reply. Ten minutes later, again no reply.

I went to the kitchen. All quiet from the cellar. I ate some cornflakes, padded restlessly about and tried the number again.

Zilch.

There was something, I thought, looking at it, that I could immediately do about the front door. It wouldn't at the moment even fit into the frame, but given a chisel and some sandpaper . . . I fetched them from the tool-rack in the garage and reduced the sharply splintered patches to smooth edges, finally shutting the door by totally removing the broken lock. It looked all right from the outside but swung inward at a touch: and we had sweet but inquisitive neighbors who called sometimes to sell us honey.

I again dialed Ted Pitts's possible number. No reply.

Shrugging I tugged a small chest of drawers across inside the front door and climbed out through the dining room window. Drove down to the pub; told Bananas the new way in.

"Do you expect *me*—?"

"Not really. Just in case."

"Where are you going?" he asked.

I showed him the address. "It's a chance."

The address was in Mill Hill on the northern outskirts of London. I drove there with my mind resolutely on the traffic and not on Cassie, unconscious, and Angelo, captive. Crunching the car at that point could be the ultimate disaster.

The house, when I found it, proved to be a middle-sized detached affair in a street of trees and somnolence; and it was empty.

I went up the driveway and looked through the windows. Bare walls, bare floors, no curtains.

With sinking spirits I rang the bell of the house next door, and although it was clearly occupied there was no one in there either. I tried several houses, but none of the people

I spoke to knew anything more of Ted Pitts than, yes, perhaps they had seen some girls going in and out, but of course with all the shrubs and trees one was shielded from one's neighbors, which meant, of course, that also one couldn't see *them*.

It was in one of the houses obliquely opposite, from where only a corner of the Pittses' front garden was visible, that in the end I found some help. The front door was opened a foot by a large woman in pink hair rollers with a pack of assorted small dogs roaming round her legs.

"If you're selling, I don't want it," she said.

I exercised on her the story I had by then invented, saying that Ted Pitts was my brother, he'd sent me his new address but I'd lost it, and I wanted to get in touch with him urgently. After six repetitions, I almost believed it.

"I didn't know him," she said, not opening the door any wider. "He didn't live here long. I never even saw him, I don't think."

"But, er, you noticed them move in, and out..."

"Walking the dogs, you see." She looked fondly down at the pack. "I go past there every day."

"Do you remember how long ago they left?"

"It must be ages. Funny your brother didn't tell you. The house was for sale for weeks after they'd gone. It's only just been sold, as a matter of fact. I saw the agents taking the board down just last week."

"You don't happen to remember," I said carefully, "the name of the agents?"

"Goodness," she said. "I must have walked past it a hundred times. Just let me think." She stared at her pets, her brow wrinkled with concentration. I could still see only half of her body, but I couldn't tell whether the forbidding angle of the door was designed to keep the dogs in or me out.

"Hunt bleach!" she exclaimed.

"What?"

"Hunt comma B L E A C H." She spelled it out. "The name of the agents. A yellow board with black lettering.

You'll see it all over the place, if you look."

I said fervently, "Thank you very much."

She nodded the pink rollers and shut herself in, and I drove around until I found a yellow board with Hunt, Bleach's local address: Broadway, Mill Hill.

The brother story brought its by-now-familiar crop of sympathetic and/or pitying looks but finally gained results. A slightly sullen-looking girl said she thought the house had been handled by their Mr. Jackman, who was now away on his vacation.

"Could you look in the files?"

She took advice from various colleagues, who doubtfully agreed under my urging that perhaps in the circumstances she might. She went into an inner office, and I heard cabinet drawers begin to open and shut.

"Here you are, Mr. Pitts," she said, returning, and it took me a moment to realize that of course I too would be Pitts. "Ridge View, Oaklands Road."

She didn't give me a town. I thought; he's still *here*.

"Could you tell me how to get there?" I said.

She shook her head unhelpfully, but one of the colleagues said, "You go back up the Broadway, around the roundabout until you're pointing toward London, then first left, up the hill, turn right, that's Oaklands Road."

"Terrific." I spoke with heartfelt relief, which they took as appropriate, and I followed their directions faithfully and found the house. It looked a small brown affair; brownish bricks, brown-tiled roof, a narrow window on each side of an oak front door, bushes screening much else. I parked in what seemed an oversized driveway outside a closer double garage and doubtfully rang the doorbell.

There was no noise from inside the house. I listened to the distant hum of traffic and the nearer hum of bees around a tub of dark red flowers, and pressed the bell again.

No results. If I hadn't wanted to find Ted Pitts so much I would have given up and driven away at that point. It wasn't even the sort of road one could inquire at a neighbor's: there were houses on only one side, with a steep wooded hillside rising on the other, and the houses themselves were far-spaced and reclusive, drawing themselves back from public view.

I rang a third time out of indecisiveness, thinking that I could wait, or come back, or leave a note begging Pitts to call me.

The door opened. A pleasant-looking woman stood there; not young, not yet middle-aged, wearing a loosely flowing green sundress with broad straps over suntanned shoulders.

"Yes?" she said inquiringly. Dark curly hair, blue eyes, the brown glowing face of summer leisure.

"I'm looking for Ted Pitts," I said.

"This is his house."

"I've been trying to locate him. I'm the brother of an old friend of his. A friend he had years ago, I mean. Could I see him, do you think?"

"He isn't here at the moment." She looked at me doubtfully. "What's your brother's name?"

"Jonathan Derry."

After the very slightest pause her face changed from watchfulness to welcome; a smile in remembrance of time past.

"Jonathan! We haven't heard from him for years."

"Are you . . . Mrs. Pitts?"

She nodded. "Jane." She opened the door wide and stepped back. "Come in."

"I'm William," I said.

"Weren't you"—she frowned—"away at school?"

"One does tend to grow."

She looked up at me. "I'd forgotten how long ago it was." She led me across a cool dark hall. "This way."

We came to a wide stairway of shallow green-carpeted steps leading downward, and I saw before me what had been totally invisible from the higher roadway—that the house was large, ultra-modern, built into the side of the hill and absolutely stunning.

The stairs led directly down to a huge room whose ceiling was half-open to the sky and whose floor was partly green carpet and partly swimming pool. There were sofas and coffee tables nearest the stairs and lounging chairs, bamboo with pink, white and green cushions, dotting the far poolside, out in the sun; and on either side wings of house spread out protectively, promising bedrooms and comfort and a life of delight. I looked at the spectacular and pretty room and thought no schoolmaster on earth could afford it.

"I was sitting over there," Jane Pitts said, pointing to the sunny side. "I nearly didn't answer the doorbell. I don't always bother."

We walked around there, passing white-trellised alcoves filled with plants and cushioned bamboo sofas with bathing towels casually thrown down. The pool water looked seagreen and peaceful, gleaming and inviting after my trudging search.

"Two of the girls are around somewhere," Jane said. "Melanie, our eldest, is married, of course. Ted and I will be grandparents quite soon."

"Incredible."

She smiled. "We married at college." She gestured to the chairs and I sat on the edge of one of the loungers while she spread out voluptuously on another. Beyond the house the lawn sloped grassily away to a wide sweeping view over northwest London, the horizon lost in misty purples and blues.

"This place is fantastic," I said.

She nodded. "We were so lucky to get it. We've only been here three months, but I think we'll stay forever." She pointed to the open roof. "This all closes over, you know. There are solar panels that slide across. They say the house is warm all winter."

I admired everything sincerely and asked if Ted were still teaching. She said without strain that he sometimes taught university courses in computer programing and that unfortunately he wouldn't be home until quite late the following evening. He would be so sorry to have missed me, she said.

"I would quite urgently like to talk to him."

She gently shook her head. "I don't honestly know where he is, except somewhere up near Manchester. He went this morning, but he didn't know where he'd be staying. In a motel somewhere, he said."

"What time would he be back tomorrow?"

"Late. I don't know."

She looked at the concern which must have shown plainly on my face and said apologetically, "You could come early on Sunday, if you like, if it's that important."

FIFTEEN

Saturday crawled.

Cassie wandered around with her plastered arm in a sling and Bananas jogged down to the cottage three or four times, both of them worried by the delay and not saying so. It had seemed reasonable on Thursday night to incarcerate Angelo, with his handiwork still appalling us in the sitting room and Cassie in pain, but by Saturday evening she and Bananas had clearly progressed through reservations and uneasiness to downright anxiety.

"Let him go," Bananas said, when he came late after closing time. "You'll be in real trouble if anyone finds out. He knows now that you're no pushover. He'd be too scared to come back."

I shook my head. "He's too arrogant to be scared. He'd want his revenge, and he'd come back to take it."

They stared miserably at each other. "Cheer up," I said. "I was ready to keep him for a week, two weeks, as long as it took."

"I just don't know," Bananas said, "how you could calmly go to the races."

I'd gone uncalmly to the races. Also to the gallops in the morning and to Mort's for breakfast, but no one I had seen could have guessed what was going on at home. Behind a public front I found it was fairly easy to hide an ongoing crime: hundreds of people did it, after all.

"I suppose he's still alive," Cassie said.

"He was up by the door swearing at four o'clock." Bananas looked at his watch. "Nine and a half hours ago. I shouted at him to shut up."

"And did he?"

"Just swore back."

I smiled. "He's not dead."

As if to prove it, Angelo started kicking the door and letting go with the increasingly familiar obscenities. I went into the kitchen and stood close to the barricade, and when he drew breath for the next verbal onslaught, I said loudly, "Angelo."

There was a brief silence, then a fierce growling shout: *"Bastard."*

"The light's going out in five minutes," I said.

"I'll kill you."

Maybe the heavily savage threat should have raised my goose bumps, but it didn't. He had been murderous too long, was murderous by nature, and I already knew it. I listened to his continuing rage and felt nothing.

"Five minutes," I said again, and left him.

In the sitting room Bananas was looking mildly piratical in his open-necked shirt and his sneakers and his four days' growth of harsh black beard, but he himself would never have made anyone walk the plank. The gloom and doom in his mind deplored what I was doing even while he condoned it, and I could almost sense him struggling anew with the old paradox that to defeat aggression one might have to use it.

He sat on the sofa and in short order drank two stiff

brandies with his arm around Cassie, who never minded. He was tired, he'd said, of us being out of his favorite tipple: he'd brought the bottle himself. "Have some ice cream with it?" Cassie had suggested, and he'd said seriously, "What flavor?"

I gave Angelo his five minutes and switched off the light, and there was a baleful silence from the cellar.

Bananas gave Cassie a bristly kiss, said she looked tired, said every plate in the pub needed washing, said "Barbados!" as a toast, and tossed back his drink. "God rest all prisoners. Good night."

Cassie and I watched his disappearing back. "He's half sorry for Angelo," she said.

"Mm. A fallacy always to think that because you feel sorry for the tiger in the zoo he won't eat you, given the chance. Angelo doesn't understand compassion. Not other people's for him. He feels none himself. In others he sees it as a weakness. So never, my darling, be kind to Angelo expecting kindness in return."

She looked at me. "You mean that as a warning, don't you?"

"You've a soft heart."

She considered for a moment, then found a pencil and wrote a message to herself in large letters on the white plaster.

REMEMBER TIGERS.

"Will that do?"

I nodded. "And if he says his appendix is bursting or he's suffering from bubonic plague, feed him some aspirins through the ventilation holes, and do it in a roll of paper, and not with your fingers."

"He hasn't thought of that yet."

"Give him time."

We went upstairs to bed, but as on the previous night I slept only in brief disturbed snatches, attuned the whole time to any noise from the cellar. Cassie slept more peacefully than before, the cast becoming less of a problem as she grew used to it. Her arm no longer hurt, she said; she simply felt tired. She said play would be resumed when the climate got better.

I watched the dark sky lighten to streaks of navy blue clouds across a somber orange glow, a strange brooding dawn like the aura of the man downstairs. Never before, I thought, had I entered a comparable clash of wills, never tested so searchingly my willingness to command. I had never thought of myself as a leader, and yet, looking back, I'd never had much stomach to be led.

In recent months I had found it easier than I'd expected to deal with Luke's five trainers, the power seeming to develop as the need arose. The power to keep Angelo in the cellar, that too had arisen not merely physically, but also in my mind. Perhaps one's capacity always expanded to meet the need: but what did one do when the need was gone? What did generals do with their full-grown hubris when the war was over? When the whole world no longer obeyed when they said jump?

I thought: unless one could adjust one's power-feelings perpetually to the current need, one could be headed for chronic dissatisfaction with the fall of fate. One could grow sour, power-hungry, despotic. I would shrink back, I thought, to the proper size, once Angelo was solved, once Luke's year was over. If one saw that one had to, perhaps one might.

The fierce sky slowly melted to mauve-gray clouds drifting over a sea of gold and lingeringly then to gentle white over palest blue, and I got up and dressed thinking that the sky's message was false: problems didn't fade with the sun and Cain was still downstairs.

Cassie's eyes, when I left, were saying all that her tongue wasn't. Hurry. Come back. I don't feel safe here with Angelo.

"Sit by the telephone," I said. "Bananas will run."

She swallowed. I kissed her and drove away, burning up the empty Sunday-early roads to Mill Hill. It was still only eight-thirty when I turned into Oaklands Road, the very earliest that Jane Pitts had said I could arrive, but she was already up and in a wet bathing suit to answer the doorbell.

"Come in," she said. "We're in the pool."

"We" were two lithely beautiful teenage girls and a stringy man going bald who swam without splashing, like a seal. The roof was open to the fair sky and a waiting breakfast of cereals and fruit stood ready on one of the low bamboo tables, and none of the Pitts seemed to mind or notice that the new day was still cool.

The stringy man slithered out onto the pool's edge in a sleek economical movement and stood shaking the water from his head and looking approximately in my direction.

"I'm Ted Pitts," he said, holding out a wet hand. "I can't see a damn thing without my glasses."

I shook the hand and smiled into the unfocused eyes. Jane walked around with some heavy black frames, which converted the brown fish into an ordinary short-sighted mortal, and he dripped around the pool beside me to where his towel lay on a lounging chair.

"William Derry?" he said, blotting water out of his ears.

"That's right."

"How's Jonathan?"

"Sends his regards."

Ted Pitts's smile was of comprehensive contentment. stopped abruptly and said, "It was you who told me where to get the form books."

All those years ago—information so casually given. I glanced around the amazing house and asked the uppermost question. "The betting system on those tapes," I said. "Did it really work?"

Ted Pitt's smile was of comprehensive contentment. "What do you think?" he said.

"All this—?"

"All this."

"I never believed in it," I said, "until I came here the other day."

He toweled his back. "It's fairly hard work, of course.

I shunt around a good deal. But with this to come back to . . . most rewarding."

"How long—" I said slowly.

"How long have I been gambling? Ever since Jonathan gave me the tapes. That first Derby . . . I borrowed a hundred quid with my car as security to raise some stake-money. It was madness, you know. I couldn't have afforded to lose. Sometimes in those days we had hardly enough to eat. It was pretty well desperation that made me do it. But of course the system looked mathematically OK, and it had already worked for years for the man who invented it."

"And you won?"

He nodded. "Five hundred. A fortune. I'll never forget that day, never. I felt so sick." He smiled vividly, the triumph still childlike in its simplicity. "I didn't tell anybody. Not Jonathan. Not even Jane. I didn't mean to do it again, you see. I was so grateful it had turned out all right, but the *strain* . . ." He dropped the damp towel over the arm of a chair. "And then, you know, I thought, why not?"

He watched his daughters dive into the pool with their arms around each other's waists. "I only taught for one more term," he said calmly. "I couldn't stand the head of the math department. Jenkins, his name was." He smiled. "It seems odd now, but I felt oppressed by the man. Anyway, I promised myself that if I won enough during the summer holidays to buy a computer, I would leave at Christmas, and if I didn't, I'd stay and use the school's computer still, and be content with a wager now and then."

Jane joined us, carrying a pot of coffee. "He's telling you how he started betting? I thought he was crazy."

"But not for long."

She shook her head, smiling. "When we moved out of our caravan into a house, bought it outright with Ted's winnings, then I began to believe it would last, that it was safe. And now here we are, so well off its embarrassing . . . and it's all thanks to your dear brother Jonathan."

The girls climbed dripping out of the pool and were

introduced as Emma and Lucy, hungry for breakfast. I was offered bran flakes, natural yoghurt, wheat germ and fresh peaches, which they all ate sparingly but with enjoyment.

I ate as well but thought inescapably of Angelo and of Cassie alone with him in the cottage. Those planks would hold. They'd kept him penned in for two whole days . . . no reason to think they'd fail this morning . . . no reason, just a strong feeling that I should have persuaded her to wait with Bananas.

It was over coffee, when the girls were again swimming and Jane had disappeared into the house, that Ted said, "How did you find me?"

I looked at him. "Don't you mean why?"

"I suppose so. Yes."

"I came to ask you to let me have copies of those tapes."

He breathed deeply and nodded. "That's what I thought."

"And will you?"

He looked at the shimmering pool for a while and then said, "Does Jonathan know you're asking?"

"Yeah. I asked him where the tapes were now, and he said if anyone knew, you would. You and only you, he said."

Ted Pitts nodded again and made up his mind. "It's fair. They're his, really. But I haven't any spare tapes."

"I brought some," I said. "They're out in the car. Can I fetch them?"

"All right." He nodded decisively. "I'll change into dry clothes while you're getting them."

I fetched the computer-type tapes I'd brought for the purpose, and he said "Six? You'll only need three."

"Two sets?" I suggested.

"Oh. Well, why not?" He turned away. "The computer's downstairs. Would you like to see it?"

"Very much."

He led the way into the body of the house and we went down some carpeted stairs to a lower floor. "Office," he said succinctly, leading the way into a normal-sized room from which one could see the same wide view of London as upstairs. "It's a bedroom really. Bathroom through there," he pointed. "Spare bedroom beyond."

The office was more accurately a sitting room with armchairs, television, bookshelves and pinewood paneling. On an upright chair by one wall stood a pair of well-used mountain-climbing boots, with the latest in thermal sleeping bags still half in its carton on the floor beside them. Ted followed my glance. "I'm off to Switzerland in a week or two. Do you climb?"

I shook my head.

"I don't attempt the peaks," he said earnestly. "I prefer walking, mostly." He pulled open a section of the pine paneling to reveal a long counter upon which stood a collection of electronic equipment. "I don't need all this for the racing programs," he said, "but I enjoy computers." And he ran his fingers caressingly over the metal surfaces with the ardor of a lover.

"I've never seen those racing programs," I said.

"Would you like to?"

"Please."

"All right." With the speed of long dexterity he fed a tape into a cassette recorder and explained he was putting the machine to search for the file name "Epsom."

"How much do you know about computers?" he said.

"There was one at school, way back. We played Space Invaders on it."

He glanced at me pityingly. "Everyone in this day and age should be able to write a simple program. Computer language is the universal tongue of the new world, as Latin was of the old."

"Do you tell your students that?"

"Er . . . yes."

The small screen suddenly announced READY? Ted pressed some keys on the keyboard and the screen asked WHICH RACE AT EPSOM? Ted typed DERBY, and the screen in a flash presented:

TWICE SHY

He put in his own name and randomly answered the ensuing questions, ending with:

HORSE'S NAME	WIN FACTOR
TED PITTS	24

"Simple," I said.

He nodded. "The secret is in knowing which questions to ask, and in the weighting given to the answers. There's nothing mysterious about it. Anyone could evolve such a system, given the time."

"Jonathan says there are several of them in the United States."

Ted nodded. "I've got one of them here." He opened a drawer and brought out what looked like a pocket calculator. "It's a baby computer with quite elegant programs," he said. "I bought it out of curiosity. It only works on American racing, of course, because one of its bases is that all tracks are identical in shape, left-handed ovals. It is geared chiefly for prize money. I understand that if you stick to its instruction book religiously you can certainly win, but of course like Liam O'Rorke's system, you have to work at it to get results."

"And never back a hunch?"

"Absolutely not," he said seriously. "Hunches are hopelessly unscientific."

I looked at him curiously. "How often do you go to the races?"

"To the races themselves? Practically never. I watch them, of course, on television, sometimes. But you don't need to, to win. All you need are the form books and objectivity."

It seemed to me a dry view of the world where I spent my life. Those beautiful creatures, their speed, their guts, their determination, all reduced to statistical probabilities and soulless microchips.

"These copies of yours," he said, "do you want them open, so that anyone can use them?"

"How do you mean?"

"If you like you can have them with passwords, so that they wouldn't work if anyone stole them from you."

"Are you serious?"

"Of course," he said, as if he were never anything else. "I've always put passwords on all my stuff."

"Er . . . how do you do it?"

"Easiest thing in the world. I'll show you." He flicked a few switches and the screen suddenly announced READY?

"You see that question mark," Ted said. "A question mark always means that the computer operator must answer it by typing something. In this case, if you don't type in the correct sequence of letters the program will stop right there. Try it. See what happens."

"I obediently typed EPSOM. Ted pressed the key marked ENTER. The screen gave a sort of flick and went straight back to READY?

Ted smiled. "The password on this tape is QUITE. Or it is at the moment. One can change the password easily." He typed QUITE and pressed ENTER and the screen flashed into WHICH RACE AT EPSOM?

"See the question mark?" Ted said. "It always needs an answer."

I thought about question marks and said I'd better not have passwords, if he didn't mind.

"Whatever you say."

He typed BREAK and LIST 10-80, and the screen suddenly produced a totally different-looking format.

"This is the program itself," Ted said. "See line 10?"

Line 10 read INPUT A$: IF A$ = "QUITE" THEN 20 ELSE PRINT "READY?"

Line 20 read PRINT "WHICH RACE AT EPSOM?"

"If you don't type QUITE," Ted said, "you never get to line 20."

"Neat," I agreed. "But what's to prevent you looking at

the program, like we are now, and seeing that you need to type QUITE?"

"It's quite easy to make it impossible for anyone to LIST the program. If you buy other people's programs, you can practically never LIST them. Because if you can't LIST them you can't make copies, and no one wants their work pinched in that way."

"Um," I said. "I'd like tapes you *can* LIST, and without passwords."

"OK."

"How do you get rid of the password?"

He smiled faintly, typed 10 and then pressed ENTER. Then he typed LIST 10-80 again, but this time when the program appeared on the screen there was no line 10 at all. Line 20 was the first.

"Elementary, you see," he said.

"So it is."

"It will take me quite a while to get rid of the passwords and make the copies," he said. "So why don't you go and sit upstairs by the pool. To be honest, I'd get on faster on my own."

Pleased enough to agree, I returned to the lazy bamboo loungers and listened to Jane talking about her daughters. An hour crawled by before Ted reappeared bearing the cassettes, and even then I couldn't leave without an instructional lecture.

"To run those tapes you'll need either an old Grantley personal computer, and there aren't many of them about nowadways—they're obsolete—or any type of company computer, as long as it will load from a cassette recorder."

He watched my incomprehension and repeated what he'd said.

"Right," I said.

He told me how to load Grantley BASIC, which was the first item on side 1 of the tapes, into a company computer, which had no language of its own built in. He again told me twice.

"Right."

"Good luck with them," he said.

I thanked him wholeheartedly, and Jane also, and as quickly as decently possible set off on the drive home.

Half a mile down the road, compelled by a feeling of dread, I stopped by the telephone booth and called Cassie. She answered at the very first ring and sounded uncharacteristically shaky.

"I'm so glad it's you," she said. "How long will you be?"

"About an hour."

"Do hurry."

"Is Angelo—?"

"He's been banging ever since you left and wrenching at the door. I've been in the kitchen. He's shaking those planks. He'll have the door off its hinges if he goes on and on. I can't strengthen the barricade. I've tried, but with one arm—"

"Cassie," I said, "go up to the pub."

"But—"

"Darling, go. Please go."

"What if he gets out?"

"If he gets out I want you safe up the road with Bananas."

"All right."

"I'll see you," I said, and disconnected. Drove like the furies toward home, taking a chance here and there and getting away with it. Across Royston Heath like a streak, weaving through pottering Sunday-outing traffic. Through the town itself; snarling down the last stretch, crossing the M11 motorway, and finally branching off the main road into Six Mile Bottom village.

Wondering all the way what Angelo would do if he did get free. Smash up the cottage? Set fire to it? Lie in wait somewhere for me to return.

The one thing he would not do was to go meekly away.

SIXTEEN

I walked carefully up the path to the lockless front door, which we no longer guarded with the chest because Cassie found climbing through the window too difficult.

The birds were singing in the garden. Would they sing if Angelo were among them, hidden in the bushes? No they wouldn't. I reached the door and pushed it open.

The cottage lay silent as if long deserted, and with spirits sinking I went through to the kitchen.

Angelo had ripped away one of the main timbers of the door and had dislodged two of the extra planks which had been wedging it shut. The door in fact was still closed, but the knife had gone from the latch.

The hole in the door was large enough to shove an arm through, but not to allow the passage of a grown man. The table and chairs and the two lowest planks hadn't shifted, but with the progress he'd made their stopping power was temporary. I had come home not a minute too soon.

"Angelo," I said.

He appeared almost instantly at the hole in the door,

scowling furiously at my return. He put both hands into the gap and violently tried to wrench away the wood from each side, and I saw that he had already been bleeding from his exertions.

"I'm going to let you out," I said. "You can save your strength."

"I'll get you." The deep growl again. The statement of intent.

"Yeah," I said. "I dare say. Now listen, because you'll want to hear."

He waited, eyes black with ferocity in the shadows.

I said, "You believe that my brother cheated you out of some computer tapes. They weren't yours to start with, but we'll not argue about that. At this moment *I* have those tapes. They're here in the cottage. It's taken me a good while to get them, which is why you've stayed here this long in the cellar. I'll give you those tapes. Are you listening?"

He wouldn't say so, but his attention was riveted.

"You spent fourteen years brooding over the fortune you lost. I'll give it to you. Fourteen years swearing to kill my brother. He's dead. You came here to do violent damage, and for that you could lose your parole. I'm prepared not to report you. In return for the computer tapes and for your continued freedom, you can clear out of here and henceforth leave me strictly alone."

He stared through the door with little change of expression, certainly without joy.

I said, "You may have been brooding over your revenge for so many years that you can't face not having the prospect of it there any longer to keep you going. You may fall apart from lack of purpose." I shrugged. "But *if* I give you liberty and the treasure you want, I'll expect the slate to be wiped clean between you and me." I paused. "Do you understand?"

He still said absolutely nothing.

"If you agree that what I'm offering is OK," I said, "you can throw out that knife you took from the door latch, and

I will give you the three tapes and the keys to your car, which is still where you left it."

Silence.

"If you choose not to accept that offer," I said, "I'll telephone to the police to come and fetch you, and they'll hear all about you breaking my friend's arm."

"They'll have you for keeping me in here."

"Maybe. But if they do you'll never get those tapes. And I mean it. *Never.* I'll destroy them immediately."

He went away from behind the door but after a long minute he reappeared.

"You'll trick me," he said. "Like your brother."

I shook my head. "It's not worth it. I want you out of my life altogether and permanently."

He made a fierce thrusting movement with his unshaven chin, a gesture which could be taken as assent.

"All right, then," he said. "Hand them over."

I nodded. Turned away from him. Went into the sitting room and sorted out one copy of each tape, shutting the three spares into a chest drawer. When I returned Angelo was still standing by the door—still suspicious, still wary.

"Tapes." I showed him. "Car keys." I held them up. "Where's the knife?"

He raised his hand and let me see it: a dinner knife, not oversharp, but destructive enough to be counted.

I laid the three cassettes on a small tray and held it out to him, and he put his arm through the hole to snatch them up.

"Now the knife," I said.

He dropped it out onto the tray. I slid it into my hand and replaced it with the keys.

"All right," I said. "Go down the steps. I'll undo the barricade. Then you can come up and go out. And if you've any thoughts of rushing me, just remember your parole."

He nodded sullenly.

"Have you still got that computer you bought fourteen years ago?"

"Dad smashed it. When I got sent up. Out of rage."

Like son, like father . . . "The tapes are still in the same computer language," I said. "Grantley BASIC. The language itself is there, on side 1. You'll need to know that."

He scowled. Beyond him entirely to be placated, let alone pleased.

"Go on," I said. "I'll unbar the door."

He disappeared from the impromptu window, and I tugged away the effective planks and pulled the table and chairs from their stations, and stood finally out of his arms' reach behind them.

"Come up," I called. "Undo the latch and be on your way."

He came out fast, clutching the cassettes in one blood-stained hand and the keys in the other, gave me a brief hard stare which nonetheless held little of the former menace, and disappeared through the sitting room toward the front door. I followed and watched him go down the path, first quickening his step and almost running as he turned into the lane and then fairly sprinting out of sight toward where he'd left the car. In a short time he came blasting back again, driving as if he feared I would still somehow stop him; but in truth all I did want was to be rid of him once and for all.

The empty cellar stank like the lair of an animal.

I looked into it briefly and decided it was a job for a shovel, a hose, a broom and some strong disinfectant; and while I was collecting those things Bananas and Cassie walked anxiously along from the pub.

"We saw you come," she said, "and we saw him go. I wanted to be here but Bananas said it might snarl things up."

"He was right." I kissed her soundly, both from love and tension release. "Angelo hates to lose face."

"You gave him the tapes?" Bananas asked.

"Yeah."

"And may they choke him," Cassie said.

I smiled. "They may not. I'd guess Ted Pitts is worth a million."

"Really?" Her eyebrows shot up. "Then why don't we—"

"It takes time and work. Ted Pitts lives right at the London end of the M1, half a mile off the country's biggest artery. I'll bet he spends countless days beating up that road to towns in the North, traipsing around betting shops, sucking his honey. It's what I guess he does, anyway. He was near Manchester yesterday, his wife said. A different town every day, so that no one gets to know him."

"What difference would that make?" Bananas said.

I explained what happened to constant winners. "I'll bet there isn't a single bookie who knows Ted Pitts by sight."

"If *you* did it," Bananas said thoughtfully, "I suppose they'd know you at once."

I shook my head. "Only on the racecourse. Round the backstreet betting shops in any big town I'd be just another mug."

They both looked at me expectantly.

"Yeah," I said. "I can just see me spending my life that way."

"Think of the loot," Bananas said.

"And no tax," said Cassie.

I thought of Ted Pitts's splendid house and of my own lack of amassed goods. Thought of him walking the upper slopes of Swiss mountains, restoring his spirit, wandering but coming home. Thought of my lack of a settled life-pattern and my hatred of being tied down. Thought of the way I'd enjoyed the past months, making decisions, running a business, knowing all the time it was just for a year, not a lifetime, and being assured by such impermanency. Thought of spending hot summer days and wet winter afternoons in betting shops, playing the percentages, joylessly, methodically making a million.

"Well?" Bananas said.

"Maybe one day, when I'm hungry."

"You've no sense."

"You do it then," I said. "Give up the pub. Give up the cooking. Take to the road."

He stared at me while he thought of it, then he grimaced and said, "There's more to life than making money. Not a lot, but some."

"One of these days," said Cassie with sweet certainty, "you'll both do it. Not even a saint could sit on a goldmine and be too lazy to pick up the nuggets."

"You think it's just lazy?"

"I sure do. Where's your buccaneering heart? Where's the glint of piracy? What about the battle cry of those old north-country industrialists—'where there's muck there's brass'?" She looked alight with enthusiasm, a glow I guessed derived as much from Angelo's absence as from the thought of an available fortune.

"If you feel the same when I've finished for Luke Houston," I said, "I'll give it a trial. Just for a while."

"Picky," she said. "That's what you are."

All the same it was in better spirits that I set about cleaning the cellar and making it fit for fishing gear to live in; and in the late afternoon all three of us sat in the sun on the cottage grass while Cassie and Bananas discussed how they would spend the loot they thought I would inevitably chase.

They already felt as I did that Angelo's revengeful lust had been at last dissipated, and they said he had even done us a favor as without his violent attack I would never have sought out Ted Pitts.

"Good can come out of bad," Cassie said with satisfaction.

And bad of good, I thought. Jonathan's conjuring tricks had trapped Angelo thoroughly and made it certain that he would be convicted empty-handed. Had ensured that for fourteen years Angelo would be unable to kill anyone else. But that particular good sequence of actions which had seemed so final at the time had proved to be only a plug for a simmering volcano. The psychopathic young man had at length erupted as a full-blown coarsened thug, no longer as Jonathan had described him, occasionally high on the drug of recklessness, but more plainly, comprehensively, violent.

Time changes perspectives. From disasters could come successes, and from successes, disasters. A pity, I thought, that one could never perceive whether to weep or cheer at the actual event.

Our lives gradually quietened to sensible proportions. Cassie went back to work in a sling, and Bananas invented a new delight involving liquid spiced beef; and I began a series of forays to stud farms to take preliminary peeks at the yearlings soon to be offered at the sales, all too aware that the climax of my year was approaching, the test by which Luke would judge me, looking back. To buy young stock that would win would be satisfactory; to buy a colt to sire a dynasty would be luck. Somewhere between the two there lay an area in which judgment would turn out to have been good, indifferent or absent, and it was there that I hoped to make as few mistakes as possible.

For about a week I moseyed around all over the place with detours to race meetings and to Luke's two trainers in Berkshire, and spent every spare waking minute with the stud book. Sim Shell said severely that he wished to be present and in full consultation whenever I bought anything for him personally to train, and Mort with every nerve twitching asked for Sir Ivor, Nijinsky and Northern Dancer, all at once, and at the very least.

Cassie came with me to the evening session on the first day of the sales, roaming about on the forever legs and listening engrossed to the gossip. Every year, Newmarket sale ring saw fortunes lost quicker than crashing stock markets, but the talk was all of hope and expectation, of slashing speed and breeding potential, all first-day euphoria and unspent checks.

"What excitement," Cassie said. "You can see it in every face."

"The joy of acquisition. Disillusion comes next week.

Then optimistic gloom. Then, if you're lucky, complacent relief."

"But today—"

"Today," I nodded. "There's still the chance of buying the winner of the Derby."

I bought two colts and a filly on that evening for staggering sums, reassured to a point by having competed against top echelons of bloodstock agents but pursued by the sapping fear that it was I who had pressed on too far, not they who had stopped too soon.

We stayed to the end of the program, partly because of Cassie's fascination with a new world but also because it was when the big buyers had gone home that a bargain sometimes arose, and I did in fact buy the last lot of the day, a thin-looking ponylike creature, because I liked his bright eyes.

The breeder thanked me. "Is it really for Luke Houston?"

"Yes," I said.

"He won't be sorry. He's intelligent, that little colt."

"He looks it."

"He'll grow, you know," he told me earnestly. "His dam's family are all late growers. Come and have a drink. It isn't every day I sell one to Luke Houston."

We went back, however, to drink and eat with Bananas, and from there to the cottage, where I sent off a Telex to Luke, for whom our midnight was three in the afternoon.

Luke liked Telexes. If he wanted to discuss what I'd sent, he would telephone after his evening dinner, catching me at six in the morning before I left for the gallops, but more normally he would reply by Telex or not at all.

The dining room was filled with equipment provided by Luke: a videodisc recorder for rewatching and analyzing past races, a print-out calculator, a photocopier, a row of filing cabinets, an electric typewriter, the Telex machine and a complicated affair which answered the telephone, took messages, gave messages, and recorded every word it heard, including my own live conversations. It worked on a separate line from the telephone in the sitting room, a good arrangement which most simply divorced our private calls from his business, allowing me to pay for one and him the other. All he hadn't given me—or had had me collect from an unwilling Warrington Marsh—was a computer.

When I came down the following morning I found the Telex had chattered during the night.

WHY DIDN'T YOU BUY. THE FISHER COLT? WHY DID YOU BUY THE CHEAP COLT? GIVE MY BEST TO CAS-SIE.

He had never actually met Cassie but only talked to her a few times on the telephone. The politeness was his way of saying his questions were simply questions, not accusations. Any Telexes which came without "best to Cassie" were jump-to-it matters.

I Telexed back.

TWO PRIVATE OWNERS WHO DETEST EACH OTHER, SCHUBMAN AND MRS. CRICKINGTON, BEAT EACH OTHER UP TO 340,000 FOR THE FISHER COLT, WAY BEYOND ITS SENSIBLE VALUE. THE CHEAP COLT MIGHT SURPRISE YOU YET. REGARDS, WILLIAM.

Cassie these days was being collected and brought back by a slightly too friendly man who lived near the pub and worked a street away from Cassie in Cambridge. She said he was putting his hand on her knee instead of the steering wheel increasingly often and she would be extremely glad to be rid of both him and the cast. In other respects than driving, the cast had been accommodated, and our nighttime activities were back to their old joy.

By day we slowly repaired or replaced everything which had been smashed, using as references the pieces Bananas had stacked in the garage. Television, vases, lamps, all as near as possible to the originals. Even six corn dollies hung again in their mobile group, dollies freshly and intricately woven from the shiny stalks of the new harvest by an elderly lady who said you had to cut the corn for them specially nowadays by hand, because combine harvesters chopped the straw too short.

Bananas thought that replacing the corn dollies might be going too far, but Cassie said darkly that they represented pagan gods who should be placated, and deep in the countryside *you never knew . . .*

I carpentered new pieces into both the damaged doors and fitted a new lock to the front. All traces of Angelo gradually vanished, all except his baseball bat which lay along the sill of the window which faced the road. We had consciously kept it there to begin with as a handy weapon in case he should come back, but even as day after peaceful day gave us a growing sense of ease we let it lie: another hostage to the evil eye, perhaps.

Jonathan telephoned me one evening, and although I was sure he wouldn't approve of what I'd done, I told him everything that had happened.

"You kept him in the *cellar?*"

"Yeah."

"Good God."

"It seems to have worked."

"Mm. I can't help being sorry that Angelo finally has the system."

"I know. I'm sorry too, after all you did to keep it from him. I really hated giving it to him. But you were right, he's dangerous, and I don't want to vanish to California; the life I want is right here on English turf. And about the system—don't forget, it isn't enough just to possess it. You'd have to operate it discreetly. Angelo knows just about nothing about racing, and he's impetuous and undisciplined, not cunning and quiet."

"He may also," Jonathan said, "think that the system gives a winner every time, which it doesn't. Old Mrs. O'Rorke said it steadily gave an average of one winner in three."

"Angelo versus the bookies should be quite a match. And by the way, I told him you were dead."

"Thanks very much."

"Well you didn't want him turning up one day on your sunny doorstep, did you?"

"He'd never get a visa."

"You can walk across the Canadian border," I said, "without anyone being the wiser."

"And the Mexican," he agreed.

I told him in detail about Ted Pitts's house, and he sounded truly pleased. "And the little girls? How are they?"

"Grown up and pretty."

"I envied him those children."

"Did you?"

"Yes. Well, there you are. It's the way life turns out."

I listened to the regret in his voice and understood how much he himself had wanted a daughter, a son... and I thought that I too would regret it one day if I didn't... and that maybe it would be terrific fun if Cassie...

"Are you still there?" he said.

"Yeah. If I get married, will you come over to the wedding?"

"I don't believe it."

"You never know. I haven't asked her yet. She might not want to."

"Keep me posted." He sounded amused.

"Yeah. How's Sarah?"

"Fine, thanks."

"So long," I said, and he said, "So long," and I put down the receiver with the usual feeling of thankfulness that I had a brother, and that he was specifically Jonathan.

More days passed. By the end of the first week's sales I'd bought twelve yearlings for Luke and lost five more to higher bidders, and I'd consulted with Sim until he was sick of it and given Mort a filly that was on her toes if not actually a Dancer, and spent two evenings in the Bedford Arms with the Irish trainer Donavan, listening to his woes and watching him get drunk.

"There's more good horses in Ireland than ever come out," he said, wagging an unsteady finger under my nose.

"I'm sure."

"You want to come over, now. You want to poke around them studs, now, before you go to the sales."

"I'll come over soon," I said. "Before the next sales, two weeks from now."

"You do that." He nodded sagely. "There's a colt I have my eye on, way down below Wexford. I'd like to train that colt, now. I'd like for you to buy that little fella for Luke, that I would."

In that particular year, as a trial, the first Newmarket Yearling Sales had been held early, at the beginning of September. The Premium Sales, when most of the bluest-blooded youngsters would come under the hammer, were as usual at the end of the month. The colt Donavan had his eye on was due to be sold two weeks ahead, but unfortunately not only Donavan had his eye on it. The whole of Ireland and most of England seemed also to have their optics swiveled that way. Even allowing for Irish exaggeration, that colt seemed the best news of the season.

"Luke would want that fella, now," Donavan said.

"I'll bid for it," I said mildly.

He peered boozily into my face. "What you want to do, now, is to get Luke to say there's no ceiling. No ceiling, that's the thing."

"I'll go to Luke's limit."

"You're a broth of a boy, now. And it's write to Luke I did, I'll admit it, to say you were as green as a pea and no good to man nor horse, not in the job he'd given you."

"Did you?"

"Well, now, if you get me that little colt I'll write again and say I was wrong." He nodded heavily and half fell off the barstool. He was never drunk on the gallops or at the races or indeed by the sale ring itself, but at all other times ... probably. The owners didn't seem to mind and nor did the horses: drunk or sober Donavan produced as many winners year by year as anyone in Ireland. I didn't like or dislike him. I did business with him before ten in the morning and listened intently in the evenings, the time when through clouds of whisky he spoke the truth. Many thought him uncouth, and so he was. Many thought Luke would have chosen a smoother man with tidier social manners, but perhaps Luke had seen and heard Donavan's intimate way with horses, as I now did, and preferred the priceless goods to a gaudier package. I had come to respect Donavan. Two solid days of his company were quite enough.

When the flood of purchasing trainers and agents and go-it-alone owners had washed out of town temporarily, Sim gave a brown short-necked filly a final workout and afterward rather challengingly told me she was as ready as could be to win the last race on St. Leger day, that Saturday.

"She looks great," I said. "A credit to your care."

Sim half scowled. "You'll be going to Doncaster, I suppose?"

I nodded. "Staying up there, Friday night. Mort's running Genotti in the St. Leger."

"Will you help me saddle mine up?" Sim said.

I tried to hide my astonishment at this olive branch of epic proportions. He usually attempted to keep me as far from the runners as possible.

"Be glad to," I said.

He nodded with customary brusqueness. "See you there, then."

"Good luck."

He was going up on the Wednesday for the whole of the four-day meeting, but I didn't particularly want to, not least because Cassie still found it difficult to manage on her own with the rigid arm. I left her on the Friday, though, and drove to Doncaster, and almost the first person I saw as I walked through the racecourse gates was Angelo.

I stopped abruptly and turned aside, willing him not to spot me, not to speak.

He was buying two racecards from one of the booths near the entrance, holding up the queue while he sorted out coins.

I suppose it was inevitable I would one day see him if he took to racegoing at all often, but somehow it was still quite a shock. I was glad when he turned away from the booth in the opposite direction to where I stood: there might be a truce between us but it was fragile at best.

I watched while he barged his way through the swelling crowd with elbows like battering rams and thighs like rocks: and he was heading not to anywhere where he could place a bet but toward the less populated area near the rails of the track itself, where supporters had not yet flocked to see the first race. Reaching the rails, he stopped beside an elderly man in a wheelchair and unceremoniously thrust one of the racecards into his hands. Then he turned immediately on his heel and bulled his way purposefully toward the serried ranks of bookmakers inside the stands, where I lost sight of him, thankfully, for the rest of the day.

He was back, however, on the Saturday. Although I seldom bothered with gambling I decided to have a small bet on Genotti in the St. Leger, infected no doubt by Mort's fanatical eagerness, and as I stood near a little Welsh bookmaker whom I'd long known I saw Angelo, thirty feet away, frowning heavily over a small notebook.

"Genotti," my bookmaker friend said to his clerk, who wrote down every transaction in the book. "Three tenners at fives, William Derry."

"Thanks, Taff," I said.

Along the row Angelo began arguing about a price on offer, which was apparently less than he thought fair.

"Everyone else is at five to one." His voice was a growl which I knew all too well.

"Try someone else, then. It's fours to you, *Mister* Gilbert."

With half my mind I was satisfied that Angelo was indeed rushing in stupidly with the system where Liam O'Rorke and Ted Pitts had taken care not to tread, but I was also uneasy that he should be arousing opposition so soon. I positively needed for him to win for a while. I'd never envisaged him sticking to the anonymous drudgery required for long-term success, but the honeymoon period should not already have been over.

Taff-the-bookmaker glanced over his shoulder at the altercation and gave his clerk an eyes-to-heaven gesture.

"What's all the fuss about?" I asked.

"He's a right gitt, that man." Taff divided his comment impartially between me, his clerk, and the world in general.

"Angelo Gilbert."

Taff's gaze sharpened on me directly. "Know him, do you?"

"Somebody pointed him out. He murdered somebody, years ago."

"That's right. Just out of the jug, he is. And *stupid*—you wouldn't credit it."

"What's he done?"

"He came up to York last week with a fistful of banknotes, laying it about as if there were no tomorrow, and us not knowing who he was at that moment. And there's us thinking we were all taking lollipops off a baby when, whammo, this outsider he'd invested about six big ones on comes cantering in from nowhere and we're all paying out and wincing and scratching our heads over where he got the info, because the trainer hadn't had as much as a quid on, as far as we knew. So Lancer, that bloke along there arguing with this Gilbert, he asks this geezer straight out who'd put him onto the winner, and that stupid gitt smirked and said Liam O'Rorke did."

Taff peered at my face, which I felt must have mirrored my feeling of inner shock, but apparently it merely looked blank, because Taff, who was a good sixty-plus, made a clicking sound with his mouth and said, "Before your time, I suppose."

"What was?"

Taff's attention was torn away by several customers who crowded to place bets, and he seemed vaguely surprised to see me still there when they'd gone.

"Are you that interested?" he asked.

"Got nothing else to do."

Taff glanced along to where Angelo had been, but Angelo had gone. "Thirty years ago. Thirty-five. Time goes so quick. There was this old Irishman, Liam O'Rorke, he'd invented the only system I ever knew that would guarantee you'd win. Course, once we'd cottoned to him we weren't all that keen to take his bets. I mean, we wouldn't be, would we, knowing he had the edge on us somehow. Anyway, he would never part with his secret, how he did it, and it went with him to the grave, and good riddance, between you and me."

"And now?"

"And now here's this geezer rocking us back on our heels with this huge win at York and then he's sneering at us and calling us mugs, and saying we don't know what's hit us yet, and what he's using on us is Liam O'Rorke's old system resurrected. And now he's all indignant and complaining that we won't give him a good price. Acting all hurt and angry." Taff laughed contemptuously. "I mean, how stupid can you get?"

SEVENTEEN

Genotti won the St. Leger by an easy four lengths.

Mort's excitement afterward seemed to levitate him visibly off the ground, the static electricity about him crackling in the dry September sunshine. He wrung my hand with bone-scrunching enthusiasm and danced around the unsaddling enclosure giving rapturous responses to all who congratulated, reacting with such uncomplicated delight to his victory that he had all the crowd smiling. It was easy, I reflected, to think of Mort as simple through and through, whereas, I had gradually discovered, he traversed tortuous routes through mental mazes where pros and cons battled like chessmen to arrive at the plans and solutions that seemed so obvious once they had turned out to be right.

I collected my winnings from Taff, who gloomily said he would never have given anyone five to one if he'd known beforehand that Genotti was Angelo Gilbert's fancy.

"Did Angelo win?" I asked.

"Of course he did. He must have had a grand on. None of us would take his money at the finish."

"So he didn't get fives?"

"More like evens," he said sourly.

At evens Angelo would still have doubled his money, but for Angelo that might not be enough. Grievance, I could see, might raise a very ugly head.

"No system could win every single time," I said. "Angelo won't."

"I dare say not," Taff said with obstinacy. "But you can take it from me that no bookie on the racecourse will in future give that arrogant so-and-so much more than evens, even if what he's backing is lame on three legs, carrying two stone overweight and ridden by my old dad."

"At evens he wouldn't win over all," I said.

"So who's crying? We're not in the loving-kindness business, you know."

"Fleece the mugs?"

"You got it."

He began paying out other successful punters with the rapidity of long practice, but it was seldom that he would go home from a racetrack with less cash than he'd brought. Few bookmakers were gamblers at heart and only the good mathematicians survived.

I drifted away from him and drank some champagne with the similarly fizzing Mort and a little later helped Sim to saddle the filly, who made it another hooray-for-Houston day by a short head. Sim took it more calmly than Mort, but with a satisfaction at least as deep, and he seemed to be admitting and acknowledging at last that I was not an ignorant bossy upstart but a well-meaning colleague and that all Luke's successes worked for our joint good. I wasn't sure how or why his attitude had changed. I knew only that a month earlier a friendly drink together in a racecourse bar to celebrate a Houston winner would have been unthinkable.

Thinking more of Mort and Sim and the horses than of the still-active specter of Angelo, I drove from Doncaster to collect Cassie, and from there to a late dinner with Bananas. He too, it appeared, had backed Genotti, more than doubling my own winnings.

"I had a hundred on," he said.

"I didn't know you ever bet."

"On the quiet, now and then. Hearing all I do, how could I not?"

"So what did you hear about Genotti?"

He looked at me pityingly. "Every time you've seen that colt work on the gallops you've come back like a kid with tickets to the Cup Final."

"More to the point," Cassie said, "if you'd used Liam O'Rorke's system, would it have come up with Genotti?"

"Ah." I read Bananas' new menu and wondered what he meant by Prisoner Chicken. Said casually, "Angelo Gilbert backed him"

"What?"

I explained about Angelo, the bookmakers, and stupidity in general.

"He's blown it," Cassie said, not without satisfaction.

I nodded. "Into fragments."

Bananas looked at me thoughtfully. "What's it going to do for the dear man's temper?"

"It's not William's fault," Cassie said.

"That trifle didn't stop him before."

Cassie looked frowningly alarmed. "What's Prisoner Chicken?" I said.

Bananas smirked. "Breast of chicken marinated in lemon juice and baked under matchstick-thin bars of herb pastry."

"It sounds dry," I said with jaundice.

"Bread and water are optional extras."

Cassie laughed, and Angelo retreated a little. We ate the Prisoner Chicken, which was predictably a delight of juice and flavor and reminded us not at all of its inspiration.

"I'm going to Ireland tomorrow," I said to Cassie. "Like to come?"

"Ireland? There and back?"

I nodded. "To see a man about a horse."

"What else?"

So we spent some of my winnings on her fare, and went down south of Wexford to see the colt all the world wanted: and half the world, it seemed, was there on the same errand, standing around an untidy stable yard with blank faces all carefully not expressing identical inner thoughts.

Cassie watched as the beautifully coupled brown yearling skittered around under the calming hands of the stud groom and unprofessionally pronounced him "sweet."

"A money machine on the hoof," I said. "Look at the greed in all those shuttered faces."

"They just seem uninterested to me."

"Enthusiasm puts the price up."

One or two of the bored-looking onlookers advanced to run exploratory hands down the straight young bones, stepping back with poker-playing noncommittal eyes, the whole procedure hushed as if in church.

"Aren't you going to feel its legs?" Cassie asked.

"Might as well."

I took my turn in the ritual and found, like everyone else, that the young limbs were cool and firm with tendons like fiddle strings in all the right places. There was also a good strong neck, a well-shaped quarter and most importantly a good depth of chest. Quite apart from his pedigree, which resounded with Classic winners, one couldn't, I thought, even imagine a better looking animal: all of which meant that the bidding at the sale on Wednesday would rise faster than Bananas Frisby.

We flew thoughtfully back to England and I sent a Telex to Luke.

BIDDING FOR THE HANSEL COLT WILL BE ASTRO-NOMICAL. I'VE SEEN HIM. HE IS WITHOUT FAULT. HOW HIGH DO YOU WANT ME TO GO?

To which, during the night, I received a reply.

IT'S YOUR JOB, FELLA. YOU DECIDE.

Ouch, I thought. Where is the ceiling? How high is disaster?

Newmarket filled up again for the new week of sales, the most important program of yearling sales of the whole season. Everyone in racing with money to spend brought determination and dreams, and the four-legged babies came in horseboxes from just up the road, from Kent and Cotswolds, from Devon and Scotland, from across the Irish Sea.

The Hansel colt from Wexford was due to be sold at the prime time of seven-thirty on the Wednesday evening, and by seven the high-rising banks of seats of the sale ring were invisible under a sea of bodies, Cassie somewhere among them. Down near the floor in the pen reserved for probable bidders Donavan was breathing heavily at my elbow as he had been all afternoon determinedly sober and all the gloomier for it.

"Now you get that little colt, now, you get him for me." If he'd said it once he'd said it a hundred times, as if repetition of desire could somehow make the purchase certain.

They brought the colt into the ring in the sudden hush of a host of lungs holding back their breath all at once, and the light gleamed on the walking gem, and he did in truth look like a prince who could sire a dynasty.

The bidding for him started not in thousands but in tens of thousands, leaping in seconds to the quarter million and racing away beyond. I waited until the first phase and raised the price by a giant twenty-five thousand, to be immediately capped by a decisive nod from an agent along to my right. I raised another twenty-five and lost it as quickly, and another, and another: and I could go on nodding, I thought, until my head fell off. Nothing easier in the world than spending someone else's money as fast as zeros running through the meter on a petrol pump.

At eight hundred thousand guineas I just stopped. The auctioneer looked at me inquiringly. I didn't blink. "Against you, sir," he said.

"Go on," said Donavan, thinking I'd merely overlooked that it was my turn. "Go on, go on."

I shook my head. Donavan turned and literally punched me on the arm in an agony of fear that my dithering would lose him the colt. "Go on, it's you. Bid, you bugger, bid."

"Any more, sir?" the auctioneer said.

I again shook my head. Donavan kicked my leg. The auctioneer looked around the silent sale ring. "All done, then?" he said. And after a lifetime's pause his gavel came down sharply, the clap of opportunity gone for ever. "Sold to Mr. O'Flaherty. Next lot, please."

Under the buzz of comment that followed the supercolt out of the ring, Donavan thrust a furious purple face toward mine and yelled uninhibitedly, "You buggering *bastard*. Do you know who bought that colt?"

"Yes I do."

"I'll kill you, so I will."

Shades of Angelo . . .

"There's no reason," I said, "why Luke should pay for your feud with Mick O'Flaherty."

"That colt will win the Derby."

I shook my head. "You're *afraid* it will."

"I'll write to Luke, so I will. I'll tell him it's you who's afraid. Bloody English. I'd kill the lot of you."

He stalked away with rage pouring visibly from every pore, and I watched him with regret because I would indeed have liked to buy him his little fellow and seen him croon over him to make him a champion.

"Why did you stop?" Cassie asked, taking my arm.

"Does it worry you?"

She blinked. "You know what they're saying?"

"That I didn't have the nerve to go on?"

"It was just that I heard—"

I smiled lopsidedly. "My first big battle, and I retreated. Something like that?"

"Something."

"O'Flaherty and Donavan hate each other so much it curdles their judgment. I meant to go as far as seven hundred and fifty thousand guineas and I thought I'd get the colt, I really did, because that's an extremely high price for any yearling. I went one bid higher still, but it wasn't enough. O'Flaherty was standing behind his agent prodding him in the back to make him carry on. I could see him. O'Flaherty was absolutely determined to buy the colt. To spite Donavan, I think. It isn't sense to go on bidding against someone compelled by raw emotion . . . so I stopped."

"But what if he *does* win the Derby?"

"About ten thousand thoroughbred colts were born last year in the British Isles alone. Then there's France and America, too. *One* colt from that huge crop will win the Derby the year after next, when he's three. The odds are against it being this one."

"You're so cool."

"No," I said truthfully. "Bruised and disgruntled."

We drove home and I sent the Telex to Luke.

REGRET UNDERBIDDER AT EIGHT HUNDRED AND FORTY THOUSAND POUNDS EXCLUDING TAX FOR HANSEL COLT. DONAVAN'S DEADLY RIVAL MICK O'FLAHERTY SUCCESSFUL AT EIGHT HUNDRED AND SIXTY-SIX THOUSAND TWO FIFTY. DONAVAN FURIOUS. SACK ME IF YOU LIKE. REGARDS, WILLIAM.

The return message came within an hour.

IF THE COLT WINS THE DERBY YOU OWE ME TEN MILLION POUNDS. OTHERWISE YOU ARE STILL EMPLOYED. BEST TO CASSIE.

"Thank God for that," she said. "Let's go to bed."

Two busy days later I dropped her at work and drove on southwestward to Berkshire to visit Luke's other trainers during the morning and to go on to see three of their horses race at Newbury in the afternoon; and there again on the racecourse was Angelo.

This time he saw me immediately before I had time to dodge; he came charging across a patch of grass, took roughly hold of my lapel, and told me the betting system didn't work.

"You sold me a pup. You'll be sorry." He looked quickly around as if hoping to find us both on deserted moorland, but as there was only concrete, well populated, he smothered his obvious wish to slaughter me there and then. He was physically tougher, I thought. Less pale, less puffy; the effects of long imprisonment giving way to a healthy tan and tighter muscles, the bull-like quality of the body intensifying. The black eyes . . . cold as ever. I looked at his re-emerging malevolence and didn't like it a bit.

I pulled his hand off my lapel and dropped it. "There's nothing wrong with the system," I said. "It's not my fault you've been trampling all over it like a herd of elephants."

His voice came back in the familiar bass register. "If I'm still losing by five tomorrow I'll *know* you've conned me. And I'll come after you. That's a promise."

He turned away abruptly and strode off toward the stands, and in a while I went in search of Taff among the bookmakers.

"The latest on Angelo Gilbert?" He looked down at me from his raised position on an inverted beer crate. "He's nuts."

"Are you still offering him rotten odds?"

"Look you, Mr. Derry, I'm too busy to talk now." He was indeed surrounded by eager customers holding out cash. "If you want to know, buy me a pint after the last race."

"Right," I said. "It's a deal." And at the end of the afternoon he came with me into the crowded bar and shouted the unexpected news into my attentive ear.

"That man Angelo's gone haywire. He won big money at York, like I told you, and a fair amount at Doncaster, but before York it seems he lost a packet at Epsom and last Monday he kissed goodbye to a fortune at Goodwood, and today he's plunged on two horses who finished out of sight.

So we're all back to giving him regular odds. Old Lancer—
he works for Joe Glickstein—Honest Joe—you must have
seen his stands at all the tracks?" I nodded. "Well, Old
Lancer, he took a thousand in readies this afternoon off that
Angelo on Pocket Handbook, what couldn't win if it started
yesterday. I mean, the man's a screwball. He's no more
playing Liam O'Rorke's system than I'm a bleeding fairy."

I watched him drink his beer, feeling great dismay that
Angelo couldn't manage the system even to the extent of
letting it find him the right horses. He had to be guessing
some of the answers to the multifarious questions instead
of looking them up accurately in the form books: skipping
the hard work out of laziness and still trusting the scores
which the computer returned. But a computer couldn't ad-
vise him, couldn't tell him that omitting an answer here and
an answer there would upset all those delicately balanced
weightings and inevitably distort the all-important win factors.

Angelo was dumb, dim, stupid.

Angelo would think it was my fault.

"They say his father's getting tired of it," Taff said.

"Who?"

"That Angelo person's father. Old Harry Gilbert. Made
a packet out of bingo halls, they say, before he got struck."

"Er, struck?"

Taff brought a lined brown outdoor face out of the beer
mug. "Struck down with arthritis, I think it is. He can't
hardly walk, anyway. Comes to the races sometimes in a
wheelchair, and it's him what has the cash."

Enlightened I thought back to the previous week at Doncaster, seeing in memory Angelo giving a racecard to an
elderly chairbound man. Angelo's father—still indulgent,
still supportive, still paying for his deadly middle-aged son.

I thanked Taff for his information. "What's this Angelo
to you?" he said.

"A long-time no friend of my brother's."

He made an accepting motion with his head, looked at

his watch and finished his beer at a gulp, saying he'd left his clerk looking after the day's takings and he'd be happier having his mitts on them himself. "We've all had a good day," he said cheerfully, "with those two odds-on favorites getting stuffed."

I drove homeward and collected Cassie, who was waiting at the hospital after a what they had called a progress assessment.

"Plaster off next week," she complained. "I wanted it off this afternoon, but they wouldn't."

The plaster by then was itching badly, the "REMEMBER TIGERS" was fading, Cassie was insisting that her arm *felt* mended and impatience had definitely set in.

We again went to the sales: I seemed to have spent half a lifetime around that sale ring, and Luke now owned twenty-eight yearlings he had not yet seen. I had signed checks on his behalf for nearly two million pounds and was tending to dream about it at night. There was only the Saturday morning left now, an undistinguished program according to the catalogue, the winding-down after the long excitements of the week. I went early by habit and with only short premeditation bought very cheaply the first lot of the day, an undistinguished-looking liver chestnut colt whose blood-lines were sounder to the inspection than his spindly legs. One couldn't have foretold on that misty autumn morning that *this* was the prince who would sire a dynasty, but that in the end was what happened. My mind, as I signed for him and arranged for him to be sent along the road to Mort's stable, was more immediately on the conversation I'd had with Jonathan on the telephone the evening before.

"I want to talk to Angelo's father," I said. "Do you remember where he lived?"

"Of course I do. Welwyn Garden City. If you give me a minute I'll find the street and the number." There was a pause while he searched. "Here we are. Seventeen, Pemberton Close. He may have moved, of course, and don't forget, William, he won't be the least pleasant. I heard he was threatening all sorts of dire revenges against me after Angelo was convicted, but I didn't hang around long enough for him to get going."

"Angelo seems to depend on him for cash," I said.

"That figures."

"Angelo's making a right balls-up of the betting system. He's losing his father's money and he's blaming me for it, and stoking up again toward volcanic eruption with me as the designated target for the lava flow."

"He's an absolute pest."

"He sure is. How does one rid oneself of a monster that won't go away? Don't answer that. Engineering Angelo back into jail permanently is all I can think of, and even then I would need to do it so that he didn't know who'd done it; and would it even on the whole be fair?"

"Provocation? Put a crime in his way and invite him to commit it?"

"As you say."

"No, it wouldn't exactly be fair."

"I was afraid you wouldn't think so," I said.

"Nothing much short of murder would put him back inside for the whole of his life. Anything less and he'd be out breathing fire again, as you said before. And however could you line up a living victim?"

"Mm," I said. "It's impossible. I still think the only lasting solution is to make Angelo prosper, so I'll see if I can persuade his old dad to that effect."

"His old dad is an old rattlesnake, don't forget."

"His dad is in a wheelchair."

"Is he?" Jonathan seemed surprised. "All the same— remember that rattlesnakes don't have legs."

I reckoned that on that Saturday afternoon Angelo would still be blundering around the bookies on Newbury race-course and that his father might have stayed at home, so it was then that I drove to Welwyn Garden City, leaving Cassie wandering around the cottage with a duster and an unac-customedly domestic expression.

The house at number seventeen Pemberton Close proved to be inhabited not by Harry Gilbert but by a stockbroker and his chatty wife and four noisy children on roller skates, all of them out in the garden.

"Harry Gilbert?" said the wife, holding a basket of dead roses. "He couldn't manage the stairs with his illness. He built himself a bungalow full of ramps."

"Do you know where?"

"Oh, sure. On the golf course. He used to play, poor man. Now he sits at a window and watches the foursomes go by on the fourteenth green. We often wave to him, when we're playing."

"Does he have arthritis?" I asked.

"Good Lord, no." She made a grimace of sympathy. "Multiple sclerosis. He's had it for years. We've seen him slowly get worse. We used to live four doors away, but we always liked this house. When he put it up for sale, we bought it."

"Could you tell me how to find him?"

"Sure." She gave me brisk and clear instructions. "You do know, don't you, not to talk about his son?"

"Son?" I said vaguely.

"His only son is in prison for murder. So sad for the poor man. Don't talk about it, it distresses him."

"Thanks for warning me," I said.

She nodded and smiled from a kind and unperceiving heart and went back to tidying her pretty garden. Surely goodness and mercy all thy days shall follow thee, I thought frivolously, and no monsters who won't go away shall gobble thee up. I left the virtuous and went in search of the sinner, and found him, as she'd said, sitting in his wheelchair by a big bay window, watching the earnest putters out on the green.

The wide double front doors of the large and still new-looking one-story building were opened to me by a man so like Angelo at first sight that I thought for a fearsome moment that he hadn't after all gone to the races; but it was only the general shape and coloring that were the same, the olive skin, graying hair, unfriendly dark eyes, tendency to an all-over padding of fat.

"Eddy," a voice called. "Who is it? Come in here."

The voice was as deep and harsh as Angelo's, the words themselves slightly slurred. I walked across the polished wood of the entrance hall and then across the lush drawing room with its panoramic view, and not until I was six feet away from Harry Gilbert did I stop and say I was William Derry.

Vibrations could almost be felt. Eddy, behind me, audibly hissed, the air leaving his lungs. The much older version of Angelo's face which looked up from the wheelchair went stiff with strong but unreadable emotions, guessed at as anger and indignation, but possibly not. He had thinning gray hair, a gray moustache, a big body in a formal gray suit with a waistcoat. Only in the lax hands was the illness visible, and only when he moved them; from his polished shoes to the great parting across his scalp it seemed to me that he was denying his weakness, presenting an outwardly uncrumbled façade so as to announce to the world that authority still lived within.

"You're not welcome in my house," he said.

"If your son would stop threatening me, I wouldn't be here."

"He says you have tricked us like your brother."

"No."

"The betting system doesn't work."

"It worked for Liam O'Rorke," I said. "Liam O'Rorke was quiet, clever, careful and a statistician. Is Angelo any of those things?"

He gave me a cold stare. "A system should work for everyone alike."

"A horse doesn't run alike for every jockey," I said.

"There's no similarity."

"Engines run sweetly for some drivers and break down for others. Heavyhandedness is always destructive. Angelo is trampling all over that system. No wonder it isn't producing results."

"The system is wrong," he said stubbornly.

"It may," I said slowly, "be slightly out of date." Yet for Ted Pitts it was purring along still; but then Ted Pitts too was quiet, clever, a statistician.

It seemed that I had made the first impression upon Harry Gilbert. He said with a faint note of doubt, "It should not have changed with the years. Why should it?"

"I don't know. Why shouldn't it? There may be new factors that Liam O'Rorke couldn't take into account because in his time they didn't exist."

A depressed sort of grimness settled over him.

I said, "And if Angelo has been hurrying through the programs, skipping some of the questions or answering them inaccurately, the scores will come out wrong. He's had some of the answers right. You won a lot at York, so I'm told. And you'd have won more on the St. Leger if Angelo hadn't scared the bookmakers with his boastfulness."

"I don't understand you." The slur in his speech, the faint distortion of all his words was, I realized, the effect of his illness. Articulation might be damaged but the chill awareness in his eyes said quite clearly that his intelligence wasn't.

"Angelo told all the bookmakers at York that he would henceforth fleece them continually, because it was he who possessed Liam O'Rorke's infallible system."

Harry Gilbert closed his eyes. His face remained unmoved.

Eddy said belligerently, "What's wrong with that? You have to show people who's boss."

"Eddy," Harry Gilbert said, "you don't know anything about anything and you never will." He slowly opened his eyes. "It makes a difference," he said.

"They gave him evens on the St. Leger winner. The proper price was five to one."

Harry Gilbert would never thank me: not if I gave him lifesaving advice, not if I helped him win a fortune, not if I kept his precious son out of jail. He knew, all the same, what I was saying. Too much of a realist, too old a businessman, not to. Angelo in too many ways was a fool, and it made him more dangerous, not less.

"What do you expect me to do?" he said.

"I expect you to tell your son that if he attacks me again, or any of my friends or any of my property, he'll be back behind bars so fast he won't know what hit him. I expect you to make him work the betting system carefully and quietly, so that he wins. I expect you to warn him that the system guarantees only one win in three, not a winner every single time. Making the system work is a matter of strict application and careful persistence, not of flamboyance and anger."

He stared at me expressionlessly.

"Angelo's character," I said, "is as far different from Liam O'Rorke's as it's possible to get. I expect you to make Angelo aware of that fact."

They were all expectations, I saw, that were unlikely to be achieved. Harry Gilbert's physical weakness, though he disguised it, was progressive, and his imperfect control of Angelo would probably only last for exactly as long as Angelo needed financing.

A tremor shook his body, but no emotion showed in his face. He said with, however, a sort of throttled fury, "All our problems are your brother's fault."

The uselessness of my visit swamped me. Harry Gilbert was after all only an old man blindly clinging like his son to an old obsession. Harry Gilbert was not any longer a man of reason, even if he had ever been.

I tried all the same, once more. I said, "If you had paid Mrs. O'Rorke all those years ago, if you had bought Liam's system from her, as you had agreed, you would legally have owned it and could have profited from it ever since. It was because you refused to pay Mrs. O'Rorke that my brother saw to it that you didn't get the system."

"She was too old," he said coldly.

I stared at him. "Are you implying that her age was a reason for not paying her?"

He didn't answer.

"If I stole your car from you," I said, "would you consider me justified on the grounds that you were too ill to drive it?"

"You prattle," he said. "You are nothing."

"Mug," Eddy said, nodding.

Harry Gilbert said wearily, "Eddy, you are good at pushing wheelchairs and cooking meals. On all other subjects, shut up."

Eddy gave him a look which was half-defiant, half-scared, and I saw that he too was dependent on Harry for his food and shelter, that it couldn't be all that easy out in the big cynical world for murderers' assistants to earn a cushy living, that looking after Harry wasn't a job to be lightly lost.

To Harry Gilbert I said, "Why don't you do what you once intended? Why don't you buy Angelo a betting shop and let the system win for him there?"

I got another stretch of silent unmoving stare. Then he said, "Business is a talent. I have it. It is, however, uncommon."

I nodded. It was all the answer he would bring himself to make. Certainly he wouldn't admit to me of all people that he thought Angelo would bankrupt any sensible business in a matter of weeks.

"Keep your son away from me," I said. "I've done more for you in getting you that system than you deserve. You've no rights to it. You've no right to demand that it make a fortune in five minutes. You've no right to blame me if it doesn't. You keep your son away from me. I can play as rough as he does. For your own sake, and for his, you keep him off me."

I turned away from him without waiting for any sort of answer, and walked hurriedly out of the room and across the hall.

Footsteps pattered after me on the polished wood.

Eddy.

I didn't look around. He caught up with me as I opened the front doors and stepped outside, and he put his hand on my arm to make me pause. He looked back guiltily over his shoulder to where his uncle sat mutely by his splendid window, knowing the old man wouldn't approve of what he was doing. Then as he saw Harry was looking out again steadfastly to the golf course he turned on me a nasty self-satisfied smirk.

"Mug," he said, speaking with prudent quietness, "Angelo won't like you coming here."

"Too bad." I shook his hand off my sleeve. He sneered back in a poisonous mixture of slyness and malice and triumph, and half-whispered his final enjoyable words.

"Angelo's bought a pistol," he said.

EIGHTEEN

"Why are you so thoughtful?" Cassie said.

"Uneasy."

We were sitting as so often at a table in Bananas' dining room with him moving about light-footedly in his sneakers seeming never to hurry yet keeping everyone fed. The plants grew with shining healthy leaves in the opulent gloom of his designedly intimate lighting, glasses and silverware gleaming in candlelight and mold spreading slowly in the dark.

"It's not like you," Cassie said.

I smiled at her thin suntanned uncomplicated face and said that I didn't want above all things a return visit from Angelo.

"Do you really think he'd come?"

"I don't know."

"We'd never get any more corn dollies," she said. "It's too late now for decent straw."

Her arm in its plaster lay awkwardly on the table. I

touched the bunched fingertips peeping out. "Would you consider leaving me for a while?" I asked.

"No, I wouldn't."

"Suppose I said I was tired of you?"

"You're not."

"Are you so sure?"

"Positive," she said contentedly. "And anyway, for how long?"

I drank some wine. For how long was an absolute puzzle. "Until I get Angelo stabilized," I said. "And don't ask me how long, because I don't know. But the first thing to do, I think, is persuade Luke we need a computer right here in Britain."

"Would that be difficult?"

"It might be. He has one in California; he might say he didn't need two."

"What do you want it for—the betting system?"

I nodded. "I think," I said, "that I'll try to rent one. Or some time on one. I want to find out what the winners should be according to O'Rorke, and what Angelo's doing wrong. And if I can put him *right*, perhaps that will keep him quiet."

"You'd have thought just giving him the tapes would be enough."

"Yes, you would."

"He's like a thistle," she said. "You're sure you've got rid of him and he grows right back."

Thistles, I thought, didn't go out to buy guns.

Bananas reverently bore his eponymous soufflé to the people at the next table, the airy peaks shining light and luscious and pale brown. The old cow, whose skill had produced it, must have stopped working to rule: Bananas Frisby had been off the menu for the last month.

"I bet he's bought her the pony," Cassie said, "*and* paid for the riding lessons."

Bananas himself, joining us later for coffee, gloomily admitted it. "She took an hour to shred carrots. Did them by hand. Ten seconds in the processor. She said processors were dangerous machinery and she'd have to negotiate a new rate for all jobs with machinery."

Bananas' new beard had grown curly, which was unforeseen in view of the lank straight locks farther up but seemed to me to be in accord with the doubleness of his nature.

"Historically," he said, "it's seldom a good idea to appease a tyrant."

"The old cow?"

"No. Angelo Gilbert."

"What do you suggest, then?" I asked. "Full-scale war?"

"You have to be sure you'll win. Historically, full-scale war's a toss-up."

"The old cow might leave," Cassie said, smiling.

Bananas nodded. "Tyrants always want more next time. I dare say next year she'll turn to motor racing."

"I suppose you don't know anyone who has a computer you can feed any language to?" I said.

"Turkish? Indochinese? That sort of stuff?"

"Yeah. Gibberish, double-speak, jargonese and gobbledegook."

"Try the sociologists."

I tried, however, Ted Pitts, early the following morning, and reached Jane instead.

"Ted isn't here," she said. "I'm afraid he's still in Switzerland. Can I help?"

I explained I wanted to borrow a computer to run a check on the racing programs, and she said sadly that she couldn't really lend me Ted's, not without him being there; she knew he was working on a special program for his classes and if anyone touched the computer at present his work would be lost, and she couldn't risk that.

"No," I agreed. Did she know of anyone else whose computer I could use?

She thought it over. "There's Ruth," she said doubtfully. "Ruth Quigley."

"Who?"

"She was a pupil of Ted's. Actually he says there's nothing he can teach her now, and when she comes here I can't understand a word they say to each other; it's like listening to creatures from outer space."

"Would she have a computer of her own?"

"She's got everything," Jane said without envy. "Born rich. Only child. Only has to ask, and it's hers. And on top of that she's brainy. Doesn't seem fair, does it?"

"Beautiful as well?"

"Oh." She hesitated. "Not bad. I don't really know. It's not the sort of thing you *notice* about Ruth."

"Well, um, where could I find her?"

"In Cambridge. That's why I thought of her, because she lives over your way. She writes programs for teaching-machines. Would you like me to call her? When do you want to go?"

I said "Today," and half an hour later I'd had my answer and was on my way, seeking out a flat in a modern apartment house on the outskirts of the town.

Ruth Quigley proved to be young: very early twenties, I guessed. I could see also what Jane meant about not noticing her looks, because the first, overpowering and lasting impression she gave was of the speed of her mind. There were light eyes, light brown extra-curly hair and a long slender neck, but mostly there was an impatient jerk of the head and a stumblingly rapid diction as if to her utter disgust her tongue couldn't speak her thoughts fast enough.

"Yes. Come in. Did you bring your tapes?" She wasted no precious words on any other greeting. "This way. Old Grantley BASIC, Jane said. You've the language with you. Do you want to load it, or shall I?"

"I'd be glad if—"

"Hand them over, then. Which side?"

"Er, first program on side 1."

"Right. Come along."

She moved with the same inborn rapidity, disappearing down a short passage and through a doorway before I'd even managed to step. She must always find, I thought, that the rest of the world went along intolerably in slow motion.

The room into which I finally followed her must originally have been designed as a bedroom, which it now in no way resembled. There was a quiet, feltlike pale green floor covering, track-lighting with spotlights, a roller blind at the window, matt white walls...and benches of machines more or less like Ted Pitts's, only double.

"Workroom," Ruth Quigley said.

"Er, yes."

It was cooler in there than out on the street. I identified a faint background hum as air-conditioning, and remarked on it.

She nodded, not lifting her eyes from the already almost completed job of loading Grantley BASIC into a machine that would accept it. "Dust is like gravel to computers. Heat, damp, all makes them temperamental. They're thoroughbreds, of course."

Racing programs...thoroughbred computers. Excellence won. Pains taken gave one the edge. I was beginning to think like her, I thought.

"I'm wasting your time," I said apologetically.

"Glad to help. Always do anything for Jane and Ted. They know that. Did you bring the form books? You'll need them. Simple programs, but facts must be right. Most teaching-machines, just the same. They bore me quite often. Multiple-choice questions. Then the child takes half an hour to get it right and I put in a bright remark like, 'Well done, aren't you clever.' Nothing of the sort. Encouragement, they say, is all. What do you think?"

"Are they gifted children?"

She gave me a flashing glance. "All children are gifted. Some more so. They need the best teaching. They often don't get it. Teachers are jealous, did you know?"

"My brother always said it was intensely exciting to have a very bright boy in the class."

"Like Ted, generous. There you are, fire away. I'll be in and out, don't let me disturb you. I'm working on a sort-listing of string arrays. They said it was taking them eighteen minutes, I ask you. I've got it down to five seconds, but only one dimension. I need two dimensions if I'm not to scramble the data. I'm poking a machine-language program into memory from BASIC, then converting the machine code into assembly-language mnemonics. Am I boring you?"

"No," I said. "I just don't understand a word of it."

"Sorry. Forgot you weren't like Ted. Well, carry on."

I had brought in a large briefcase the tapes, the racing form books, all sorts of record books and all the recent copies of a good racing paper, and with a feeling that by Ruth Quigley's standards it was going to take me a very long time, I set about working out which horses were *likely* to have won according to Liam O'Rorke, and checking them against those which had actually reached the post first. I still needed a list of the horses which Angelo had backed, but I thought I might get that from Taff and from Lancer on the following day: and *then* I might be able to figure out where Angelo had messed everything up.

FILE NAME?

CLOAD "DONCA," I typed. Pressed the "ENTER" key, and watched the asterisks; waited for "READY?" Pressed "ENTER" again and got my reward.

WHICH RACE AT DONCASTER?

ST. LEGER, I typed.

DONCASTER: ST. LEGER. TYPE NAME OF HORSE AND PRESS 'ENTER'.

GENOTTI, I typed. Pressed "ENTER".

DONCASTER: ST. LEGER.
GENOTTI.
ANSWER ALL QUESTIONS YES OR NO OR WITH A
NUMBER

AND PRESS 'ENTER .
HAS HORSE WON AS A TWO YEAR OLD?

YES, I typed. The screen flashed a new question leaving the headings intact.

HAS HORSE WON AS A THREE YEAR OLD?

YES, I typed.

HOW MANY DAYS SINCE HORSE LAST RAN?

I consulted the daily newspaper which always gave that precise information, and typed in the number which had appeared there on St. Leger day: 23.

HAS HORSE WON OVER DISTANCE: ONE MILE SIX FURLONGS?

NO, I typed.

HAS HORSE RUN OVER DISTANCE: ONE MILE SIX FURLONGS?

NO.

TYPE LONGEST DISTANCE IN FURLONGS OVER WHICH HORSE HAS WON.

12.

HAS HORSE RUN ON COURSE?

NO.

TYPE IN PRIZE MONEY WON IN CURRENT SEASON.

I consulted the form books and typed Genotti's winnings, which hads been fairly good but not stupendous.

HAS HORSE'S SIRE SIRED WINNERS AT THE DISTANCE?

I looked it up in the breeding records, which took much longer, but the answer was YES.

DAM DITTO?

YES.

IS HORSE QUOTED ANTE-POST AT TWELVE TO ONE OR LESS?

YES.

HAS JOCKEY PREVIOUSLY WON A CLASSIC?

YES.

HAS TRAINER PREVIOUSLY WON A CLASSIC?

YES.

ANY MORE HORSES?

YES.

I found myself back at the beginning and repeated the program for every horse which had run in the race. The questions weren't always precisely the same, because different answers produced alternative queries, and for some horses there were far more questions than for others. It took me a good hour to look everything up, and I thought that if I ever did begin to do it all seriously I would make myself a whole host of more easily accessible tables than those

available in the record books. When I at last answered NO
to the final question ANY MORE HORSES? I got the clear
reply that left no doubt about Liam O'Rorke's genius.

Genotti headed the win factor list. An outsider turned up
on it in second place, with the horse that had started favorite
in third: and the St. Leger result had been those three horses
in that order exactly.

I could hardly believe it.

Ruth Quigley said suddenly, "Got the wrong result? You
look flummoxed."

"No . . . the right one."

"Disturbing." She grinned swiftly. "If I get the results I
expect I check and check and check. Doesn't do to be
complacent. Like some coffee?"

I accepted and she made it as fast as she did everything
else.

"How old are you?" I said.

"Twenty-one. Why?"

"I'd have thought you'd have been at the university."

"Degree at twenty plus one month. Nothing unusual.
Cheated my way in, of course. Everything's so slow nowadays. Forty years ago, degrees at nineteen or less were
possible. Now they insist on calendar age. Why? Why hold
people back? Life's terribly short as it is. Master's degree
at twenty plus six months. Did the two courses simulta-
neously. No one knew. Don't spread it around. Doing my
doctorate now. Are you interested?"

"Yes," I said truthfully.

She smiled like a summer's day, come and gone. "My
father says I'm a bore."

"He doesn't mean it."

"He's a surgeon," she said, as if that explained much.
"So's my mother. Guilt complexes, both of them. Give to
mankind more than you take. That sort of thing. They can't
help it."

"And you?"

"I don't know yet. I can't give much. I can't get jobs I
can do. They look at the years I've been alive and make

judgments. Quite deadly. Time has practically nothing to do with anything. They'll give me the jobs when I'm thirty that I could do better now. Poets and mathematicians are best before twenty-five. What chance have they got?"

"To work alone," I said.

"My God. Do you understand? You're wasting time, get on with your programs. Don't show me what I should do. I've got a research fellowship. What do I seek for? What is there to seek? Where is the unknown, what is not known, what's the question?"

I shook my head helplessly. "Wait for the apple to fall on your head."

"It's true. I can't contemplate. Sitting under apple trees. Metaphorical apple trees. I've tried. Get on with your nags."

Philosophically I loaded YORK and worked through the three races for which there were programs, and found that in two of them the highest scoring horse had won. Three winners from the four races I'd worked through. Incredible.

With a feeling of unreality I loaded EPSOM and went painstakingly through the four races for which there were programs; and this time came up with no winners at all. Frowning slightly I loaded NEWBU for Newbury and from a good deal of hard accurate work came up with the win factors of the race in which Angelo had backed the absolute no-hoper Pocket Handbook.

Pocket Handbook, who had finished exhausted and tailed-off by at least thirty lengths, was at the top of the win-factor list by a clear margin.

I stared distrustfully at the rest of the scores, which put the race's actual winner second from the bottom with negligible points.

"What's the matter?" Ruth Quigley said, busy at her own machine and not even glancing my way.

"Parts of the system are haywire."

"Really?"

I loaded GOOD and sorted through five races. All the top scorers were horses which in the events had finished no nearer than second.

"Are you hungry?" Ruth said. "Three-thirty. Sandwich?"

I thanked her and went into her small kitchen where I was interested to see that her speed stopped short of dexterity with slicing tomatoes. She quite slowly for her made fat juicy affairs of cheese, chutney, tomatoes and corned beef which toppled precariously on the plate and had to be held in both hands for eating.

"Logical explanations exist," she said, looking at my abstracted expression. "Human logic's imperfect. Absolute logic isn't."

"Mm," I said. "Ted showed me how easy it is to add and delete passwords."

"So?"

"It would be pretty easy, wouldn't it, to change other things besides?"

"Unless it's in ROM. Then it's difficult."

"'ROM'?"

"Read Only Memory. Sorry."

"He showed me how to LIST things."

"You've got RAM, then. Random Access Memory. Change what you like. Kids' stuff."

We finished the sandwiches and returned to the keyboards. I loaded the Newbury file, chose the Pocket Handbook race and listed the program piece by piece.

LIST 1200-1240, I typed, and in front of the resulting screenful of letters, numbers and symbols sat figuring out the roots of trouble.

```
1200 PRINT "TYPE IN PRIZE MONEY IN CURRENT
SEASON"
1210 PRINT W: IF W < 1000 T = T + 20.
1220 IF W > 1000 THEN T = T: IF W > 5000
THEN T = T
1230 IF W > 10000 THEN T = T: IF W > 15000
THEN T = T
1240 GOSUB 6000
```

Even to my ignorant and untutored eyes it was nonsense. Liam O'Rorke wouldn't have meant it, Peter Keithly wouldn't have written it, Ted Pitts would never have used it. In plain language what it was saying was that if the season's winnings of a horse were *less* than one thousand pounds, the win factor score should be increased by 20, and if they were *more* than one thousand, and however much more, the win factor score would not increase at all. The least successful horses would therefore score most highly on that particular point. The weighting was topsy-turvy and the answers would come out wrong.

With the hollow certainty of what had happened staring me in the face I loaded the Epsom file and searched the LISTS of the programs for the four races on which Angelo had lost. In two cases the weightings for prize money were upside down.

Tried Goodwood. In three of the five listed races, the same thing.

Depressed beyond measure I loaded the files for Leicester and Ascot, where races were to be held during the week ahead. Typed in the names of all the races to be run there and found there were programs for eight of them: one at Leicester, seven at Ascot. LISTed each of the eight programs in sections and found that in four of them the score for amassing much prize money was zero, and the score for prize money of under one thousand pounds was anything up to 20.

There were programs for some races at all the tracks which I knew for a certainty were not fourteen years old. Modern races, introduced since Liam O'Rorke had died.

The programs were no longer pure O'Rorke, but O'Rorke according to Pitts. O'Rorke updated, expanded, renewed. O'Rorke, on these particular tapes, interfered with, falsified, mangled. Ted Pitts . . . one had to face it . . . had wrecked the system before he'd handed it to me. And had delivered me defenseless to the wrath of Angelo Gilbert.

I thanked the frustrated and brilliant Miss Quigley for her day-long patience and drove home to Cassie.

"What's the matter?" she said immediately.

I said wearily, "The ess aitch i tee has hit the fan."

"What do you *mean?*"

"Angelo thinks I've tricked him. That the betting system I gave him was wrong. That it produces too many losers. Well, so it does. Normally it must be all right but on these tapes it's been altered. Ted Pitts has rigged so many of the programs that anyone using them will fall flat on his greedy face." And I explained about the reversed scores of winning, which produced scatty results. "He may also have changed some of the other weightings to get the same effect. I've no way of knowing."

She looked as stunned as I felt. "Do you mean Ted Pitts did it on *purpose?*"

"He sure did." I thought back to the time he'd taken to make my "copies"; to the hour I'd spent sitting by his pool talking to Jane, leaving him, at his own request, to work alone.

"But why?" Cassie said.

"I don't know."

"You didn't tell him, did you, what you wanted the tapes for?"

"No, I didn't."

She said doubtfully, "Perhaps it might have been better if you'd said how vital they were."

"And perhaps he wouldn't have given them to me at all if he'd known I had Angelo locked in the cellar. I mean, I thought he might not want to be *involved.* Most people wouldn't, with something like that. And then, if he was like Jonathan, he might have changed the weightings anyway, just to prevent Angelo from profiting. You never know. Jonathan himself would somehow have tricked Angelo again. I'm sure of it."

"You don't think Ted Pitts asked Jonathan what he should do, do you?"

I thought back and shook my head. "It was before nine in the morning when I went to the Pitts house. That would make it about one A.M. in California. Even if he had his number, which I doubt, I don't think he would have telephoned Jonathan in the middle of the night. And Jonathan anyway sounded truly disappointed when I told him I'd given Angelo the tapes. No, Ted must have done it for his own reasons, and by himself."

"Which doesn't help much."

I shook my head.

I thought of the certainty with which I'd gone to Harry Gilbert's house on the previous day. Hell's teeth—how wrong could one be, how naive could one get?

If I warned Angelo not to use the tapes in the week ahead, he would be sure I had tricked him and was now scared to death of his revenge.

If I didn't warn him not to use the tapes he would most likely lose again and be more sure than ever that I'd tricked him...

If I wrung the right answers out of Ted Pitts and told them to Angelo, he would still think I had deliberately given him useless tapes...on which he had already lost.

Ted Pitts was in Switzerland walking up mountains.

"Would you care," I said to Cassie, "for a long slow cruise to Australia?"

NINETEEN

Jane Pitts on the telephone said, "No, terribly sorry, he moves about and stops in different places each night. Quite often he sleeps in his tent. Is it important?"

"Horribly," I said.

"Oh, dear. Could I help?"

"There's something wrong with those tapes he made for me. Could you by any chance lend me his own?"

"No, I simply can't. I'm frightfully sorry but I don't know where he keeps anything in that room and he positively hates his things being touched." She thought for a few minutes, puzzled but not unwilling, friendly, anxious to help. "Look... he's sure to call me one day soon to say when he'll be home. Would you like me to ask him to call you?"

"Yes, please," I said fervently. "Or ask him where I can reach him, and I'll call him. Do tell him it's really urgent. Beg him for me, would you? Say it's for Jonathan's sake more than mine."

"I'll tell him," she promised, "as soon as he calls."

"You're unscrupulous," Cassie said as I put down the receiver. "It's for your sake, not Jonathan's."

"He wouldn't want to weep on his brother's grave."

"William."

"A joke," I said hastily. "A joke."

Cassie shivered, however. "What are you going to do?"

"Think," I said.

The basic thought was that the more Angelo lost the angrier he would get, and that the first objective was therefore to stop him betting. Taff and the others could hardly be persuaded not to accept such easy pickings, which left the source of the cash, Harry Gilbert himself. Precisely what, I wondered, could I say to Harry Gilbert which would cut off the stake money without sending Angelo straight around to vent his rage?

I could tell him that Liam O'Rorke's system no longer existed: that I'd got the tapes in good faith but been tricked myself. I could tell him a lot of half-truths...but whether he would believe me, and whether he could restrain Angelo even if he himself were convinced, of those imponderables there was no forecast.

Realistically, there was nothing else to do.

I didn't particularly want to try to trap Angelo into being sent back to jail: fourteen years was enough for any man. I only wanted, as I had all along, for him to leave me alone. I wanted him deflated, defused...docile. What a hope.

A night spent with my mind on pleasanter things produced no cleverer plan. A paragraph in the *Sporting Life*, read over a quick breakfast after an hour with the horses on the Heath, made me wish that Angelo would solve my problems himself by bashing someone else on the head: about as unlikely as him having a good week on the system. Lancer, the bookmaker, said the paper, had been mugged on his own doorstep on returning from Newbury races on Friday evening. His wallet, containing approximately fifty-three pounds, had been stolen. Lancer was OK; police had no leads. Poor old Lancer, too bad.

I sighed. Whom, I wondered, could I get Angelo to bash? Besides, of course, myself.

On account of the knee-groper I was driving Cassie to work whenever possible, and on that morning after I'd dropped her I went straight on to Welwyn Garden City, not relishing my prospects but with not much alternative. I hoped to persuade both Harry Gilbert and Angelo that the havoc the years had caused to the O'Rorke system couldn't be undone, that it was blown, no longer existed, couldn't be recovered. I was going to tell him again that any violence from Angelo would put him back in a cell, to try to make them believe it . . . to fear it.

I was taller than Angelo and towered over a man in a wheelchair. I intended slightly to crowd them, faintly to intimidate, certainly to leave the physical impression that it was time for them to back off. Even on Angelo, who must have known how to frighten from childhood, it might have some effect.

Eddy opened the front doors and tried at once to close them again when he saw who had called. I pushed him with force out of the way.

"Harry isn't dressed," he said fearfully, though whether the fear was of me or of Harry wasn't clear.

"He'll see me," I said.

"No. You can't." He tried to bar my way to one of the wide doors at the side of the entrance hall, thereby showing me which way to go: and I walked over there with Eddy trying to edge me out of my path by leaning on me.

I thrust him again aside and opened the door, and found myself in a short passage which led into a large bedroom which was equipped most noticeably with another vast window looking out to the golf course.

Harry Gilbert lay in a big bed facing the window, ill and growing old but still in some indefinable way not defenseless, even in pyjamas.

"I tried to stop him," Eddy was saying ineffectually.

"Take this tray and go away," Harry Gilbert said to him,

and Eddy picked from the bedclothes the half-eaten breakfast which I had interrupted. "Shut the door." He waited until Eddy had retreated and then frostily to me said, "Well?"

"I've discovered," I said with urgency, "that Liam O'Rorke's betting system has the equivalent of smallpox. It should be treated like a plague. It'll bring trouble to all who touch it. The old system has been through too many hands, been adulterated by the years. It's gone bad. If you want to save your cash you'll stop Angelo using it, and it's pointless getting angry with me on any counts. I got the system for you in good faith and I'm furious to find it's useless. Bring Angelo in here and let me tell him."

Harry Gilbert stared at me with his usual unreadable face, and it was without any visible consternation that he said in his semi-slurred way, "Angelo isn't here. He is cashing my check at the bank. He is going to Leicester races."

"He will lose," I said. "I didn't need to warn you, but I am. Your money will be lost."

Thoughts must have traversed the brain behind the cold eyes but nothing much showed. Finally, and it must have been with an inner effort, he said, "Can you stop him?"

"Stop the check," I said. "Call the bank."

He glanced at a clock beside him. "Too late."

"I can go to Leicester," I said. "I'll try to find him."

After a pause he said, "Very well."

I nodded briefly and left him, and drove toward Leicester feeling that even if I had managed to convince Harry, which was in itself uncertain, I was facing the impossible with Angelo. The impossible all the same had to be tried: and at least, I thought, he wouldn't actually attack me on a busy racecourse.

Leicester races on that cold autumn day turned out to be as busy as a well-smoked beehive, with only a scattering of dark-coated figures trudging about doggedly, head-down in the biting wind. As sometimes happens on city-based tracks on weekdays the crowd was thin to the point of embarrassment, the whole proceedings imbued with the perfunctory and temporary air of a ritual taking place without fervor.

Taff was stamping about by his beer crate, blowing on his fingers and complaining that he would have done better business if he'd gone to the day's other meeting at Bath.

"But there's the Midlands Cup here," he said. "It'll be a good race. I thought it would pull them. And look at them, not enough punters to sing 'Auld Lang Syne' around a teapot." The Welsh accent was ripe with disgust.

"What are you making favorite?" I said smiling.

"Pink Flowers."

"And what about Terrybow?"

"Who?"

"Runs in the Midlands Cup," I said patiently. Terrybow, the computer's choice, top of the win factors. Terrybow with a habit of finishing tenth of twelve, or seventh of eight, or fifteenth of twenty: never actually last but a long way from success.

"Oh, Terrybow." He consulted a notebook. "Twenties, if you like."

"Twenty to one?"

"Twenty-fives then. Can't say fairer than twenty-five. How much do you want?"

"How much would you take?"

"Whatever you like," he said cheerfully. "No limit. Not unless you know something I don't, like it's stuffed to the eyeballs with rocket dust."

I shook my head and looked along the row of cold disgruntled bookmakers who were doing a fraction of their usual trade. If Angelo had been among them I would have seen him easily, but there was no sign of him. The Midlands Cup was the fourth race on the program and still an hour ahead, and if Angelo was sticking rigidly to the disaster-laden system, Terrybow would be the only horse he would back.

"Have you seen Angelo Gilbert here today, Taff?" I asked.

"No." He took a bet from a furtive-looking man in a raincoat and gave him a ticket. "Ten at threes, Walkie-Talkie," he told his clerk.

"How's Lancer?" I asked. "Can't see him here."

"Cursing muggers and rubbing a lump." He took another tenner from a purposeful woman in glasses. "Ten at eights, Engineer. Some kids rolled old Lancer on his own doorstep. I ask you, he carries thousands around the racecourse, pays it in to his firm at the end of the day, and then goes and gets himself done for fifty quid."

"Did he see who robbed him?"

"One of Joe Glick's other boys who's here says it was a bunch of teenagers."

Not Angelo, I thought. Well, it wouldn't have been. But if only he *would*...

I looked speculatively at Taff, who worked for himself and did carry his takings home at the end of the day. Pity one couldn't catch Angelo in the act of trying to retrieve his stake money after Terrybow had lost. Pity one couldn't arrange for the police to be on hand when Angelo mugged Taff on the way home.

I'm down to fantasies, I thought: it's depressing.

The time passed and Angelo, who had been so ubiquitous when I had been trying to avoid him, was nowhere to be seen. I walked among the bookmakers and asked others besides Taff, but none of them had seen Angelo at all that afternoon, and there was still no sign of him during the run-up to the Midlands Cup. If he had gone to Bath after all, I thought, I was wasting my time...but the only race that day on the O'Rorke tapes was the Midlands Cup; its only designated horse, Terrybow.

With less than five minutes to go, when the horses were already cantering down to the start, a tremendous burst of tic-tac activity galvanized the men with white gloves high on the stands who semaphored changes of odds. With no direct link like telephones or radio the bookmakers relied on tic-tac to tell them if large sums had been placed with their firms on any particular horse, so that they could bring down the offered price. Taff, watching his man signaling frenziedly, rubbed out the 20 written against Terrybow on his blackboard and with his piece of chalk wrote in 14. Along the row all the other bookies were similarly engaged. Terrybow fell again to 12.

"What's happening?" I said to Taff urgently.

He cast an abstracted eye in my direction. "Someone down in the cheap ring is piling a stack on Terrybow."

"Damn," I said bitterly. I hadn't thought of looking for Angelo anywhere but around his usual haunts: certainly not in the comfortless far enclosure away down the course where the entrance fee was small, the view of the races moderate, and the expectation of the few bookmakers trading there modest to the point of not being worth standing in the cold all afternoon. And even if I'd thought of it I wouldn't have gone there, because it would have meant risking missing Angelo in the paddock. Damn and blast, I thought. Damn Angelo today and all days and for the whole of his life.

"You knew something about this Terrybow," Taff said to me accusingly.

"I didn't back it," I said.

"Yeah, that's right, so you didn't. So what's going on?"

"Angelo Gilbert," I said. "He's betting where he isn't known in case you wouldn't give him a good price up here."

"What? Really?" He laughed, rubbed out the 12 against Terrybow and replaced it with 20. A small rush of punters resulted and he took their money with relish.

I went up on the stands and watched in a fury while Terrybow ran true to his form and drifted in twelfth of fifteen. Ted Pitts, I thought bleakly, might as well have shoved me under the wheels of a truck.

I did see Angelo that afternoon, and so did practically everyone else who hadn't gone home before the sixth race.

Angelo was the angrily shouting epicenter of a fracas going on near the weighing room: a row involving several bookmakers, a host of racegoers and some worried-looking officials. Disputes between bookmakers and clients were traditionally dealt with on that spot by one particular Jockey Club official, the ring inspector. Angelo appeared to have punched him in the face.

The milling crowd parted a little and shifted, and I found myself standing near the front of the onlookers with a clear view of the performance. The ring inspector was holding his jaw and trying to argue around his winces, six bookmakers were declaring passionately that money once wagered was lost forever, and Angelo, waving his hard bunched fist, was insisting they give it back.

"You tricked me," he shouted. "The whole bloody lot of you, you stole my cash."

"You bet it fair and square," yelled a bookmaker, wagging a finger forcefully in Angelo's face.

Angelo bit the finger. The bookmaker yelled all the harder.

A man standing next to me laughed, but most of the onlookers had less objectively taken sides and it seemed that a general brawl needed only a flashpoint. Into the ugliness and among the angrily gesturing hands and violent voices walked two uniformed policemen, both very young, both slight, both looking poor opponents in size and in forcefulness for the prison-taught Angelo. The ring inspector said something to one of them which was inaudible to me in the hubbub, and to his immense and visible surprise Angelo suddenly found himself wearing, on the wrist he happened not to be waving in the air at the moment, a handcuff.

His bellow of rage fluttered the pigeons off the weighing room roof. He tugged with his whole weight and the boy-policeman, whose own wrist protruded from the other cuff, was jerked off his feet onto his knees. It looked not impossible that Angelo could pick him up bodily and simply run off with him, but the second constable came to the rescue, saying something boldly to Angelo and pulling his radio communicator out of the front of his uniform jacket to bring up reinforcements.

Angelo looked at the ring of spectators through which he had little real hope of pushing and at his unexpectedly adroit captor, now rising from his knees, and at the seething bookmakers who were showing signs of satisfaction, and finally straight at me.

He took a step toward me with such strength that the half-risen policeman lost his balance again and fell on his back, his arm twisting awkwardly over his head, stretching in the handcuff. There was about Angelo suddenly such an extraordinary growth of menace, something so different from a mere racecourse argument, that the thronging voices fell away to silence and eyes looked at him with age-old fright. The monstrous recklessness seemed to swell his whole body, and even if the words were banal, his gritty voice vibrated with a darkness straight out of myth.

"You," he said deliberately. "You and your fucking brother."

There was an awareness in his face of the attentive crowd of witnesses around us and he didn't say aloud what was in his mind, but I could hear it as clearly as if he'd woken the sleeping hills.

I'll kill you. *I'll kill you.*

It was a message not so much new as newly intense. More than ever implacable. A promise, not a threat.

I stared back at him as if I hadn't heard, as if it wasn't there looking at me out of his eyes. He nodded however as if savagely satisfied and turned with a contemptuous shrug to the rising policeman, jerking him the last few inches to upright; and he went, after that, without fighting, walking away between the two constables toward a police car which was driving in through the gates. The car halted. They put him in the back seat between them and presently rolled away, and the now strangely quiet crowd began to spread and disperse.

A voice in my ear, the Welsh voice of Taff, said, "You know what set all that off?"

"What?" I asked.

"The bookies down in the cheap ring told Angelo he was a right mug. They were laughing at him, it seems. Joshing him, but friendly like to start with. They said they'd be happy to keep on taking his money, because if he thought he'd bought Liam O'Rorke's old system he'd been robbed, duped, bamboozled, made a fool of and generally conned from here to Christmas."

Dear God.

"So then this Angelo sort of exploded and started trying to get his stake back."

"Yes," I said.

"Well," Taff said cheerfully. "It all makes a change, though I reckon those goons in the cheap ring would have done better to keep their mouths shut. That Angelo was a bit of a golden goose and after this he won't lay no more golden eggs."

I drove home with a feeling that the seas were closing over my head. Whatever I did to try to disentangle myself from Angelo it seemed that I slid further into the coils.

He was never, after this, going to believe that I hadn't tricked him on purpose. Even if I could at last get him the correct system, he wouldn't forgive me the bets lost, the sneers of the bookmakers, the click of those handcuffs.

The police might hold him overnight, I thought, but not much longer: I doubted if one punch and a few yells would upset his parole. But to the tally in his mind would be added a night in the cell to rankle with those in my cellar . . . and if he'd come out of prison angry enough to attack me with nothing against me but the fact of my being Jonathan's brother, how much more would he now come swinging?

Cassie had long been home when I finally got there and was buoyantly pleased with the prospect of having the cast off her arm on the following afternoon. She had arranged a whole day off from work and had thanked the groper for the last time, confident that she would be able to drive more or less at once. She was humming in the kitchen while I cooked some spaghetti for supper, and I kissed her abstractedly and thought of Angelo and wished him dead with all my heart.

Before we had finished eating, the telephone rang and

most unexpectedly it was Ted Pitts calling from Switzerland. His voice, on the whole, was as cool as the Alps.

"Thought I'd better apologize," he said.

"It's kind of you."

"Jane's disgusted with me. She told me to ring you at once. She said it was urgent. So here I am. Sorry, and all that."

"I just wondered," I said hopelessly, "why you did it."

"Mashed up the weightings?"

"Yes."

"You'll think I'm mean. Jane says I'm so mean she's ashamed of me. She's furious. She says all our wealth is due to Jonathan, and I've played the most rotten trick on Jonathan's brother. She's hardly speaking to me she's so cross."

"Well... *why?*" I said.

He did at least seem to want me to understand. He spoke earnestly, explaining, excusing, telling me the destructive truth. "I don't know. It was an impulse. I was making those copies, and I suddenly thought I don't want to part with this system. I don't want anyone else to have it. It's mine. Not Jonathan's, just mine. He didn't even want it, and I've had it to myself all these years, and I've added to it and made it my own. It belongs to me. It's *mine*. And there you were, just asking for it as if I would give it to you as of right, and I suddenly thought, why should I? So I just quickly changed a lot of the weightings. I didn't have time to test them. I had to guess. I altered just enough, I thought, but it seems I did too much. Otherwise you wouldn't have checked. I intended that when you used the system you wouldn't win enough to think it worth all the work, and you'd get tired of it." He paused. "I was jealous of you having it, if you really want to know."

"I wish you'd told me—"

"If I'd said I didn't want to give it to you, Jane would have made me. She says I must now. She's so cross."

"If you would," I said, "you might save me a lot of grief."

"Make your fortune, you mean." The apology, it seemed, hadn't come from the heart: he still sounded resentful that I should be learning his secrets.

I thought again about telling him about Angelo but it still seemed to me that he might think it the best reason for *not* giving me the system, so I said merely, "It could work for two people, couldn't it? If someone else had it, it wouldn't stop you yourself winning as much as ever."

"I suppose," he said grudgingly, "that that's true."

"So . . . when do you come home?"

"The week after next."

I was silent. Appalled. By the week after next heaven knew what Angelo would have done.

Ted Pitts said with half-suppressed annoyance, "I suppose you've betted heavily on the wrong horses and lost too much, and now you need bailing out a lot sooner than the week after next?"

I didn't dispute it.

"Jane's furious. She's afraid I've cost you more than you can afford. Well . . . I'm sorry." He didn't truly sound it.

"Could she find the tapes to give to me?" I said humbly.

"How soon do you need them?"

"More or less at once. Tonight, if possible."

"Hmph." He thought for a few seconds. "All right. All right. But you can save yourself the journey, if you like."

"Er, how?"

"Do you have a tape recorder?"

"Yes."

"Jane can play the tapes to you over the telephone. They'll sound like a lot of screeching. But if you've a halfway decent recorder the programs will run all right on a computer."

"Good heavens."

"A lot of computer programs whiz around the world on telephones every day," he said. "And up to the satellites and down again. Nothing extraordinary in it."

To me it did seem extraordinary, but then I wasn't Ted

Pitts. I thanked him with more intensity than he knew for his trouble in ringing me up.

"Thank Jane," he said.

I did thank her, sincerely, five minutes later.

"You sounded in such *trouble*," she said. "I told Ted I'd sent you to Ruth because you'd wanted to check the tapes, and he *groaned*, so I asked him why... and when he told me what he'd done I was just *furious*. To think of you wasting your precious money when everything we have is thanks to Jonathan."

Her kindness made me feel guilty. I said, "Ted said you could play the real tapes to me over the telephone, if you wouldn't mind."

"Oh yes, all right. I've seen Ted do it often. He and Ruth are always swapping programs that way. I've got the tapes here beside me. I made Ted tell me where to find them. I'll go and get the recorder now, if you'll hang on, and then I'll play them to you straight away."

I had called her from the office because of the message recorder already fitted to that telephone, and when she returned I recorded the precious programs on Luke's supply of fresh unused tapes, which might not have been of prime computer standard but were all the same a better bet, I reckoned, than trying to record new machine language on top of old.

Cassie came into the office and listened to the scratchy whining noises running on and on and on.

"Horrible," she said: but to me, sweet music. A ransom to the future. Passport to a peaceful world. In a sudden uprush of optimism entirely at variance with the gloom of my drive home from Leicester, I convinced myself that this time, now that we had the genuine article, our troubles would come to an end. The solution was still, as it had always been, to make Angelo rich, and at last it could be done.

"I'll give these tapes to Angelo," I said, "and we'll go away from the cottage for just a while... a few weeks... just until he's won enough not to want his revenge. And we'll be free of him at last, thank God."

"Where shall we go?"

"Not far. Decide tomorrow."

When three tapes were full and the noises fell quiet, I switched off the recording part of the machine and spoke again to Jane.

"I'm very grateful," I said. "More than I can say."

"My dear William, I'm so sorry . . ."

"Don't be," I said. "You've saved my life." Quite literally, probably, I thought. "Everything," I said, "will be all right."

One shouldn't say such things. One really shouldn't.

TWENTY

Cassie came with me in the early morning to see the horses work on the Heath, shivering a little in boots, trousers and padded husky jacket, but glad, she said, to be alive in the free air and the wide spaces. Her breath, like mine, like that of all of the horses, spurted out in lung-shaped plumes of condensing vapor, chilled and gone in a second and quickly renewed, cold transformed to heat within the miracle of bodies.

We had already in a preliminary fashion left the cottage, having packed clothes and necessaries and stowed the suitcases in my car. I had also brought along a briefcase containing the precious tapes and a lot of Luke's paperwork and had rerouted my telephone calls by a message on the answering system, and it remained only to make a quick return trip to pick up the day's mail and arrange for future postal deliveries to be left at the pub.

We hadn't actually decided where we would sleep that night or for the nights to come, but we did between us have a great many friends who might be cajoled, and if the traditional open-house generosity of the racing world failed us, we could for a while afford a hotel. I felt freer and more light-hearted than I had for weeks.

Sim was positively welcoming on the gallops, and Mort asked us to breakfast. We shivered gratefully into his house and warmed up with him on toast and coffee while he slit open his letters with a paperknife and made comments on what he was at the same time reading in the *Sporting Life*. Mort never did one thing at a time if he could do three.

"I've rerouted my telephone messages to you," I told him. "Do you mind?"

"Have you? No, of course not. Why?"

"The cottage," I said, "is at the moment uninhabitable."

"Decorators?" He sounded sympathetic and it seemed simplest to say yes.

"There won't be many calls," I promised. "Just Luke's business."

"Sure," he said. He sucked in a boiled egg in two scoops of a spoon. "More coffee?"

"How are the yearlings settling?" I asked.

"Come and see them. Come this afternoon; we'll be lungeing them in the paddock."

"What's lungeing?" Cassie said.

Mort gave her a fast, forgiving smile and snapped his fingers a few times. "Letting them run around in a big circle on the end of a long rein. Give them exercise. No one rides them yet. They've never been sadddled. Too young."

"I'd like that," Cassie said, looking thoughtfully at the cast and clearly wondering about the timing.

"Where are you staying?" Mort asked me. "Where can I find you?"

"Don't know yet," I said.

"Really? What about here? There's a bed here, if you like." He crunched his teeth across half a piece of toast and ate it in one gulp. "You could answer your own phone calls. Makes sense."

"Well," I said. "For a night or two . . . very grateful."

"Settled then." He grinned cheerfully at Cassie. "My

daughter will be pleased. Got no wife, you know. She scarpered. Miranda gets bored, that's my daughter. Sixteen, needs a girl's company. Stay for a week. How long do you need?"

"We don't know," Cassie said.

He nodded briskly. "Take things as they come. Very sensible." He casually picked up the paperknife and began cleaning his nails with it, reminding me irresistibly of Jonathan, who throughout my childhood had done his with the point of a rifle bullet.

"I thought I'd go to Ireland at the weekend," I said, "and try to make peace with Donavan."

Mort gave me a blinding grin. "I hear you're a turd and an ignorant bastard, and should be dragged six times round the Curragh by your heels. At the least."

The telephone standing on the table by his elbow rang only once, sharply, before Mort was shouting "Hullo?" down the receiver. "Oh," he said, "hullo, Luke." He made signaling messages to me with his eyebrows. "Yes, he's here right now, having breakfast." He handed over the receiver, saying, "Luke rang your number first, he says."

"William," Luke said, sounding relaxed and undemanding. "How are the new yearlings?"

"Fine. No bad reports."

"Thought I'd come over to see them. See what you've gotten me. I feel like a trip. Listen, fella, do me a favor, make me some reservations at the Bedford Arms for two nights, fourteenth and fifteenth October?"

"Right," I said.

"Best to Cassie," he said. "Bring her to dinner at the Bedford on the fourteenth, OK? I'd sure like to meet her. And, fella . . . I'll be going on to Dublin. You aiming to go to the Ballsbridge Sales?"

"Yeah, I thought to. Ralph Finnigan died. They're selling all his string."

Luke sounded appreciative. "What would you pick, fella? What's the best?"

"Oxidize." Two years old, well-bred, fast, a prospect for

next June's Derby and bound to be expensive.

Luke gave a sort of rumbling grunt. "You'd send it to Donavan?"

"I sure would."

The grunt became a chuckle. "See you, fella, on the fourteenth."

There was a click and he was gone. Mort said, "Is he coming?" and I nodded and told him when. "Most years he comes in October," Mort said.

He asked if we'd like to see the second lot exercise, but I was anxious to be finished at the cottage so Cassie and I drove the six miles back to the village and stopped first at the pub. Mine host, who had been invisible earlier, was now outside in his shirtsleeves sweeping leaves off his door-step.

"Aren't you cold?" Cassie said.

Bananas, perspiring in contrast to us in our huskies, said he had been shifting beer barrels in his cellar.

We explained about going away for a while, and why.

"Come inside," he said, finishing the leaves. "Like some coffee?"

We drank some with him in the bar, but without the ice cream and brandy he stirred into his own. "Sure," he said amiably. "I'll take in your mail. Also papers, milk, whatever you like. Anything else?"

"How absolutely extravagantly generous are you feeling?" Cassie said.

He gave her a sideways squint over his frothy mugful. "Spill it," he said.

"My little yellow car is booked in today for service and a road test, and I just wondered—"

"If I'd drive it along to that big garage for you?"

"William will bring you back," she said persuasively.

"For you, Cassie, anything," he said. "Straight away."

"Plaster off this afternoon," she said happily, and I looked at her clear gray eyes and thought that I loved her so much it was ridiculous. Don't ever leave me, I thought. Stay around forever. It would be lonely now without you. It would be agony.

We all went in my car along to the cottage, and I left it out in the road because of Cassie wanting Bananas to back her little yellow peril out of the garage onto the driveway. She and he walked toward the garage doors to open them, and I, half watching them, went across to unlock the front door and retrieve the letters which would have fallen on the mat just inside.

The cottage lay so quiet and still that our precautions seemed unnecessary, like crowd barriers on the moon.

Angelo is unpredictable, I told myself. Unstable as Mount St. Helens. One might as well expect reasonable behavior from an earthquake, even if one does ultimately wish him to prosper.

REMEMBER TIGERS.

There was a small banging noise out by the garage. Nothing alarming. I paid little attention.

Six envelopes lay on the mat. I bent down, picked them up, shuffled through them. Three bills for Luke, a tax notice for the cottage, an advertisement for books and a letter to Cassie from her mother in Sydney. Ordinary mundane letters, not worth dying for.

I gave one final glance around the pretty sitting room, seeing the red-checked frills on the curtains and the corn dollies moving gently in the breeze through the door. It wouldn't be too long, I thought, before we were back.

The kitchen door stood open, the light from the kitchen window lying in a reflecting gleam on the white paint: and across the gleam a shadow moved.

Bananas and Cassie, I thought automatically, coming in through the kitchen door. But they couldn't. It was locked.

There was hardly time even for alarm, even for primeval instinct, even for rising hair. The silencer of a pistol came first into the room, a dark silhouette against the white paint, and then Angelo, dressed in black, balloon-high with triumph, towering with malice, looking like the devil.

There was no point in speech. I knew conclusively that he was going to shoot me, that I was looking at my own death. There was about him such intention of action, such a surrender to recklessness, such an intoxication of destructiveness, that nothing and no one could have talked him out of it.

With a thought so light-fast that it wasn't even conscious I reached out to the baseball bat which still lay on the windowsill. Grasped its handle end with the dexterity of desperation and swung toward Angelo in one continuous movement from twisting foot through legs, trunk, arm and hand to bat, bringing the weight of the wood down toward the hand which held the pistol with the whole force of my body.

Angelo fired straight at my chest from six feet away. I felt a jerking thud and nothing else and wasn't even astonished, and it didn't deflect my swing even a fraction. A split second later the bat crunched down onto Angelo's wrist and hand and broke them as thoroughly as he'd broken Cassie's arm.

I reeled from the force of that impact and spun across the room, and Angelo dropped the gun on the carpet and hugged his right arm to his body, yelling one huge shout at the pain of it and doubling over and running awkwardly out of the front door and down the path to the road.

I watched him through the window. I stood in a curious sort of inactivity, knowing that there was a future to come that had not yet arrived, a consequence not yet felt but inexorable, the fact of a bullet through my flesh.

I thought: Angelo has finally bagged his Derry. Angelo has taken his promised revenge. Angelo knows his shot hit me straight on target. Angelo will be convinced that he has done right, even if it costs him a lifetime in prison. In Angelo, despite his smashed wrist, despite his prospects, there would be at that moment an overpowering, screaming, unencompassable delirium of joy.

The battle was over, and the war. Angelo would be satisfied that in every physical, visible way, he had won.

Bananas and Cassie came running through the front door and looked enormously relieved to see me standing there, leaning a little against a cupboard but apparently unhurt.

"That was Angelo!" Cassie said.

"Yeah."

Bananas looked at the baseball bat which lay on the floor and said, "You bashed him."

"Yeah."

"Good," Cassie said with satisfaction. "His turn for the dreaded plaster."

Bananas saw Angelo's gun and leaned forward to pick it up.

"Don't touch it," I said.

He looked up inquiringly, still half-bent.

"Fingerprints," I said. "Jail him for life."

"But—"

"He shot me," I said.

I saw the disbelief on their faces begin to turn to anxiety.

"Where?" Cassie said.

I made a fluttery movement with my left hand toward my chest. My right arm felt heavy and without strength, and I thought unemotionally that it was because some of the muscles needed to lift it were torn.

"Shall I get an ambulance?" Bananas asked.

"Yes."

They didn't understand, I thought, how bad it was. They couldn't see any damage, and I was concerned mostly about how to tell them without frightening Cassie to death.

It wasn't that at that point it felt so terrible . . . but I still knew in a detached fashion that it soon would be. There was an internal disintegration going on like the earth shifting, like foundations slipping away. Accelerating, but still slow.

I said, "Ring Cambridge hospital."

It all sounded so calm.

I slid down, without meaning to, to my knees, and saw the anxiety on their faces turn to horror.

"You're really hurt," Cassie said with spurting alarm.

"It's, er, er..." I couldn't think what to say.

She was suddenly beside me, kneeling, finding with terrified scarlet fingers that the entry wound that didn't show through the front of my padded husky jacket led to a bigger bleeding exit at the back.

"Oh, my *God*," she said in stunned absolute shock.

Bananas strode over for a look and I could see from both their faces that they did know now. There was no longer any need to seek the words.

He turned grim-faced away and picked up the telephone, riffling urgently through the directory and dialing the number.

"Yes," he was saying. "Yes, it's an emergency. A man's been shot. Yes, I did say shot. Through the chest. Yes, he's alive. Yes, he's conscious. No, the bullet can't be in him." He gave the address of the cottage and brief directions. "Look, stop asking damn fool questions. Tell them to shift their arse. Yes, it does look *bloody* serious, for God's sake stop wasting time. *My* name? Christ Almighty, John Frisby." He crashed the receiver down in anger and said, "They want to know if we've reported it to the police. What the hell does it matter?"

I couldn't be bothered to tell him that all gunshot wounds had to be reported. Breathing, in fact, was becoming more difficult. Only words that needed to be reported were worth the effort.

"That pistol," I said. "Don't put it...in a plastic bag. Condensation...destroys...the prints."

Bananas looked surprised and I thought that he didn't realize I was telling him because quite soon I might not be able to. I was beginning to feel most dreadfully ill, with clamminess creeping over my skin and breaking into a sweat on my forehead. I gave a smallish cough and wiped a red streak from my mouth onto the back of my hand. An enveloping wave of weakness washed through me, and I found myself sagging fairly comprehensively against the cupboard and then half lying on the floor.

"Oh, William," Cassie said. "Oh, *no*."

If I'd ever doubted she loved me, I had my answer. No one could have acted or feigned the extremity of despair in her voice and in her body.

"Don't . . . worry," I said. I tried a smile. I don't suppose it came off. I coughed again, with worse results.

I was trying to breathe, I thought, through a lake. A lake progressively filling, fed by many springs. It was happening faster now. Much faster. Too fast. I wasn't ready. Who was ever ready?

I could hear Bananas saying something urgent, but I didn't know quite what. My wits started drifting. Existence was ceasing to be external. I'm dying, I thought, I really am. Dying too fast.

My eyes were shut and then open again. The daylight looked odd. Too bright. I could see Cassie's face wet with tears.

I tried to say, "Don't cry," but I couldn't get the breath. Breathing was becoming a sticky near-impossibility.

Bananas was still talking, but distantly.

There was a feeling of everything turning to liquid, of my body dissolving, of a deep subterranean river overflowing its banks and carrying me away.

Dim final astringent thought . . . I'm drowning, God damn it, in my own blood.

TWENTY-ONE

Cassie's face was the next thing I saw, but not for more than a day, and it was no longer weeping but asleep and serene. She was sitting by a bed with me in it, surrounded by white things and glass and chromium and a lot of lights. Intensive care, and all that.

I woke by stages over several hours to the pain I hadn't felt from the shot, and to tubes carrying liquids into and away from my log of clay and to voices telling me over and over that I was lucky to be there; that I had died and was alive.

I thanked them all, and meant it.

Thanked Bananas, who had apparently picked me up and put me in my own car and driven me at about a hundred miles an hour to Cambridge because it was quicker than waiting for the ambulance.

Thanked two surgeons who it seemed had worked all day and then again half the night to stanch and tidy the wreckage of my right lung and stop blood dripping out of the drainage as fast as the transfusions flowed into my arm.

Thanked the nurses who clattered about with deft hands and noisy machinery, and in absentia thanked the donors of blood type O who had refilled my veins.

Thanked Cassie for her love and for sitting beside me whenever they'd let her.

Thanked the fates that the destructive lump of metal had missed my heart. Thanked everyone I could for anything I could think of in gratitude for my life.

The long recurring dreams that had come during unconsciousness faded, receded, seemed no longer to be vivid fact. I no longer saw the Devil pacing beside me, quiet but implacable, the master waiting for my soul. I no longer saw him, the Fallen Angel, the Devil with Angelo's face, the yellow face with frosted hair and black empty holes where the eyes should have been. The Presence had gone. I was back in the daft real enjoyable world where tubes were what mattered, not concepts of evil.

I didn't say how close I had been to death because they were saying it for me, roughly every five minutes. I didn't say that I had looked on the spaces of eternity and seen the everlasting Darkness and had known it had a meaning and a face. The visions of the dying and the snatched-from-death were suspect. Angelo was a living man, not the Devil, not an incarnation or a house or a dwelling place. It was delirium, the confusion of the brain's circuits, that had shown me the one as the other, the other as the One. I said nothing for fear of ridicule: and later nothing from feeling that I had in truth been mistaken and that the dreams were indeed . . . merely dreams.

"Where is Angelo?" I said.

"They said not to tire you."

I looked at the evasion in Cassie's face. "I'm lying down," I pointed out. "So give."

She said reluctantly, "Well . . . he's here."

"*Here?* In this hospital?"

She nodded. "In the room next door."

I was bewildered. "But why?"

"He crashed his car." She looked at me for signs, I supposed, of relapse, but was seemingly reassured. "He drove into a bus about six miles from here."

"After he left the cottage?"

She nodded. "They brought him here. They brought him into the emergency unit while Bananas and I were waiting there. We couldn't believe it."

It wasn't over. I closed my eyes. It was never going to be over. Wherever I went, it seemed that Angelo would follow, even onto the slab.

"William?" Cassie said urgently.

"Mm?"

"Oh. I thought—"

"I'm all right."

"He was nearly dead," she said. "Just like you. He's still in a coma."

"What?"

"Head injuries," she said.

I learned bit by bit over the next few days that the hospital people hadn't believed it when Bananas and Cassie told them it was Angelo who had shot me. They had fought as long and hard to save his life as mine, and apparently we had been placed side by side in the Intensive Care Unit until Cassie told them I'd have a heart attack if I woke and found him there.

The police had more moderately pointed out that if it was Angelo who woke first he might complete the job of murdering me: and Angelo was now in his unwaking sleep along the hallway, guarded by a constable night and day.

It was extraordinary to think of him being there, lying there so close. Unsettling in a fundamental way. I wouldn't have thought it would have affected me so badly, but my pulse started jumping every time anyone opened the door. Reason said he wouldn't come. The subconscious feared it.

Bodies heal amazingly quickly. I was free of tubes, moved to a side ward, on my feet, walking about within a week: creeping a bit, sure, and stiff and sore, but positively, conclusively alive. Angelo too, it seemed, was improving. On the way up from the depths. Opening unseeing eyes, showing responses.

I heard it from the nurses, from the cleaners, from the woman who pushed a trolley of comforts, and all of them watched me curiously to see how I would take it. The piquancy of the situation hit first the local paper and then the national dailies, and the constable guarding Angelo started drifting in to chat.

It was from one of them that I learned how Angelo had lost control of his car while going around a roundabout, how a whole queue of people at a bus stop had seen him veer toward the bus as if unable to turn the steering wheel, how he'd been going too fast in any case, and how he had seemed at first to be *laughing*.

Bananas, when he heard it, said trenchantly, "He crashed because you broke his wrist."

"Yes," I said.

He sighed deeply. "The police must know it."

"I expect so."

"Have they bothered you?"

I shook my head. "I told them what happened. They wrote it down. No one has said much."

"They collected the pistol." He smiled. "They put it in a paper bag."

I left the hospital after twelve days, walking slowly past Angelo's room but not going in. Revulsion was too strong even though I knew he was still lightly unconscious and wouldn't be aware I was there. The damage he had caused in my life and Cassie's might be over, but my body carried his scars, livid still and still hurting, too immediate for detachment.

I dare say I hated him. Perhaps I feared him. I certainly didn't want to see him again, then or ever.

For the next three weeks I mooched around the cottage doing paperwork, getting fitter every day and persuading

Bananas to drive me along to the Heath to watch the gallops. Cassie went to work, the plastered arm a memory. My blood was washed almost entirely off the sitting room carpet and the baseball bat was in the cellar. Life returned more or less to normal.

Luke came over from California, inspected the yearlings, met Cassie, listened to Sim and Mort and the Berkshire trainers, visited Warrington Marsh, and went off to Ireland. It was he, not I, who bid for Oxidize at Ballsbridge and sent the colt to Donavan, and he who in some way smoothed the Irish trainer's feelings.

He came back briefly to Newmarket before leaving for home, calling in at the cottage and drinking a lunchtime scotch.

"Your year's nearly through," he said.

"Yeah."

"Have you enjoyed it?"

"Very much."

"Want another?"

I lifted my head. He watched me through a whole minute of silence. He didn't say, and nor did I, that Warrington Marsh was never going to be strong enough again to do the job. That wasn't the point: the point was permanence—captivity.

"One year," Luke said. "It's not forever."

After another pause I said, "One year, then. One more."

He nodded and drank his drink, and it seemed to me that somewhere he was smiling. I had a presentiment of him coming over again the next year and offering the same thing. One year. One year's contract at a time . . . leaving the cage door open but keeping his bird imprisoned: and as long as I could go, I thought, I might stay.

Cassie, when she came home, was pleased. "Mort told him he'd be mad to lose you."

"Did he?"

"Mort likes you."

"Donavan doesn't."

"You can't have everything," she said.

I had quite a lot, it was true; and then the police telephoned and asked me to see Angelo.

"No," I said.

"That's a gut reaction," a voice said calmly. "But I'd like you to listen."

He talked persuasively for a long time, cajoling again every time I protested, wearing down my opposition until in the end I reluctantly agreed to do what he wanted.

"Good," he said finally. "Wednesday afternoon."

"That's only two days—"

"We'll send a car. We don't expect you to be driving yet."

I didn't argue. I could drive short distances but I tended to get tired. In another month, they said, I'd be running.

"We're grateful," the voice said.

"Yeah..."

I told Cassie and Bananas, in the evening.

"How awful," Cassie said. "It's too much."

The three of us were having dinner alone in the dining room as the restaurant didn't officially open these days on Mondays: the old cow had negotiated Mondays off. Bananas had done the cooking himself, inventing soufflé of whitefish, herbs, orange and nuts to try out on Cassie and me: a concoction typically and indescribably different, an unknown language, a new horizon of taste.

"You could have said you wouldn't go," Bananas said, heaping his plate to match ours.

"With what excuse?"

"Selfishness," Cassie said. "The best reason in the world for not doing things."

"Never thought of it."

Bananas said, "I hope you insisted on a bullet-proof vest, a six-inch-thick plate-glass screen and several rolls of barbed wire."

"They did assure me," I said mildly, "that they wouldn't let him leap at my throat."

"Too kind," Cassie murmured.

We poured Bananas' exquisite sauce over his soufflé and said that when we had to leave the cottage we would camp in his garden.

"And will you bet?"

"What do you mean?"

"On the system."

I thought blankly that I'd forgotten all about that possibility: but we did have the tapes. We did have the choice.

"We don't have a computer," I said.

"We could soon pay for one," Cassie said.

We all looked at each other. We were happy enough with our own jobs, with what we had. Did one always, inevitably, stretch out for more?

Yes, one did.

"You work the computer," Bananas said, "and I'll do the betting. Now and then. When we're short."

"As long as it doesn't choke us."

"I don't want diamonds," Cassie said judiciously, "or furs, or a yacht . . . but how soon can we have a pool in our sitting room?"

Whatever Luke said to my brother when he got home to California, I never knew, but it resulted in Jonathan telephoning that night to say he would be arriving at Heathrow on Wednesday morning.

"What about your students?"

"Sod the students. I've got laryngitis." His voice bounced the distance strong and healthy. "I'll see you."

He came in a rented car looking biscuit-colored from the sun and anxious about what he would find, and although I was by then feeling well again it didn't seem to reassure him.

"I'm alive," I pointed out. "One thing at a time. Come back next month."

"What exactly happened?"

"Angelo happened."

"Why didn't you tell me?" he demanded.

"I'd have told you if I'd died. Or someone would."

He sat in one of the rockers and looked at me broodingly.

"It was all my fault," he said.

"Oh, sure." I was ironic.

"And that's why you didn't tell me."

"I'd probably have told you one day."

"Tell me now."

I told him, however, where I was going that afternoon, and why, and he said in his calm positive way that he would come with me. I had thought he would: had been glad he was coming. I told him over the next few hours pretty well everything which had happened between Angelo and me, just as he had told me all those years ago in Cornwall.

"I'm sorry," he said, at the end.

"Don't be."

"You'll use the system?"

I nodded. "Pretty soon."

"I think old Mrs. O'Rorke would be glad. She was proud of Liam's work. She wouldn't want it wasted." He reflected for a bit and then said, "What make of pistol? Do you know?"

"I believe . . . the police said . . . a Walther .22?"

He smiled faintly. "True to form. And just as well. If it had been a .38 or something like that you'd have been in trouble."

"Ah," I said dryly. "Just as well."

The car came for us as threatened and took us to a large house in Buckinghamshire. I never did discover exactly what it was: a cross between a hospital and a civil service institution, all long wide corridors and closed doors and hush.

"Down there," we were directed. "Right along at the end. Last door on the right."

We walked unhurriedly along the parquet flooring, our heels punctuating the silence. At the far end there was a tall window, floor to ceiling, casting not quite enough daylight; and silhouetted against the window were two figures, a man in a wheelchair with another man pushing him.

Those two and Jonathan and I in due course approached

each other, and as we drew nearer I saw with unwelcome shock that the man in the wheelchair was Harry Gilbert. Old, gray, bowed, ill Harry Gilbert who still consciously repelled compassion.

Eddy, who was pushing, faltered to a halt, and Jonathan and I also stopped, we staring at Harry and Harry staring at us over a space of a few feet. He looked from me to Jonathan, glancing at him briefly at first and then looking longer, more carefully, seeing what he didn't believe.

He switched to me. "You said he was dead," he said.

I nodded slightly.

His voice was cold, dry, bitter, past passion, past hope, past strength to avenge. "Both of you," he said. "You destroyed my son."

Neither Jonathan nor I answered. I wondered about the genetics of evil, the chance that bred murder, the predisposition which lived already at birth. The biblical creation, I thought, was also the truth of evolution. Cain existed, and in every species there was survival of the ruthless.

It was only by luck that I had lived, by Bananas' speed and surgeons' dedication. Abel and centuries of other victims were dead: and in every generation, in many a race, the genes still threw up the killer. The Gilberts bred their Angelos forever.

Harry Gilbert jerked his head back, aiming at Eddy, signaling that he wanted to go; and Eddy the look-alike, Eddy the easily led, Eddy the sheep from the same flock, wheeled his uncle quietly away.

"Arrogant old bastard," Jonathan said under his breath, looking back at them.

"The breeding of racehorses," I said, "is interesting."

Jonathan's gaze came around very slowly to my face. "And do rogues," he asked, "beget rogues?"

"Quite often."

He nodded and we went on walking along the corridor, up to the window, to the last door on the right.

The room into which we went must once have been finely proportioned, but with the insensitivity of government departments it had been hacked into two for utility. The result was one long narrow room with a window and another inner long narrow room without one.

In the outer room, which was furnished only by a strip of mud-colored carpet on the parquet leading to a functional desk and two hard chairs, were two men engaged in what looked like unimportant passing of the time. One sat behind the desk, one sat on it, both fortyish, smallish, bored-looking and with an air of wishing to be somewhere else.

They looked up inquiringly as we went in.

"I'm William Derry," I said.

"Ah."

The man sitting on the desk rose to his feet, came toward me, shook hands, and looked inquiringly at Jonathan.

"My brother, Jonathan Derry," I said.

"Ah."

He shook hands with him too. "I don't think," he said neutrally, "that we'll need to bother your brother."

I said, "Angelo is more likely to react violently to my brother than to me."

"But it was you he tried to kill."

"Jonathan got him jailed . . . fourteen years ago."

"Ah."

He looked from one of us to the other, his head tilted slightly back to accommodate our height. We seemed to be in some way not what he'd expected, though I didn't know why. Jonathan did certainly look pretty distinguished, especially since age had given him such an air of authority, and he had always of the two of us had the straighter features; and I, I supposed, looked less a victim than I might have. I wondered vaguely if he'd been expecting a shuffling little figure in a dressing gown and hadn't reckoned on clothes like his own.

"I think I'll just go and *explain* about your brother," he said at last. "Will you wait?"

We nodded and he opened the door to the inner room parsimoniously and eeled himself through the gap, closing it behind him. The man behind the desk went on looking bored and offered no comment of any sort, and presently his colleague slid back through the same-sized opening and said they were ready for us inside and would we please go in.

The inner room was lit brightly and entirely by electricity and contained four people and a great deal of electrical equipment with multitudinous dials and sprouting wires. I saw Jonathan give them a swift sweep of the eyes and supposed he could identify the lot, and he said afterward that they had all seemed to be standard machines for measuring body changes—cardiograph, encephalograph, gauges for temperature, respiration and skin moisture—and there had been at least two of each.

One of the four people wore an identifying white coat and introduced himself quietly as Tom Course, doctor. A woman in similar white moved among the machines, checking their faces. A third person, a man, seemed to be there specifically as an observer, since that was what he did, without speaking, during the next strange ten minutes.

The fourth person, sitting in a sort of dentist's chair with his back toward us, was Angelo.

We could see only the top of his bandaged head, and also his arms, which were strapped by the wrists to the arms of the chair.

There was no sign of any plaster on the arm I'd broken: mended, no doubt. His arms were bare and covered sparsely with dark hairs, the hands lying loose, without tension. From every part of his body it seemed that wires led backward to the machines, which were all ranked behind him. In front of him there was nothing but a stretch of empty brightly lit room.

Dr. Course, young, wiry, bolstered by certainties, gave me an inquiring glance and said in the same quiet manner, "Are you ready?"

As ready, I supposed, as I would ever be.

"Just walk around in front of him. Say something. Anything you like. Stay there until we tell you it's enough."

I swallowed. I had never wanted to do anything less in

all my life. I could see them all waiting, polite, determined, businesslike—and too damned understanding. Even Jonathan, I noticed, was looking at me with a sort of pity.

Intolerable.

I walked slowly around the machines and the chair and stopped in front of Angelo, and looked at him.

He was naked to the waist. On his head, below a cap of fawn crepe bandage, there was a band of silvery metal like a crown. His skin everywhere gleamed with grease and to his face, his neck, his chest, arms and abdomen were fastened an army of electrodes. No one, I imagined, could have been more comprehensively wired; no flicker of change could have gone unmonitored.

He seemed as well-fleshed and as healthy as ever, despite his earlier two weeks in a coma. The muscles looked as strong, the trunk as tanklike, the mouth as firm. The hard man. The frightener. The despiser of mugs. Apart from his headdress and the wires, he looked just the same. I breathed a shade deeply and looked straight into his black eyes, and it was there that one saw the difference. There was nothing in his eyes, nothing at all. It was extraordinary, like seeing a stranger in a long-known face. The house was the same . . . but the monster slept.

It was five weeks, all but a day, since we had last faced each other; since we had brought each other near death, one way or another. Even though I had been prepared, seeing him again affected me powerfully. I could feel my heart thudding: could actually hear it in the expectant room.

"Angelo," I said. My tongue felt sticky in my dry mouth. "Angelo, you shot me."

In Angelo, nothing happened.

He was looking at me in complete calm. When I took a pace to one side, his eyes followed. When I stepped back he still watched.

"I am . . . William Derry," I said. "I gave you . . . Liam O'Rorke's betting system." I said the words slowly, clearly, deliberately, trying to control my own uneven breath.

From Angelo there was no reaction at all.

"If you hadn't shot me . . . you'd have been free now—and rich."

Nothing. Absolutely nothing.

I found Jonathan standing beside me, and after a pause Angelo's gaze wandered from me to him.

"Hello, Angelo," Jonathan said. "I'm Jonathan, do you remember? William told you I was dead. It wasn't true."

Angelo said nothing.

"Do you remember?" Jonathan said. "I tricked you sideways."

Silence. A dull absence of all we had endured for so long. No fury. No sneers, no threats, no towering hurricane of hate.

Silence, it seemed to me, was all that was appropriate. Jonathan and I stood there together in front of the shell of our enemy and there was nothing in the world left to say.

"Thank you," Tom Course said, coming around the chair to join us. "That should do it."

Angelo looked at him.

"Who are you?" he said.

"Dr. Course. We talked earlier, while we were fixing the electrodes."

Angelo made no comment but instead looked directly at me.

"You were talking," he said. "Who are you?"

"William Derry."

"I don't know you."

"No."

His voice was as deep and as gritty as ever, the only remnant, it seemed, of the old foe.

Dr. Course said heartily, "We'll take all those wires off you now. I expect you'll be glad to get rid of them."

"Who did you say you are?" Angelo said, frowning slightly.

"Dr. Course."

"Who?"

"Never mind. I'm here to take the wires off."

"Can I have tea?" Angelo said.

Dr. Course left the taking off of the wires to his woman colleague and led us around to look at the results on the machines. The observer, I noticed, was also consulting them acutely, but Course paid him scant attention.

"There we are," he said, holding out a yard-long strip of paper. "Not a flicker. We had him stabilized for an hour before his visitors came. Breathing, pulse rate, everything rock steady. Quiet in here, you see. No interruptions, no intrusions, no noise. That mark, that's the point at which he saw *you*"—he nodded at me—"and as you can see, nothing altered. This is the skin temperature chart. Always rises if someone's lying. And here"—he moved across to a different machine—"heart rate unchanged. And here"—to another—"brain activity, very faint alteration. He couldn't have seen *you*, his hated victim, suddenly and unexpectedly standing in front of him, and yet show no strong body or brain changes, not if he'd known you. Absolutely impossible."

I thought of my own unrecorded but pretty extreme responses, and knew that it was true.

"Is this state permanent?" Jonathan asked.

Tom Course gave him a swift look. "*I* think so. It's *my* opinion, yes. See, they dug pieces of skull out of his brain tissue. Brilliant repair job on the bone structure, have to hand it to them. But there you are, you can see, no memory. Many functions unimpaired. Eat, talk, walk, he can do all that. He's continent. He'll live to be old. But he can't remember anything for longer than about fifteen minutes, sometimes not even that. He lives in the absolute present. Loss of capacity for memory is not all that rare, you know, after severe brain damage. But with this one, there were *doubts*. Not *my* doubts, official doubts. They said he was faking, that he knew he'd go to a hospital, not a prison, if he could persuade everyone he'd lost his memory."

Tom Course waved a hand around the machines. "He couldn't have faked today's results. Conclusive. Settle the arguments once and for all. Which is why we're all here, of course. Why they gave us this facility."

His woman colleague had taken the silver band off Angelo's forehead and the straps off his wrists, and was wiping the grease from his skin with pieces of cotton wool.

"Who are you?" he said to her, and she answered, "Just a friend."

"Where will he go?" I said.

Tom Course shrugged. "Not my decision. But I'd be careful. I'm not a civil servant. My advice, I don't suppose, will be taken." His remark was clearly aimed at the observer, who remained obstinately impassive.

I said slowly, "Could he still be violent?"

Tom Course gave me a swift sideways glance. "Can't tell. He might be. Yes, he might be. He looks harmless. He'll never *hate* anyone, he can't remember anyone long enough. But the sudden impulse..." He shrugged again. "Let's say I wouldn't turn my back on him if we were alone."

"Not ever?"

"How old is he? Forty?" He pursed his mouth. "Not for another ten years. Twenty perhaps. You can't tell."

"Lightning?" I said.

"Just like that."

The woman finished wiping the grease and was holding out a gray shirt for Angelo to put on.

"Have we had tea?" he said.

"Not yet."

"I'm thirsty."

"You'll have tea soon."

I said to Tom Course, "His father was outside. Did Angelo see him?"

Course nodded. "No reaction. Nothing on the machines. Conclusive tests, the whole lot of them." He looked slyly at the observer. "They can stop all the arguing."

Angelo stood up out of the chair, stretching upright, seeming strong with physical life but fumbling with the buttons on his shirt, moving without total coordination, looking vaguely as if not quite sure what he should be doing next.

His wandering gaze came to rest on Jonathan and me.

"Hello," he said.

The doors from the outer room opened wide and two white-coated male nurses and a uniformed policeman came through them.

"Is he ready?" the policeman said.

"All yours."

"Let's be off, then."

He fastened a handcuff around Angelo's left wrist and attached him to one of the nurses.

Angelo didn't seem to mind. He looked at me uninterestedly for the last time with the black holes where the eyes should have been and walked as requested to the door.

Diminished, defused . . . perhaps even docile.

"Where's my tea?" he said.

ABOUT THE AUTHOR

Dick Francis is a former champion steeple-chase jockey who rode for some years for Queen Elizabeth, the Queen Mother. When age and injury grounded him at thirty-six, he was asked to write a weekly racing column for the London *Sunday Express*. From this experience he branched out into fiction, using his knowledge of the inside world of horses as the background for his novels. Dick Francis is married, lives in Oxfordshire, England, and still rides whenever he can.